A Stage in Our Past,

*English-language theatre in Eastern Canada
from the 1790s to 1914: Murray D. Edwards*

UNIVERSITY OF TORONTO PRESS

Published on the occasion of
the Centennial of Canadian
Confederation and subsidized
by the Centennial Commission.

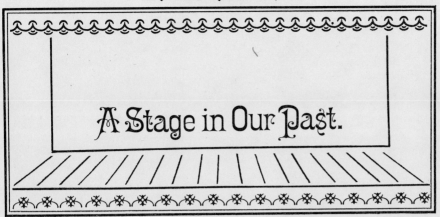

A Stage in Our Past.

Contents.

Foreword.

MAVOR MOORE
GENERAL DIRECTOR, ST. LAWRENCE CENTRE FOR THE ARTS

Some years ago the Canadian Theatre Centre, of which I was then the chairman, was asked to arrange for the Stratford Festival an exhibition to be called "100 Years of Canadian Theatre (English)." One didn't know where to look. The embarrassment was due less to the want of a past, than to the almost total lack of a record of it. Our historians have always been fascinated with politics to the near exclusion of everything else – a mania shared, it must be confessed, by most of their readers. As for the part played in our lives by one of the oldest of man's arts, there were a few scattered articles and tattered memoirs long out of print, unsorted references in American and British publications, and the beginnings of a picture collection at the Toronto Public Library. Beyond that a fellow could whistle – which is bad luck in the theatre.

About the same time, fortunately, I had a visit from a young CBC radio producer, trying to finish in his spare time a university thesis on early Canadian theatre. His name was Murray Edwards, and we promptly made him Archivist for the Centre. The post was unpaid, but as recompense he was allowed to appropriate whatever we collected. He has obviously been working at Canadian theatrical history ever since.

Murray Edwards and I spent many happy hours tracking down leads, piecing together clues and identifying pictures of people and places. But while I went on to other things, he has persevered in the hunt, and succeeded in establishing himself as that rarest of scholars, a Canadian theatrical historian.

My own interest in the subject dated back to childhood, and reading these pages has brought those days vividly back to me. From about the age of four on I was regularly taken to the theatre by my mother who, as Dora Mavor, had first gone on the stage in 1910. The first Canadian graduate of London's Royal Academy of Dramatic Art, she returned to Canada in that year to play in a stock company in Ottawa, and then after diverse experiences in New York and Chicago joined the famous touring company of Philip (later Sir Philip) Ben Greet. First playing "bits" and later as his leading lady, she toured with Ben Greet through several states of the U.S.A. and Ontario until the onset of war in 1914 – the same event which ends Dr. Edwards' study.

These days, using the transparent excuse that she is now past eighty, my mother will claim that her memory is less than perfect – and follow with a demonstration of total recall. I know, because I remember so vividly the tales she told in my boyhood . . . Robert Mantell as Richard III angrily stabbing a recalcitrant stagehand during a strike . . . a thin (then) Sydney Greenstreet disappearing through a fractured stage-board . . . assorted extras ducking out of the range of William Faversham's spit as he launched into "Friends, Romans and countrymen" . . . playing Rosalind on a slag-heap before rapt coal-miners . . . introducing Yeats to Toronto audiences at the old Princess Theatre . . . and the names: Sybil Thorndike, Maude Adams, Laurence Irving (who stayed with my grandfather in Toronto), Margaret Anglin, Constance Collier, and the rest.

Like others of my generation, whose memories also will be awakened by these pages, I remember as a boy seeing the aging Nazimova as a creaky but still glamorous Hedda Gabler, Martin Harvey in "The King's Messenger" nobly supporting his untalented wife, Walter Hampton gallantly giving Richelieu and Caponsacchi to an audience which no longer cared – but when I saw them in the twenties they were relics of a bygone age of theatre.

It is that age which Murray Edwards recreates for us in this book. He has modestly called it "A Stage in our Past" – a play on words which allows him to disclaim any intention to write a definitive history of either plays or players. In fact he gives us a little of both – and in addition some valuable Appendices. He closes this collection of essays reasonably, if regrettably, with the onset of World War I. It is to be hoped that either he or others will take up the story from there: how the professional stage in Canada had a lively if brief renaissance in the twenties, almost died out in the depression, and then – spurred on by national confidence in World War II – arose again to bring us Stratford, and finally several genuinely native plays and theatres, in modern times.

We have no crystal ball to predict the future, but as always it can only be built upon the past. And one of the things we learn from Dr. Edwards' history is that Canadians, of all people, appear to have been moving toward "their own thing" for quite a long time.

Introduction.

Most people with a knowledge of Canada's cultural past will agree with Nathan Cohen when he says, "theatre as something of value to a discerning public has never counted in the life of English-language Canada."[1] This opinion has a familiar ring. Canadians have been constantly reminded of their lack of achievement in the arts, and, strangely enough, in almost the same breath, they have been encouraged to believe that the future will be bright. Few concrete examples are adduced to describe the sad condition or hopeful signs. Generalizations have proved the rule, and this is perhaps understandable because there is a degree of protection in vague terms. We can talk about the twentieth century belonging to Canada, and be comforted in the knowledge that the "giant" will eventually awake. When we turn to the past we can blandly accept the fact that we have been culturally retarded for we can point to broad, familiar causes: pioneer life, cold weather, and lack of population.

But surely the time has come to examine Canada's theatrical past and look for some of the details. If it is true, for example, that the theatre has never counted in English-speaking Canada, then obviously it would be of value to know more specifically to what degree it has failed. The main purpose of this book is to do simply this: to reveal something of our culture by digging up the facts. These were not collected in the hope of proving Cohen and other deductive writers wrong. I was not working under the delusion that I would find a Canadian Ibsen, Shaw, or Shakespeare hidden in the archives. It was quite obvious to me that my conclusion would merely confirm the suspicion that early Canadian theatre lacked literary significance. To steal a phrase from Northrop Frye, most of our early dramatic writing is "as innocent of literary intention as a mating loon."[2] But this doesn't mean that the early theatre should be neglected. It represents an important segment of our cultural history and for this reason alone deserves more attention than it has received to the present. Serious critical appraisal is possible when we accept the fact

[1] Nathan Cohen, "Theatre Today: English Canada," *The Tamarack Review*, XIII, 24 (Autumn 1959).
[2] Northrop Frye, *Literary History of Canada* (Toronto: University of Toronto Press, 1965), p. 822.

that the Canadian theatre can be studied not necessarily in an international context but as a part of the Canadian way of life.

This book was designed to open up some avenues of research in the Canadian field. When a foreign actor or playwright steps into our history, I am, therefore, more concerned with the role he played in this country than the part he played on the world stage. Theatre movements are considered primarily from a Canadian point of view. Since facts concerning the theatres themselves have played a reasonably important part in the history of Canadian theatre, I have devoted the first chapter to the playhouses and the social conditions in which they were fostered. Touring companies, foreign and native, have been extensively discussed as they generally represent the most prevalent type of theatre in Canada during the latter part of the period under consideration. Poetic drama has been examined not only as an interesting development in the English theatre but as a particularly apt reflector of Canadian attitudes.

Of course all of these subjects are large, and the reader may wonder why I have chosen to spread myself over such a broad area, rather than concentrate on a single aspect. The reason, I must confess, is chiefly personal. Of the various ways of approaching history, I have always preferred the broader perspective. There are disadvantages. Experts in some of the fields will miss the detail they may expect to find, and certainly the theatrical history of someone's home town is bound to be ignored. I trust, however, that by extending the limits of this study, I have been able to make a respectable beginning from a number of different vantage points. Indeed, it is my hope that I will encourage other theatre students to make more detailed and critical analyses of these categories.

Although initially allowing myself a good deal of liberty in my research, I have naturally been forced to organize the material within certain boundaries. Canada has two languages and, one day, ideally, we will be able to write about the Canadian theatre without undue reference to this fact. But at the time of writing, I felt that it was still best to treat each culture separately. I am, for example, an English-Canadian, a product of our educational system, and thus it was natural for me to decide to write about the English-speaking theatre. This was a major decision. Another important decision was concerned with the geography of the country. Because Canada is large, I have found it necessary to limit this work mainly to the eastern provinces. I should, however, point out that a liberty has been taken with the expression, "eastern." Winnipeg from early times has commonly been known as the gateway to the West, but in theatrical terms during this period it was recognized as the end of a "road" which began in the east. Companies on the eastern circuit often included Winnipeg. To the theatre manager of those early days Canada was divided into roughly three zones: the East which included the Maritimes (also part of the New England circuit), Quebec, Ontario and Winnipeg; the Middle West which was represented by Saskatchewan and Alberta; and British Columbia in the Far West. During the touring days, the east was fed mainly from New York, and the west received most of its entertainment from the cities along the west coast of the United

States. It was obvious that I should choose the eastern zone, because <u>Ontario was (and still is) the centre of theatrical activity.</u>

The period for examination was chosen only after research had shown the way. It was found, for example, that 1914 was a suitable year to end this particular study of the theatre because <u>from approximately 1912 onward the movies began to threaten the stage, and in 1914 the war in Europe ended a phase in our professional theatre.</u> In searching for the appropriate time to begin, I was faced with one simple problem: either I could begin when dramatic writing started to appear, or I could push farther back to the beginnings of the popular theatre. I chose the latter. However, I did not feel obliged to relate the story of <u>"Neptune's Theatre" in 1606,</u>[3] or the <u>performances put on by Admiral Parry in the Arctic.</u>[4] Although interesting in themselves, these early events have only intrinsic value. References to some performers and to the theatres they acted in will take the reader back to the <u>1790s,</u> but most attention is paid to the succeeding years, <u>the years approaching the turn of the century when the professional groups began to appear in the larger cities and touring companies were reaching out across the country.</u>

No systematic research could begin until a chronology of performances had been established, and as there was no publication in Canada that could serve the purpose, aid had to be solicited from the United States. The first step was to make <u>a detailed examination of theatrical news</u> contained in the <u>*New York Dramatic Mirror*</u> and the <u>*New York Clipper*</u>, two papers which recorded the happenings in the theatre world during this period, and although concentrating on the United States, did include eastern Canada. The order of events was noted and then attention was directed to the Canadian source material. Here difficulties stood in the way. Many of the newspapers still preserved in the small centres, and referred to in this book, were not mentioned in the central listings of the National Archives. The only solution was to visit the numerous and far-flung towns and search out the specific newspaper. Some of the past issues, if they were found at all, were quite often discovered buried in a damp basement or rotting in a barn. Information as to performers and other theatre people was gained, whenever possible, through interviews, generally with surviving relatives.

It remains for me to thank all the people who became involved with my search for Canadian theatre. Sometimes the aid was a kindly favour or a routine task, as I imagine it was for many of the editors throughout Ontario who probably only vaguely remember a strange character who sat in their back rooms or basements and read old newspapers, or the library staffs in almost every province who received and struggled with my various requests. More particularly I am indebted to Miss Heather McCallum and her staff at the Theatre Collection, Metropolitan Toronto Public Library, and Mr. Paul

---

[3]See Marc Lescarbot, *The Theatre of Neptune in New France*, trans. Harriette Taber Richardson (Boston, 1927).

[4]On November 5, 1819, in a harbour in the Arctic Circle, Admiral Sir Edward Parry and some of his crew performed *Miss In Her Teens*. Some time later, when they had used up all their plays, they turned to writing their own. Parry was apparently "co-author of a piece entitled 'The North-West Passage, or Voyage Finished'. . . ." Ann Parry, *Parry of the Arctic* (London, 1963), p. 60.

Meyers of the New York Public Library. To Ernest Marks Jr. and Robert Marks Jr., who spent many hours reminiscing about the famous Marks Brothers, and to the late Mrs. McLeish, daughter of Albert Tavernier and Ida Van Cortland, who was tireless in her aid, I owe a special debt of gratitude. My thanks also to the many friends and associates whose observations and suggestions are now buried in the text. Their aid, of course, in no way makes them responsible for my opinions, errors and omissions. Finally I must thank my father, Frank Edwards, for being a constant critic of my work, and my wife, who has not only prodded me along the way, but has acted as my collaborator.

It is notoriously difficult to identify the first source of theatrical illustrations, which lead a peripatetic life just as actors do. I remain grateful to many people who have from time to time dipped into their archives and personal diaries for pictures, posters and programs (some originals, some prints), which could be

copied and used on television and in exhibits. The Theatre Collection of the New York Public Library has kindly provided pictures of William MacReady, Rose Coghlan, Robert Lorraine, and Charlotte Cushman. The opportunity to secure prints of a number of pictures related to the Marks Brothers tours and the Tavernier companies was part of the generous sharing of reminiscences by the Marks family and the late Mrs. McLeish which I have mentioned above. The Metropolitan Toronto Public Library has been the source of a number of illustrations: posters of the Royal Opera House; the John Ross Robertson Collection for those of Frank's Hotel, John Nickinson, Mrs. Morrison, the Royal Lyceum (Toronto); the Theatre Collection for the Royal Lyceum poster, the masthead from the Toronto Opera House; the Toronto and Early Canada Picture Collection for the Grand Opera House (Toronto). The Public Archives of Canada have provided pictures of Charles Mair, D'Arcy McGee, Sarah Anne Curzon, Bliss Carman, and William Wilfred Campbell. The picture of the old Grand Theatre in London, Ontario, comes from the archives of the *London Free Press*. Pictures of early theatres in the west may be seen in the collections of the British Columbia and Saskatchewan archives, among others. Finally, I am deeply grateful for the opportunities to see and obtain information and illustrations which came to me through my activities at various times with the Canadian Broadcasting Corporation, the Stratford Shakespearean Festival, and the Canadian Theatre Centre. In particular, the experience of gathering material for a special exhibition by the Centre, to which Mavor Moore refers in his Foreword, was a rewarding and pleasurable one.

The moving spirit of this book has always been shared by members of the staff of the University of Toronto Press with whom my relations have been cheerful and helpful. I gratefully acknowledge a grant from the Centennial Commission for assistance in my final preparation of the manuscript and of another from the Canada Council towards the production costs of the book.

A Stage in Our Past.

Players and Playhouses.

The history of the Canadian theatre has had little interest for the scholar. It is a pity this is so, because a study of this subject provides a fascinating insight into the life and cultural needs of a new country. One reason for the neglect can be found in the fact that there have been no artistic triumphs. Although Canada has experienced rapid economic growth during the period under discussion, it has lagged noticeably in cultural development. In the early stages, economic concerns naturally took precedence over cultural needs, and there was also the fact that the English-speaking population (our main concern here) grew rather slowly. The loyalist immigration into British North America after the American Revolution started the trend that was eventually to lead to a British majority over the French.

According to *A Historical Atlas of Canada*, it is estimated that 20,000 loyalists finally settled in Nova Scotia, 14,000 in New Brunswick, 6,000 in Upper Canada and 1,000 in Lower Canada. The move to the interior was gradual, and it is therefore natural to find the first evidence of theatrical activity to be in the Maritimes. In most communities, the local citizens rose to the occasion and developed flourishing amateur theatres. Their popularity, however, was generally short-lived. A study of early records reveals a sudden move from amateur to professional theatre. The interesting and unfortunate point concerning this abrupt transition is that the professional theatre which supplanted the local efforts was invariably American or English. The native talent failed to mature and was apparently unable to compete with the attractions offered by the older cultures. We should add, however, that there seems to be reason to suspect that Canadians preferred to assume the role of passive observers. At the time local amateur groups should have been developing to professional status, encouraging playwrights, actors and directors of their own, Canadians were sitting back and applauding the American or English stars, with the result that the growth of theatre in Canada was largely an artificial one. This is not to say that the pattern of development from the amateur to foreign professional theatre was entirely consistent. There were exceptions, of course. In some cities, such as Montreal, the amateur and professional seemed to grow side by side, and at times it is difficult to distinguish between them. Generally, however, the local amateur development ends when the foreign professional begins, and this pattern can be observed as we trace the growth of the theatre in eastern Canada.

A close look at the beginnings of the theatre in the Maritimes provides us with an example. According to an article by A. R. Jewitt, the first drama to be performed in Halifax was an amateur production of *The West Indian* by Richard Cumberland. Jewitt estimates that this performance took place on March 14, 1787, which would make it possibly the first amateur production in English in Canada. The local inhabitants were very much pleased with the production and expected greater triumphs to follow. Something of the seriousness of the occasion is reflected in a notice that was published at the time:

> The avidity with which the tickets for this play have been purchased up marks the high sense the public entertain of its merit and proves the choice of the gentleman under whose care the entertainment is conducted to be perfectly judicious.[1]

The group was obviously determined to keep up the standard of their plays. In 1789 we find them presenting *The Beaux' Stratagem* at the New Grand Theatre. An amusing piece of instruction given to the ladies and gentlemen who attended the play is preserved in Beamish Murdoch's *A History of Nova Scotia*. They were asked to "give directions to their servants, when they come to take them from the theatre, to have their horses' heads towards the parade." Ladies were also requested to dress their heads "as low as possible."[2]

His Royal Highness, Prince Edward, arrived in Halifax on May 10, 1794, and because of his desire, The Gentlemen Amateurs presented *The Mock Doctor* (*The Doctor in Spite of Himself* by Molière?) at the Halifax Theatre on December 30, 1794. The Prince, apparently, was a theatre buff and through his encouragement, the amateurs attempted a new play every fortnight. A casual glance at this period is rewarding; the amount of theatre activity is impressive, and the quality of the plays is high. Murdoch mentions one performance which bears testimony to the Amateurs' concern about high standards. On January 13, 1795, they presented *Love à la Mode* which we may assume was Dryden's *Marriage à la Mode*. The management felt obliged to remind their customers that "No children in laps to be admitted."[3]

After this performance, there appear to be many barren years. It isn't until 1816, well after the War of 1812, that we discover Price, Charnock, Placide, and Young presenting plays at the new theatre which was "fitted up in a large wooden store on Fairbanks' warf."[4] The Americans had come to town; it was time for the amateurs to retire. During the years that followed it can be assumed that productions by this company and others continued, but the record does not indicate that any of them established notable standards. Indeed, the next information of any importance concerning activities in Halifax is the announcement of the arrival of two English professionals, Powell and Baker who, in 1897, created a theatrical stir there.

[1]A. R. Jewitt, "Early Halifax Theatres," *Dalhousie Review*, v, 444–59 (January, 1926).
[2]Beamish Murdoch, *A History of Nova Scotia or Acadie* (Halifax, 1867), III, 78.
[3]*Ibid.*, p. 141.
[4]*Ibid.*, p. 393.

New machinery was added to the theatre to allow such special effects as "A Ship in Distress, etc. stranded on the Coast." Plays were given more frequently. In March 1898, for example, four different bills were advertised. The theatre fare was enlarged to include operas (the first opera in Halifax was Sheridan's comic opera *The Duenna*), spectacles, and pantomimes, and the length of the evening's entertainment was extended. The size, variety and quality of the entertainment can be gathered from the following playbill contained in Jewitt's article:

---

*Collins Evening Brush for Rubbing
off the Rust of Care*

CHIEF SUBJECTS OF LAUGHTER

Modern Spouters, Stage Candidates, Tragedy
Struck Taylors, Butchers in Heroics, etc., etc.

Interspersed with a variety of Comic Songs. Between the parts,
Mr. Baker will speak a Prologue in the Character of a Country
Boy; ditto in Character of a Covent Garden Buck, and Garrick's Epilogue in Character of a Drunken Sailor.

A typical evening consisted of a regular play, a farce, and an interlude called *The Stage Coach*, a title which described that part of the entertainment given over to variety.

The low quality of the productions at this time was noted by one observer who considered the theatrical attempts "foreign Novelties, these Gin shops of the Stage that intoxicate its Auditors and dishonor their understanding with a levity for which I want a name." Whether he voiced a common opinion or was merely speaking for himself, this remark suggests that the "foreign" performer was not beyond criticism. Nevertheless there seems to have been no attempt by the local citizens to improve the standards. Halifax, from the 1890s to recent times, accepted generally the type of amusement that was provided by the foreign professionals.[5]

In another isolated little pocket, Saint John, New Brunswick, we can see a similar development of the theatre, and again the presence of the loyalists is a cultural stimulant. Leaders such as Colonel Edward Winslow and the Honourable Ward Chipman supported the efforts of the amateurs with some enthusiasm. The Colonel was known to have made the 80-mile trip to Saint John from Kingsclear merely to attend a performance, and Chipman, who had been unable to attend that particular programme, managed to get to a different performance, presumably by the same company, at a later date. He wrote to Winslow on March 3, 1789:

We were highly pleased with your theatrical jaunt – the description reached us just as we were setting off for the entertainment given us last evening by Miss

---

[5]I am aware of one thesis at present being prepared which will examine the theatre in Halifax in detail, and in doing so, may find proof to the contrary.

Doyley and Company. Everything went off exceedingly well, and will, I hope from the success of it, be a prelude to other exhibitions of the same kind.[6]

It is possible that Winslow had seen and may have given the "description" of the performance which had been put on for "Public Charity" on Saturday, February 28, 1789. It was, as J. R. Harper points out, the first dramatic performance in Saint John.[7] An advertisement had been placed in *The Royal Gazette*:

At Mallard's Long Room, King Street
will be performed

THE COMEDY OF

THE BUSY BODY

to which will be added

WHO'S THE DUPE

The doors to be opened at half past Five.
To begin precisely at half past Six O'clock.
Tickets at three shillings each, to be had at Mallard's.

Some days later there appeared in *The Royal Gazette* a criticism – or more correctly – a review of the show. This is probably the first of its kind in the history of Canadian theatre, and for that reason alone deserves to be preserved:

Saturday evening last, was presented before the most numerous and polite assembly which has appeared in this Town "The Busy Body" and "Who's the Dupe?" by a company of gentlemen. Mallard's Long Room on this occasion was converted into a pretty theatre. The scenes, the decorations and the dresses were entirely new, and in general, well cast, and the characters supported with great life and humor. Some of the company displayed comic talents which would have done honor to the British theatre and it is justice to say that all exceeded the expectations of the most favorable of friends. The applause of the assembly manifested the highest gratification in this the first dramatic exhibition in this Province.

The "theatre" was typical for its time. It was space in a building that usually served another purpose. Actual buildings will be considered in more detail later. It is sufficient here to note that the building had two storeys, the upper storey being the place where the performances were given.

The "gentlemen" actors of Saint John continued to put on plays for some time. We note, for example, that when the City Hall was erected in 1795, the amateurs were preparing a theatrical season and later in 1816 we find

---

[6]Many details of the early theatre in the Maritimes are to be found in the *Winslow Papers, 1776–1826*, ed. Rev. W. O. Raymond (Saint John, 1901). The excerpt used here was already selected by J. R. Harper in his article, "The Theatre in Saint John," *Dalhousie Review*, xxxiv, 260–69 (Autumn, 1954).

[7]A good deal of information about the early theatre in Saint John was received through correspondence with J. R. Harper, when he was Archivist of the New Brunswick Museum.

that they had moved into Mr. Green's store where they planned to put on *The Magpie and the Maid* and *Raising the Wind*. But in 1810 the inevitable foreign professional had arrived in town. He was performing at the Drury Lane theatre, the first proper theatre to be built in Saint John. It is curious to note that his name was Powell and his programme was very similar to the one that heralded the coming of professionals to Halifax. The mystery is, of course, the eighty-eight years that separate the two events. It may be co-incidence that the names are the same, or it is possible that the Powell of the Powell and Baker team that performed in Halifax in 1897 was a relative carrying on the tradition.

In Saint John, Mr. Powell was performing for "one night only." His repertoire is impressive:

For one Night only

Theatre, Drury-Lane, Saint John

On Wed. May 16th

Mr. Powell will give his Attick Entertainment

THE EVENING BRUSH

For

Rubbing Off the Rust of Care

Subject for Laughter

Butchers in Herocks—Tragedy Tailers—Wooden Actors—

Blunderers and Bogglers—An Actor reading his part without

Eyes, Etc.

To be interspersed with several appropriate

Comic Songs, viz

Shakespeare's Seven Ages of Human Life,

Darby Logan's Passage from Dublin to London,

The Coach Box,

The Golden Days of good Queen Bess

To which there will be added a Whimsical and Critical

Dissertation on Noses:

The Ruby Nose,

Roman Nose of old Ben Blunderbuss,

The prognosticating Snout of Goody Screech Owl, Etc. Etc.

The whole to conclude with a song

Modernized by Mr. Powell

Giving a Whimsical description of the

BATTLE OF THE NILE,

To be sung in the character of a French Officer.

In 1816, a professional group moved into Saint John and started productions of a fairly high standard, but the letters to the paper demanded that they be removed because of the "ribald nature" of the plays. Considering that one of the plays was Shakespeare's *Romeo and Juliet*, our first reaction is to question the intelligence of Saint John's citizens. Actually, it was an American company, and anti-Yankee sentiments may well have been running high in Saint John.

In the *Courier*, September 6, 1817, the comedy *Every One Has His Faults* by Mrs. Inchbold was advertised, and we find, when checking the cast list, that it was the same company that had been playing in Halifax. Mr. Placide was a rather well-known American actor of the time. T. A. Brown, in his *History of the American Stage*, describes him as an actor of "the good old school – a school wherein is taught the lesson that a strict adherence to truth in the delineation of a character, constitutes one of its chief, if not the most essential, feature of the dramatic art." But Mr. Placide and his company obviously impressed the theatre public of Saint John unfavourably, and the amateurs, as usual, were unable to offer an alternative.

As the years went by more theatres were built, such as Hopley's, Lanergan's, The Academy of Music, and the Saint John Opera House, and they were built as a rule to serve the touring professionals from England and the United States. The rise of commercial activity in Saint John in the 1830s and later did not create an atmosphere in which the theatre arts could grow. The members of the *nouveaux riches* manifested a shallow and superficial interest in cultural activities, a condition in which only the professional touring companies could survive. After the great Saint John fire of 1877, it would appear that the arts suffered another decline just as the decline in ship building and lumbering at approximately the same time resulted in the loss of her position as a leading commercial city.

In Montreal and Quebec, as might be expected, the first attempts to stage an entertainment were made by the French-speaking Canadians, and plays in French generally dominated the stage until the first half of the 1790s. By the latter part of that decade, however, as A. R. M. Lower observes in his *Canadians in the Making*, the trend to performances in English had become obvious.[8] Amateurs and travelling performers vied for attention, and in 1798 the citizens were offered an exhibition of " – a giraffe!" Although Lower doesn't mention it, the appearance of this animal may well have signalled the arrival of John B. Ricketts' Circus. A record of the travels and experiences of this circus in Montreal and Quebec is preserved in the reminiscences of its star performer, Mr. John Durang.[9] He was an original member of the Ricketts' Circus which had been performing circus acts, ballet, opera and serious drama in Philadelphia and New York since 1792. In the early summer of 1797, Ricketts decided to explore less populated areas, and to do this he divided his company into two: his brother, in charge

[8] Arthur R. M. Lower, *Canadians in the Making* (Toronto, 1958), p. 154. Lower is specifically speaking about Quebec. However, the same conditions existed in Montreal.
[9] *The Memoir of John Durang, American Actor, 1785–1816* (Pittsburgh: University of Pittsburgh Press, 1967). The manuscript copy of the Durang memoirs is held by the Historical Society of York County, York, Pennsylvania.

of one company, went off in the direction of the Atlantic States, and John Ricketts himself led the other company to Albany and then to Canada.

Daniel R. Porter, who has traced Durang's early career, and written a short article, "The Circus First Comes to Albany, 1798," about the first leg of the journey, lists the many talents of this man. [During his career, which began in 1784 and ended in 1821, he was "at one time or another a dancer, actor, mime, translator, manager, author, clown, puppeteer, designer, acrobat, rider, slack wire performer, musician, singer, promoter, property man, and choreographer."[10] And he apparently needed all these talents to survive in the backwoods of Canada.] The trip alone was rather extraordinary. The Circus no doubt tried to keep to the paths used by the American and British forces during the American Revolutionary War, but as Durang confesses, they often found it necessary to hire a guide. A Mr. Dailey saw them through a ten-mile stretch: "Sometimes thro' swamps then over mountains, then thro' a thick woods, then for a long part of the way on the beach sinking in the sand, the sun scorching and flies biting."[11] And here and there they saw log cabins, which, as Durang notes, were "inhabited by Canadians." In due course, they finally reached Montreal where they immediately built a circus-theatre, and settled down for an indefinite stay.

Before leaving Montreal, Durang was allowed a benefit performance and for this occasion he "brought out" an English comedy called *The Ghost*. He also presented a number of Indian dances which he describes:

I performed the *pipe dance*. The manner is graceful and pleasing in the nature of savage harmony. Next the *Bagle Tail Dance*. I concluded with the *War Dance*, descriptive of their exploits, throwing myself in different postures with firm steps with hatchet and knife representing the manner they kill and scalp and take prisoners, with the yells and war hoops. I was told by the officer that I excelled as their native Indian dances were more simple. I jumped through a barrel of fire and concluded with an exhibition of fireworks. I had eight hundred dollars in the house.[12]

His costume was also "most compleat" having been purchased from an Indian for rum.

The Circus's last production in Montreal was on May 3, 1798. It then travelled to Quebec where it performed for two months before returning to the United States. The first invasion of Lower Canada by the foreign professional was over. Ricketts' Circus had actually proven that a trip to Montreal and Quebec was possible and reasonably profitable.

Other intrepid travellers were bound to follow, but it was not until sometime in 1803 that the next American actor arrived. Mr. Ormsby also came via Albany and presumably made the trip alone. With the assistance of some of the Montreal citizens he built the city's first theatre which was located on the second storey of a stone building situated on St. Sulpice Street, near St. Paul Street. His first performance, on November 19, 1804, was *The*

[10]Daniel R. Porter, "The Circus First Comes to Albany, 1798," *New York History*, XLIV, No. 1, 50 (January, 1963).
[11]*Durang Memoir*.
[12]*Ibid*.

Busy Body and *Sultan* for which he charged 5/ for boxes, 2/6 for the gallery. As Franklin Graham says in his *Histrionic Montreal*, it was "an unprofitable season!"[13] But thespians are an indomitable breed, and we find, in 1807, that a <u>Mr. Seth Prigmore</u> had arrived in Montreal, determined to start producing regular dramas. He rebuilt the existing theatre, calling it the Montreal Theatre and taking care that stoves be placed in different parts of the house. He also saw to it that "the gallery frequenters were kept in strictest subjection, and <u>no</u> intoxicants sold." For his first play, Colman's *Heir-at-Law* which was presented on January 7, 1808, the price of admission was in dollars. A box cost a dollar, the pit fifty cents, and the gallery twenty-five cents. For a later production of *Othello* (the first time in this country) he returned to English currency: the boxes costing 5/-; pit 2/6; and gallery 1/3. He was probably pressing on with his theatrical affairs when John Bernard arrived in the city.[14] His opinion of Prigmore's company is short and to the point: "I found a company playing at Montreal as deficient in talent as in numbers." Prigmore didn't succeed in Montreal, nor anywhere else as far as I can determine. One rather amusing picture of him is recorded by Graham. Charles Durang, who was following in his father's footsteps, recalls meeting him on tour:

> We met Mr. P. in a huge sleigh near Trois-Rivières. He was wrapped up in a buffalo robe, a *bonnet rouge* was on his head, such as the Canadian peasantry wear; a wampum belt was buckled around his waist and Indian moccasins were on his feet. With his red face and burly form, he appeared like one of the ancient French landed proprietors, or like one of the half-breed chiefs. He had some three or four persons with him, whom he called his company, and was then *en route* to play at Quebec.

As Montreal grew in importance as a theatre town, Quebec City declined. In the latter city, the stage facilities were extremely limited, and as a result the citizens were only able to attract the third-rate companies. Graham notes the experience of one such company, of which Durang was a member. The story must reflect the low point of cultural development in Quebec City in the fall of 1810. The company was led by a Mr. John Mills:

> ... on the opening night Mills acted scenes from "Macbeth," although the company did not possess means beyond the compass of a farce. In the dagger scene he used two white-handled dinner knives borrowed from Mrs. Armstrong, a good-natured, little, fat lady who kept the tavern under the theatre. The kilt was borrowed from an officer and fellow lodger. Taken as a whole, the play, as presented on this occasion, was a direful affair. It had not the redeeming merit of being ludicrous or funny, unless the amusement was furnished by a very tall Scotchman with a huge aquiline nose and a bald head, the very personification of a bald eagle topping a human skeleton. . . . The Governor-General and his pretty young wife were there. All the married officers and their wives were

---

[13]Franklin Graham, *Histrionic Montreal* (Montreal, 1902). There is a wealth of information in this book which is of interest mainly to the theatre historian. There is no index, and it is generally difficult to follow, but if you know the names of some of the early actors and want to trace their careers, this book is invaluable.

[14]John Bernard was an English actor who was manager of the Boston Theatre in 1806. He passed through Canada on his way home where he died in "destitute circumstances," November 29, 1828.

present, besides the fashion of Quebec. A collection of refinement that had been used to the most superb theatres of Europe were thus assembled in a large upper storey of a building which was in a state of dilapidation. It was fixed up with tiers of boxes, but the auditers could shake hands across the area. . . . This brilliant audience, although they seemed to enjoy the performance with becoming grace and good humour, gradually withdrew. . . .

Little improvement in the facilities was made as the years passed. It is, therefore, strange to note that Henry Irving saw fit to perform here in 1884 during his second American tour. His secretary reported:

The theatre here would make you shriek. It is a cross between a chapel and a very small concert room and the stage is about half the size of that of St. George's Hall. The entrance is being washed now, but no amount of soap and water will repair the broken windows. The kind of people who play here as a rule are of the least intellectual order – we found two members of the preceding troupe on the stage – they were *two hens*![15]

And so we can leave this early theatre in Quebec City, as Irving surely did, with little reason to return.

Montreal continued to grow in size and in cultural attainment. The first proper theatre in Montreal was the Theatre Royal which was built in 1825 with John Molson being the principal shareholder. The cost of construction was approximately $30,000. It was two storeys high with a Doric portico, and inside it had two tiers of boxes, a pit and a gallery. The Royal (also affectionately called The Theatre Molson) opened on Monday, November 21, under the management of Frederick Brown, a professional tragedian from the United States. It is worth noting that in the early productions at this theatre there was a constant mixing of the amateur and professional. The core of the company consisted of Brown's professional friends from Boston; the minor actors were selected from the amateur ranks in Montreal. He was, apparently, still the manager in 1826 when Edmund Kean made his first appearance there as Richard III, and in the succeeding nights presented *The Merchant of Venice*, *King Lear*, and *Othello*. A list of some of Kean's supporting cast in this latter play remains. We find Brown playing Iago and his wife cast in the role of Emilia. Cassio was performed by a Mr. William Lee, Roderigo by Thomas Placide (brother of Harry Placide, who according to Brown's *History of the American Stage* made his first appearance on the stage in 1828, at the Park Theatre, New York) and Desdemona by a Miss Riddle. With such a cast, hastily assembled (a common procedure), the effectiveness of the production depended primarily upon the abilities of the star, who at all times was meant to be the centre of attention. To move from scene to scene, constantly being faced with a variety of acting styles, temperament, and misplaced cues, would have been enough to tempt even the most hardened performer to fortify himself against the ordeal. Many, in fact, did carry a bottle as a "prop" for all occasions.

The year 1833 was a notable one for the Theatre Royal and the citizens of Montreal, for in that year Charles Kemble and his daughter made their

---

[15]Laurence Irving, *Henry Irving: The Actor and His World* (London, 1951), p. 445.

appearance. We are indebted to Graham for saving an interesting piece of correspondence. In a letter to Charles Mathews, Sr., Fanny describes some of the conditions she was faced with and hopes that he will take her advice and stay away. The letter was written on December 21, 1834:

We went to Canada, I believe, upon the same terms as everywhere else—a division of profits. Vincent de Camp had the theatres there, and of the horrible strolling concerns I could ever imagine, his company and scenery and getting-ups were the worst. . . . Heaven knows the company would have been blackguardly representatives of the gentry in "Tom and Jerry;" you can fancy what they were in heroicals. Our houses were good; so I think, yours would be; but though I am sure you would not have to complain of want of hospitality . . . the unspeakable dirt and discomfort of the inns, the scarcity of eatables and the abundance of eaters (fleas, bugs, etc.), together with the wicked (limb) dislocating road from St. Johns to Laprairie would make up a sum of suffering, for which it would be difficult to find adequate compensation. . . . The heat while we were in Montreal was intolerable – the filth intolerable – the bugs intolerable – the people intolerable – the jargon they speak intolerable. I lifted my hands in thankfulness when I again set foot in these United States.

Obviously, in Fanny's eyes, Montreal had not achieved much in the way of cultural stature. But her remarks were personal and were no doubt meant to bring a smile to old Mathews. Still, in assessing the standards in Canada in these early times, it's wise to remember that they were considerably lower than those that existed in England or the United States.

In 1835, Molson presented the use of the Royal to the Amateurs of the 24th Regiment. This is of particular interest to researchers in Canadian theatre because in the ranks of the principal players we find the name Nickinson. It was with the Amateurs that John Nickinson, who was later to become the manager of the Royal Lyceum in Toronto, made his first appearance. He probably spent at least eight years in the vicinity of Montreal for in 1843 he is referred to as manager of the Theatre Royal. Determined to spend his life in the theatre, he bought his discharge from the army and left for the United States where he made his first stage appearance in Albany. He then became prominent as a member of Mitchell's Olympic Company, and when this company closed he pursued the fashion of the day and went on the "road." It is at this point that he began to play an important role in the early theatre of Toronto.[16]

However, in the early days of his career, it is rather fascinating to note that Nickinson was probably part of the company that met Charles Dickens during his first American visit in 1842. Dickens was giving a series of readings, but in Montreal he decided to act. He had always wanted to be an actor, of course. His readings were apparently staged with great care and on his lecture tours he was known to take along a gas-man to ensure proper lighting for his facial expressions. It may have been that Dickens considered Montreal sufficiently in the backwater to allow him to test himself as an actor without fear of public criticism, or else that Nickinson and his fellow actors, having spent some time with Dickens talking about the theatre, had

[16]See p. 25.

12

eventually persuaded him to join them on the boards for a night or two. We'll probably never know. The fact is, Dickens' memorable connection with amateur theatricals had its beginnings in Montreal. He acted the part of Alfred Highflyer in *A Roland for an Oliver*, Mr. Snobington in *Two O'Clock in the Morning*, and Gallop in *Deaf as a Post*. He was also part-time director, and approached this role with enthusiasm. In a letter to a friend he described the scene of a rehearsal in his inimitable fashion:

I would give something . . . if you could stumble into that very dark and dusty theatre in the day-time (at any minute between twelve and three), and see me with my coat off, the stage manager and universal director, urging impracticable ladies and impossible gentlemen on to the very confines of insanity, shouting and driving about, in my own person, to an extent which would justify any philanthropic stranger in clapping me into a strait-waistcoat without further inquiry, endeavouring to goad H. into some dim and faint understanding of a prompter's duties, and struggling in such a vortex of noise, dirt, bustle, confusion, and inextricable entanglement of speech and action as you would grow giddy in contemplating.[17]

Unfortunately no further information about this amateur group has been found.

Two years later, in 1844, the Theatre Royal was made available to William Charles Macready, one of the first English stars to tour in America. He presented *Hamlet* on July 15, and a reporter from the *Montreal Gazette* took this occasion not only to praise the play and the actors' performances but to make some interesting observations about the interior of the theatre. He observes that the manager had "renovated the second tier of boxes, covered the seats etc. for the accommodation of those who are unable to procure seats in the first." He doesn't mention the pit, but we can assume that there was one because he goes on to say that "to prevent any improper persons from entering that portion [the private area, obviously], there will be several citizens placed at that door." Class distinctions were being faithfully observed!

The first Theatre Royal was closed in 1845 and from this time on there is a certain amount of confusion as to the names of the subsequent theatres. The next theatre was built in 1847 and was generally called the Royal or Hays Theatre. This name doesn't become a problem until 1852 when an immense fire destroyed this theatre but spared another theatre which had been erected in 1851 and was also called the Theatre Royal. We can only assume that the citizens of Montreal had a clear idea as to where they were going when they went to the theatre in 1851.

The Hays Theatre, or as it was sometimes referred to, the Theatre, opened its doors to the public on July 10, 1847. This information is taken from a slim volume written by a Mr. John Gaisford, who was there at the time and became the prompter of the Theatre Royal, Montreal, in 1848.[18] He had

---

17T. Edgar Pemberton, *Charles Dickens and the Stage* (London, 1888), p. 203.
18John Gaisford, *Theatrical Thoughts* (Montreal 1848). It was dedicated to Major Granville, 23rd (Royal Welch) Fusiliers and the Officers of the Garrison of Montreal. On the front page is also inscribed "Theatre Royal, Montreal, 10th April, 1848," and the date of the author's benefit: "Theatre Royal, Thursday, December 23, 1848."

arrived in Montreal to accept the position offered to him by the business manager, Mr. Skerrett, who had control of a number of theatres throughout eastern Canada. The job was to have begun on May 3, 1847, at a theatre in Hamilton, but because of a "deficiency in the circulating medium," and "in consequence of another one," he arrived in Montreal about the middle of June. It was a poor start for Mr. Gaisford. But he was not the type to remain idle. While he was waiting for the prompter's position (which he eventually assumed) he promptly wrote a book about the theatre called *Theatrical Thoughts*.

It is an odd little book, a hodgepodge of various ideas and thoughts. Among other things, he reproduces some of the material from a benefit he had given at the theatre on December 23, 1848. Part of the evening consisted of the reading of conundrums submitted by the Montreal citizens. All those who participated by sending in their rhymes were expected, quite naturally, to attend the theatre that evening to hear Gaisford read them aloud. The applause which followed each reading was noted by Gaisford and at the conclusion, he chose the winner by determining which conundrum received the greatest response. The invitation was welcomed by certain wits and wags, and, wits and wags being what they are, not all the conundrums were read. As he notes in his apology:

I received several other Conundrums, some of which being decidedly immoral were immediately destroyed.

Some conundrums that may have been read out by Gaisford at the benefit were not printed in the book because they were of a "party political, temporary local, and decidedly personal nature." His excuse was that "it is not convenient for me to walk the streets in armour, beneath my clothing, and I have a great antipathy to legal proceedings." There were no repercussions, and apparently Gaisford's little trick to get an audience was quite successful.

Theatrical Thoughts is divided into two main parts. In the first half the author considers the various expenses of the theatre, and in the latter part he amuses himself by making some remarks about the new Hays Theatre, professional and amateur theatricals, a make-believe world of a rich and poor dramatist, and an evening at the "Shakespeare Club." Both halves are disappointing, mainly because no names are mentioned. Although employed as a prompter to the Theatre Royal, and as a box-keeper for the amateur societies, he never mentions the names of his associates, and he is quite proud of this fact:

The careful reader will at once perceive that in no one instance are individuals even hinted at throughout these pages; neither are the virtues of the influential Star painted in glowing colors, nor his private character probed, for the discovery of blemishes – names are not mentioned.

Thus a book that could have been invaluable was thereby reduced to a playful exercise.

In part one of *Theatrical Thoughts*, Gaisford's comments are of a very broad nature. In naming the various positions in a theatre, he always uses the title and never the specific name. The proprietor is noted as being a capitalist who, "if he did not actually build, at all events, has bought the edifice, and paid for it a handsome sum of money, on the rent of which he depends for the interest on his Capital." The stage manager, as Gaisford points out, was "a very important person." But other than insisting that he should be a gentleman of good education and one "acquainted not only with the Classics, but able to read and converse freely in French, German and Italian language," he makes few specific references to the important daily duties. Who was this exceptional individual at the Theatre Royal in 1848? The chances are he didn't exist. As Gaisford admits, few members of the profession could reach the standard he drew. His definition of a prompter is not too strict which leads us to believe that he may have used himself as a yardstick. The man had to be "well educated, energetic, sober, straightforward, punctual and systematic, well gifted with application, perseverance, and endurance." Other members of a well-run theatre are: the call boy, who "should be a young lad, who can read and write pretty well, and being smart, active and intelligent, with a taste that way inclined, promises some day to make an actor"; a scenic artist, who has "the knack of making unseemly daubs appear at a distance like beautifully delineated pictures"; a carpenter and machinist, who "in addition to being an able workman at his craft, must be able to invent or contrive all the numerous machinery connected with the stage"; a property man, who "must be a genius of a peculiar nature, a sort of Jack-of-all-trades, and master of them all; no matter what is required, he is expected either to beg, buy, borrow, or steal it, and oftentimes has to display his taste in the manufacture of inanimate animal objects from a mouse to an elephant." The last member of the profession to receive his scrutiny was the treasurer. This gentleman's personality during business hours seems to have remained constant through the years. Gaisford suggests that you "Go to the Box Office in the morning if you would see the cool indifference with which he invariably treats you and your money. . . . He has no time for compliments, so never thinks of paying them to you."

The subtitle of the second half of *Theatrical Thoughts*, "The Drama in Montreal," would lead one to believe that some exciting "inside" stories of the acting world in early Montreal might be divulged. Some facts do come to light, but Gaisford cautiously refuses to go much beyond the simple relating of events that happened in 1847. For a description of the new Hays Theatre he recommends his readers to "pay a dollar each for a view of its interior." He does, however, give some details about the seating capacity and scenery. The theatre accommodated "comfortably about five hundred persons in the Boxes, eight hundred in the Pit, and eight hundred in the Gallery." Most of the audience could have "a good view of the stage," which was "furnished with a moderate stock of very good scenery." On the whole, he was very impressed with this "magnificent Temple of the Muses," which, in his opinion, stood "unrivalled on this side of the Atlantic as a Provincial Theatre," and reflected "a great deal of credit upon Mr. M. J. Hays, the proprietor, for his enterprise, and the various artists for their several exertions." In his article, "Les Théâtres et les lieux d'amusements à Montréal," which appeared in the 1908–9 edition of *L'Annuaire Théâtral*, M. E. Z. Massicotte adds to our knowledge of its interior. He quotes from the *Monde illustré*:

A l'intérieur du théâtre il y avait trois galeries, des loges de face, de côté, d'avant-scène et même des baignoires. Son jeu de scène, un des meilleurs en Amérique, était évalué a $40,000. Seul le rideau, peint par l'italien Martanni, coûtait $6,000.

According to Gaisford, the programme on the theatre's first opening night consisted of an opening address by the lessee, the national anthem, *Much Ado about Nothing*, a dance by Miss St. Clair, and the farce of *Tom Noddy's Secret*. This contradicts slightly Jean Beraud's description of the occasion in his *350 Ans de Théâtre au Canada français*, in which he notes that the opening productions were *Beaucoup de bruit pour rien* and *Le Marchand de Venise*.[19] They both agree, however, that the star was James W. Wallack, who played there for three weeks. Various other troupes arrived, but business was generally bad. Skerrett, the business manager, was unable to sustain his bookings of professional companies, and we find in 1848 that the theatre was given over a great deal to the amateurs. Gaisford says that this happened on fourteen occasions, "six times by the Officers of the Garrison – four times by the Garrison Amateurs – twice by the Canadian, and twice by two different parties of Gentlemen Amateurs." Although highly critical of amateur productions as a whole, he was very favourably impressed by the efforts of the Gentlemen Amateurs. He was willing to state that "there are few *Dramatic Corps* at present in existence which are able to compete with the Gentlemen who performed in the *Heir-at-Law, London Assurance*, and *The Rivals*." He felt that the reason for their success lay in the fact that they essayed characters, "so essentially those of gentlemen, that the polished drawing-room manners, and easy unassumed behaviour of the Performers told to great advantage. They wisely eschewed anything of a heavy tragic character, confining their labors to these comedies and farces within scope of their abilities." The standard of the Garrison Amateurs, on the other hand, was dismally low, their company consisting of "stage struck Sergeants, Corporals and Privates." At this point one cannot help but remember the early career of John Nickinson, who had passed through Montreal some years ago and was, by this time, acting in the United States.

Gaisford probably went back home after a few years; he had come originally from Savannah, Georgia. We can imagine the tales he must have told about his years in the frozen North. Hopefully at this time he would have been mentioning names![20]

The second Theatre Royal, built in 1851, was still standing when Graham published *Histrionic Montreal* in 1902. It had undergone many structural changes, the most important one being the removal of the pit. In the 60s, this area, called the "twenty-five-cent pit," extended from the stage to the back of the house. Sometime in 1873, a Mr. Ben De Bar converted this space

16

---

[19] Jean Beraud, *350 Ans de théâtre au Canada français* (Ottawa, 1958), p. 40.
[20] In his *Theatrical Thoughts* he breathes life only into one little story and that is his recounting of events on the night he went to "The Shakespeare Club."

into what we now consider the orchestra, and the "pittites" were sent upstairs to the top gallery. We trust that this move put an end to a "game"
frequently played by the pittites and called "Tossing." A young person who
happened to be on one of the back benches would shout, "Toss me," and he
would be immediately picked up by his neighbours and tossed over the heads
of the customers directly in front. He would receive this treatment for the
full length of the hall, eventually landing on the front bench where he would
be allowed to remain as a reward for his hazardous trip. Tossing in the
gallery would have been a very dangerous game.

The New Dominion Theatre was also opened in 1873, and like the
Theatre Royal catered to the touring professional. By 1876 it had become a
home for vaudeville troupes, and in 1878 burlesque moved in. The Academy
of Music, situated on the east side of Victoria Street a few doors above St.
Catherine Street, was built in 1875. The interior consisted of four boxes,
four stalls, two galleries and had a seating capacity of about 2,000. It was
at this theatre in 1880 that W. H. Fuller's Canadian musical *H.M.S. Parliament* had its first important performance.[21]

After 1890 theatres in Montreal began to multiply. The Queen's Theatre
started its career in 1891 and after a varied but not distinguished career
closed in 1898. The Théâtre Français, first opened in 1884, was rebuilt and
renamed the Empire Theatre in 1891. For the next three years it was
managed by a syndicate of prominent French Canadians who intended to
make it a house of grand opera and high-class French drama. But it passed
back to an English-speaking company after three years of financial loss. The
last and most important theatre built and operated during the period of this
study was Her Majesty's Theatre which opened its doors in 1898 and
brought down the last curtain on May 27, 1963. As a theatre it was ranked
among the finest in America. There were two galleries, of which the upper
was divided and contained the family circle and the "gods." There were ten
boxes on each side of the stage, six being a part of the proscenium arch. An
American, Mr. Frank Murphy, secured the first lease and opened the theatre
with a production of E. E. Rice's *The Ballet Girl*. It was a very social
occasion – as almost all openings are – and so the performance was preceded
by poetry recitations and an address from the mayor. One or two lines in a
poem which had been prepared for the occasion caught my eye:

> That all we offer shall be clean and pure;
> "Immodest scenes admit of no defence,
> For want of decency is want of sense."

A perfectly proper thing to say, and as usual in the Canadian theatre these
sentiments were no doubt respected!

The Ballet Girl, a now unknown play by a forgotten playwright, was
performed by an undistinguished cast. But it was a climax in the eyes of
Franklin Graham.

How different the scene ninety-four years before! when, during the same month,

[21]As far as I know, W. H. Fuller was not himself a part of the theatrical scene in
Montreal. His plays have, therefore, been treated separately. See pp. 149–56.

our forefathers gathered [to see] Centlivre's "Busybody," an obsolete comedy by a forgotten playwright, and directed by an actor-manager whose name has no place in the list of *biographia dramatica*.

The surroundings were more opulent, that is true. But on stage, the play and the performers were still unimpressive. No Canadian themes were struck for this auspicious occasion, and no Canadian star was among those on the stage.

Following the path of immigration along the Great Lakes and into the interior of Upper Canada we find evidence of early play-making in the little towns and cities. But the growth is slow and uncertain. Writing in 1820, Robert Gourlay found that Upper Canada was:

too young for regular theatric entertainments and these delicacies and refinements of luxury which are the usual attendants of wealth. Dissipation, with her fascinating train of expenses and vices, has made but little progress on the shores of the lakes.[22]

Such conditions were not destined to last, and as the towns and cities appeared, a growing insistence to entertain and be entertained began to make itself felt.

As in the Maritimes, the plays were at first put on by the citizens. And as the years pass we find the same transition from the local amateur to the foreign professional. The speed with which this took place was directly related to the rate of improvement in communication. In the late 30s and early 40s, the amateur reigned, but by the middle of the 60s the iron monster was carrying the American and English professional into all the major towns in Ontario. Ottawa, Kingston, Toronto, Guelph, Hamilton, London and Stratford were important stops on a theatrical tour. And as the spur lines were pushed out, other, smaller towns were inevitably brought into the circuit.

Ontario was literally invaded by the professionals, although we should note that they were usually of the "touring" type; there are, strangely enough, few examples of dramatic companies taking up residence in a city or town outside of the Maritimes. Some of the most interesting and amusing descriptions of early theatre conditions were made by two such travelling performers, Mrs. Sam Cowell, and Captain Horton Rhys, alias Morton Price.

Mrs. Cowell kept a diary which contains a day-by-day report of the Canadian tour she took with her husband in the year 1860. She reflected at the end of their Canadian travels: "It will quite be a relief to get into a City like Detroit, after these half savage villages."[23] Her description of the "theatre" and its environment in Ottawa (soon to become Canada's capital) supports the general impression that Canadians were not making much effort to nourish the theatrical arts:

It was very dark when Sam and I set off to find the "Theatre" where the Concert was to take place. Over wooden pavements, and no pavements, and deep ruts,

---

[22]Robert Gourlay, *A Statistical Account of Upper Canada* (London, 1822), p. 250.
[23]Information about the Cowells comes from Willson M. Disher's *The Cowells in America* (London, 1834). See pp. 193, 176, and 169.

and thick pools of mud, we picked our way till we were in the fields. . . . Across a dismal road lay the Theatre, "A rat-hole below and a swallow's nest above." We knocked in vain for admittance for a long time. At last got into the den. Dismal crackling, brown "evergreens" decorated the Theatre in the audience part. The dust clogged one's throat, and the gas leaked so badly that half had to be put out. – Sam dressed half in sight of the audience, and Miss German had a cellar (full of rats) assigned to her, so Sam let her dress (first) in his room. – One or two fellows were very noisy in the gallery. . . . We had $80.00.

Two typical characteristics of the theatre in Canada which persisted through the years are referred to by Mrs. Cowell in her comments about the Music Hall in Quebec. On arriving at the theatre the company discovered one of their baskets missing. In their search for this article they looked under the stage where they "found a door, knocking at which, and on its being opened, we found ourselves in a drinking saloon." Having found the basket there, they went "upstairs to the stage." Most early theatres were, in fact, extensions of drinking parlours. This being the case, it is not surprising to discover that the theatre was deplored by the respectable majority. Edwin C. Guillet, in his examination of social life in early Upper Canada, notes the close association between saloons and entertainment, and he cites a contemporary publication to indicate that the saloon (and probably much of the entertainment presented there) was a source of embarrassment to many of the residents of York:

. . . we believe there is no city of its size on the continent which is pestered with so many saloons and taverns; and, if the morals and habits of our people were to be judged by this criterion, the stranger would form a very unfavourable and unjust opinion.[24]

A second common characteristic of theatre buildings in Canada noted by Mrs. Cowell was that the stage was usually upstairs. We can assume that in buildings serving a number of purposes, the theatre was considered the least important. The stores and the drinking establishments were entered by walking through a door, but to gain admission to the theatre one had often to climb rickety stairs. The first characteristic disappeared over the years because of social pressure, but the habit of second-floor theatres persisted (see appendix B).

Captain Horton Rhys arrived in the New World at approximately the same time as the Cowells. Like Mrs. Cowell, Rhys kept a diary, and shortly after his return to England, he published a book called *A Theatrical Trip for a Wager*. As the title implies, the Captain's venture was the result of a bet. When a number of his friends doubted his ability to survive as a performer in a country in which he was not known, Rhys insisted he could. Eventually a legal document was drawn up stating the facts of the wager of which the following is an excerpt:

We, the undersigned A. Smith and B. Brown, conjointly bet Captain H. R., the sum of five hundred pounds that he does not, in any country other than Great Britain or Ireland, by his talents as an actor, author, singer, or composer, separ-

[24]Edwin C. Guillet, *Early Life in Upper Canada* (Toronto, 1933, 1963).

ately or collectively, clear the sum of five hundred pounds over and above all expenses other than those of Board and Lodging and personal expenditure. . . . It is further stipulated that Captain H. R. shall travel and make and play his engagements under an assumed and fictitious name.[25]

Rhys accepted and chose to tour in the United States and Canada. The similarities to *Around the World in Eighty Days* are obvious, and indeed the Captain himself does remind one of Philias Fogg. Unlike Fogg, however, Rhys had as his companion a lady, a talented young singer, whose stage name was Miss Catherine Lucette.

Of all the theatres Rhys played in, Nordheimer's Hall in Montreal seems to have been the best.[26] He found Quebec's Music Hall in much the same condition as Mrs. Cowell had reported, and referred to it merely as a "wretched contrivance." Kingston's stage facilities were limited to a city hall which, he noted rather sadly, rented at twelve dollars a night. Belleville's theatre was new, but "so new that it consisted of simply lath and plaster; the lessee, a Mr. Lester, did all he could to make it endurable, but – ye gods! I never *was* so cold, and Lucille and myself to this day regret having taken fifty dols. a night to play at Belleville." In Cobourg he was reduced to playing in a hotel.

Although he doesn't mention the name of the theatre in which he performed in Toronto, it was most likely the Royal Lyceum. We will be examining this theatre later when we consider the Toronto scene. It is perhaps sufficient to note here that when it was partially destroyed by fire in 1883, a reporter for the Toronto *Globe*, April 24, 1883, took the occasion to review its past. In the early days it was "used as a drill shed by the 10th Royals during the stirring times of the American War, and in the winter used for skating under the name of the Victorian Skating Rink." According to the article, which is certainly not specific, it did have its moments as a theatre. The writer mentions one detail of interest. In 1853 "Cool Burgess rented it and fitted it up as a minstrel hall with great success." It is possible, therefore, that Cool was in or around the theatre when Rhys arrived on the scene. The Toronto engagement, by the way, was not successful and Rhys left after one performance, taking with him some unfavourable opinions of the city:

I, however, didn't care much about Toronto; there was too much assumption of exclusiveness, without just grounds to go upon, and I left the place then, as I do now, without any intention of returning to it.

Other cities in which he performed were Hamilton, Port Hope, and Ottawa, but Rhys unfortunately left no descriptions of the theatres in these towns.

We should note that his arrival in Canadian towns and cities as an entertainer was the cause of some concern to the inhabitants. As the Captain remarked, "Actors in Canada are a little too much of the Fly-by-night order to hold a *high* social status." The theatre still played a small part in the

[25]Captain Horton Rhys, *A Theatrical Trip for a Wager* (London, 1861). This book has now been reprinted with an introduction by Robertson Davies.
[26]It was essentially a concert hall and is not mentioned in *Histrionic Montreal*. Charles Heavysege gave a reading of *Saul* in Nordheimer's Hall.

1 / Neptune approaches New France, and so the theatrical
invasion of Canada began. This first play in Canada was
performed partly in canoes, partly at a feast, in 1606. Drawing
by C. W. Jefferys, from the Imperial Oil collection.

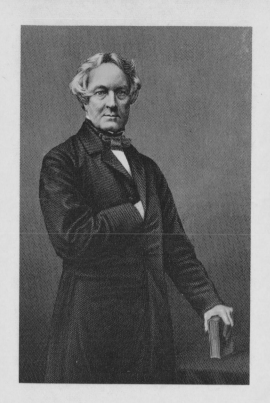

2 & 3 / Important theatrical names as well as little known performers started visiting Canadian cities and towns well before Confederation. William Charles Macready (*left*) was playing Hamlet in Montreal in 1844, and Captain Horton Rhys (*right*), the extraordinary Englishman who made a theatrical tour of North America on a bet, arrived about twenty years later.

4 / In the gold-rush town of Barkerville, British Columbia, the Williams Creek Fire Hall served as the local theatre.

5 / Frank's Hotel, as the name implies, did not survive from its "take" at the box office. The second floor of this building provided the first regular theatre in York (Toronto).

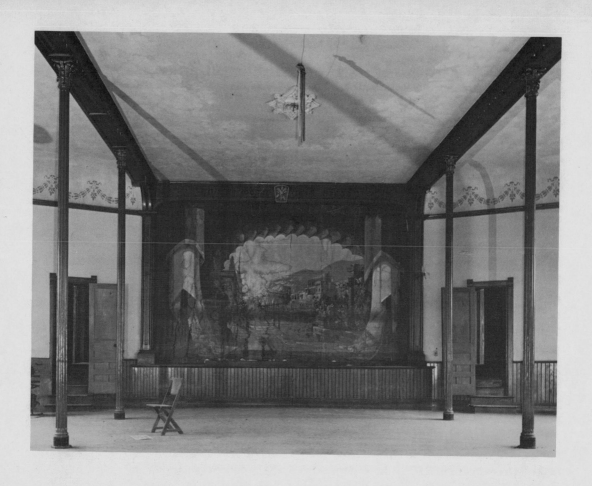

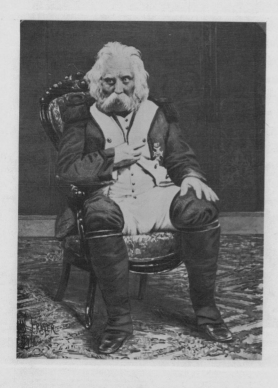

6 / Here in the Opera House in Thamesville, Ontario, Robertson Davies, as a youngster, made his stage *début*. Many theatres like this have lasted to our own time.

7 / John Nickinson, here seen costumed and made up for a now unknown role, was the manager of the Royal Lyceum, Toronto, in the 1850s.

social life of Canadians at this time and was quite often looked upon with much distrust. The fact that the Captain was able to make five hundred pounds and return to England at the appointed hour may be considered as something of an achievement.

It is rewarding to look back to the early theatres of Toronto, to the time when this city was known as "Little York." One is able to find articles and documents which produce not only the facts but something of the spirit of the time.[27] Beginning in 1820, Frank's Hotel on the northwest corner of West Market Street and Market Lane (Colborne Street) provided the first regular theatre in York. Performances were apparently held in a room with a low ceiling, sometimes referred to as a loft and at other times as the ballroom. According to an article in the *Colonial Advocate* in 1825, the "confined space" did house boxes and a pit. In the boxes there were generally found people such as "the Hon. Mr. Allan, the Hon. Mr. Macaulay, Colonels Adamson and Ingersoll, Major Heward, Messrs. Matthews, Hamilton, Clark, Fothergill, Lefferty, Gordon, Morris, D. Jones, and Wilkinson, M.P.'s. . . ." In the pit sat "the barristers' clerks, attorneys' apprentices and shopkeepers." There is no indication of the capacity of the house, but we can assume that it seated something under a hundred people. This was presumably quite adequate, because as the writer points out, "puritanism triumphed over jollity, mirth and frivolity," in the "pious town of York." Some of the plays performed were *Barbarossa or The Siege of Algiers*, *Ali Baba or The Forty Thieves*, *The Lady of the Lake*, and *The Miller and His Men*. This last production was seen by the writer from the *Colonial Advocate* and on that night (December 28, 1825) he reports, there was a full house which included His Excellency's eldest son and many of the "fashionable people," such as "Messrs. C. Jones, Proudfoot, Lee, J. Jones, [and] Lyons."

On stage there was an interesting blend of the professional and the amateur. So-called professionals such as Mr. and Mrs. Talbot arrived and put on performances with the aid of amateurs drawn from the garrisons and the city. One receives the impression that the theatrical group was small and exclusive. Occasionally the man who sat in the box one week was on stage the next. A Mr. Allan, who was singled out as one of the audience by the reporter from the *Colonial Advocate*, was also an actor of such ability that he was, according to a remark in Robertson's *Landmarks of Toronto*, "seriously advised to become a professional actor." He was, of course, Sir Allan MacNab, who finally chose the political arena to display his acting skills. Three other amateurs who on one occasion had the honour of being noticed and praised in the *Colonial Advocate* were Mr. Davis, Mr. Gilbert, and Mr. Smith who played the major roles in a production of *Richard III*. The ladies didn't fare so well:

. . . if the manager would choose his loving maidens from among the females beyond eight years of age, and give Mrs. Gilbert the hint to bestow on her pretty face certain appropriate streaks, and on her hair a little hair-powder, when she condescends to appear as the representative of wintry three-score, it would, we think, be well enough. The chief beauty of an opera is its close resemblance to

[27]A history of the theatre in Toronto is now in the process of being written.

scenes in real life; and the strength of a company is shewn to great disadvantage when young women wont [*sic*] grow old, and babies play the parts usually allotted to their mothers.

In October 1826 the first professional performance of *Taming of the Shrew* was given in Frank's ballroom by an indomitable couple, Mr. and Mrs. Emmanuel Judah. They were on tour at the time and Toronto (York) was just one of the stops along the road. According to the *York Gazette*, they had received "liberal support" in Kingston and Montreal. But whether the York community came out to applaud or criticize remains a mystery. Hye Bossin, author of *Stars of David*, has traced the history of Jewish participation in the theatre of Toronto and admits to have searched in vain for any sign of newspaper response to their performance.

Sometime in 1828–29 a second "dramatic company" arrived in York. The actor-manager was Sol Smith, who had been on and off the road for a number of years. He had spent a summer in Brunswick, N.J., playing the organ for the Episcopal church and giving singing lessons when the lure of the stage tempted him to venture out again on a tour of the West. His first performance in "his majesty's dominions" was at Niagara. He at once ran into trouble:

Our performance was interrupted by a dozen well dressed fellows, who took a room immediately adjoining ours, and amused themselves and annoyed us by roaring out "God save the King," "Rule Britannia," and other loyal tunes.[28]

After they had finished the play and farce, Smith and his company "proceeded to the bar-room in a body, determined to 'thrash them'," as their "American blood was up." Unfortunately, the Canadians had got word of Smith's intentions and had reinforced their numbers. The actors were at a disadvantage. An Englishman, seeing their plight, jumped into the fray. Smith recalls the words of the Englishman and the conclusion of the fight with relish:

Stop! hear me out; what, you are determined are you? Very well, boys, just as you please. I fought against the Yankees during the war (d—n me if I think any of *you* did!) I am a true Englishman; these Yankees are STRANGERS on our shores, and therefore entitled to kindness and protection. You are twenty without the niggers; they are twelve. Boys (addressing us), do your best; I am on your side, and you are now a "baker's dozen!" The parties met. The Englishman dealt his blows right and left, and fought like a hero, as he was; and the Colonists, sailors, lords, half-breeds and negroes were routed.

The next day the company set off for Little York, where, Smith confesses, they made "a most miserable season." Their bills were printed, by the way, by Mr. Mackenzie, "afterward so notorious for the part he took in the Canada rebellion." Smith doesn't mention the theatre, but we can assume that it was at Frank's Hotel. One evening, Smith recalls, they met "the once celebrated Jack Dwyer." This was probably John Hambury Dwyer, the actor, who, as Brown mentions in his *History*, dropped out of sight in the United States for about twelve years. Smith was astounded to discover that

[28]Solomon Franklin Smith, *Theatrical Management* (New York, 1868), p. 40.

Dwyer was "at this place teaching elocution," and he recalls a particular evening that involved Dwyer:

He came to the theatre in company with about thirty gentlemen of the place, who were, like himself, "full of wine." We had dismissed our audience that night (two men and a boy), but the jovial party insisted we should light up and go through with the performance, for which they would give us thirty dollars. We consented, and played the BROKEN SWORD and some after piece.

After his one disastrous season, Smith and company left York presumably never to return.

Although Frank's Hotel is given the credit for being the first permanent home for the theatre in Toronto, we must recognize the fact that stage productions preceded this date. We are fortunate to have a letter written by Maria L. Jarvis to her grandfather, the Rev. Samuel Peters, which recalls a night she spent in the theatre in February 1809. This letter is reprinted in Edith Firth's *The Town of York* and offers some delightful comments on the time. The play was *The School for Scandal* and was, according to Maria, "well calculated . . . my dear Sir, to excite the risible faculties of some tho horrible faces in others." After noting that the audience included "many of the York scandal hunters," she goes on to describe the scene in more detail:

I have nothing to recount very material, such as Coaches run away with, squeesing to death, fainting fits caused by the crowded audience and confined air – headlong tumbles from the Gallery's that to be sure I did not see owing I suppose to my not being very observing at the best of times – particularly at such a critical moment as that in which the most of the inhabitants of York were so admirably Depicted—.

These boisterous affairs were often advertised as beginning at "early Candlelight."

The York theatres which were built during the 30s and 40s are hardly distinguishable. Indeed, most of them had no particular names, and are recognized only by their street location. A certain fascination remains, of course, in being able to find on a current city map the approximate spot where the old theatre was built. The second theatre, for example, erected in 1834, was set in what appears to have been a field on the north side of Colborne Street, west of the St. Lawrence Market. It was merely the second floor of an old frame building which housed a shop on the main floor. The third house of amusement, in operation between 1834 and 1837, was a converted chapel on the south side of King Street west of Jordan. Around this time there was a barn-like theatre on the north side of Front Street east of Church. In the 40s, two other theatres vied for audiences: Dearing's Theatre, which was situated on the east side of Scott and extended from Front to Wellington Street, the main entrance being on Front Street, and the William Street Theatre which was operated by a group of amateurs and was naturally on William Street, just above Queen.

With the erection of the Royal Lyceum in the mid-forties, Toronto could boast of its first proper theatre. There is some confusion as to the actual date on which it started operations, and this is only natural because it never had an official opening. There is sufficient evidence to indicate, however, that plays were performed there before 1848, the time usually referred to by most historians. George M. Harrington, in his article "Toronto and Its Early Theatrical Entertainments," suggests that the Lyceum was opened to the public on Monday evening, January 12, 1846, with a performance of *The School for Scandal* presented by the Toronto Amateur Theatrical Society, a group which also performed in Hamilton.[29] Later, on June 1, 1846, "Mr. Skerrett, who hailed from different theatres in the north of England, grasped the helm of theatrical affairs in Toronto by opening the Lyceum for a short season."[30] Sometime after January 12, therefore, the amateur and professional were integrated, and it was probably the Toronto-Hamilton circuit that Skerrett was referring to when he hired John Gaisford. But as we have already seen, Gaisford went to Montreal by mistake. If he had arrived in Toronto, he may have been depressed by the conditions that were facing Skerrett. He was having trouble, as Harrington says:

His expenses were far in advance of his receipts, and the season came to an abrupt close before the date at first appointed. The fault was not his own, for he had brought a good dramatic company, in which was included his wife; but his efforts to provide a high class of dramatic entertainments were not sufficiently appreciated, and he left the city with an unfavourable impression of its inhabitants.

Whether his impression changed or not, we find him back in Toronto in 1847. An advertisement in the *Globe*, May 29, 1847, advises the public that on the evening of this date at the Royal Lyceum there would be a performance of *The Iron Chest* and a farce, *'Twas I*. Mrs. Skerrett was in the cast, and it was mentioned that Mr. Skerrett would make his first appearance for the season on the following Monday. During his absence from Toronto, he was probably in Montreal. On his return to Toronto on June 9, 1847, we find him introducing his star, Mr. James W. Wallack, who was to perform at the Lyceum for six nights. Very little more is known about Skerrett. If he is the George Skerrett mentioned by Brown in his *History*, then he left Canada in or around 1852 and became a member of the Lyceum, New York, dying in Albany on May 17, 1855.

The next manager at the Royal Lyceum was a Mr. T. P. Besnard who, as Guillet points out in his *Early Life in Upper Canada*, ran one of the first circuses in York in 1827. His main attraction seems to have been his wife, who was an expert at "tossing of balls and knives." There is, however, no sign of his wife when he took over the Royal Lyceum around 1850. We can assume that Mrs. Besnard did not aspire to be a legitimate actress, or the Lyceum, under Besnard's management, was not interested in the ball-tossing type of entertainment. Unfortunately, we have no record of the plays performed. A variety of performers were featured by the Lyceum at this time; there was Cool Burgess, for example, already mentioned, and the irascible

[29]George M. Harrington, "Toronto and Its Early Theatrical Entertainments," *Canadian Monthly and National Review*, VIII, 603 (January, 1882).
[30]*Ibid.*, p. 604.

Captain Horton Rhys. Approximately two years later, however, an important partnership was formed. Besnard's name became linked with John Nickinson, who had recently arrived from the United States. This date is something of an occasion in Canada's theatrical history, because from this time on Toronto was linked to the professional theatre in New York and London.

Why did Nickinson come to Toronto? Brown's *History of the American Stage* says that he "collected a company among which was W. J. Florence and Charles Peters (his son-in-law), and paid a visit to Canada, playing in Quebec, Montreal, and Toronto, which proved so successful that he was induced to lease the Royal Lyceum." Frank N. Walker in his *Four Whistles to Wood-Up* recalls that a William Huckett, engineer for the Erie Railroad, had known Nickinson when he had lived in Buffalo, and that it was Huckett who "induced him to lease the Lyceum."[31] Walker goes on to note that the company opened on March 28, 1853, with *The Rough Diamond* and the following night presented *Faint Heart Never Won Fair Lady*.

It was probably not necessary to plead with Nickinson. He knew the situation in Toronto quite well, and would have been aware that there was little competition. A great deal of the "legitimate" entertainment was provided by amateur groups. Huckett and his brother Josiah, for example, were part of a little amateur society which could claim Frederic Cumberland, chief engineer for the Northern Railways, as one of their leading actors! Cumberland's theatrical fame rested on the fact that he was related to Richard Cumberland and through this connection was presumably able to get acting scripts from England. There is, however, no evidence to suggest that any of "Sir Fretful's" plays were ever performed by this group in Toronto.[32]

Nickinson was also no doubt aware that the common run of entertainer could prosper in this thriving little city; that, in fact, the night life at this time was very active. Saloons dotted the streets in much the same fashion as our service stations do today. The Apollo Saloon which charged twelve and one-half cents for admission (this included a drink or a smoke and the opportunity to watch the show) was quite well known and should be singled out for attention. It was here in the late 1850s that one could be entertained by a Mr. Burgess [Cool] and a Mr. Den Thompson. The former is described as a negro minstrel singer. George Ham, who seems to have remembered most of everything theatrical he ever heard or saw, recalls some facts about this early pioneer of the theatre:

Cool, by the way, was one of the best of the earlier burnt cork artists, his Nicodemus Johnson being irresistibly funny. He began as a local song and dance performer, lending added humor to his terpsichorean efforts by reason of the length of his feet, which, it is hardly necessary to say, were artificially prolonged.[33]

[31]Frank Norman Walker, *Four Whistles to Wood-Up* (Toronto, 1953), p. 39.
[32]Frank Norman Walker, *Sketches of Old Toronto* (Toronto, 1965). Huckett would appear to be important in any consideration of the amateur theatre in Toronto. Walker notes on p. 283: "Having a flair for showmanship, Huckett redesigned the interior of the theatre, and staged some successful amateur performances."
[33]George H. Ham, *Reminiscences of a Raconteur* (Toronto, 1921), pp. 175–6.

The man with whom Cool Burgess worked was no doubt the same Mr. Denman Thompson who later became internationally famous as the author of *The Old Homestead*. When he was at the Apollo he was referred to as a "broth of a boy from the Emerald Isle," indicating an early start in show business. In the 70s, according to Hector Charlesworth's *Candid Chronicles*, he was still in Toronto playing in a "not very reputable saloon and dance hall on Bay Street." Charlesworth also recalls that in the early 80s he saw a play called *Uncle Josh* which, although already full length, was still only the crude beginnings of the popular play to come. (Graham records in his *Histrionic Montreal* that Thompson appeared in *Joshua Whitcomb* at the Dominion on August 17, 1876.) Thompson, of course, played the lead: a Yankee farmer called Joshua Whitcomb. It is aggravating but typical that Thompson, who spent so much time in Canada and who obviously developed his skill as an actor performing for Canadians, should have chosen to develop an American character. However, this was, and still seems to be, the trend. A Canadian performer who reaches a certain stature inevitably seeks wider acclaim. To achieve international importance he must conquer the theatrical centres of the English-speaking world, and to do this he must develop his material and style in a manner accepted by those centres. In the 1880s there would have been little sense in creating a Canadian character if the creator wished eventually to star on American stages, and Thompson, as so many performers to follow, obviously looked forward to the larger audiences and bigger purses below the border.

Another important centre of theatrical activity at this time was the Grand Opera House, and we are fortunate to have an eye-witness report of the performance of *The Old Homestead* when it was presented there in November 1887. The report, which appeared in the *Evening Telegram* on Saturday, July 23, 1887, is by a man who identifies himself only as "the Man in the Front Row." He enjoyed the play thoroughly, and because in many respects it represents the type of play that was popular at the turn of the century in America, England and Canada, we take the liberty of quoting at length. "The Man in the Front Row" was particularly impressed by the sense of nostalgia in Thompson's play:

Den Thompson takes one by the hand and leads him gently back to boyhood day on the hillside farm. In the glare of the footlights one sees the moonbeams glistening on the hard snows of a bitter winter or the heat rays dancing above the parched cornfields. In the music of the orchestra one hears the wind in its many moods. During the performance one breathes again the very essence of home life and is surrounded again by the purest of home influences. The curtain rises on the farmyard. In the background is the old sun-baked barn bursting at the corners with its golden stores. Real hens cackle in the foreground, a blessed if unmusical note. A party of young people from the city burst into the yard and sniff the air from the kitchen. "Bacon," says the leader. "I didn't like it a bit at home, but I could eat a pound here." Uncle Josh appears and learning his visitor's identity says to the young man: "A how de do. I knew your father." His honest grasp brings tears to the youth's eyes. Says Uncle Josh, "You may stay at my house if you call me uncle. Now run in to tea." The old man is called out in a few minutes to attend to a tramp, a real American tramp, if one was ever seen. Careless, jovial, dirty, but with a heart under his pachydermic epidermis. Uncle Josh leads him to talk of his life. He tells of its glories. "Well," says the old man, "I reckon you are like the singed cat; ye feel a good deal better'n ye look." The tramp goes on to tell of a loving mother left in sorrow "because I couldn't have my own way." A five dollar bill pressed in the ragged young fellow's hand more than meets its equivalent in a promise to seek that aged mother. Uncle Josh sits looking far away. "I wonder where my own boy is" says he, for his son has gone to seek his fortune in Gotham and has long been silent. As the old man speaks a sweet-voiced choir in concealment sings "Where is my boy tonight?" and at the back of the stage is seen while the curtain falls a vision of three or four young fellows holding down the mahogany bar of a . . . liquor saloon.

The boy is found, of course, in the last act, and falls into his father's arms "while the church organ peels forth and the church choir sings." "The Man in the Front Row" was emotionally moved and we get a clue to the reason why in his concluding remark: "Den Thompson preaches a sermon better than most parsons. He reaches one's inner heart." This was, to a degree, the spirit of the age. The sentimental was linked to the religious. It was good to see God's will being done; it was right to weep. Today the temptation is to laugh.

During Nickinson's management (1852–58) many of the great actors of the day visited Toronto, and on the Lyceum stage a number of stars-to-be took their first steps. Nickinson's daughters, Mrs. Charles Walcott and Mrs. Charlotte Morrison, made their debut here under the directorial eye of their father. In 1857, Clara Morris, then eight years old, is said to have made her first appearance in a pantomime. She was later to make her name as "America's most famous emotional actress." Ida Van Cortland followed her a few years later and patterned her acting after Clara, especially in the role of Cora the Creole in *Article 47*. In 1858 the famous Charles Mathews, Jr., passed through Toronto. On a pair of playbills in my collection it is advertised (with an ominous warning: "Positively Last Appearance") that he would perform in *Trying It On, Dowager, He Would be an Actor, A Handsome Husband* and *Twenty Minutes with a Tiger*. It was in this year that Nickinson, for some unknown reason, returned to the United States. During his absence his son-in-law, Owen Marlowe, assumed the management. On April 30, 1860, in anticipation of the Prince of Wales's visit, the Lyceum was renamed the Prince of Wales. According to Harrington, Nickinson was at this time again managing the theatre. A short while later, however, we find that he has left his daughter Charlotte Nickinson in charge.

The theatre continued to attract the stars, but while acting as manageress Miss Nickinson (who sometime in the 60s became Mrs. Morrison) apparently became interested in developing a stock company in Toronto. By 1874 she had achieved this end, and the city, in a community-spirited gesture, built for her the first Grand Opera House. The theatre was opened on September 21, 1874, with a presentation of that old favourite, *The School for Scandal*. The cast was an all-Canadian one, with Mrs. Morrison playing the role of Lady Teazle. One of the members of the cast was probably Ida Van Cortland, and when we examine her career later in this book, we will have occasion to take a closer look at the plays and the rehearsal procedures of this forgotten but rather important Toronto stock company. It is sufficient to mention here that the first Grand Opera House was burned in 1879 and this date marks the end of Mrs. Morrison's local company. With the opening of the new Grand Opera House in 1880, the touring stars from the United States and England again assumed the prominent position in the weekly fare.

This is not to say that the Grand was the only theatre in Toronto. There was also the Queen's Theatre, which was probably built in 1858, and changed its name to the Lyceum (not to be confused with the Royal Lyceum) sometime in the 70s before falling into a decline and finally being destroyed by fire in 1883. The Royal Lyceum struggled along until around 1885 when it was put to a variety of uses, including that of a warehouse and a kitchen utensil factory. In 1874 when it suffered from a fire, it was rebuilt and apparently known as the Royal Theatre for a number of years. Whether it was also referred to as the Theatre Royal is not certain. It is, in fact, difficult to establish the dates of many of the early theatres mainly because of the confusion of names. The Grand Opera House stands as an example, being completely rebuilt at least three times. The Opera House, a strong competitor of the Grand, probably went through as many changes, and to compound the confusion, was known as Jacob and Sparrow's Theatre for some time. One thing we are sure of is that these two theatres, the Grand and the Opera House, along with the Princess Theatre and the Academy of Music, housed the majority of the important attractions that came to Toronto from the 1880s until the First World War.

We must remember that although many handsome theatres were built in Toronto and other cities throughout Canada in the latter part of the nineteenth century, the prevailing mood was essentially anti-theatre. There was little interest in the business world, the universities or local government in providing a home for native talent. For the most part, theatre buildings were built to attract touring companies. Many structures were, in fact, put up with American money to serve their own interests. Few Canadians were active in the theatre; they attended the shows but rarely supported the actor. They didn't go to the theatre; rather they went, euphemistically, to the Opera House, and when the play was over, they hardly ever talked seriously about it. Indeed so little comment remains, we are tempted to believe that to talk about the theatre or the play, let alone to write about it, must have been considered low and in bad taste. Are the reasons for this difficult to trace? Many people, of course, were under the influence of their church, and whichever church they attended they almost invariably found that their spiritual adviser regarded the stage as the gate of Hell. Even among the latitudinarians there were comparatively few who were moved by the magic of the stage. The theatre was regarded as sinful to a large and influential section of the community. The weight of the prejudice may be judged by the fact that as late as 1894 the deed of gift forbade use of costumes in any entertainment on the stage of Massey Hall. The proviso was devised to strike at the very root of the "evil." On May 4, 1880, a Reverend J. B. Silcox read a paper (and it was printed in the *Evening Telegram*) on "The Church and the Theatre" at a meeting of a Toronto Ministerial Association, in which he contended that "the Stage was opposed to morality as proved by its history." Enough amusement-seekers remained, however, to ensure comparative success for the theatrical ventures; they did not constitute a critical theatre audience but were simply looking for an evening's entertainment. This uncritical attitude was also apparent in the journals of the day.

The first serious attempt to comment on the state of the drama in Toronto was not made until 1874. It was in October of this year that *The Canadian Monthly and National Review* decided to examine the theatre as a part of the social scene and the conclusion drawn was hardly one to inspire the reader. Even at this date the editor felt obliged to introduce himself and the column with an apology. He realized that the subject-matter would cause offence in some quarters, and being aware of this, assured his readers that the step was taken only after cautious deliberation. He conceded that the amusements of the community were "subordinate to weightier interests," but insisted that they were not "to be passed over as undeserving of attention." It appears that his interest had been drawn to the worthwhile activity which was taking place at the Grand Opera House under the management of Mrs. Morrison. Actually the editor proved to be an ardent defender of the theatre. In the April 1875 issue he made a direct answer to those who were "denying a place to the drama as an accredited and legitimate educator of the age." His feelings on the subject were strong:

The world is full of strange puzzles. A large class of the public whose appetite is tickled by the reports of Brooklyn Scandals and criminal trials in the morning newspaper satisfies its moral scruples by declining to attend the evening play, and by denouncing those who do.

This attitude disturbed the critic and encouraged him to make a more detailed examination of the public. His comments are perhaps unique; at least they are the only organized observations of this nature available today.

He came to the conclusion in his October 1875 issue that there was no such thing as a "recognized class of play-goers [in Toronto], except those frequenters of the theatre that belong to the more frivolous and unemployed section of society, and the audience that is drawn from those visiting the city. . . ." His remarks in December of the same year have a prophetic ring familiar to anyone concerned with the theatre in Canada today:

"We take our amusements sadly," someone has said, and the remark is one that may truly be made of the manner in which the patrons of the drama in Canada enjoy their occasional evening at the theatre. . . . But with even the best entertainments provided at our opera houses, their success owes little to the sympathy and appreciation of the audience. The houses are cold in their recognition of effort: the audience spiritless and indifferent in showing its acceptance of the play, and utterly lacking in that contagious feeling of pleasure and satisfaction which good acting merits, and is entitled to receive. . . . There is little desire to come to the play actuated by an intelligent interest in the drama, or from sympathy with its history and traditions, or from the motive of comparing actor with actor, in the rendition of their parts. Only from the lower motives of seeking an easily satisfied pleasure, or to pass an otherwise tedious evening, do we find the bulk of our theatre audiences drawn to the house.

Some critics of the theatre today would be willing to argue that the picture of the Canadian audience has not changed a great deal. However, in fairness, we must admit slight gains. Canadian playwrights, for example, are today frequently able to have their plays performed, and audiences have been known to be warm in their "recognition of effort." This was not the case in the 1870s. The two major theatres, the Royal Opera House and the Grand Opera House, seemed to have been willing to receive only English and American productions.

The Royal Opera House stressed melodrama, but the Grand Opera House did attempt a broader selection and was thought to be progressive. Considering this, it is rather disappointing to note a number of the attractions during the year 1876. The season opened on September 23 with *A Scrap of Paper*. Following this Henry Ward Beecher arrived and on September 25 lectured Torontonians on the subject *Ministry of Wealth*. From September 26 to 29, Dominick Murray presented two of his favourites, *Willy Rielly* and *Escape from Sing Sing*. On October 4 there was *The Great Divorce Case* followed on October 10 by *Kit, the Arkansas Traveller*. The Grand Italian Opera performed in *Faust* and *Il Trovatore* between October 18 and 26 and on October 27 there was a presentation of *Romeo and Juliet*. Miss Kate Claxton was seen in *Conscience* on November 13 and 14. On December 15 Professor Baldwin held his *Seances* which required "fifty young ladies to be selected from the audience." Starting December 27 and lasting a full week, was the production of Gilbert's *The Palace of Truth*.

Not one of the presentations of this progressive theatre was the product of a Canadian writer. The Canadian dramatist, and especially the poetic dramatist, was rarely able to have his play staged. Canadians from early times were conditioned to accept the outsider and reject their own.

As I have suggested above, the pattern of growth in the smaller centres in Upper Canada and later in Ontario is similar in that they all demonstrate with little variation the movement in Canadian theatre from the native amateur to the foreign professional. However, until the touring companies became a dominant force in the 70s and 80s, the theatres in the little towns developed in isolation. It is probably something in the vague "spirit" of the country that caused them to grow in much the same fashion despite their remote locations.

A glimpse at Ancaster, a little town at the head of Lake Ontario, is rewarding. Sol Smith, who had just completed his miserable season in York, passed through Ancaster on his way back to the United States. He records that a thespian society had been in existence there for about two years before his arrival. He was told the following story by a member who approached him with a request to perform:

Two hundred pounds had been subscribed by the members for purchasing scenery, wardrobe, and books. The association met one night in each month for rehearsal, their first play intended for performance being *She Stoops to Conquer*.

They had met probably twenty times, and never had progressed in the rehearsal farther than the second scene in the comedy, for the following reason: The landlord of the hotel where they performed, had *liquor*, and that of the very best kind, so that before the actors could get through the scene, they were too tipsy to proceed any farther, and generally broke up in a row.[34]

Thus the "spirit" was with them in more than one way. Ancaster gradually became a sleepy village, but if it had grown it would have taken its rightful place on the "road" as a stop for the travelling companies.

The town of Galt is another example. Its early history was recorded by a resident, James Young, who, unlike many early Canadian historians, made a point of recalling some of the events of the theatre. It was, presumably, in the summer of 1843 that a group called the Galt Thespian Amateurs was formed and in the fall "broke out into open performance."[35] These were held in the fire hall and here they were apparently able to compete favourably with the occasional attraction of a fire. Some of the plays presented were *The Castle Spectre*, with *Strap, the Cobbler*, as an after-piece, *The Mountaineers*, *The Secret Panel*, *The Illustrious Stranger*, and *No Song, No Supper*.

Again we find no significant development of the amateur theatre in this little town. The local residents, however, eventually built their own town hall and following the custom, erected a stage and auditorium on the second floor of the building. Having the necessary facilities, the town quickly adopted the accepted procedure and opened its doors to touring entertainers.

Initially London had an active local theatre. In 1844 the amateurs joined ranks and performed in a converted barn, and previous to this date the British Garrison officers had amused themselves and the town people with the odd play such as *Rent Day* and *You Can't Marry Your Grandmother*.[36] By 1845 the Shakespeare Club had been formed "for the encouragement of drama and the promotion of rational amusement." The fact that it never produced a play by Shakespeare did not seem to disturb anyone. In the 50s, a man by the name of Brunton established himself as an acting-manager, and produced plays which featured his wife who was "undoubtedly the most talented member of the company." In the spring of 1856 his company presented *The Tragedy of Charles II*, *The Poor Gentleman*, *The Married Rake*, *Richelieu* and *Hamlet*. Other local groups appeared and were active for varying lengths of time in the succeeding years, but by the 1880s London had primarily become a stop for the touring companies, and as the amateurs gradually left the stage, the foreign professionals stepped into the limelight. We find in September, 1881 that the new opera house was under the control of C. J. Whitney, a businessman who lived in the United States. London became part of his circuit and the citizens were thereafter provided with all commercial successes from Broadway. It wasn't until the 1930s, when the

[34]Solomon F. Smith, *Theatrical Management*, p. 42.
[35]James Young, *Reminiscences of the Early History of Galt and the Settlement of Dumeries* (Toronto, 1880), p. 191.
[36]Information about the theatre in London may be found in an article by F. Beatrice Taylor in the centennial edition of the *London Free Press*, June 15, 1955. More detailed information can be expected from Orlo Miller of the same city who is currently conducting research in this field.

Dominion Drama Festival and the London Little Theatre were organized, that the amateurs again came into prominence.

Ottawa, or Bytown, as it was called in the early days, was given its first theatrical performance by a group of soldiers from the 15th Regiment on February 6, 1837. The play was *The Village Lawyer* and the money collected went for charity.[37] It was an inauspicious beginning, and the future development of the theatre in Canada's capital was disappointing. Theatres were built, and Ottawa became one of the stops along the road for touring companies. In 1850 a little theatre club, organized by Mr. William Pittman Letts, staged performances in the town hall. It didn't last long for in 1854 the first American touring actors arrived. They probably presented their plays in the new Her Majesty's Theatre which was built in this year. This may have been the theatre that shocked and horrified Mr. and Mrs. Sam Cowell. The Grand Opera House opened on February 4, 1875, and ended its days in a typical way, being consumed by fire on the night of July 5, 1913. The first production was *The Bohemian Girl*. A few years later, in 1879, the curtain went up on a Canadian play, F. A. Dixon's *Canada's Welcome*. Other important events included the appearance of the Holman Opera Company, a completely Canadian organization which originated in Toronto. E. A. McDowell was also a frequent attraction. The Grand Opera House remained Ottawa's leading theatre until 1897 when the Russell was erected.

From 1897 on, however, the Grand went into a steady decline. It followed the typical downward steps; melodramas sustained it for a while, then variety with the odd bioscope, and finally lectures and slides. The Russell was the centre of dramatic art in the Capital, and remained in this position until after the First World War. It stands as a link between the early professional theatre and the Little Theatre movement which gained prominence after the war. It was at the Russell Theatre on November 15, 1913, for example, that the Drama League began with the presentation of three one-act plays.

Unlike the small towns in Ontario, which accepted isolation as a matter of course, isolation was forced upon Winnipeg. It was inclined to be rough, as most pioneering towns are, but this doesn't allow it any singular distinction. As A. R. M. Lower points out, Winnipeg shared an honour with Barrie, Ontario. According to a report from the women's temperance society in the 1870s, they were "the two wickedest places in Canada."[38] More specifically, Winnipeg should be treated as an extension of eastern theatrical development. Touring companies eventually spread out from the main centres in the East and generally travelled as far as Winnipeg. Beyond this, only the foolish or dyed-in-the-wool romantic would dare to venture.

In fact, the Middle West was truly left to fend for itself with the result that no theatrical endeavour of any consequence materialized. On the far west coast, the theatre had a development similar to that of the east, its rise and fall probably depending on the vicissitudes of the mining companies in

[37]A few pertinent facts about Ottawa's early theatre can be found in Lucien Brault's *Ottawa Old and New* (Ottawa, 1946).
[38]Arthur R. M. Lower, *Canadians in the Making*, p. 319.

much the same manner as the theatre in the east was dependent upon other forms of industry and the establishment of military garrisons. The professional touring companies in British Columbia were mainly from the west coast of the United States, and, as in the East, gradually supplanted what little amateur activity there was.[39]

Information about Winnipeg's first theatre, built in 1871 and called the Red River Hall, has been preserved in the published recollections of "an Old Timer." His article was included in a pamphlet which was distributed at the formal opening of the Walker Theatre in 1907.[40] The building appeared to be typical of most early theatres in Canada:

It was the plainest, most unfinished and unpretentious affair possible to imagine as a theatre. It had a stage consisting of a platform raised about a foot above the floor, was lighted by oil lamps, and heated by a couple of stoves. The sole entrance and exit was a narrow plank staircase running transversely across one end of the building on the outside.

The stage area was very small and this made it necessary to place the dressing rooms in a shop directly beneath the stage. Access to these rooms was gained through "a very precipitous trap stair immediately behind the lilliputian scenes."

Other makeshift theatres followed with impressive names such as Theatre Royal, Dufferin Hall, Winnipeg Opera House; but it was not until 1876 that the city finally had a theatre of any substance. As usual in Canadian towns, this first notable theatre occupied the second floor of the town hall. The auditorium seated about five hundred people. According to the Old Timer, it had a gallery which extended across one end of the hall, was heated by hot air, lighted by oil lamps, and was entirely devoid of emergency exits. In 1877 the first professional, Cool Burgess, whom we have already met, arrived in town and from that day on Winnipeg became a stop for the professional touring companies. By the early 1900s the little city of Winnipeg, which became known as The Gateway of the West, could boast of four theatres: The Winnipeg Theatre, The Winnipeg Opera House, the Dominion Theatre, and the Walker Theatre.

Of these four theatres, the Walker Theatre was the most impressive. The owner, the enterprising C. P. Walker, had by the turn of the century made himself well known to touring company agents in both Canada and the United States. His daughter, Ruth Harvey, recalls in her book *Curtain Time* his first trip to New York for the purpose of booking a show:

"Winnipeg!" the manager said it with disbelief and derision. "How do they get there – by dog sled? What do they play in – an igloo?"[41]

[39]Michael Booth has written a good deal about the theatre in British Columbia. See "Pioneer Entertainment: Theatrical Taste in the Early Canadian West," *Canadian Literature*, 4 (Spring, 1960), 52– 8; "Gold Rush Theater: The Theater Royal, Barkerville, British Columbia," *Pacific Northwest Quarterly*, 51 (July, 1960), 97–102; "The Beginnings of Theatre in British Columbia," *Queen's Quarterly*, 24 (October, 1960), 22–6.

[40]Anonymous, "The Early Play Houses of Winnipeg," *Formal Opening of the Walker Theatre*, Winnipeg, Manitoba, February 18–19, 1907. One copy of this pamphlet is held in the Theatre Collection at the New York Public Library.

[41]Ruth Harvey, *Curtain Time*, Boston: Houghton Mifflin Co., p. 291.

As the years passed, however, Walker was able to overcome the many difficulties the remoteness of Winnipeg presented by offering touring companies extended runs through his chain of theatres linking Winnipeg with Minneapolis through the towns of the Red River Valley. This route became very popular with the touring stars, as Ruth Harvey indicates:

This circuit represented the northern limit to which touring companies traveled. It lay on the edge of wilderness, with nothing beyond it but a scattering of villages, then forest, tundra, Hudson's Bay and the Arctic Ocean. Winnipeg, its most eastern city, was two thousand miles by rail from New York, and twice as far from London. But there was no need then to go to New York or London to enjoy the theatre. The shows came to us.[42]

With the stars from England and the United States, there was the occasional Canadian. For a few years at the turn of the century Walker was able to support an all-Canadian company. The actor-manager of this company was Mr. Harold Nelson who became well known in the West for his portrayals of Petronius in *Quo Vadis*, and of Hamlet and Richelieu. He was, apparently, an "intelligent" actor and was particularly "adept in the art of making love." Walker was obviously something more than a business manager. A reviewer in Winnipeg's *Town Topics* wrote, "In Mr. Nelson, Manager Walker has a theatrical star worthy his attention, and Canada has an actor, scholar and gentleman of whom she may justly feel proud." Walker and Nelson were probably partners. However, Canada as a whole was hardly aware, let alone proud, of this new star. As far as research can determine, Nelson's Canadian Dramatic Company performed in and around Winnipeg only, in the theatres which formed part of Walker's Red River Valley circuit.

In spite of Walker's efforts, the native theatre in Winnipeg did not develop. The city remained essentially a receiver of culture. Indeed, in all matters coming under the general heading of culture, the city was indebted to outside sources, particularly to the countless touring companies.

At the turn of the century, more theatres on the scale of the Walker Theatre were constructed throughout eastern Canada. Many of them, as we have noted, were operated by Americans: Whitney's chain, for example, finally included opera houses in Toronto, London, Hamilton, Woodstock, Guelph and St. Thomas. They varied in size and shape, the façade and front of the house usually receiving the most consideration. The size of the building actually had little importance in the development of the drama in Canada. In the United States, and particularly in England, the dimensions of the auditorium did affect the drama. The larger theatres with proscenium widths of 40 feet or more and audience capacities of 1500 and up were generally devoted to the spectacular. The intimate reviews, and serious drama as a whole, were kept alive in the smaller theatres. In England, the most famous example was the Court Theatre which housed the earlier productions of Shaw. But in Canada, the size of the auditorium was never, as far as I can ascertain, determined by artistic considerations.

[42]A casual record of performances from 1897 to 1911 was kept by Walker. It is reproduced, with considerable editorial comment and rearrangement, in Appendix A.

In general, theatres in Canada during this period fall into the category of private theatres. This is one of five categories listed by Edwin Sachs in his large and comprehensive examination of European playhouses, *Modern Opera Houses and Theatres*. He was writing in 1896, and he notes that in Europe (excluding England), most theatres were subsidized. They received support from the court, the national government, municipal funds, or through subscription from interested groups. The fifth category, the private theatre, was found to be prevalent only in England and the United States. His remarks about the business arrangements in the private theatre, although based on his observations in England, accurately describe conditions as they existed in Canada:

The private theatre is sometimes owned and managed by the same person, who is a manager by profession, or an actor-manager; more often, however, the owner leases it for terms varying in length from a few nights to several years, to managers or "star" actors and actresses. In the first case the theatre is conducted directly as a matter of business, whilst in the latter the owner of the building chiefly considers his property an investment, leaving the lessee to employ it for what purpose he will.[43]

35

The relatively rapid growth of opera houses and theatres in Canada from the 1890s until the First World War did little for the would-be Canadian playwright or scenic designer. In a limited way it provided a beginning stage for the actor, who, if he achieved any eminence at all, did so in the United States or England. Generally the theatres were built as business investments to serve the touring companies.[44] Just how they were used by these companies will be the subject of the next chapter.

[43]Edwin O. Sachs, *Modern Opera Houses and Theatres* (London, 1896), I, p. 3.
[44]As a guide and reference some of these theatres are listed in Appendix B.

Touring Days.

The pattern of development of the theatre was relatively the same in every
town and city in Canada. Maturity, in the theatrical sense, was reached
when the community was recognized by the touring company. Indeed, to
have become a regular stop on the road was a proud achievement. English
and American companies, always searching for a larger audience, naturally
took advantage of the lack of local competition, and by the turn of the
century, Canada had become not much more than an appendage of the
two older cultures.[1] This cannot be construed as a surprising development:
it was inevitable. People normally require entertainment and if the community fails to provide it, they welcome the outsider. Unfortunately once
this trend was established, the growth of native talent was severely curtailed.
Canadians developed the habit of waiting for the foreign stars and neglected
their own potential leading actors. There were many reasons and pressures
which forced Canada into becoming a receiver of culture. Theatre practices
were undergoing change. In the 1880s and 90s, the theatre in England and
the United States revolved around the actor-manager. These men were
dictators in their own theatre; consequently the acting community was
influenced by their methods and styles, and the audiences were conditioned
to receive the kind of play which suited their taste. Unfortunately, most of
them had lost touch with the latest cultural developments. In the larger
centres the taste in theatre was directly affected by the works of new playwrights, the actor-manager's authority was under-cut, and gradually his
popularity waned. But cultural revolutions spread slowly, and the actor-
manager soon discovered that his magic was still strong in the provinces.
The tour soon became the thing, and Canada proved to be lucrative terri-
tory. Only a strong native theatre could have withstood the onslaught.

We must remember, as Ernest Reynolds has pointed out in his *Modern
English Drama*, that the commercialization of the theatre took place at this
time.[2] In England and the United States this phenomenon was balanced by

[1] A list of touring companies is recorded in Appendix c.
[2] Ernest Reynolds, *Modern English Drama*, 2nd edition (Norman: University of Oklahoma Press, 1951), p. 16.

a concern for the art of the drama: there were two streams. In Canada, on the other hand, the artistic stream was missing and when the commercial theatre started to grow few Canadians reaped the profit. The American and English touring companies, similar to the movie companies of today, sent the shows in and took the money out. Certainly the presence of the foreign touring companies in such numbers in Canada suggests that there were not many Canadian businessmen who could foresee a tidy profit in the business of theatre, and that the theatrical visionary who may have seen the value of introducing professional theatre as a cultural stimulant, was lacking as well. Generally, we must concede that Canadians were passive partners in the business; the Americans and the English were the aggressors.

As the business of putting on shows grew into an entertainment industry, large organizations came into being. The Theatrical Syndicate, formed in 1896 by a group of American businessmen, soon controlled the major theatres throughout eastern Canada. The main opposition to this "octopus" was formed by another American firm, the Shubert Theatre Corporation. Canada's contribution to the development of theatre cartels was The Canadian Theatrical Managers' Association, which in May 1906 elected Ambrose Small president and decided to hold their next convention in New York. Apart from the proposed site of their convention, the irony is that Small was under contract to Klaw and Erlanger, the major partners in the Theatrical Syndicate. Western Canada was fed generally by the Northwestern Affiliated Theatrical Circuits. C. P. Walker of Winnipeg owned one of the circuits which operated theatres in northern Minnesota, North Dakota, and western Canada. But we should note that the Canadian theatres were a part of an American branch.

The touring companies which covered Canada from roughly the 1880s to 1913 were mainly American. Ownership of the Canadian opera house gradually passed into the hands of the American businessman, who quite naturally turned to the Syndicate as a reliable booking agent. Canadians couldn't compete, but they did complain, and as usual, when they had a problem, they looked to England. A direct result was the formation of the Anglo-Canadian Booking Office with plans to tour large "combinations" across the country. It was also determined not to play any American cities on the way. The battle was on, and the year was 1913. As one theatre critic put it: "Canada for the English is becoming an issue which will merit the attention of the producing and booking powers of the United States." Another newspaper man shared with his readers the "inside" story that "It is the intention to increase the number of British theatrical visitors by one hundred per cent, thereby seriously reducing the extent of American bookings throughout Canada."[3] The English competitors took a major step with the formation of The British and Canadian Theatre Organization Society. The well-known English actor, Mr. Lewis Waller, was an important member. Their first organized tour presented Sir John Martin-Harvey in his *The Only Way*. But time was against the Association. With the advent of the First World War, the English theatrical invasion of Canada ended.

[3]*New York Dramatic Mirror*, April 29, 1914.

The Americans continued to send companies to Canada, but the power of the syndicates waned as a result of the war. Eventually only the larger cities were privileged to receive the Broadway successes. The field was now open to the Canadian companies, but alas it was too late. The golden age of the touring company was ending and there was nothing to look forward to. It was a time to reminisce, and Canadians did not have much of their own to remember.

The effect of the touring company on Canadian theatre was not, of course, entirely deleterious. As patrons of these companies, Canadians were able to keep reasonably in touch with the commercial theatre of the time. The changing styles of Shakespearean production were faithfully reflected in the town halls and opera houses throughout the country. The latest farces, the countless musicals and melodramas, were played and re-played for as long as they held box-office appeal. Moreover, Canadians were occasionally able to see one of the "new" plays which were being written by dramatists of the so-called New Movement.

Following Ibsen's lead, some playwrights were beginning to dispense with stultifying theatrical conventions and deal with the complexities of human nature. Their attention was focused on the individual in society and their methods were realistic. As the plays of this New Movement represented an important development in the theatre, I shall pay particular attention to those touring companies which dared present some of the new thoughts to the Canadian public. Strangely enough, most contemporary historians of the theatre in Canada are content to assume that there was very little, if any, stage experience of the New Drama. Their remarks are obvious generalizations, because no one has ever made the effort to examine theatre events in detail. Actually a number of plays by Ibsen and his followers were presented on Canadian stages and a record of them should be kept. By doing this, we should be able to establish, with a degree of accuracy, this country's place in the history of the theatre. It is my purpose, therefore, to note these various performances and thereby to reveal something of the reactions and preconceptions of the audiences whose support determined the direction which the Canadian theatre was to take. They represent an important part of the touring days.

A touring company is, of course, essentially a business operation, and success is measured by receipts at the box-office. Anyone who organizes and produces a company for the road must therefore have a shrewd sense of mass appeal; the merchandise must please the largest segment of the population. As a result, managers of touring companies usually pick from the common denominator. The members of the company must also subscribe to this commercial philosophy, albeit in varying degrees. One thing is certain, everyone from the actor-manager to the eager young spear-holder must be prepared to endure physical exhaustion. He must also steel himself to the fact that, although he will be developing his stage technique, he will most often be practising his talents on poor play material. Moreover, because of the arduous routine, the occasions are rare when he can sit back and study the subtleties of his own part let alone muse about the intentions of contemporary writing. A touring company is also geared to the long run. Once the cast is set and the scenery is ordered, the objective is to last as long as possible. As a result, actors have been known to age beyond the requirements of their role during an extended tour. (This aspect of the tour, by the way, has also become the blight of Broadway successes.) Touring companies have rarely played an important part in the development of the theatre. Actors wither in the routine; no new trends in playwriting have emerged.

Canada, as we have seen, did not develop a strong local theatre during the early crucial years. In England around the turn of the century, it was the growth of the repertory system which acted as a catalyst for new ideas. A company such as Miss Horniman's which established itself in the community was able to encourage and foster the regional playwright. The writer and the company worked together to produce plays with a point of view. This did not happen in Canada. Melodrama, generally written to fit the requirements of a touring star and shaped to please the masses, poured into the Dominion from England and the United States and filled the opera houses across the land until the outbreak of the First World War.

The Canadian touring companies did not prove to be exceptional in any way. They did not establish any significant standards in presentation or in acting and their choice of plays is disappointing to the student of theatre history. No experiments were made. No play by Ibsen, Shaw, Galsworthy or Pinero was produced by them. Of the three companies to be considered, apparently only one presented any plays by a Canadian. And this last fact is the most discouraging.

CANADIAN PLAYERS OF THE PAST

Of the hundreds of touring companies travelling in Canada during this period, few were Canadian. Both the lack of interest on the part of Canadians in native talent and the fact that local groups were unable to compete financially with the more established English and American companies accounts for this. Touring a play was, after all, a highly competitive business.

There were some Canadian companies, of course. But as time goes by it becomes more and more difficult to collect information about these various groups. The Summers Stock Company established a permanent home in Hamilton around the turn of the century. They also went on tours periodically, playing melodramas and farces. Their *repertoire* was mentioned when they performed in Ottawa in November 1903. Some of the more familiar titles are *Pawn Ticket 210, Resurrection, Rip Van Winkle, A Wife's Honor, La Belle Marie,* and *True Irish Hearts.* One play that they were known to have presented a few years later has the intriguing title of *The Man From Ottawa.* Unfortunately, no information about this play has been found. It's possible that it was written by George Summers, who fancied himself as something of a playwright as well as a leading comic actor. But apart from these few details, nothing remains of this active little company.

Three other companies stand out, and we are fortunate to have more information about them: The McDowell Company, the Marks Brothers, and the Tavernier Company.

E. A. McDowell, although born in the United States, spent most of his active life in Canada and was probably one of the first to organize and operate a Canadian touring company. Unfortunately, we have little information about this man and his career. Franklin Graham remembers him with affection:

Eugene A. McDowell was a conscientious actor and a painstaking manager, never grumbling at the cost of mounting a play properly. He was a favorite with every one, being most affable and courteous, and was a staunch friend.

As we have already noted, he was the first manager of The Academy of Music in Montreal. This was in 1875, and may have been, as Graham points out, his first important administrative position. We can only assume that he stayed in this post until 1877 when a Mr. Charles Arnold came to town. No information remains about Arnold other than the fact that he and McDowell formed a touring company and sometime in this year set off for western Canada and the United States. We are missing most of the details about this group; no cast or play lists have survived. But we do have a little word picture of an experience they had in the town of Emerson, south of Winnipeg. Graham records in his *Histrionic Montreal* that at the time the population of the town numbered about 1,000. He continues:

The "theatre" was an old warehouse full of farming implements and boxes. The place had but two exits one of which was from the platform to the prairie, where tents had been rigged up for the company. There was not a house nearer than a mile, and, as everybody came on horseback, the outside was like a horse fair. Soap and candle boxes formed the back seats, champagne and brandy cases being in front. The Inhabitants were anxious for the company to remain a second night, which they could not do on account of being booked elsewhere, so another performance was given that same night at 11.15. A Canadian political burlesque, "H.M.S. Parliament," written to "Pinafore" music was given. The orchestra consisted of a church organ.

H.M.S. Parliament is the musical which was written by W. H. Fuller of Montreal, and I shall be considering it in more detail later. Notice of this early performance suggests, however, that these two men knew each other and may have collaborated on the script. McDowell was probably trying out the musical while on the road. There is, unfortunately, no other recorded performance of *H.M.S. Parliament* between this one in Emerson in 1877 and the opening in Montreal in 1880.

According to the "Old Timer" in the *Formal Opening of the Walker Theatre,* McDowell's company arrived back in Winnipeg on May 17, 1879. The plays presented by them were recorded and are worth noting, for they generally represent the best of the commercial successes of the time. Dion Boucicault's *Arrah-na-Pogue, The Shaughraun* and *Colleen Bawn* were prominently advertised. Two plays by T. W. Robertson were included: *Caste* and *Ours. Pygmalion* and *Galatea,* and the more recent *Engaged* of W. S. Gilbert, are found in the repertoire of this little company. The rest

were typical popular melodramas, *East Lynne, Field of the Cloth of Gold,*
Uncle Tom's Cabin.

McDowell was obviously interested in contemporary drama during his career. The fact that he produced Fuller's *H.M.S. Parliament* also indicates that he was aware of the possibility that Canadian plays could be successful. An item in the *New York Clipper* of November 27, 1886, draws our attention to his production of *The Big Boom.* This play, which will be referred to again, was written by Charles W. Handscomb, the Winnipeg drama critic. McDowell was trying, in the early stages of his career, to involve Canadian writers in the theatre. It seems, however, that his ambitions waned and by 1889 we find that as manager of the stock company at the Lansdowne Theatre in Saint John, New Brunswick, he produced "grand revivals of all the old standard plays." Such fare as *The Two Orphans, The Lyons Mail, Little Em'ly* and *A Wife's Peril* filled the bill at the theatre during the summer season.

41

The stock company in Saint John was disbanded on August 15, 1889, and at that time the future plans of the company members were listed in the columns of the *New York Dramatic Mirror* of June 29, 1889. Most of them were doing quite well, having received offers from a variety of companies. Fanny Reeves, McDowell's wife, was going back to a Winnipeg stock company. McDowell had been offered the part of supporting actor for Clara Morris. Mrs. Jamieson, Mrs. Mowat, and Mrs. Linda Bainbridge had accepted positions with the Hoyt and Morris Company. A Miss Mary Hampton was joining William Gillette's *Held by the Enemy* company, and a Mr. T. D. Frawley was expected to report immediately to an American company which was planning to present a play called *The Soldier's Web.* And so the company separated and it is very unlikely that they were ever reunited. No further sign of McDowell or his company remains.

But the Marks Brothers did stand out. Under a variety of titles which always included their name, this little group of brothers – seven, in fact – retained a secure and respectable position on the road for some thirty years. Driving north today on Highway 7 towards Canada's Capital, you pass through a little town called Maberly. Within a few miles is Christie Lake, the original home of the Canadian Marks Brothers. No physical evidence remains to show that it was once the base of operation for that famous theatrical company. The pavilion in which they planned their tours and rehearsed their plays has disappeared. But with the aid of relatives, and diligent searching through scrapbooks and newspaper files, a history of this theatrical family can be pieced together.

Bob Marks, the eldest boy in a family of seven, left home, probably in 1876 or 1877, to venture into the world as a salesman. While attempting to sell his five-octave harmonicas to the citizens of Maberly, he met a travelling magician who called himself "King Kennedy, the Mysterious Hindu from the Bay of Bengal." Intrigued by the novelty of the King's profession, Marks attended a performance and at the conclusion introduced himself with the intention of suggesting a partnership. It isn't difficult to imagine the meeting. The King was getting old and his prospects were bleak. Bob Marks was young and energetic. An agreement was reached: in exchange for knowledge of some of the magic, Bob Marks bought an interest in the "Company," and the two set off to make their fortune in a fashion strongly reminiscent of the Duke and the King in *Huckleberry Finn.*

After a successful season of touring with the magic act, Bob Marks returned to Christie Lake confident that he had found his life's work. In his travels he had considered the possibilities of an actual touring company that would perform plays for the public, and realizing this would require more people, it seems likely that he had his younger brothers in mind when he returned to the farm. The boys were no doubt tempted, but at that time only Tom decided to break from the home and venture on the road. Being limited once more to two, they obviously did not perform any plays, and it is quite likely that Bob merely passed on some of the magic secrets, thereby retaining in the new company the essential characteristics of the old.

In 1879 they set off with a team and buggy and a determination to take what they termed "drama" to the West. The c.p.r. had not been completed, so they drove to Owen Sound where they boarded the Northern Belle for Parry Sound; they then proceeded to Copper Cliff, Manitoulin Island, Port Arthur, and finally Winnipeg. They held performances on the way, but it was in the town of Winnipeg that they made their greatest impression. Here, according to a newspaper clipping in the Marks scrapbook, their arrival was chronicled by an article entitled: "Hurrah, we're not in the backwoods any more. A Show has come to town."

Theatre-goers in Winnipeg at that time, of course, would have recalled other professional entertainers. As we have seen, E. A. McDowell had been there. Cool Burgess had also played Winnipeg in 1877, and the *Free Press,* conscious of this significant event, had commented: "The visit of the first professional troupe to this province will long be remembered as an interesting era [*sic*] in the social history of Winnipeg."[4]

Normally the Marks Brothers would have rented the city hall as their predecessor had done, but according to an article in the scrapbook, they put their show on in one of the smaller halls. This could very well have been the case, for at that time in Winnipeg there were places other than the city hall in which performances could be staged. These were the halls, common in most Canadian towns, that were the extensions of the bars and saloons. One of these houses, the Pride of the West Saloon, "was proud of its piano," and supported a "high-class vaudeville show." Perhaps Bob and Tom Marks performed in these elegant surroundings.

From Winnipeg, they proceeded to the mining towns of the western United States and then gradually worked their way east and so home again. One by one the other brothers were enticed into the business, and by the mid-eighties, Bob Marks's dream began to come true. With the addition of two women to the troupe, he was able to produce plays, the first one probably being *The Bird in a Gilded Cage.* Other unpretentious plays followed and soon a repertoire was established.

The nineties proved to be the decade during which the Marks Brothers

42

[4]Irene Craig, "Grease Paint on the Prairies," *Historical and Scientific Society of Manitoba,* iii, 46 (1947).

achieved recognition. The other brothers had entered the field and now with more than one company on the road their name became a familiar sign in countless towns throughout Canada and the United States. The major companies, all called The Marks Brothers, were managed by Bob, Ernie and Tom. They did not perform in the large cities nor did they attempt to interest the intellectuals. It was natural that they should have concentrated on melodrama. Many of the scripts still remain and the private reminders and stage directions pencilled in by the actors help to recall the style and flavour of their performances. The plays, on the whole, followed the familiar pattern, cut to suit the morality of the little Victorian towns. The villains were truly despicable with their black mustachios, black riding boots, and black sombreros. In contrast, the heroes were magnificent with wavy blonde hair and open-necked white shirts. It wasn't difficult for the audience to distinguish the good from the bad! The contrast was equally great between the bouncing calico-clad heroine and the slinky siren in satin or velvet. And when the hero or heroine spurned temptation, it was with a resounding declaration that could not have failed to implant a moral lesson in the heart of every spectator.

Some of the plays seem to have been ordered especially by Robert Marks, and were performed by his company. But the titles and plots are of such a general nature that it is difficult to view them as original. *The Little Minister*, for example, was written specifically for Bob Marks, but it is a far cry from the play of the same name by James Barrie. Nor did the Marks's "property," *The Village Blacksmith*, bear any relation to W. S. Gilbert's widely known play. The use of familiar titles was good business. Indeed, most of the plays which were presumably the property of R. W. Marks have a suspicious familiarity about them. Some of them, noted as "copyrighted in Washington," are *Children of the Slums*, *Paradise Regained*, *Harvest of Sin*, and *A Mother's Heart*.

Other plays, the common stock-in-trade for many other touring companies and part of the Marks Brothers' repertoire, were *The Black Flag*, *A Celebrated Case*, *Uncle Tom's Cabin*, *The Two Orphans*, *The Ticket-of-Leave Man*, *Ten Nights in a Bar-Room*, *East Lynne*. Whether it was original or common property, there was no deviation from melodrama, and, according to Bob Marks, this preference was deliberate: "The great appetite of the masses of show-goers is for melodrama. Despite what the 'experts' say, melodrama is one of the great perennials in the theatrical business."[5] He went on to explain that it was a particular type of melodrama which accounted for the tremendous success of the Marks Brothers:

For the lifetime of the Marks enterprises our people have absolutely refused to compromise on honest and orderly entertainment. Companies must depend on family patronage, and the vast majority of Canadian and American families are founded on wholesome standards.[6]

This was a sensible argument. Marks was referring to the fact that the

[5]A quotation by R. W. Marks, included in an article entitled "Ten, Twenty, Thirty" by Robson Black. No source or date.
[6]*Ibid.*

people in the towns, in comparison to big city dwellers, retained a particular Victorian viewpoint. Entertainment took place at home, with the whole family participating, and when the evening out gradually became recognized as an alternative, it merely became an extension of the home life. If a play was performed in the town opera house, it was an occasion for the whole family to attend. Naturally there was an insistence that the drama be morally correct, and companies such as the Marks Brothers soon gained favour for their reliability.

When considering plays not suitable for his company, Marks singled out those of Ibsen, in particular *A Doll's House*. In 1908 he had followed directly behind Jane Corcoran's production of this play and he had no doubt heard sufficient comment on the play and the immorality of Ibsen to have convinced himself of the righteousness of his own melodramatic ways. From the articles available, a reaction can be compiled somewhat along these lines:

It must be remembered that to a farmer or small town dweller in Canada at the turn of the century, melodrama was, in a sense, realism. It dealt with life as he understood it, and the problems that he feared, such as an erring daughter. Such a thing had happened to a neighbour; the disgrace to the family, the outraged parent's reaction, "Out in the snow!," the snow, of course, being for dramatic effect! And then the explanation to show that it wasn't as bad as it seemed to be, or perhaps the reassertion of natural kindness, so that life would become tolerable again, even pleasant! reconciliation, everything as it should be. Life was like that.

In Ibsen's plays, on the other hand, Marks could very well have felt that life was not honestly portrayed. Comparing *East Lynne* with *A Doll's House*, for example, he could have argued that the former would have been considered much more natural and true to life than the latter.

Mrs. Wood can be said to have accepted the conventions of her time. "When lovely woman stoops to folly" – what remained for her to do but die, as surely as women taken in adultery in the time of the ancient Hebrews. Although the Victorians, being kindly people, only cast stones in a metaphorical sense, the end was the same, though it was delayed. Lady Isabel, in *East Lynne*, overwhelmed by circumstances that she has not been trained to meet, curls up and dies. This is very sad and unfortunate, of course, but under the circumstances quite natural. But Nora! This commonplace Norwegian lady is suddenly endowed with powers of rhetoric generally assumed to be the accomplishment of the male, and rather than remain submissive to her husband, decides to leave him. Although this may have been considered wonderful by the experts, the man in the pioneer country could only view it as unforgivable and incredible, and if given the choice of an Ibsen play or a Marks Brothers play, he didn't hesitate to choose the latter.

By 1900 the Marks Brothers touring system was well organized. During the summers at Cedar Lodge, Christie Lake, the brothers gathered to plan for the following season. The plays were chosen and distributed among the three companies and the routes planned in detail. Although they all opened their seasons at approximately the same time, they took care to begin at an appropriate distance from each other. In 1902, for example, when Tom Marks was opening in Battle Creek, Michigan, Bob Marks began his operations close to home at Peterborough, Ontario, and Ernie Marks started at

Morrisburg, Ontario. Then, in a well-planned scheme, the companies dove-tailed their tours, covering the country in such a fashion that in any one town at any one time, the citizens were either welcoming or waving goodbye to a Marks Brothers production.

The individual companies were also well organized. R. W. Marks was the manager of No. 1 Company, his wife, May A. Belle, was the leading lady, and George Marks, apart from being "the heavy," was the company's treasurer. There was also a property man, a musical director (and orches-tra), a stage manager and a business manager. The company was com-posed of about twelve members. The No. 2 Company included Joe Marks, with Alex as advance agent, Ernie as stage manager and Ernie's wife Kitty as the leading lady. The third company was led by Tom Marks. All three companies were of about the same strength and they each started off on the road with the same amount of money, duly recorded in their central records. It was an efficient business operation. In fact their business ability was noted by C. J. Whitney in a letter which Bob Marks proudly carried at all times:

I have played the Marks Brothers Dramatic Company over my circuit. They broke all week stand records at popular prices and broke their own record on return weeks. They are gentlemen actors, bustlers and money getters.

In business terms, public relations was probably the most important aspect of their operations. The people wanted melodrama as far as R. W. Marks and his brothers could ascertain, and working on that assumption, they never varied their bill. The people enjoyed the excitement and colour of a circus, so the Marks Brothers adopted the policy of entering a town with a parade and a brass band. The people respected the church, so the entire troupe was ordered to church at least once every Sunday. In towns where the denominations were more evenly divided, they were expected to go two and even three times, each time to a different church. The Marks Brothers wisely followed the policy that the customer was always right, and they would go to any lengths to provide what was wanted. In some towns, for example, in an attempt to please all the people at one time, they would hire a three-storey building, and put vaudeville on the first floor, drama on the second, and a freak show on the top. They were also very much aware of the value of the dollar in the smaller towns, and to be assured of a full house, or as they would have argued, to give every one the privilege of seeing their productions, it is very likely that they originated the "ten, twenty, thirty, show." This would appear on the bill boards and of course referred to the price of admission. The idea became popular in the United States in the early part of the century.

Although they spent a great deal of their time studying the ways and means of public persuasion, the Marks Brothers did not forget to lavish attention on their plays. The costumes, for example, were always selected with great care. In *Anona the Indian Maid*, which was presumably the property of R. W. Marks, the hero was costumed in "a broad-brimmed black hat, ringlet wig, white cravat, full-shirt, blue coat trimmed with gold lace, long red waist coat, trunk breeches, buff boots, belt and hanger." The heroine was in a "light petticoat with red feather trimming, gold bracelets and anklets with feathers, moccasins, head dress of beads and feathers, beads and ornaments around neck, long gold earrings." The settings were also very important and unlike most touring companies of the time, which would merely reshuffle the flats to give the impression of a new scene, the Marks Brothers took pains to create (and the trouble to transport) expensive and elaborate scenery. Every new scene had to be visually correct, and rather than limit the number of different settings in one play, as would have been expected of a touring company, they deliberately increased the number as an added attraction. In fact, a scene painter usually accompanied the troupe who could, on short notice, create a completely new scene. This practice was occasionally employed by Bob Marks when he was playing for an extended time in one city. Something of the variety and extent of the scenery can be seen from the description, again from *Anona the Indian Maid*, of the first scene. It is set "on the main deck of the Urania, with ladders, mist, yards and shrouds." From there the scene changes to "a plain of ice; heavy lurid horizon, a few stars seen." The audience was then treated to a change of pace and temperature as "the coast of Mexico" spread before them. Finally, a magnificent saloon, and through the window a splendid view of Paris. That these directions were fully carried out is evident in the photographs of the play which still remain.

The necessity for realism, as they understood it, was a major consideration and it took the form of presenting on the stage actual farm machinery, livestock, trees and grass, etc. In *Huldah*, for example, a complete farm setting was simulated. A cow and a chicken coop with live chickens apparently vied with the actors for the attention of the audience. The little details were not forgotten, as can be seen in the direction that there be "soap for the wash tub." The doors, of course, were also practical, perfected even to the latch. In fact all the effects in a Marks production were planned to startle or convince with accuracy. The Marks Brothers productions bear a similarity to the touring companies of a slightly earlier date in England, one such company being immortalized by Dickens as "Vincent Crummles and Company."

The sensational element was duly incorporated into most of their melodramas. The situations were generally copies of a type which were the familiar stock-in-trade of almost every touring company. An episode from *The Village Blacksmith* serves to illustrate the typical sensational scene and at the same time reveal something of the quality of the average Marks Brothers production. The villain, Dorman, has managed to overpower the hero, Rhodes. Rescue is on the way in the person of Walton, the honest and kindly village blacksmith. However, the question of lasting suspense remains: will he get there in time? The action takes place in the old mill:

DORMAN: Do you see that wheel there?

RHODES: Yes, but what of that?

DORMAN: I'm going to tie you to it, set the machinery of the mill in motion, and you will be drawn toward it with every revolution, until at last, you will be ground into a shapeless mass. (*Bus. of tying Rhodes*)

RHODES: Oh my God! Have you no mercy, man? No mercy?

DORMAN: Mercy! Ha! Ha! I never knew what mercy meant!

RHODES: But Mark, Mark, I'm your own brother, think of our mother in heaven, think of . . .

DORMAN: Shut up. I think of nothing. I only remember that you stood between me and all my plans when we were boys, for dissipated though you were, you were the favorite of the family, and I have always hated you for it. But tonight, I have my sweet revenge! (*Sets wheel in motion*). Goodbye my dear Rockford. I wish you a pleasant journey to the devil.

Enter Walton

WALTON: What! Mark Dorman!

DORMAN: Out of my way, John I'm a desperate man, and if you attempt to hinder me, I'll shoot you down like a dog.

WALTON: Out of your way, you scoundrel, never! for you settle your account with me, here and now! (*Springs at Dorman—clench*).

Revolver is discharged harmlessly in air, and finally wrenched from Dorman's grasp, falling upon the floor. Terrific struggle, which is at last won by Walton. Walton stops wheel by seizing lever just as Rhodes' head is about to be drawn into the pit. Walton leans panting on the lever.

This play, and many others of the same kind, belong to a type of drama that has long since disappeared from the stage. Today there is little chance of finding an audience sufficiently unsophisticated to require their return. It is true that in recent years old melodramas have been revived as comedies, but in such productions the spirit that originally sustained them is lost. Melodramas truly belong to a stage in our past, a stage, by the way, of intense theatrical vitality.

The life of the company on tour also echoes the past. One amusing story has added value as it provides a glimpse of the type of audience the early touring companies had to contend with. The incident apparently occurred not long after the formation of the parent company. Robert Marks, Sr., and his fellow actors were fulfilling an engagement in a small town called Napinka, a typical cow-town in those days, close to the Dakota boundary. Cowboys, equipped with the inevitable six-shooters, came to their performance, but alas! though these gentlemen were looking for entertainment, it was really of a different kind than that which the Marks Company had in mind. In true western fashion they proceeded to shoot up the scenery and put holes in the kerosene footlights. Perhaps this would have been the finish of the show for some companies, but Bob Marks had encountered and overcome trouble before. Before the next show he drew aside some of the trouble-makers and appointed them as ushers. Never before or since were the duties of an usher so ardently performed. They would have no noise! Noise, even in the form of laughter or applause, was sternly rebuked. The Marks Company performed in silence, almost as nerve-racking an affair for them as the destruction of the scenery had formerly been. No guardians of the peace could have performed their duties more conscientiously.

Many indeed were the misfortunes and hardships as well as triumphs experienced by the intrepid Marks Brothers during their long career on the

Canadian road. Ernie was the last to leave the road, and that was in 1922.[7] There were no artistic achievements; they were strictly entertainers and as such gave a great deal of happiness to a vast number of people. They gave their audiences what they wanted, and in return were paid handsomely for their efforts. As R. W. Marks remarked on recalling his touring days, "You might say that we were benefactors on the road to fortune."

The only other Canadian touring company of note during the period under discussion was that formed by Albert Taverner (who subsequently assumed the name Tavernier as more suitable for the dignity of his profession), and his wife Miss Ida Van Cortland. This company, it must be conceded, in spite of the undeniable attractiveness of the redoubtable Marks Brothers, was superior in many respects to that company, save possibly in the field of finance. Rather than produce freely adapted copies of second-rate melodramas, or plays written by themselves, they generally presented the successes of the day: the classic melodramas such as *The Ticket-of-Leave Man, Under the Gaslight, Arrah-na-Pogue, Colleen Bawn,* and *Camille.*

There was also a great difference in the beginnings of these two companies. The Marks companies grew out of a circus atmosphere in which the steps from selling five-octave harmonicas, through performing feats of *legerdemain* and finally to producing full-scale melodramatic productions were a logical result of business acumen rather than of artistic aspirations. With the Taverniers, however, the situation was reversed. From the beginning both Albert Tavernier and Ida Van Cortland revered the theatre and looked on the acting profession in the highest possible terms. They tended to dismiss considerations of monetary return and sought rather to dignify themselves by assuming the roles of dedicated artists.

According to notes held by his daughter Mrs. Ida C. McLeish,[8] Albert Tavernier owed his initial interest in the theatre to his father who, on getting married, had given up his acting career for the more reliable profession of elocution teacher. He did not, however, manage to become a very reliable husband and father for, as Mrs. McLeish says on recalling her grandfather, "He was a wanderer more or less, and would sometimes be gone for weeks or months and the family would not know his whereabouts." He died of yellow fever in Kingston, Jamaica, October 20, 1885. When the family came to Toronto, young Albert was persuaded by his mother to continue his studies at college. She encouraged her son to get a degree in civil engineering to prepare for a respectable profession. Albert, however, concentrated his attention on the college amateur productions and usually could have been found at the Grand Opera House, the home of Mrs. Morrison's Stock Company. In 1877 when the actor C. W. Couldock was appearing at this theatre, Albert made his bid for the professional stage. He recalled this little episode in some notes which appear to have been the tentative beginnings of an autobiography:

48

[7]*Daily Times-Gazette,* Oshawa, February 16, 1952.
[8]Most of the material from this section is derived from an interview with the late Mrs. Ida C. McLeish, daughter of Albert Tavernier and Ida Van Cortland, and the scrapbooks in her possession. The other main source is the Tavernier Theatre Collection in the Toronto Public Library.

I was acquainted with the famous old actor C. W. Couldock – then connected with Mrs. Morrison's Toronto Stock Co. from which so many good actors graduated. I called on Mr. Couldock and recited for him by way of something light, Marc Antony's oration over the dead body of Caesar. He was evidently favorably impressed and secured my first engagement with his old time friend John A. Ellsler of Cleveland.

His first speaking part with this company was in the old play *A Heroine in Rags* which was performed in the 1877–78 season. In 1879 he returned to Canada and became a member of the E. A. McDowell Touring Company.

Whereas Albert Tavernier's career apparently started with the touring company, Ida Van Cortland, as we have noted, gained her early experience as a member of Mrs. Morrison's Stock Company in Toronto. It was at this theatre in 1877 that Miss Van Cortland took her first tentative steps under the watchful eye of Mrs. Morrison. As Miss Van Cortland mentioned many years later in an address, she started at the bottom, in the ballet. She explained the term and the work it involved:

By Ballet, I don't mean the dancing ballet, but the extra men and women that were always members of the company, and from whose ranks were drawn the people to fill unforeseen vacancies. . . . I was expected to "go on" without a line to say, perhaps to carry a banner or be of a crowd to shout myself hoarse; but every night, I was on the stage in some capacity, learning how to enter, exit, walk, stand still, hold my hands or speak a few lines.[9]

She was no doubt holding a spear on stage or watching from the wings during Couldock's performances, for she was an earnest student, and seized on every occasion to study her profession. Something of the dedicated atmosphere of which she was a part is revealed in her recollections:

As I watched in the wings, and listened, in those old days, it seems to me the actors were never weary of discussing readings, expressions, emphasis and action. The Couldock reading of a line was contrasted with a Booth interpretation; and the phrase was discussed pro and con, the meaning analyzed word by word, and the methods of inflection necessary to bring that meaning out.

On September 21, 1877, Ida had the opportunity to "speak a few lines," and seemingly acquitted herself quite admirably. She had appeared in Fanny Davenport's production of *As You Like It*, and according to the critic for the *Toronto Globe* of September 17, 1877, her Amiens was the best that he had seen at the Grand Opera House. It was a thrilling evening for Miss Van Cortland, and as she recalled in her address, it was her first real step forward in her profession:

I satisfied Miss Davenport, and I was happy. So I began to know what life upon the stage meant, its hard work, its long rehearsals, its lonely going to and from the theatre at all hours of the night, standing about in the wings wearily waiting hours while important scenes were being rehearsed.

The popular *As You Like It* was again performed at the Grand Opera

[9]From a copy of the address given to the University Women's Club of Ottawa, around 1918, and in the possession of Mrs. Ida C. McLeish, p. 2.

House on October 9, 1877, and on this occasion there was no opportunity for the members of Mrs. Morrison's Company because Miss Louisa Pomeroy was the leading lady and she travelled with a full supporting cast. The arrival of this company was, in fact, something of an occasion, for it was probably one of the first of its kind to appear in Toronto.[10] From then on, however, the appearance of the touring company was to become more frequent. The speed at which the transition took place can be observed in the fact that the Grand Opera House, when it closed its doors at the end of this season, never again opened as a stock company.

Miss Pomeroy's company gains some importance for us not only because it was one of the first of its kind to arrive in Canada, but because in its cast list we find Albert Tavernier playing the role of Duke Frederick. The two probably met at this time, but there is no evidence of a romance, and after the performances, Albert no doubt left town with the company.

50

Miss Van Cortland remained with the stock company and was evidently kept quite busy. The touring company had not yet ousted the touring star. As she noted: "In quick succession came Frederick Robinson, Dominick Murray, J. T. Raymond, Cecil Rush, McKee Rankin, Modjeska, William H. Leake, George Rignold, Fred Warde, Robert McWade and others." Further insight into the busy routine of this stock company can be gained from her invaluable reminiscences.

There was a change of bill by the regular company as a rule, once a week; but when stars came, the change of bill depended upon the *repertoire* of the star. If a legitimate star, the change was generally nightly. Out of 30 weeks [a regular stock season] 10 were devoted to Shakespeare; *As You Like It, Macbeth, Henry V, Twelfth Night, Romeo and Juliet, Richard III, Merchant of Venice, Othello,* – all in one season.

The term "legitimate" usually referred to Shakespearean actors and productions, but as with most terms, it generally had a broader meaning, and it is safe to assume that Miss Van Cortland included in this category most blank-verse plays which formed the repertoire of the leading actors of the time.

The Grand Opera House, according to Miss Van Cortland's description, was rarely dark. If no star arrived, productions were put on by the resident actors, and, of course, there was always Toronto's favourite, Mrs. Morrison, to assume the leading roles. At other times the honours were shared, as was the case in performances of *Englishmen in India* and *To Parents and Guardians*, in which no one actor was given top billing.

Mrs. Morrison's Company apparently provided excellent training for the aspiring young actor. Miss Van Cortland, for instance, was privileged to act

[10]Arthur Hobson Quinn, in his *History of the American Drama, from the Beginning to the Civil War*, pp. 387–8, notes that the development of the travelling company with one play was due to the initiative of Dion Boucicault. Sometime in 1860, he apparently "conceived the idea that instead of sending a star around the theatrical circuit of that day, a second company could be sent out from New York in a successful play and the drama itself could be billed as the attraction."

with the leading actors of the time and as a resident actress was obliged to accept a wide variety of roles. As she noted:

In that one season I worked under twenty different stars, and played at least forty parts, ranging from broad comedy to serious tragedy, from the soubrette part in *Mickey Free* with Dominick Murray, to the 2nd witch in *Macbeth* with Fred Warde and Frederick Robinson.

That she was progressing in her profession was commented upon by the critic for the *Toronto Mail* on March 27, 1878, who had witnessed her performance in one of the leading parts in *The Two Orphans*:

Miss Van Cortland has long since given the public proof of her unquestionable powers as an actress but few would have imagined she could have acquitted herself so well in the onerous part of Louise. . . . The character of the poor blind girl, with its transitions from despair to hope, the unobtrusive resignation with which she bears her troubles and the quite unmistakable joy manifested at their happy close – all these marked the true artist, and indicate for this young lady a still more successful future.

Her student days at the Grand Opera House lasted until the end of the season. She would probably have continued on at this stock company, gradually developing her skills and moving steadily up into the more important roles, if it had not been for the fact that Mrs. Morrison obviously ran into a number of problems which caused her to close the theatre. As Miss Van Cortland recalled, "The season toward the end was very disastrous." It seems that the theatre was not prospering and "Salaries were unpaid." And within the company there was unrest: "Mr. W. S. Harkins and his wife Lenore Bigelow playing the juvenile left the company, and everything was in a state of confusion." This state was a familiar one in those days in the theatre, and when it occurred there was nothing to do but go out and seek employment at another theatre. Mrs. Morrison no longer required their services, and that was the end of it.

Miss Van Cortland went to New York and there she was auditioned by Mr. Nannery for his theatrical company in Halifax, and in January, 1879, she commenced her duties as a member of his company. The first play of the season was *The Romance of a Poor Young Man*, which was performed on January 15, 1879. It set the tone, and from that time until the end of March, the company presented a series of melodramas and light farces, such as *The Marble Heart*, *The Lyons Courier*, *Under the Gaslight*, *All that Glitters is Not Gold*, *Hurricanes*, and *Pocahontas*. It seems that Miss Van Cortland was still gaining experience from a variety of roles, for in the last-mentioned play she was cast as Captain John Smith.

After establishing himself in Halifax, Nannery took his company to St. John's, Newfoundland. It was obviously his plan to alternate between these two cities, but first he had to discover whether or not the Newfoundland people would appreciate his efforts. The initial visit was therefore a limited engagement and the play chosen was once again *The Romance of a Poor Young Man*. Something of the atmosphere with which theatrical entertain-

51

ment had to contend may be gathered from the fact that they performed in the Total Abstinence Hall. The play was a success, and according to the local drama critic the "St. John's public never had such a talented company." Encouraged by this reception, Nannery proceeded with his arrangements to alternate between the two cities. His decision to do so is worth noticing for it marks the first time that Newfoundland had been linked to Canada by a touring company. Many years were to elapse before Newfoundland was to be again so honoured. C. Nick Stark noted in the *New York Dramatic Mirror* of June 17, 1914, that W. S. Harkins, the juvenile who had left Mrs. Morrison's Company, was at this time performing with his company at St. John's, and Stark felt obliged to refer to the Harkins Company as the first of its kind to arrive in Newfoundland.

Nannery's Company returned to Newfoundland in September, 1879, and in the cast we find once more the name of Albert Tavernier. The first play in which he and Miss Ida Van Cortland performed together would seem to have been *The Ticket-of-Leave Man*, on September 19, 1879, in which Ida played the part of May Edwards opposite the leading man, Frank Roche, and Albert was cast in the role of Maltby. Sometime during this season in Newfoundland, Albert and Ida fell in love and in the following summer in New York they were married.

It should be noted in passing that the season in Newfoundland ended with a scandal which, trivial as it may have been, did bring about the close of the company and put an end to theatre in Newfoundland, as far as touring companies were concerned, for a considerable length of time. The only remaining clues to this scandal are the two letters printed in the St. John's newspaper: a denunciation by Bess Jefferson Fisher, an actress in the company, and a reply to it by Nannery himself. Miss Fisher's letter, which is quoted in part, certainly attempted to obliterate Mr. Nannery's reputation in Newfoundland:

The cowardly attack of Mr. Nannery upon two unprotected ladies, should pass without a word from us – with silent contempt which the *bully* deserves. But that his reputation is not so well known here as in Halifax, and I think it necessary to point out why he selects women as his opponents. The encounter which resulted in a sound thrashing last summer from a gentleman in Halifax has taught him it is best to try his skill on the weaker sex; at least from them he need fear no personal chastisement. . . . In my dealings with Mr. Nannery, I have found him a trickster. Not one week's salary was ever received at the time specified – always one week later.

All this is rather vague, for it seems impossible to believe that Mr. Nannery physically assaulted the ladies of his company with the intent, as the letter suggests, or for the pleasure of spoiling their beauty or otherwise impairing their ability as actresses. Nevertheless, whatever the quarrel and whatever the justifications, a scandal was created. Mr. Nannery felt compelled to resign, but before he left he wrote a reply to the newspaper letter, and his reference to his career, though it ignored particular charges, has a certain impressive dignity.

8 / Most performers from the United States and England made only temporary visits to Canada. John Nickinson was an exception: he chose Toronto as his home, and, as an actor-manager, gave the city its first real taste of professional theatre.

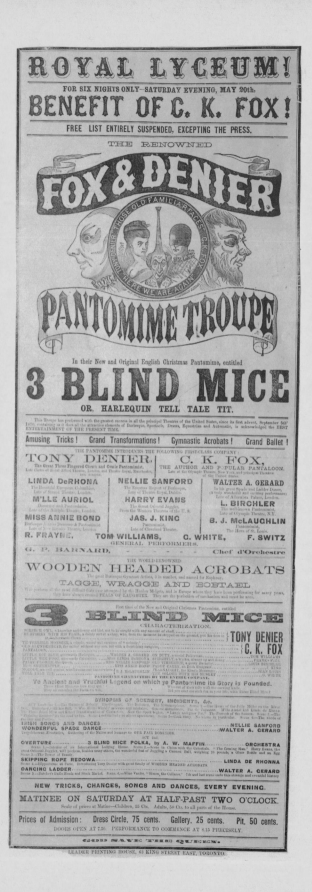

9, 10, 11 / Under John Nickinson's management, a wide variety of performers from England and the United States visited Toronto. His own daughter, Charlotte (shown at right with her husband, Daniel Morrison), was probably the most important addition to the Toronto scene. Under her guiding hand a stock company was formed giving an opportunity to Canadian talent. Her efforts were recognized in the "Grand Complimentary Benefit" given her by "prominent citizens of Toronto."

12 / The Royal Lyceum, Toronto, although under various managements during the 1850s and 60s, can generally be considered the home of the Nickinson family. It was on the south side of King Street between Bay and York, and was built by John Ritchey in 1848.

I have managed successfully for a number of years the largest operatic and dramatic companies in Canada. I have paid as high as $4,750.00 per week in salaries, and have had over a hundred people employed in various theatres at one time; but in ten years, with the exception of this summer, I have had no trouble like the present. I write this letter reluctantly and wish no hostile feeling to any one member of the company.

Actually the fact mentioned in Miss Fisher's letter, that he always paid his cast one week late, only testifies to his honesty, for in those days it was not uncommon for the manager to disappear in times of financial duress with what little money remained and leave the actors to fend for themselves. Neither Albert Tavernier nor Ida Van Cortland commented on the affair. They apparently did not side with Nannery for they remained with the company, which lasted out the season and then disbanded.

In the next two or three years Tavernier and his wife found employment in a variety of touring companies, the longest association probably being with Mr. Harry Lindley. This gentleman was a rather extraordinary character who remained on the Canadian road for many years. Walter McRaye, a professional entertainer who toured throughout Canada, met Lindley during his travels and at one time had the opportunity of performing with him. Lindley was presenting a play called *The Man from Galway*, which he claimed to have written himself. McRaye doubted Lindley's authorship but said "it didn't matter much for it was rotten anyway."[11] As to the rest of the plays in his repertoire, McRaye had very little to say except that they were just a "lot of pirated plays stolen from New York." His further comments are quite amusing and throw some light on the small-town touring companies of those days.

Adelaide Flint was his leading lady and she was clever and pretty. Her husband was old Doug Secord, a member of the family at Niagara that had given Laura Secord to Canada. Doug was general factotum with the company and doubled in so many parts that the auditors finally forgot his original name. He had even played "Mobs " offstage. Harry Lindley owed nearly every hotel man in Canada. Once in the Maritimes a landlord seized the company and travelled with it until his money was paid.

Strangely enough the Taverniers remained with Lindley for almost a year. In 1881 they returned to the Grand Opera House in Toronto, then under the management of O. B. Sheppard, and took parts in a play called *Cherry Ripe* which was produced on October 22, 1881, by the Florence Company. They were at this time appearing in notices as Mr. M. A. Tavernier and Mrs. Ida Tavernier.

Everything appeared to be going along well. Others in the profession, viewing their constant employment, would no doubt have considered them highly successful. But although financially secure, the Taverniers were not happy, and when *Cherry Ripe* closed, they decided "that it was professional suicide to continue playing with a one-piece company." The time had come to form their own company, and this they did, calling it the New York

11Walter McRaye, *Town Hall To-night!* (Toronto, 1929), p. 26.

Comedy Company with Ida Van Cortland as the star. The initial performances were held in Halifax. In the years that followed they toured mostly
in the East, travelling west as far as Winnipeg, and south into the bordering
towns and cities of the United States.

Their partnership in this theatrical endeavour was a perfect combination.
Miss Van Cortland was the natural choice for a leading lady, and Tavernier,
apart from being an excellent character actor, proved himself a capable
manager. Their chief aim was to please the public and quite naturally the
only way of achieving this goal was to favour the popular plays of the time.
There was a concentrated effort to produce plays in which Miss Van Cortland could excel, some of which are noted by her son, P. A. Taverner, in
his letter contained in the Tavernier Theatre Collection:

Her greatest parts were Mercy Merrick in *The New Magdalen*, Stephanie in
Forget-me-not, Antonio in *Two Nights in Rome*, Lucretia Borgia, Cora in *Article
47 or The Creole*, and *Camille*. She also made an acceptable Juliet, and was also
good in certain light comedy parts as Mrs. Gilffory in *The Mighty Dollar*, Lady
Gay Spanker in *London Assurance*, and as Galatea in *Pygmalion and Galatea*.

Other plays in their repertoire were *Under the Gaslight, The Ticket-of-Leave
Man, East Lynne*, and *Hazel Kirke*.

In Miss Van Cortland's reminiscences we glimpse something of the technique involved in the acting methods of her time. Her remarks are not
extensive but they do indicate how she struggled to achieve and express
emotion. The role of Cora the Creole in *Article 47* apparently presented an
interesting problem. This was the part made famous by Clara Morris in
which a woman who has had her face and neck disfigured by a bullet fired
by her lover gradually goes mad. Miss Van Cortland spoke of her approach
to the part:

I went to the asylums at Toronto and Kingston to study those awful aggregations
of human woe. I noted the general symptoms common to all mad people, the
insane laugh, the frequent mutterings, the restless hands, and when George tears
the veil from the disfigured face, I crouched down to the floor of the stage with
a long, low, agonized moan, trying vainly to cover up the scar, but mad, mad.

She was a strong believer in what was later (and loosely) called the Stanis-
lavsky approach. She would probably have claimed full agreement with
Sarah Bernhardt's declaration that an actress "must weep real tears, suffer
real anguish, laugh a real laugh and a laugh which is contagious."[12] Her
approach to Camille is indicative:

Camille was one of my strongest parts. I had knelt at the feet of Modjeska, and
had won my inspiration from her, for while playing Nanine with her in this piece,
at Mrs. Morrison's, I had sobbed my heart out with my head in her lap. . . . Nor
was this girlish hysteria, for even after years of experience, emotion aroused by
such parts, in me at least, was real. If I had to move the people, I had first to
move my own heart, and many a night, I have been so overcome I have been
carried off the stage when the curtain fell.

Miss Van Cortland no doubt was sincere in the expression of her emotions,

[12]Sarah Bernhardt, *The Art of the Theatre* (London, 1924), p. 200.

but it is likely that though the tears were real, the pose and gesture were conventional. Whatever the case, the style proved popular.

Little is recorded of this company's touring days. We do know, however, that they used to rehearse the plays for the coming season at a cottage in the Muskoka district of Ontario. Mrs. McLeish still has the guest book of that cottage, and in it is an entry for the year 1895 in which Albert Tavernier made a few comments on the events of the season.

Company played *Mighty Dollar* at Bracebridge, June 28th and made a big hit. Performance was for the benefit of the orchestra. House was rather bad. Mr. J. M. Hyde, our new manager for season '95–'96, arrived to commence booking June 25th. Company played at Rosseau July 11, *Forget-me-not*. Mr. Hyde saw the performance and was much delighted and encouraged. . . . Company left Rosseau for Parry Sound by stage, 24 miles, to play there a week. The stage road is frightfully rough but we enjoyed it on account of the novelty and interesting scenery and farm incidents, and being favored by a cool day for the trip. Favored by fine cool weather in Parry Sound, we did a fair business for the town and the season of the year. We cleared about $100.00, and returned to Gibraltor by way of Port Cockburn, arriving home everyone tired out after our 12 hour jump.

We can see from this note that the Tavernier Touring Company did not always travel in the greatest of style. Indeed, their attainments fell far short of their dreams. In the opinion of P. A. Taverner, his mother especially failed to achieve the recognition she deserved. Her mistake, according to him, was "in adhering to a sure moderate success, instead of going to New York," where she would have undoubtedly taken her place "alongside the notables of the profession."

Miss Van Cortland, on the other hand, was inclined to think that her decision was not a mistake. She forfeited metropolitan success for a life on the road and was proud of it. The fact that she was idolized in all the little towns on their circuit was ample reward. In later years she recalled her experiences with pleasure.

The annual appearance of the company in each town was an event looked forward to by old and young. The children met me at the stage door and clung to my skirts. I had the following of the "home" or "family public," which is the best public upon which any manager can depend.

These pleasant conditions lasted for a number of years, and then, in 1896, quite abruptly, she left the stage and the Tavernier Dramatic Company was disbanded. The specific cause of her leaving is not apparent. There were the children, of course, and it is quite likely that the company was not making enough money. Miss Van Cortland's suggestion, made many years after her retirement, that the public's taste had changed and that she had bowed out with the advent of farce in comedy was only partially true. Serious presentations of *East Lynne* and *Camille* continued well into the twentieth century. It may have been that they were crowded out by the increase of the smaller touring companies, which were by this time reaching the communities with their stock of musicals and farce.

Albert Tavernier remained with the profession and his later career is marked by the inevitable ups and downs of an actor's life. His last engagement was with Katharine Cornell in *The Age of Innocence*. He died of a heart attack in 1929, after a performance in Philadelphia. According to his daughter, he became, like his father, a wanderer. He had some success in New York, and was heard from in Kingston, Jamaica; St. John's, Newfoundland; London, England; and a variety of cities throughout the United States.

Mrs. Tavernier turned her back on the stage and found employment with an insurance company. She cherished her memories and, according to her daughter, could be found quite often sitting with her scrapbook recalling her triumphs. Once she had been an idol in countless Canadian towns, and the thought was comforting. A would-be poet wrote a tribute for her which held a special place in her book.

> If for Ida I'd a pen
> As gifted as my theme is, —
> For Ida I'd array it then
> In compliment extremis,
> To tell how fourteen days ago
> When first I stood beside her,
> I felt the spell which all must know
> For Ida, if they eyed her.

Ida, when she was reaching the end of her life, was able to recall her decision to remain in Canada. If she had gone to New York or London would she have become one of the leading ladies of the theatre? She died believing that she would, and to the end she was serenely happy to know that she had "sacrificed metropolitan success for the wee bit of domestic life accorded to [her] by a life on the road."

More information about Canadian touring companies will, no doubt, be revealed in the years to come. My examination is restricted to these few, with the result that it is impossible to draw firm conclusions. However, there are a number of obvious points that can be made. We can observe, for example, that on the whole the companies remained loyal to Canada. There was no urgent desire among the stars to seek their fortune in the United States or England; Ida Van Cortland actually resisted this move in spite of the fact that she was sure she would be successful. The companies, and the actors involved, seemed content to remain Canadian. This is not to say that they restricted their activities to Canada. A second point to note is that the Canadian touring companies of this early period were part of the North American theatre. All of them considered it quite natural to extend their circuits below the border, just as many American companies looked upon Canada as merely a northern part of their own country. From a commercial stand point there wasn't much difference between Canada and the United States.

But there was, naturally, a difference between Canadian companies and foreign companies. Generally, the Canadian groups were quite conservative in their choice of material. The American and English companies tended to be more adventurous. As a result, it was through the efforts of the foreign touring companies that Canadians gained the opportunity of seeing some of the plays of the New Movement. The reaction of the Canadian public to this exposure is now to be considered.

THE NEW MOVEMENT ON TOUR

The New Movement in drama might be said to have had its beginnings with the plays of T. W. Robertson, the playwright now commonly recognized as the first modern English dramatist. Ernest Reynolds, in listing the precursors to Shaw in his *Modern English Drama*, draws our attention to the important position Robertson holds in England's history of the theatre:

His earliest herald in England had been T. W. Robertson, whose domestic "cup-and-saucer" comedies, *Caste, Play, School, Ours,* and others, had introduced a breath of real life into the silk-fringed air of the London theatres in the 1860's.[13]

57

The movement was essentially a withdrawal from the old Victorian stage tradition, and, as it grew, it encompassed a wide variety of writers with a number of similar aims. They all endeavoured to increase the naturalness of the stage setting, to develop the authentic accents of ordinary speech in their dialogue, and to reflect something of their own society and times. As George Rowell notes in his excellent survey of this period, *The Victorian Theatre,* "The thirty years which followed the opening of the Bancrofts' management at the Prince of Wales's witnessed the theatre's gradual achievement of respectability."[14] This period saw the work of Robertson's successors, among whom Tom Taylor, H. J. Byron, and Sydney Grundy were outstanding. It was the next twenty years, or as Rowell points out, "the era separating the first performance of *The Second Mrs. Tanqueray* from the outbreak of the Great War," that marked "the full flowering of the fashionable theatre." This was the era of prestige for the playwright; the time of Oscar Wilde, Arthur Wing Pinero, Henry Arthur Jones, James M. Barrie and John Galsworthy. It was also the time for the growth of the intellectual drama. With the opening of the Independent Theatre in 1891, English playgoers were introduced to the works of Henrik Ibsen and George Bernard Shaw.

Indeed there was a steady growth of the New Drama in England from the time of T. W. Robertson to the outbreak of the First World War. In view of this it would be natural to assume that there would have been a reflection of this theatrical activity in Canada. Some evidence of the New Drama does indeed exist, but diligent research has revealed the Canadian counterpart to be a dim copy. Of Ibsen and Shaw, a few plays were presented. Of the other dramatists, six were found to be represented: Thomas W. Robertson, Arthur Wing Pinero, James M. Barrie, Sydney Grundy, Henry Arthur Jones, and John Galsworthy.

Canadian attitudes toward the element of realism in the New Drama are reflected in the drama columns of the *Canadian Monthly* during 1875–76.

[13]Ernest Reynolds, *Modern English Drama*, p. 124.
[14]George Rowell, *The Victorian Theatre* (London, 1956), p. 103.

Although the critic, writing about Robertson's *Ours*, appeared to be happy with the development, and thought that the attention to realism was "delightful to witness," he was not entirely convinced of the final value of such a trend. The following is a typical example of his reasoning:

The temptation to fill a theatre by means of attractions which dramatic art will not sanction has always been very strong. The temptation exists no less today. Indeed, it seems stronger than ever; for the rage increases for . . . the realism of the modern stage. . . . In this state of things, one might well question what the drama of the future is to be. . . . The art of filling the house with the voice, by the play of the features, or with the subtle and varied mental action of the player, is in danger of being lost. . . . Cheap sentiment, common-place incident, and violent situation, however presented, are not the attractions one would wish to see the public satisfied with. Neither does the importunity of the public eye for realistic productions and elaborate provision of scenery and setting, indicate health in its demand, nor give a hopeful assurance of its result.[15]

His intention is clear; the ideal of the "romantic" in drama was to be cultivated in opposition to the growing demands of realism.[16]

The Canadian critic, and the public as a whole, were (and still are, for that matter) conservative in their choice of theatre. Plays by a new dramatist would receive popular acceptance in Canada only after they had become commonplace in other English-speaking countries. Robertson's plays, for example, were still considered quite modern enough for Canadians in 1896, and touring stars were wise to keep this in mind when they ventured into this country. The famous actor-manager, John Hare, for example, was fortunate in his choice of plays. For his tour of eastern Canada in the winter of 1896, he presented Robertson's *Caste*, and the public approved of his conservative taste. The play was a respectable twenty-nine years old, having been first performed in 1867, the year of Canada's Confederation. A writer for the *Daily Mail and Empire*, November 26, 1896, remarked:

Mr. John Hare, both as actor and manager, has always been conservative in making additions to his repertoire of plays, and by the admirers of the advanced school of playwrights he has been accused of being a reactionary – a charge no doubt suggested by his refusal to produce *The Second Mrs. Tanqueray*.

The fact that his refusal was commended is significant. Canadians were not yet prepared to accept Pinero's recent drama. It was, after all, only three years old, having had its first performance in London in 1893.

One other production of Robertson's *Caste* took place in Canada during

---

[15]"Music and the Drama," *Canadian Monthly*, ix, 346 (April, 1876).

[16]Canadians generally turned a deaf ear to new movements in the arts. The dominant theatrical trend of the nineteenth century was realism, not romanticism. Zola's manifesto, appended to his play *Thérèse Raquin*, produced in 1873, had sounded an alarm: ". . . I defy the last of the romanticists to put upon the stage a heroic drama; at the sight of all the paraphernalia of armor, secret doors, poisoned wines and the rest, the audience would only shrug its shoulders. And melodrama, that bourgeois offspring of the romantic drama, is in the hearts of the people more dead than its predecessor; its false sentiment, its complication of stolen children and discovered documents, its impudent gasconnades, have finally rendered it despicable so that any attempt to revive it proves abortive." But this was not so in Canada; here the old guard was prepared to fight for romance.

the period under consideration. It was presented by the E. A. McDowell Touring Company at the Grand Opera House in Hamilton in April, 1885. There was no comment from the press. *School* was presented by the Dramatic Branch of the Winnipeg Operatic Society in March, 1889. It was noted by the *Daily Mail and Empire* of April 25, 1889, as being a performance for a "fashionable" audience. *Ours* had a relatively early production at Mrs. Morrison's Grand Opera House, Toronto in March 1877. It received little critical comment.

Sydney Grundy was represented by his play *A Pair of Spectacles*. It was apparently suitable for Canadian taste. The critic for the *Daily Mail and Empire*, who viewed the show at Toronto's Grand Opera House when it played there in November, 1896, remarked: "It would be difficult to find a comedy that teaches so wholesome a lesson, or that leaves an audience at its conclusion so well disposed towards mankind."

In 1896, then, Pinero's *The Second Mrs. Tanqueray* was difficult for Canadians to accept, and John Hare's refusal to produce the play had received much enthusiastic approval. However, some years later, in February 1903 the play was presented in Toronto by Mrs. Patrick Campbell. Even at this late date the production caused a disturbance. During an interview after the performance, Mrs. Campbell was forced to defend herself, and in answer to a question put to her by an irate spectator who wondered why she never condescended to present "some type of wholesome, pure and lovable woman instead of the female with a past," she replied, "A good woman is a dramatic impossibility." In defence of the play she suggested that "human dramas are of public benefit rather than damaging to the morals of the people." The Toronto public was not kindly disposed to such attitudes, however, and said so, according to the reporter who attended the interview. Pinero's *The Notorious Mrs. Ebbsmith*, which was also part of her repertoire, was presented in Winnipeg[17] where it caused no disturbance.

Some of the early plays of Pinero were, of course, quite acceptable. For example, a local group presented *Sweet Lavender* in March 1908 in Toronto. The performance, as reported in the *Daily Mail and Empire*, was part of a drive by the management to "produce pure and wholesome comedies," which would "meet with the approval of the theatre-going public of Toronto."

None of the controversial plays of Henry Arthur Jones was performed in Canada. He was represented only by *The Silver King*, a perennial melodrama which lasted as long as the road. Of John Galsworthy's plays only *The Silver Box* found its way to Canada. It was presented by the Horniman Players in Montreal on February 22–24, 1912, and it did not cause any adverse criticism.

One does not have to be a particularly astute reader to note in most of the above-mentioned reviews the frequent use of the word "wholesome." It is worth pointing out as a quality which played a large part in Canada's cultural growth. As we shall see, wholesomeness became a basic ingredient of

[17]See Appendix A.

the poetic drama, and was commonly used as a yardstick for measuring the value of Ibsen's and Shaw's plays.

IBSEN ON THE ROAD

In the past, a growth in Ibsen's popularity always encouraged argument. This was the case not only in his own country but also in France, Germany, England, the United States, indeed in any country in which his plays were performed. The cause for the excitement was usually the subject-matter.

In England the controversy was possibly more heated and lengthy than in any other country, and the probable reason was that the English, on the whole, were not only displeased by the subject-matter, but were shocked by the new non-Shakespearean dramatic form. Also, the plays, quite often presented in poor translations, had a false ring for the play-goer, in much the same way as "dubbing" in modern foreign films can strike a false note. The English play-goer's irritation and even anger is even more understandable when we consider that he had little preparation for Ibsen's stark problem dramas.

Since Ibsen did not arouse widespread interest in England until his plays appeared on the stage, the performance of *A Doll's House* in 1889 by Janet Church and Charles Charrington in London marks the beginning of the Ibsen controversy. Arguments for and against Ibsen and his plays appeared steadily in periodicals and newspapers. Some of the critics, reacting with their public, voiced what they felt to be the opinion of the majority. Clement Scott, for many years a drama critic on a variety of papers (the *Daily Telegraph*, the *Sunday Times* and the *London Illustrated News*), was the leader of such hostile critics as J. F. Nesbit, Alfred Watson and Edward Morton. There were critics on the other side, too, of course. The most outstanding were probably William Archer and Edmund Gosse. The latter, who had spent some time in Norway, wrote the first significant criticism of Ibsen published in England. Other critics who followed this lead were A. B. Walkley, drama critic of *The Times*, George Bernard Shaw, J. T. Grein, Arthur Symons, Havelock Ellis, George Moore, and Allen Monkhouse.

In America the early information about Ibsen came primarily from the English journals and periodicals in which criticisms and reviews were published. But Americans were not entirely dependent upon England. Performances were soon taking place in the United States, and the critics inevitably took sides. One who exerted the greatest influence during the time when knowledge of Ibsen was spreading was William Winter. He never changed his opinion and over the years he used all his journalistic skill in the fight against the advance of Ibsen in America. There were, to be sure, a number of Ibsen supporters who attempted to interpret the plays and educate the public. Some of them were well known, such as Clayton Hamilton, Brander Matthews, Archibald Henderson, and H. L. Mencken.

Since there was a good deal of comment about Ibsen and his plays in English and American publications, the educated Canadian public presumably was able to keep informed on the controversy. In Canada only the odd person in the daily newspapers was interested enough to express his views on the matter. Granting the fact that Canadian literary journals at the turn of the century were not notably progressive, it is nevertheless disappointing to find only one article which comments on Ibsen. It was written by E. W. Patchett and appeared in the *Queen's Quarterly* in 1907. It is a dispassionate review. Patchett is quite obviously trying to give a sane academic view; to give, as it were, an unbiased summing up. But this he finds difficult to do, for Ibsen's social comment is at variance with Patchett's romantic leanings. As he says, Ibsen "exposes the hideous ulcers which disfigure society, with the idea that men will come to detect them," but, he continues, possibly a more valuable alternative would be to seek out the beautiful.[18] Although preferring the latter course, he concludes with good grace:

Yet, even admitting Ibsen to be entirely mistaken in the course he adopted, his high moral aim and the seriousness with which he pursued it, combined with unusual dramatic insight, fully deserve the meed of praise which is beginning to be bestowed on him.

An examination of Canadian fiction also reveals a similar lack of interest in the Ibsen controversy. The short excerpt which follows is from the novel, *Peevee*, written by Fred Jacob in 1928, and set at the beginning of the century:

"Pretty immoral chap, that fellow Ibsen!"
Peevee was feeling chagrined, or he would not have asked abruptly:
"What has he been up to now?"
Immediately he regretted his words, but the Reverend Rodd did not regard them as rudeness.
"Oh, he may be a very decent fellow for all I know!" he explained. "But his plays are far too disturbing for Canadians."[19]

As far as present research can verify, this is the only critical reference to Ibsen in early Canadian fiction. Jacob, looking back, as he says in the Foreword, to "depict the period when Canada was growing self-conscious in the arts!" recalls something of the general commotion caused by the New Movement in the drama, but his reference is certainly not specific, certainly not as specific as could have been expected from an author who was, from 1910 to the 1920s, the head of the drama department for the Toronto newspaper the *Mail and Empire*. Ibsen disturbed the world, and so it is safe to assume that he would disturb Canadians.

Actually the reaction of Canadians to the plays of Ibsen has never been specifically considered. C. F. Klinck, for example, in his book *Wilfred Campbell*, implies that Canadians knew of Ibsen only through reading reviews from the United States:

Echoes of the revolution reached Ontario in reviews of the New York season printed for readers of *The Canadian Magazine*. At the time when Campbell was penning his protest, that journal was recording Madame Nazimova's great success in *A Doll's House* and *Hedda Gabler*, Ibsen's highly controversial plays.[20]

[18]E. W. Patchett, "Ibsen," *Queen's Quarterly*, XIV, 275 (April, 1907).
[19]Fred Jacob, *Peevee*, Toronto 1928, p. 167.
[20]C. F. Klinck, *Wilfred Campbell* (Toronto: Ryerson Press, 1942), p. 144.

We should note, however, that twelve years before Campbell wrote his protest, "Shakespeare and the Latter-Day Drama," in 1907, Julia Stuart and her American company had performed *A Doll's House* in most of the major cities and many of the towns throughout eastern Canada.

As in England, Canada's introduction to Ibsen was through his controversial plays. The list is not long, however. Of all Ibsen's plays, only *A Doll's House, Ghosts, Hedda Gabler, Rosmersholm* and *The Pillars of Society* were seen in Canada, and *A Doll's House* was the first. It was in 1895 that Miss Julia Stuart and her company boldly included the play in their repertoire and ventured into Ontario. There is no evidence to indicate that this company performed in the United States, making the Canadian tour, as it were, a mere extension of an American tour. Indeed it seems possible that they set off almost immediately to the north with the zeal of pioneers, intent on educating their backward cousins. However, their idealism was restrained somewhat by business considerations, for in their repertoire they wisely retained a number of bread-and-butter plays such as *Camille* and *East Lynne*.

Very little is known of Julia Stuart. She is noted by George Odell in his *Annals of the New York Stage* as playing opposite Frank Karrington in *The White Slave* (1891–92). The performance "aroused tears in showery April (4th–9th)," and then again was noted as a "first-rate second-rate attraction" in February (8th–13th). A bare outline of her career can be found in a clipping from the *Toledo Blade*, now held in the files of the theatre collection of the New York Public Library:

Her father, David, was a popular actor in Scotland, where she was born, and her mother was a premier dancer in the Covent Garden Ballet. She made her first stage appearance in London at the age of three. At fifteen, she became a member of the Haymarket Theatre Company in London. Coming to America she played Juliet in New York and for six years headed her own road company.

It was obviously at this time, during her six years on the road, that we pick up her trail in Canada. To complete her story, it should be added that some time after her adventure in Canada she retired from the stage and "devoted herself to political work in Boston." One wonders whether her experience of playing in *A Doll's House* in the backwoods of Canada influenced her decision.

The route that this company took can be traced in the pages of the *New York Dramatic Mirror*. They started out in the winter of 1895 and their first stop was Ottawa. From there they went to Brockville and then on to the Princess Theatre in Toronto. After Toronto they played in such smaller towns as Brantford, Berlin, Guelph, and Peterborough. Unfortunately the reviews from the smaller centres no longer exist. In Brantford, Berlin, Peterborough, and Brockville the play was advertised, but no critic deigned to review it. The Guelph newspaper for this period has been destroyed by fire. There was no trace of the performance in Ottawa. The performance in Toronto, which took place on October 28, 1895, was well covered by all the major newspapers and it is to them that we must turn to recapture the reaction on this notable occasion.

It was not very impressive. The critic of the *World*, for example, was merely sympathetic. He informed the reading public that Miss Stuart was "a charming little lady," and that "in the many trying scenes throughout the performance," she had "earned the sympathy and friendship of her audience." One gets the impression that this critic did not receive Ibsen's message. He went on to note a particular scene, and by his remarks we may gain some insight into Julia Stuart's approach to the play: "Probably no more touching scene has ever been witnessed in a Toronto playhouse than the separation which occurs between Nora and her husband at the conclusion of the drama." The unmistakable shades of melodrama are evident.

According to the critic of the *Evening News*, the audience was incapable of understanding the play, and this in spite of the fact that in it were many so-called followers of Ibsen:

Ibsen's disciples in Toronto had the first sight of the master last night at the Princess Theatre. The play was *A Doll's House*, perhaps the one of all the great Norwegian's most suited for dramatic presentation. In this, as in other plays of Ibsen's, the plot is subsidiary to the moral lesson taught and the problem solved. As audiences are impatient of being lectured, and Ibsen preconceives a capacity for ideas, it is not to be wondered at, that the greater portion of the audience were perplexed at the Northman's philosophy.

Obviously only a few people approached the play in all seriousness. For the majority it was a drama of no particular significance. The confusion no doubt arose when it was found to be a serious play, and the perplexity of the audience revealed itself in the form of an embarrassment evident in their misplaced laughter. As the critic pointed out, their confusion "was lamentably shown in their entire misapprehension of the character of Dr. Rank, the consumptive. The audience failed entirely to grasp the pathos of his love declaration to Nora and seemed to regard the scene as the comic relief of the play."

The *Daily Mail and Empire* was content to note that "a large audience attended, an audience attracted chiefly by curiosity, and they were rewarded by seeing a poor play very cleverly played." The article concluded with a dour prophecy:

This is a play, excellently presented, but as a play, founded largely on false and meretricious sentiment. As this is the first time one of Ibsen's productions has been given in Toronto, we advise people to go and see it; they will not probably much desire to see another from the same pen.

It is difficult now to ascertain whether Miss Stuart was faithful to the play as written by Ibsen, or whether she took liberties with the script. Such liberties were, of course, an accepted practice in those days. In one of the first performances of *A Doll's House* in the United States, for example, presented possibly under the title *Nora*, Helena Modjeska, the leading lady, saw fit to give the play a happy ending.[21] And then there was Henry Arthur Jones's adaptation, *A Butterfly on the Wheel*, which actually was recorded as having been played at London, Ontario, on March 6, 1913. There is, however, no mention of it in the *London Free Press*.

The smaller companies which filled the road ignored the rights of the playwright. Plays were vehicles for actors and they reserved the right to re-write them at will. Indeed, the playwright was lucky if he received his royalties. Ibsen, it seems, was particularly ill-used by these pirates. Hector Charlesworth, one of Canada's best-known journalists in the early years of this century, recalled a story in his *Candid Chronicles* which illustrated Ibsen's feelings with respect to this situation. Most of the celebrities touring America at the turn of the century were employed by a gentleman called Major Pond, and a close friend of Charlesworth's, William J. Wright, was at one time Pond's European representative. Wright, on one occasion, received an order to get Ibsen for a lecture tour:

Wright, knowing that he might be received with insult, went to Christiania, and had the good luck to run across a Norwegian whom he had known in Minneapolis, who, having accumulated a fortune, had returned to his native land. This friend said he knew Ibsen and would introduce Wright to him in the café where the dramatist was accustomed to sit for an hour or two every afternoon. Ibsen proved to be in a pleasant mood and, after champagne had been served once or twice, grew expansive. Wright then made his proposition, and the dramatist at once flew into a rage. "No, I will not go to America," he said, "it is a nation of thieves." Then he drew from his pocket a list of managers, actors, and actresses, very comprehensive, who had produced plays of his without paying him royalties. He had probably obtained these through his son, Dr. Sigurd Ibsen, at one time an attaché at Washington. "All thieves, all pirates!" he said. "If I went there they would rob me again."[22]

It is quite possible that Julia Stuart was on his list. Whether or not she paid the royalties is of no importance to us, although it seems, on this occasion at least, to have been Ibsen's main concern. It is likely, however, that she would have incurred Ibsen's wrath on another count. The door that slammed in the Toronto productions certainly did not produce much reverberation. Indeed, the reference to the sad and touching scene in which Nora takes her leave of Torvald conjures up a vision of the noble heroine's gentle departure, the brave little woman's facing the world alone! Miss Stuart may have been playing Nora in her best *East Lynne* fashion, and this could very well have been the reason why there was no outburst of indignation from the Canadian audience. Furthermore, it should not be forgotten that the freedoms generated by the pioneering way of life produced a more liberal opinion of woman's place. A. R. M. Lower refers to this aspect of Canadian culture when considering the development of education in the pioneer democracy. He reminds us in his *Colony to Nation* that in this young country legal equality was stressed at the expense of old-world traditions, and the rules which separated the sexes in so-called polite societies were put

[21]H. L. Mencken, "Et-Dukkehjemiana," *The Theatre Magazine*, XII, 41 (August, 1910).
[22]Hector Charlesworth, *Candid Chronicles* (Toronto, 1925), p. 300.

aside in favour of equal rights and privileges for all. For example, girls and boys were given the same opportunities in school, and by the 1880s co-education was accepted at the university level. Possibly, therefore, the shock of Nora's decision might have appeared less radical and this, combined with Miss Stuart's carefully modulated version of the play, no doubt tended to reduce the likelihood of a fervent reaction from the audience.

The next actress to champion Ibsen in Canada was Mrs. Minnie Maddern Fiske. As was the case with most of the leading artists of the stage, her trips to Canada were confined to the larger cities, and on this occasion she visited only Toronto. Her company presented *A Doll's House* at the Grand Opera House on February 21, 1896.

The role of Nora was familiar to her. Although she had first acted in the play in 1894, she had actually become interested in it several years earlier, as an incident described in the *Theatre* of August, 1919, reveals. Apparently Mrs. Fiske discovered the play while performing in Minneapolis. She handed it to William Faversham, who was acting with her at the time, saying it was "the greatest modern drama she had ever read."[23] He was equally impressed, and so they decided to give a private performance for their own pleasure, casting the various roles among the members of the company. The manager of the Gibson Hotel, where they were staying, offered to clear the dining room for one night, and the play went on "without scenery, with the actors in their street clothes." The audience was made up of a number of employees of the hotel and those of the theatre company who were not appearing in the drama, and, although the performance started at midnight and lasted until three in the morning, "not a single person of the unique audience left the 'theatre.'"

H. L. Mencken was one of the first to suggest that Mrs. Fiske's performance in the New York production of *A Doll's House* placed her at the forefront of her profession, and at the same time revealed Ibsen as no longer a curiosity but a master playwright. It is rather disconcerting to turn from this praise to the review of February 22, 1896, by the critic for the *Daily Mail and Empire*, written after the performance of *A Doll's House* in Toronto. He rather pompously concludes that "the most clever actress in the world cannot make this absurdly over-drawn tale of 'domestic infelicity' a dramatic success." He observes also that:

Mr. Neil – intentionally, or unintentionally, of course we cannot say – made Thorwald such a pronounced cad that the surprise was not that his wife ultimately found him the utter fool with whom no self-respecting woman would live, but, how any woman, with the latent capacity for unpleasant analytical discovery which Nora possessed, could ever have married such a man is a "problem" Henrik Ibsen and his adaptors have not attempted to solve.

Criticism such as this would lead one to believe that the play had been badly directed; that Ibsen's values had been distorted. However, the critic for the *Toronto World*, a faithful admirer of Ibsen, presented the opposite point of view in his review of the same performance. He admitted that "It

23Ray Abthorpe, "Some Unique Performances," *The Theatre Magazine*, xxx, 102 (August, 1919).

is almost impossible to find actors who can grasp the subtleties of Ibsen," but insisted that in this performance "Mr. Neil as Helmer . . . showed the fullest possible grasp of Ibsen's humor and truthfulness." And for a neutral opinion, the drama critic of the *Evening Star* refused to take sides, and commented instead on the play's theme:

About *A Doll's House*, with which Toronto is familiar, I shall say nothing more than that it is a serious play in which a serious problem of marriage and separation is discussed by a serious philosopher who chose to teach through drama. The subject is treated with the virile gravity of a Norwegian and leaves behind a profound legacy of reflection.

As we can see, criticism of the early performances of *A Doll's House* in Toronto was not exciting. The play did not shock the critics as it had done in other countries. But the controversy, although not heated, was consistent with world opinion. Ibsen had his supporters and his detractors, and generally speaking, the latter were in the majority.

For the first performance of *Ghosts* in Ontario, a small town was chosen, rather than the usual centre, Toronto, and again we find Ibsen's champion to be a woman: Miss Edith Ellis Baker. According to the route list published in the *New York Dramatic Mirror*, Miss Baker opened *Ghosts* in Berlin, Ontario, on September 16, 1903. Other towns on her route were Lindsay, Barrie, Woodstock, Chatham, London and Guelph. Her status in the theatre world is indicated by the fact that, like most actresses of lesser fame, she avoided the large cities. As the newspaper files in a small town are rarely complete, it has been difficult to trace her career. Moreover, the drama critic of a large newspaper almost never went to a small town simply to see a certain production. Left to the mercy of the town newspaper, a performance, whether poor or outstanding, was therefore quite often passed over without a word. Such appears to have been the fate of Miss Baker in almost every town she visited. There is no record of her performance in Barrie, Woodstock, Chatham, or Guelph. An advertisement for the play appeared in Lindsay's *Weekly Post*, September 18, 1903, and the *London Free Press*, September 3, 1903, but no comment on the play was found.

The drama critic for the *Berlin News Record* was at the theatre, however, and has faithfully recorded his impressions. His review of Miss Baker's *Ghosts* is the only one that remains, and it is amusing to consider that this gentleman from Berlin, who may very well have been the sports writer (sports and drama shared the same page), had the honour of speaking for Canada on the occasion of the first performance of *Ghosts* in this country. He apparently had no preconceived ideas about the play. The following, in part, is his review:

The three act family drama, *Ghosts*, by Henrik Ibson [*sic*], as put on the boards last evening at Berlin's playhouse, is one of the strongest productions Berlin has seen. The title is misleading, before you see the play. . . . It points many a moral, but ever and always its text is "The Wages of Sin is Death." It is subtle, suggestive, always restrained by a proper delicacy of treatment.

This is a far cry from the original reviews in England which compared *Ghosts* to "an open drain," and a "dirty act done in public." Indeed, our *Record* reporter seems to have regarded it merely as a rather strong melodrama. He referred to the leading lady, for example, as playing the part of a "widowed mother." Possibly Miss Baker's interpretation tended to capitalize on the romantic and sensational aspects of the production, but even so it seems remarkable that the play received such a pleasant reception.

Edith Ellis Baker, like Julia Stuart, never rose to prominence, and when her days on the stage were over, she quietly disappeared. The only information about her theatrical life, apart from the review in Berlin, Ontario, appears in a clipping from an unknown newspaper of May 1903, now in the files of the Theatre Collection at the New York Public Library:

She appeared as the child in *East Lynne* at the age of six, and from that time until she was fourteen was constantly before the public. Then followed a period in school after which she starred in a piece called *The Ships of State*, and later in Lotta's play, *Pawn Ticket 210*. Then came two years of ill health, during which she took up playwriting. In 1901 she leased the Park Theatre, Brooklyn, and presented the Baker Stock Company there. Last year Mrs. Baker wrote *The Point of View* and, determined to put it to the test before a New York audience, took a lease of Mrs. Osborn's Play House.[24]

There is no record of her play. Indeed, there is no further mention of Miss Baker as a playwright or an actress. However, she does have the honour of being the person to introduce *Ghosts* to Canada.

The Canadian career of *Ghosts* was not entirely tranquil. It is true that Miss Baker's tour proved, as far as we know, to be uneventful, but had she travelled as far west as Winnipeg the production would have been reviewed by the formidable critic Mr. C. W. Handscomb of the *Manitoba Free Press*. When Alberta Gallatin, yet another lady champion of Ibsen, performed in *Ghosts* on March 9, 1904, Handscomb's criticism the following day was blunt. "*Ghosts* is unwholesome, degrading – disgusting! His play is smut – just plain smut!" And with those opening remarks Handscomb registered the normal reaction to this controversial play. He stressed, of course, its unwholesome qualities: "Those of us who were at the Winnipeg Theatre last night were relieved to get out to breathe again in the pure, wholesome prairie atmosphere." He was aware that the New York critics had been writing of this play as "the greatest drama of modern times," but this did not deter him from making his own judgment!

High art they called it! Perhaps it is – perhaps in this wild and wooly west we lack the intelligence to discern high art. To me it is dirt – just dirt! The audacious daring with which the sex questions are discussed in this play has no stage precedent – not even the *risqué* problem plays have gone this far – while the utter depravity of the character is astounding. . . . But why write of the ghastly thing. Let's forget it if we can. The Ibsen cult may be all right but in this morally healthy western community we want none of his gruesome dissections.

[24]Quotation from her obituary, *New York Herald-Tribune*, August 27, 1948.

Two days later, a letter to the editor draws our attention to the fact that Mr. Handscomb's opinion did not necessarily reflect all of Winnipeg:

Sir:

In your paper of Thursday, March 10, appears an article by Mr. C. W. Handscomb on Ibsen's *Ghosts*. In the beginning he says "Ibsen is a genius they tell us. Perhaps so!" Why not acknowledge right out that he is a genius, and a splendid one at that. . . .

I can assure you that on the writer it made a deep impression, and if it did not have this effect on the general public, it is time that it did. I earnestly wish that the Winnipeg Press will see their duty just as plainly as Ibsen does and try and make thinking, broadminded men and women.

Perhaps the Winnipeg people are not ripe to understand this Ibsen drama. If not, I feel sorry. I do not see what vileness and dirt there is in the realistic drama written with the plain purpose of improving morals. If there was anything I felt shocked about last night it certainly was the public who did not understand and who offended both players and author by their misplaced laughing and jokes. It is to you, Mr. Newspaperman, to teach your public a better understanding of morals, and if they cannot understand the moral part, they should understand the dramatic part of Ibsen's *Ghosts* and every vile thought would be banished out of their minds.

G.H.

This writer was probably one of the minority. Perhaps he belonged to the "Ibsen cult" and, as there was no other critic in Winnipeg, felt it his duty to defend his hero. The critic did not reply and the whole matter was dropped.

But Handscomb did not allow the heat of his emotions concerning Ibsen's *Ghosts* to distort his judgment of Miss Gallatin as an actress. His praise of her as an artist of high rank was lavish and echoed the opinion of Alexander Woolcott, who considered her to be one of the best American actresses. There is no evidence that Miss Gallatin played in any other Canadian city. This is curious, for Winnipeg was not a big city and was far from the normal touring routes of Ontario. We can only assume that she was persuaded to make the trip by C. P. Walker, one of the most active theatre managers in Canada at that time.

This early history of *Ghosts* in Canada concludes with an examination of the various productions by Claus Bogel. In 1905, he left the American theatrical routes for an extended tour of eastern Canada. He opened in Toronto on January 23, subsequently playing in Guelph, Hamilton, London, Berlin and Woodstock. His tour ended in Ottawa.

Bogel's company appears to have given the first performance of *Ghosts* in Toronto. On the whole, the reaction to the play was very sophisticated, and seems to confirm the supposition that Ibsen was by this time generally accepted in larger centres. The critic for the *News* was enthusiastic in his praise. "Ibsen's *Ghosts*," he wrote on January 24, 1905, "is a great play, a nerve thrilling tragedy, brought by gradual stages to a climax of distilled horror." His comment concerning the play's acceptance by the audience also indicates a popular trend toward Ibsen:

13 a & b / The Academy of Music, Saint John, New Brunswick, suggests the opulence of the theatres that were built primarily to house the touring companies that invaded Canada in the latter part of the 19th century. (*Canadian Illustrated News*)

14 / Sir Johnston Forbes-Robertson in the role of *Hamlet*. His production of Shaw's *Caesar and Cleopatra* had its first performance in Canada in 1907. (See page 77.)

15 / Maude Adams as Lady Babbie in Barrie's *The Little Minister*, one of her most famous roles.

16 / Rose Coghlan, the famous American actress who played *Mrs. Warren's Profession* and outraged a critic in Winnipeg in 1907. (See page 75.)

17 / Robert Lorraine, who came to Canada with *Man and Superman*. (See page 74.)

18 / Mrs. Minnie Maddern Fiske, one of the
most popular leading actresses in America.
Her company presented *A Doll's House* in
Toronto. (See page 65.)

19 / Grand Opera House, London, Ontario. It was in imposing establishments like this that the Canadian public saw their favourite international stars. At other times local talent would take the stage. (See page 136.)

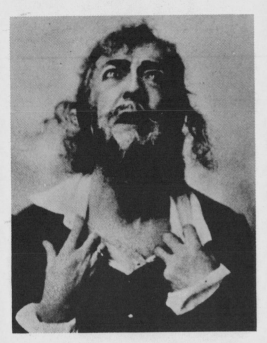

20 / Robert Bruce Mantell, "perhaps the handsomest of romantic actors," once was a box-office competitor of Sir Henry Irving in eastern Canada. (See pp. 158–159.)

21 / Helena Modjeska, a Polish actress who spent most of her acting life in the United States, included Toronto in her tours. (See page 50.)

22 / Ellen Terry was a leading lady with Sir Henry Irving from 1878 to 1902. She performed in *Captain Brassbound's Conversion* in Canada in 1907. (See pp. 77, 78.)

23 / Sir Henry Irving, the famous English actor-manager, who made a number of trips to Canada. (See pp. 11, 105.)

Toronto Opera House

JACOBS & SPARROW,
Proprietors and Managers.

✤✤PROGRAMME✤✤

AMBROSE J. SMALL,
Representative.

WEEK COMMENCING SEPTEMBER 28TH, 1896.

G. M. ROSE & SONS,
Publishers, 25 Wellington St. West

Across Canada towns and cities built their opera houses and
waited for the touring companies to arrive. 24 / The masthead
for the programme of the Toronto Opera House bears the name
of Ambrose J. Small (see p. 181).

25 & 26 / Two famous old theatres in Toronto: the Grand Opera House (*left*) and the Royal Opera House. (*Right*) A poster for a performance at the Royal Opera House.

ROYAL OPERA HOUSE

KING STREET WEST.

J. H. McKINLEY..MANAGER & LESSEE.
CHAS. A. WATKINS..BUSINESS MANAGER.
ED. ABERCROMBIE..TREASURER.
H. A. DAWSON..ADVERTISING AGENT.

THURSDAY EVENING, FEB. 10, 1876.

The Best Bill of the Season!

THE GREAT DRAMA, ENTITLED THE

LITTLE DETECTIVE

BARRY MALLINSON, *alias* PERCY ALLEN...MR. CHAS. J. FYFFE
SIR GERVASE LANGTON, a rich English Baronet.................................MR. CHAS. DeGROAT
MR. RODERICK TRACY, a Bow Street Runner in disguise.................MR. B. C. SMITH
LORD JU'ST ST'U'VESANT, a German sharper and swindler.................MR. BELVIL RYAN
PHŒLUS ROCKAWAY, light-hearted and light-fingered.................MR. B. H. BAIRD
DOCTOR STRASFELDT, a German physician.................MR. E. A. WHITE
STEPHEN HARDCLIFF.................MR. H. R. LONSDALE
DOZEY, an ancient and somniferous watchman.................MR. TODD
NAP.................} His companions in vigilance,.................MR. COWPER
SNOOZE.................MR. NEILSON
CAPT. GUSTAVE KOENIG, of the Baden City Guard.
FLORENCE LANGTON, with song.................'MISS AGGIE WOOD
GRIZZLE GUTTERIDGE, a Somersetshire witch, with song
MRS. GAMMAGE, an ancient nurse
MR. HARRY RAUKET, a fast young man, with song
BARNEY O'BRIAN, from the bogs of Ballynaggle.................MISS VIOLET CAMPBELL
MADAME RETZDOFF, a wealthy merchant's daughter.................MISS MARIE LE BRUN
STELLA, her daughter, travelling for the benefit of her health.................MISS ELIZA GLASSFORD
UNA LANGTON, betrothed to Barry Mallinson.

ACT I.

MAGNIFICENT SALOON of the Hotel Russe at Baden-Baden. QUADRILLE by the Characters. The Card Sharpers. The Dying Child. The inquisitive Daughter. The Detective on the Track. SONG by FLORENCE. The Oath. TABLEAU.

ACT II.

THE LITTLE DETECTIVE ON THE TRACK.

The BOAT-HOUSE ON THE LAKE. By Moonlight. THE MURDER. The Floating Spirit of the Murdered Girl.

ILLUMINATED TABLEAU.

ACT III.

SIX MONTHS ELAPSE.

The Plotters at work. The Little Detective on hand. Irish Song and Irish Jig.

TRACKED TO DEATH by the LITTLE DETECTIVE.

Monday Evening, February 14th, 1876,

THE GREAT DRAMA OF THE

ORANGE GIRL!

With New Scenery, Properties, &c., &c.

Grand Saturday Matinee, at 2 P.M.

Every Evening this week, and Saturday Matinee,

Miss Ellise Simpson

—AND—

MR. HARRY BROWN,

The Celebrated London Comique, will appear in a Choice Selection of Songs and Ballads.

POPULAR PRICES,

Gallery	25 cents.
General Admission	50 "
Balcony	50 "
Orchestra	75 "
First three rows Orchestra Circle	75 "

NO EXTRA CHARGE FOR RESERVING SEATS.

BOX OFFICE OPEN DAILY from 9 A.M. to 5 P.M.

Reserved Seats can be secured at Nordheimer's Music Store, King Street East, and at all the principal Hotels.

GOD SAVE THE QUEEN.

Globe Printing Company, 26 & 28 King Street East, Toronto.

29 / The Walker Theatre of Winnipeg (*right*), through its manager, C. P. Walker, drew travelling stars from as far away as New York. (See page 73.)

27 & 28 / Touring stars from the western states performed on the stage of the Vancouver Opera House (*above*). The Regina Opera House (*below*) was a regular prairie stop for Canadian companies such as the Marks Brothers.

THE WALKER THEATRE

WINNIPEG, MANITOBA, CANADA

31 / Mrs. Patrick Campbell, the English
actress whom Shaw described as being
"perilously bewitching." She toured Canada
in *The Second Mrs. Tanqueray*. (See
page 59.)

30 / Richard Mansfield (*left*). This
American actor created mainly romantic
roles in which he toured successfully
throughout the United States and Canada.

32 / James O'Neill (*right*), father of Eugene
O'Neill, toured in romantic dramas and
enchanted actors and audiences alike with
his "fatal gaze." (See page 157.)

33 & 34 / Sir John Martin-Harvey, for many
years a member of Sir Henry Irving's
company, formed his own company in 1899.
He was renowned for his role of Sydney
Carton in *The Only Way*, a moving adaptation of *A Tale of Two Cities*, with which he
toured Canada in 1913. (See page 37.)

The audience was a large one and a most appreciative one when the character of the play is considered, and only one indignant householder went out in the middle of the second act. This is an indication of the spread of the Ibsen cult, for in the past at least half a dozen conventionalists were likely to go out at every performance.

The critics for the *Daily Mail and Empire* and the *Daily Star* were also very much pleased with the play and the performance. The critic of the latter newspaper drew attention to the fact that the university circle was "especially well represented." There was one dissenting voice, however. The reviewer in the *Evening Telegram* was not convinced that *Ghosts* had found a popular audience in Toronto. His comment provides an interesting contradiction to that of the writer in the *News*:

The audience which applauded *Ghosts* at the finish, at its initial presentation last night, was the product of the process of selection otherwise known as the survival of the fittest. The house was two-thirds full at the commencement . . . but there was a continual withdrawal as the play progressed. The bulk of those who remained applauded vigorously, even rapturously.

Despite these remarks, it is apparent that by 1905 Ibsen had a respectable number of enthusiastic supporters in Toronto.

Such was not the case in the smaller towns. There an Ibsen production was still, on the whole, battling for the approval of the critic and the public alike. Claus Bogel ran into this situation in London, Ontario. Although London was generally considered to be a good theatre town, he found himself playing, according to the *London Free Press* of January 27, 1905, to "a very small audience." The people either were not interested or, having been warned of the play's immorality, stayed away deliberately. The drama critic of the *Free Press* assured them that they had not missed much. Indeed, he felt that they were wise to have avoided a production which depicted "gross immorality in terms coarse and bordering on the vulgar."

Hamilton, unlike London where Edith Ellis Baker had performed *Ghosts* two years earlier, had had no previous experience with this play. Although the reaction was not violently antagonistic, it was probable that the small-town audience agreed with this review in the *Hamilton Spectator* of February 2, 1905:

Before a fair-sized audience at the Grand last night, Ibsen's much discussed play, *Ghosts*, was presented. There are five characters in the play, not one of whom is worthy of respect. This is not due to the lack of histrionic ability in the players nor to the merits of the play itself, which has been admitted and certainly is a masterpiece of dramatic workmanship, but rather to the revolting and abnormal pictures of life it seeks to portray. That such plays exhibit truthful pictures of some phases of human nature no one will deny, but is it wise to select the vile and loathsome for presentation on the stage? No good purpose would be served by narrating the story of the plot. The lesson sought to be enforced is the severity with which the laws of heredity visit the sins of the parents upon the children.

The writer further commented that although it was difficult to discover what the feelings of the spectators were, if they were pleased "it was scarcely manifested by the applause which greeted the performers."

One last record of a performance of Bogel's company appeared in the *Berlin Daily Telegraph,* January 31, 1905. The audience, as usual, found it difficult to accept the serious purpose of the play:

It is true that upon some of those present last night, the lesson of the play was lost but that was not the fault of the play or the players. At the most awe-inspiring moment of the whole performance, in the last act, when with the bright sun of a glorious day streaming through the window and upon his face, Oswald Burns turns to his mother and says, "Give me the sun, mother," some found it possible to laugh.

The production two years earlier by Miss Baker was not mentioned and apparently forgotten.

A presentation of *Hedda Gabler* by Jane Corcoran in London on March 1, 1908, seems to have been the first performance of the play in Canada. Her plan to alternate this play with *A Doll's House* proved to be a happy arrangement, at least according to the critic of the *Free Press* for March 2, 1908:

A second session with Ibsen was enjoyed by local patrons when Miss Corcoran and her company presented *Hedda Gabler* Saturday night following *A Doll's House* of the evening before.

If the latter play proved to abound with sordidness and misanthropism, the following was a revelation to those who attended the performance to absorb the Ibsen style of play. To state that those present wended their different homeward ways permeated to the marrow with the Norwegian playwright's style is but to put things mildly.

Miss Corcoran repeated her successful portrayal of Hedda Gabler at the Russell Theatre in Ottawa, where, according to the review in the *Ottawa Free Press* of March 21, 1908, she "captivated an audience." We have no record in the early period to 1914 of any other performance of *Hedda Gabler* except for these two by Jane Corcoran. It is a pity that the reviewers did not examine these performances in more detail. The play may have been readily accepted because the audiences shared Ibsen's distaste for the kind of woman Hedda Gabler represented, and her death as a payment for her sins gave the work a morally correct conclusion.

A Doll's House, on the other hand, was still generally unpopular and it is difficult to understand why Miss Corcoran continued to present it rather than *Hedda Gabler.* On her tour she performed the part of Nora at Chatham, Kingston, Woodstock, St. Catharines, Peterborough, and Berlin for generally small and unreceptive audiences. It is likely that her own preference caused her to persevere. The *Ottawa Free Press* for March 14, 1908, telling of the research she undertook while in Italy, reveals something of the interest she must have felt for the role:

During her stay in Rome . . . Miss Jane Corcoran learned to dance the tarantella, the sinuous wild dance of the Italian peasants. . . . After her instruction in Rome, Miss Corcoran spent two weeks in the villages of Southern Italy where she studied the peasants at their play and obtained the local color which she injects into her performance and dance in Ibsen's *A Doll's Dream* [*sic*]. The costume which Miss Corcoran wears in the performance of the dance is an exact copy of those worn by the peasant women.

In an effort to interest the general public, Miss Corcoran also spent a great deal of time and money on her advance publicity, a practice not followed by the previous Ibsen performers. In Berlin, for example, her arrival was advertised throughout the town with large posters. Her manager, Mr. Aiston, had also arranged to have her picture placed on the front page of the newspaper. To ensure that the people went to the play in the right frame of mind, they were invited to attend a free lecture on Ibsen's work at the Opera House on February 26, 1908, to prepare for her performance on March 4. The talk was, according to the *Berlin Daily Telegraph* of February 26, 1908, to "clear away many of the false impressions some people have of Ibsen's works." The lecturer, Mrs. Sarah E. Dunbar, was reputed to know "more about the literature of the drama than any other person in America." Those attending left reassured that although Ibsen was undoubtedly "very plain," all his dramas were "strictly moral."

The advance publicity had very little effect. Miss Corcoran played to "a small and not a particularly enthusiastic audience." The company found the same lack of response in Hamilton, as the critic remarked in the *Hamilton Spectator* of March 10, 1908:

It is regrettable that Hamilton should have showed so little appreciation of the opportunity to see and hear a production of the great Norwegian dramatist who is admittedly the most interesting and wonderful of modern playwrights, for it was a very small audience which greeted Miss Jane Corcoran last evening in Ibsen's *A Doll's House*.

The lack of enthusiasm, of course, was to be expected. *A Doll's House*, as we have seen, was not the type of play to interest the majority in a small Canadian town. In the United States, however, *A Doll's House* had by this time become commonplace. As W. P. Eaton remarked in *The American Stage of Today*, "that drama, indeed, figures every week in the program of some stock company through the country."[25]

Rosmersholm was presented by Mrs. Fiske on a return visit to Toronto on April 25, 1908. Evidence of a change in the attitude toward Ibsen is revealed by the critic for the *Evening Telegram* of April 25, 1908:

Whatever its justification, this much is sure; that *Ghosts* haunted the rest of Ibsen's plays for two decades, and only now is the playgoing public taking an interest in the Norwegian's legacy. In Toronto, for instance, though of course Mrs. Fiske's *Rosmersholm* is not the first Ibsen play seen here, it is the first time that the production has been offered not with hesitancy, but boldly as an event.

Oddly enough *Rosmersholm* was not given any other performances at this time nor did Mrs. Fiske tour with it in Canada.

Mrs. Fiske did present, however, the last Ibsen play to be produced in Canada in this early period. *The Pillars of Society* was given in Winnipeg at

25W. P. Eaton, *The American Stage of Today* (Boston, 1908), p. 132.

the Walker Theatre on August 17, 1910. Ibsen had received his most thorough condemnation in this city when C. W. Handscomb reviewed *Ghosts* in 1904, but *The Pillars of Society* drew from the same critic of the *Manitoba Free Press* quite a different response:

Friend and foe alike can combine in applauding *Pillars of Society*. It is a tremendously strong play, but it is entirely wholesome and the principal offender of the story is allowed to find grace in the public confession of his wrong doing.

It is worth noting that those features of *The Pillars of Society* which Handscomb lauded were no doubt scorned by most sophisticated critics of the time. For example, Handscomb remarked that "if Ibsen had found it possible to give all his plays the wholesome flavour of *Pillars of Society* and to teach the glorious lesson of renunciation of the self, or some other great similar truth, he would have been an uplifting power for all time to all men." Otto Heller, a professor of literature at Washington University, perhaps reflected more faithfully the contemporary temper when he suggested that Ibsen, in this play, "though struggling for artistic freedom, still seemed wedded to certain false idols of the stage, notably the haunting spectre of 'poetic justice,' that is, the distribution of rewards and punishments at the close of the action." He went on to note that critical modern audiences would be "apt to disclaim in the very name of Ibsen the elaborate climax, the spectacular *grand scène* with its tearful pathos, and above all other things the audacious improbabilities that bring about quite unexpectedly an all's-well-that-ends-well conclusion. . . ."[26] Although Handscomb was obviously not an astute literary critic, his appraisal of Ibsen's work is of particular interest to us as it seems to reflect the sentiments of the people of the West.

The Russian actress Alla Nazimova made what appears to have been her first Canadian appearance in the part of Nora in *A Doll's House* in Winnipeg, June 9, 1909. The critic for the *Manitoba Free Press* found the production to be excellent but expressed dismay that "the foremost actress of the present day should have been insulted with so poor a house." Even Nazimova was unable to make this play palatable to the people of Winnipeg. When Nazimova performed in Toronto on March 1, 1910, however, it was "before a brilliant audience [which] almost taxed the seating accommodation of the Princess Theatre." On this happy note we come to the end of our survey of early Ibsen productions in Canada.

What then can be concluded as to the effect of Ibsen's plays in Canada? Between 1877 and 1899 Ibsen wrote his realistic social dramas. Between 1895 and 1910 about half of these were introduced to Canada. That is, between 1895 when Julia Stuart brought *A Doll's House* to Ottawa and 1910 when Nazimova was acclaimed in the same play in Toronto, a number of different audiences in various favoured locales had viewed one or more of five plays by Ibsen. From these few dozen performances it is difficult to determine the importance of Ibsen's contribution to Canadian culture. It is true that Ibsen's plays gradually came to be more easily accepted as audiences became more familiar with them and understood their motivation

[26]Otto Heller, *Henrik Ibsen* (Boston, 1912), p. 125.

better. It is also true that city audiences tended to accept and understand them sooner than small-town audiences, and that as time passed the revelations about human character and the individual's conflict with society became less shocking and more a part of common knowledge. However, this experience was no different from that of any country which witnessed the growth of Ibsen's popularity.

In fact, Ibsen's influence in Canada was slight, and for a number of particular reasons. Because his plays were introduced to the Canadian public in a haphazard fashion by foreign touring companies, in widely separated areas and to largely unprepared audiences, it is natural that their effect should have been diffused. Certainly there is no evidence that his plays were sought after by any interested group. The influence of Ibsen's plays was also limited because the problems raised in them were largely outside the experience of most Canadians. The unsophisticated were generally inclined to criticize not the manners and morals of society, but offences against social convention. It was not social injustice that concerned them but how to conform to the rules. This Victorian conservatism prevented Canadians from accepting realism in the theatre. If in life it was proper to be conventional, it was certainly not the prerogative of the theatre to be unconventional. As a critic for the *Globe* said on December 10, 1892, three years before an Ibsen play was performed in Canada, "This we demand, the worthy must be rewarded and the villain punished. The playwright would have an empty house if the rewards and punishments were concealed." The random seeding of Ibsen on Canada's uncultivated soil produced no vigorous crop of new playwrights and actors. No serious Canadian writer was stimulated to examine Ibsen's contribution to modern thought. The Canadian universities ignored him. No Canadian actor or company attempted to present his plays. In fact the general attitude in Canada toward Ibsen's revolutionary ideas in the theatre was one of apathy.

SHAW AND THE CANADIAN REACTION

George Bernard Shaw was represented in this period of Canadian theatre by six plays: *Candida, Man and Superman, Mrs. Warren's Profession, Widowers' Houses, Caesar and Cleopatra,* and *Captain Brassbound's Conversion.* It is not a wide selection, and the fact that productions of these few plays were spread out geographically and chronologically to the extent of having a nine-year gap between the performance of *Candida* in Winnipeg in 1904 and its next appearance in Ottawa in 1913, provides us with some indication of why Shaw remained, in the opinion of most people, a mere curiosity.

Such was the case on the occasion of *Candida's* appearance in Winnipeg on December 24, 1904. This was the first play by Shaw to be performed in Canada. In the same year *Candida* had been produced by Vedrenne and Barker in London, and Arnold Daly in New York.[27] C. W. Handscomb was obviously confused for, as he noted in his review in the *Manitoba Free Press*

---

[27]Raymond Mander and Joe Mitchenson, *Theatre Companion to Shaw* (London, 1954), p. 42.

the next day, "Why this chap, Shaw, seems bent on puzzling us. Indeed, puzzle and paradox constitute the very kernel of the nut he gives us to crack." He further remarked, "*Candida* may be serious in motive, the philosophy of a genius or it may be just the brilliant buncombe of a jesting cynic without any underlying purpose." The tone of this review indicated that he felt it to be the latter. The point is that he did not feel that *Candida* held any *risqué* or even serious message. If he had, we can be sure he would have questioned Shaw's right to express it. However, he hesitated to recommend the play to the average play-goer. It required a select audience, one which could appreciate a "highly intellectual farce." It was a play "for the intellect – not for the eye."

According to Handscomb, Lester Lonergan,[28] the young man who managed the company and played the lead, "portrayed the heart-hungry idealist with an appealing force," and although the critic obviously disliked Marchbanks, he had nothing but praise for Lonergan's "faithful portrayal" of the part.

Such praise no doubt pleased Lonergan very much, for he took great pride in his ability to fathom an author's meaning. Very little is known of Lester Lonergan, but we do have his comments on this aspect of his profession: "As I see it, an actor should be able to place his personality within the shells of many characters, and give them souls in accordance with the author's vision and creation."[29] Whether or not his interpretation of the part of Marchbanks would have pleased Shaw, we shall never know. It is highly unlikely that Shaw was informed of the production. One thing is certain, however: Lonergan had little opportunity to study many other actors in the role. Evidently Richard Mansfield some years previously had considered playing the part and, as Shaw had noted, "went so far as to put the play actually into rehearsal before he would confess himself beaten by the physical difficulties of the part."[30] Lonergan could have seen Arnold Daly's production in New York which ran from December 8, 1903, into January 1904. But this would have been his only model as Daly's performance was the first in North America and Lonergan's own was the second. There is no indication that he played *Candida* in any other Canadian city.

Man and Superman was the second Shaw play to come to Canada. It was brought over by the English star, Robert Lorraine, and played for the first time in Montreal on January 21, 1907. According to the critic for the *Montreal Daily Star* of January 22, it was a great success:

Last night a new star rose in the theatrical firmament of Montreal, or rather two new stars, those of Bernard Shaw and Robert Lorraine. A new playwright and a new actor. *Man and Superman* is the first of Mr. Shaw's plays to be seen in this city and last night was its first appearance as it was also that of Mr. Lorraine.

Although the critic had not seen any other of Shaw's plays on the stage, he

[28]Lonergan is not to be confused with Lanergan, who was, during the 50s and 60s, the "father of theatricals" in Saint John, New Brunswick.

[29]Newspaper clipping from the *New York Sun*, May 18, 1919. Contained in the Locke Collection, Theatre Collection, New York Public Library.

[30]George Bernard Shaw, *Plays Pleasant*, 2nd edition (Harmondsworth, Middlesex: Penguin Books, 1949), p. ix.

had obviously read them and possibly also the reviews as they came in from
England and the United States. He was aware of Shaw's reputation. He
accepted *Man and Superman* as a delightful farce but warned his readers
that Shaw was capable of being naughty; that at times he was likely "to
become the Intellectual Slap-stick Man, the vulgarian who in philosophic
jargon deals on the public stage with delicate questions which in common
decency should not be treated in such a manner." But in *Man and Superman*, with the third act omitted, all was well. It is, after all, without the
episode in hell, as Eric Bentley points out, "a farce of the order of *You
Never Can Tell*."[31]

In warning the public against Shaw "the vulgarian," the Montreal reviewer may very likely have had *Mrs. Warren's Profession* in the back of
his mind. Unfortunately there is no record of a performance of this play in
Montreal. To find a Canadian reaction to it we must turn back to Winnipeg.

Mrs. Warren's Profession was played for the first time in Canada by Rose
Coghlan's Company at the Walker Theatre on April 21, 1907, and, as far as
diligent research can discover, this was its only appearance in this early
period. Only two years previously it had been given its first public performance. Arnold Daly had tried it in New Haven, Connecticut, and had
caused quite a sensation. At the end of the first performance the police
walked in and closed the theatre. When it arrived in New York the play was
closed and, for good measure, the cast was arrested.

The Canadian première was very dull by comparison. According to
Walter McRaye, who was present and recalled the evening briefly in his
book *Town Hall Tonight!*, the reaction of the audience was apathetic. He
remembered that the play had been banned before it came to the West, and
went on to say:

The prudes and press said "Taboo," the undercurrent of gossip about its character attracted a crowd of people who looked for something *risqué*. Couched in all
the subtle humour of Shaw it passed over their head, and they sat wondering
what it was all about.

Unfortunately McRaye did not discuss any of the stage aspects of the production; he merely noted that it was the last time he ever saw Rose Coghlan.
It remains something of a mystery, however, why an actress famous for her
Lady Teazle and for feature roles in such plays as *The Silver King*, *Masks
and Faces*, *Diplomacy*, and *A Woman of No Importance*, and who had
presumably never before performed in a Shaw play, should have chosen the
role of Mrs. Warren, played it once, and then dropped it from her repertoire. Although the play was "booked" for three nights, there is no evidence,
in either advertisements or comments, to indicate that the company stayed
in town. It seems likely that *Mrs. Warren's Profession* fell victim to a form
of private censorship.

Handscomb damned the show in the *Manitoba Free Press* of May 1,
1907. As the moral mentor of Winnipeg he found he was no longer dealing
with a "jesting cynic without any underlying purpose." At the Walker

[31]Eric Bentley, *Bernard Shaw* (New York, 1947), p. 155.

Theatre he felt he had witnessed a shocking exhibition and that it was his duty to warn the public of this play's immorality. His violent reaction three years earlier to *Ghosts* apparently forgotten, he assured his readers that "No more unwholesome, nor repulsive play has ever been seen in Winnipeg." He confessed to "one or two smart lines and a certain sort of brilliancy which one has learned to term Sawian [*sic*]," but he added, "The bitter sewerlike flavour one carries away in the mouth is not compensated for by a false and mere meretricious glitter." The play was plainly a "beatification of evil living, a sermon on the advantages of vice and the story of a woman who, to term a courtesan, would be a compliment." In support of his contention that the play was a conglomeration of "false sentiment and batholic [*sic*] bosh," he turned to a scene in the last act "when the mother expatiates to the daughter on what an exemplary parent she has been and begs her to go on living on the money derived from her malodorous profession."

76

So appalled was Mr. Handscomb by what he termed the immorality of the play, that he failed to consider its criticism of the Victorian economic structure. He certainly could never have shared the view, always held by some and lately expressed by St. John Ervine, that "*Mrs. Warren's Profession* is an entirely moral play, written with no other intent than to expose a grave social evil."[32]

It was while trying to have this play performed in England that Shaw first came upon that formidable obstacle, the censor. As he noted in his preface to *Plays Unpleasant*, in order to have permission to perform a play he had to submit it to the Lord Chamberlain's Examiner of Plays and

obtain from him an insolent and insufferable document, which I cannot read without boiling of the blood, certifying that in his opinion – *his* opinion! – my play "does not in its general tendency contain anything immoral or otherwise improper for the stage," and that the Lord Chamberlain therefore "allows" its performance (confound his impudence!).

It would be far better, contended Shaw, that the play be allowed to take its chances before the ordinary laws of the land. Shaw here omitted to refer to a third force which might operate as a censor – public opinion. If the play was not immoral, or "otherwise improper for the stage," the public would "allow" its performance to continue simply by attending. If it did not receive their approval, they would stay away. In this respect a local critic or prominent citizen could exercise a good deal of influence. Perhaps this early production of *Mrs. Warren's Profession* was censored in this way.

At approximately the time at which *Mrs. Warren's Profession* was shocking or confusing the people of Winnipeg, Toronto was playing host to *Widowers' Houses*. On May 27, 1907, Herbert Kelcy and Miss Effie Shannon opened at the Princess Theatre. On May 28 their production received the following review:

Several conspicuously good actors were wasted upon a tiresome and futile play enjoying the name of *Widowers' Houses*. They are all made the victims of a

---

[32]St. John Ervine, *Bernard Shaw: His Life, Work and Friends* (New York, 1956), p. 253.

debaters.

It is difficult to imagine what Shaw would have thought if he had had the opportunity of reading these comments. He was able to look back on the first performance of this play in England with obvious glee and remarked in the preface to *Plays Unpleasant*: "I had not achieved a success; but I had provoked an uproar; and the sensation was so agreeable I resolved to try again." But no such excitement would have greeted him in Canada. Perhaps Canadian apathy might have discouraged even Shaw's indomitable spirit. The indifference exhibited by the Toronto critic is more exasperating when we realize that the production in Canada preceded the first public performance in England by approximately five months. Such a casual dismissal was a much more painful form of censorship than that which so angered Shaw in England.

Caesar and Cleopatra was brought into Canada by the Klaw and Erlanger Syndicate, and opened at the Princess Theatre, Toronto, on February 18, 1907. Klaw and Erlanger had a rather unenviable reputation in Canada. As a drama critic in the *Evening Telegram* for March 17, 1906, had remarked in passing, "they do peddle around considerable junk." It would seem strange therefore that they should have sponsored a play by Shaw. But the reason is clear. The play was a vehicle for their star, Johnston Forbes-Robertson. In the review in the *News* of February 19, 1907, Robertson's integrity in choosing such a play is questioned: "It is disappointing that Mr. Robertson should take advantage of Shaw's momentary popularity to litter a stage with so much inconsequential incident and flippancy of design as are contained in this tedious drama." The critic also preferred the nobility of the heroes of poetic drama to Shaw's Caesar, and regretted the waste of Mr. Robertson's talents on this slight role: "The stage needs more such cultivated poetic minds as Mr. Robertson's and it is truly a gratification to see him struggle to impart unity, conviction and dramatic purpose to Shaw's vernacular Caesar, bereft of real dignity and all the enshrinement which a B.C. existence has habitually accomplished for him." Shaw's mocking or light-hearted attitude toward historical figures and traditions shocked many, and to those Canadians who held the past in almost religious awe, his approach was blasphemous.

The conviction that Shaw was riding to fame on the backs of the "stars" persisted. When *Captain Brassbound's Conversion* was presented at His Majesty's Theatre in Montreal on April 6, 1907, the critic for the *Gazette* of April 9 opened his review by saying:

It was not so much Shaw's play that people went to see last night . . . as Miss Ellen Terry. *Captain Brassbound's Conversion* was a mere incident. No one cared whether he was converted or not – the more so after they had made his acquaintance. It was Ellen Terry and her art they went to see.

Shaw had written this play as a vehicle for Ellen Terry. That she was not quick to grasp the meaning of the role, however, is evident in the correspondence which passed between them. Eventually the actress and the part became one, and this was to be expected for in Shaw's eyes, Ellen Terry *was* Lady Cicely Waynflete. But the writer for the *Gazette* could not bring himself to view her as a character. He had come to see Ellen Terry, and, for this pleasure, was willing to put up with Bernard Shaw, just as he was convinced Miss Terry was doing:

On the whole it can scarcely be said that Miss Terry is at her best as an exponent of Shaw. She probably presents his ideas in a more lovable manner than he conceived . . . Miss Terry triumphed despite all, and turned the part of the innocent domineering girl into a most lovable character – even when she gave vent to the typical Shavian ironies, they were given with a childish insouciance that not only robbed them of their sting, but gave them an added charm.

In this the critic showed himself akin to Blawner Bannal, the reviewer in *Fanny's First Play*, who had to be told by whom a play was written before he knew whether it was good or bad. Lady Cicely was certainly not "innocent" except probably in the technical sense. And had Miss Terry enacted the part with "childish insouciance," she would not have "robbed" the part of its "sting" but of its sense.

The last appearance of a Shaw play in the period under consideration took place at the Russell Theatre in Ottawa on April 15, 1913. It was the reappearance of *Candida*, as performed by Miss Horniman. Evidently it was a great success but, again, a success for the players, not the playwright. The reviewer for the *Ottawa Free Press* of April 16, apparently thinking that the actors were working under a handicap, said:

The actors make the Shaw characters actually live and have their being. This presumably is very difficult to do. The fact that they were capable of creating the transformation was sufficient testimony for the company.

The opinion that Shaw created puppets instead of characters still forms a subject of discussion, but during the time with which we are concerned it was a general and persistent accusation. Shaw was considered a playwright incapable of producing real people for the stage. Most Canadian critics would have agreed with the American who noted:

Audiences like to see on the stage men and women of flesh and blood in action, controlled by strong passions and responsive to conflicting emotions. Shaw, on the contrary, uses his characters as mere lay-figures to exploit his philosophy.[33]

Indeed, in Canada, Shaw was considered a poor playwright and was condemned for his argumentative, unemotional and dull disquisitions. Shaw's plays were designed to make one think, and apparently very few Canadians went to the theatre for that purpose. His attack on the economic and political structure of society thus had little effect. Serious discussions on such subjects were expected to come from the pulpit, not from the stage, and Shaw's insistence on using the theatre for his moral and social reforms was not acceptable. His plays, as theatre, were disliked; his lessons ignored. Certainly no Canadian prose dramatists were persuaded to follow his example.

[33]Joseph M. Rogers, "Some Aspects of George Bernard Shaw," *Lippincott's Monthly Magazine*, LXXVIII, 446 (October, 1906).

To be fair, it must be admitted that there were undoubtedly some Canadians who had studied Shaw, read his plays, and welcomed the opportunity of seeing them in production, but this minority was too small to find a voice. They did not constitute an *avant-garde* – those already in revolt against conventions in general and conventional plays in particular – capable of enjoying Shaw as they eventually did in England and the United States. Canadians were not ready for the man who blatantly questioned their values and the structure of their society. They preferred to remain faithful to the conventional idealism that abounded in the melodrama of the time. And so, despite approval in both England and the United States, Shaw's popularity in Canada did not grow. The only concentrated effort to exhibit Shaw's plays was undertaken by Hart House Theatre in Toronto between 1924 and 1934. Even here, however, comparatively few plays were presented over a ten-year period. They were *Great Catherine*, May 1926; *The Shewing-up of Blanco Posnet*, November 1924; *Misalliance*, December 1924; *Heartbreak House* (first showing in Canada), May 1926; *The Man of Destiny*, November 1927; *How He Lied to Her Husband*, March 1927; *The Doctor's Dilemma*, November 1927; *Major Barbara*, January 1931; *The Devil's Disciple*, October–November 1934.

In considering Shaw's lack of impact on the Canadian scene, we should not forget that much critical opinion was concerned with that rather intangible quality: wholesomeness. However it may have been defined in the individual critic's mind, Shaw was rarely able to pass the test. Furthermore, Shaw was enigmatic, and this, to audiences who were used to the straightforward melodrama where good was rewarded and evil punished, was inexcusable. Walter McRaye probably made an accurate estimate of Canadians at large when he offered the remark about the Winnipeg audience which viewed *Mrs. Warren's Profession*: "They sat wondering what it was all about." It is likely that most theatre-goers and critics across Canada watched the other Shaw plays in a similar state of confusion. Is it a sign of our growing "sophistication" that Shaw is today possibly our best box-office dramatist next to Shakespeare?

CENSORSHIP

Before turning our attention to the plays written by Canadians during this period, the reader may be able to draw some conclusions about theatrical conditions in Canada by taking a brief look at the business of censorship. Although censorship was but one among many influential factors which discouraged the healthy development of theatre in Canada, it should be considered if only as a reflection of the strong puritanical strain that existed in this country. By examining some cases of censorship, and the methods by which they were handled, we can observe Canadians in one of their favourite pastimes, the pursuit of wholesomeness.

In most Canadian cities, censoring a performance was the responsibility of the morality officer of the police department. In Toronto, a city which fairly represents theatrical conditions in English-speaking Canada, his authority was outlined in a city by-law which allowed him to "enter any theatre, hall, or other place of public amusement or entertainment, and if . . . [at his request] such immoral or indecent play, sketch, or performance [was] not forthwith stopped, to apprehend the performer or performers without warrant, and carry him, her, or them as soon as practicable before a justice of the peace."[34] It was, in fact, the police officer's duty to ascertain whether a play was immoral or indecent and then take appropriate action.

Such a person existed in Toronto when *Blanco Posnet* was brought here by a visiting company in 1914. We find in an article in the *Mail and Empire* of May 2, 1914, headed "Toronto is Ridiculed," that the play was banned:

Toronto has a municipal censor for its theatres, one Banks, and, following in the distant wake of his prototype in London, he forbade the performance of *Blanco Posnet* on the grounds that the play contained blasphemous and immoral matter.

80

The fact that *Blanco Posnet* was forbidden a performance in Canada does not necessarily reflect a particular Canadian attitude, but stands as a sign post in the growth of censorship. *Blanco Posnet* likely had its first Canadian presentation at Hart House Theatre in 1924 in Toronto. By this time it appears to have lost its blasphemous and immoral character. A review of the play in the *Evening Telegram*, November 18, 1924, merely noted that "the fun approaches the ribald at times but the whole play is one large gesture of good-humoured irony."

Naturally there were as many different views as there were policemen, and so, eventually, in an effort to correct the situation, exact definitions were presented to the officer as a means of simplifying his task. A play was to be censored, for example, if it included scenes of violence. Such a law, of course, if carried out to the letter, could soon lead to ridiculous extremes. Robson Black, Canadian correspondent for the *New York Dramatic Mirror*, May 14, 1910, related the following story which, he assured his readers, was "God's truth."

Staff Inspector George Kennedy, play censor of Toronto, told the *Mirror* that according to the law no Shakespearean tragedy could be given in Toronto on pain of arrest of all actors and management. Why was this? Because, in the Inspector's words: "*Hamlet, Macbeth* and *Richard III* come under the head of 'spectacles of violence' and are unfit for modern audiences to see." These were his very words: "So you look on the slaying of Polonius and the death of Laertes and that sort of thing as against the Toronto by-law?" questioned the *Mirror* man. "Necessarily," was his reply.

There is no evidence that Mr. Kennedy ever arrested a company on such a charge, but the fact that he was prepared to stand by this ruling draws attention to the absurdity of censorship laws in Toronto at this time.

Generally, there was no attempt to ascertain the nature of a production before it appeared. Any conceivable form of entertainment was allowed free entry and continued performances until for some reason or other a patron felt compelled to complain to the police. On receiving the complaint, the

[34]Toronto By-law, Sub-section 8a, as partially printed in the *Montreal Gazette*, April 20, 1907.

morality officer would witness the play and then pronounce his judgment. The play, of course, could have been having daily performances for a week before this occurred. There was, moreover, always the chance that the morality officer would consider the objection unfounded, and allow the public to continue to enjoy the show, as he perhaps had done himself. There was no guarantee for the moral objector that his complaint would be taken seriously. *The Merry Wives of Windsor*, for example, was presumably sanctioned by the police when it was quite obvious to the critic who wrote in the *Canadian Monthly* of May 1877, that the play contained "all the coarseness of the age which produced it," and was "hardly fit for presentation before a modern audience."

The morality officer was certainly not a dictator. Indeed, his decisions were generally unavoidably swayed by pressure groups. He would have to placate both the irate theatre manager and the protests of ardent moralists and do-gooders. It is understandable that his final decisions were rarely his own. In many cases his authority was challenged by members of the various churches. On one occasion in Montreal, for example, Archbishop Bruchési took it upon himself to censor a play called *La Rafale*, which was being produced by the Théâtre des Nouveautés.[35] Unable to persuade the theatre manager to discontinue the play, the Bishop sent out a pastoral letter in which he forbade the faithful to attend this particular theatre in future. The ban was effective, and the theatre had to close. It remained closed until the management gave the Bishop assurance that further plays would be selected with more care. The original permission granted by the recognized censor was, in this case, of little importance.

Sarah Bernhardt became the centre of a controversy between the censor and the church in 1880. It was one of those rare occasions in which the argument took place before the performance. The censor, along with the critics and the public, had voiced his happy approval of her impending visit. The Presbyterian church, however, demanded that her performance be prevented. Whatever the reason, it had little to do with her ability as a performer.

Probably the most aggressive defender of public morals in the history of Canadian theatre was the Reverend John Coburn. His first appearance as a censor in his own right was heralded by a headline in the Toronto *Mail* of May 23, 1913. The reader was informed that Mr. Coburn was going "over the head of the Censor," and would "cause summons to be issued." He had taken this action after witnessing at the Princess Theatre a play called *Deborah*, which had been approved by the official censor, Mr. William Banks. The case was eventually taken to the courts and placed before Judge Morson, who decided to hold the court proceedings in the theatre. This decision caused a great deal of excitement. The *Ottawa Free Press* of June 6 described the event:

In an empty theatre before a half a hundred ministers, newspaper men, and representatives of women's societies, and last, and most important, his Honor, Judge Morson, *Deborah* was presented again at the Princess Theatre . . . more

[35]Details of the incident were carried by the *Montreal Star*, April 3, 1907.

powerfully than ever before. The occasion was unique in Toronto's theatrical annals, the performance being really a session of the Division Court, and the acting, evidence on which the Judge was to base his opinion whether the play was moral or immoral.

Much to Coburn's astonishment and consternation, Judge Morson ruled that the play was not immoral, and thus put an end to the first legal battle involving the theatre in Canada. News of the Court's decision was the signal for some editorial comment from the papers. The editor writing for the *Toronto World* on June 7, 1913, for example, felt that Judge Morson "had done the community a great service in vindicating the purpose of high-minded dramatists like Mr. Legrand Howland, and clearing the reputations of the ladies and gentlemen who presented his play, of the stigma cast upon them by an ignorant and incompetent critic like Mr. Coburn."

But Mr. Coburn was not discouraged. Shortly after this initial failure, he helped organize a protest meeting at Massey Hall and there a resolution was passed naming a committee of forty whose duty it was to "clean up the theatres of the city."[36] No one objected. The committee was finally accepted by the city as semi-official censors, and it lasted in this capacity for some years. As Coburn pointed out, it was while the committee was active and co-operated with the Toronto Board of Police Commissioners that Toronto gained the reputation of having "the cleanest stage of any city of its size on the North American continent."

We should probably note at this point that the stress was laid on the quality of "cleanness." At no time did Coburn refer to the merits of a play. Indeed, it would be safe to assume that he knew very little about the theatre, and had no interest in it, except that from a moral standpoint it needed constant watching.

The official censor was influenced and at times overrun by the persuasions of the clergy and various groups. There was no ruling from the top, as in England where there was an examiner of plays to irritate the playwright as well as the producer. Canada's system of censorship resembled that of the United States. In both these countries there was no pre-judging of plays. As I have pointed out, a first-nighter frequently took upon himself the role of judge and censor. If he felt it necessary, he would inform the morality officer and so the battle was on. We can note that under this system, the censor inevitably reflected the temper of the people.

Canadians as a whole have seldom been concerned with the art of the theatre. A play at the opera house rarely stood for anything other than entertainment, and thus their attendance was affected by minor considerations. If the play was thought to be morally questionable the average Canadian put it out of his mind. He stayed home; whether or not it was a play by a prominent writer of the time had little bearing on his actions. If a play criticized England and praised the United States, it was doomed. *Nathan Hale*, for example, was brought to Canada by an obviously naïve manager of an American touring company, and soon died on the road. One of the last performances was in Hamilton on January 21, 1903. The remarks of

[36]John Coburn, *I Kept My Powder Dry* (Toronto, 1950), p. 119.

the critic for the *Hamilton Spectator* recall the general feeling at the time: "A piece of dramatic clap trap perpetrated by Clyde Fitch, for consumption in Yankeeland, was foisted on a small and quite chilly house last evening." Of course it wasn't "clap trap" but a play that praised the Americans at the expense of the English was damned before the curtain went up. The value Canadians have attached to the theatre is also reflected in their particularly harsh treatment of their own playwrights and performers. Only now is this attitude beginning to change. But during the period we have been discussing, the Canadian play or the Canadian star had little chance of success at the box office.

Censorship was generally directed against American and English productions. The Canadian touring companies, as we have seen, selected their plays with caution. Their repertoires consisted of the standard plays, vehicles which served the romantic actor and pleased the general public. Apart from this preference to "play it safe" which protected them from the censor, we should also note that they generally chose, with few exceptions, to avoid plays by Canadians. Their lack of interest may be better understood after examining the body of work produced by a number of Canadian writers usually referred to as poetic dramatists.

The Poetic Drama.

In an article called "A Canadian Playwright's Lighthearted Look at How General Wolfe Took Louisbourg" (the *Star Weekly*, June 6, 1964), the writer took a brief and "lighthearted" glimpse at the accomplishments of Halifax's Neptune Theatre. In referring to his play that ended the first season, *Louisbourg*, John Gray reminds the reader that it demands "a lot of nerve for a new theatre company to put on that well-known box office anaesthetic, a new Canadian play." The truth of this statement is, unfortunately, borne out by the history of Canadian theatre. John Gray is not the first man to try to write a Canadian play, but, we should note, he can be placed in that small company of dramatists who have had the interest of a local theatrical group. The collaboration of the playwright and producer is essential, and it is encouraging to see that the present-day trend is in this direction. Looking back into the past, we will find little evidence of a *rapport* between Canadian actors and Canadian writers. There are many reasons for this, no doubt, but perhaps the main cause was the lack, among the practising theatre people, of dedicated souls who viewed the drama as an art form. There was the actor-manager E. A. McDowell, who was apparently interested in the Canadian writer, but his efforts were limited and he failed to establish a trend. The Marks Brothers and even the Tavernier Company were mainly concerned with earning a living. Thus it is rather remarkable, that in such an atmosphere, so many writers actually wrote plays.[1] There were generally two areas open to the serious Canadian playwright: he could compete in the commercial field by supplying the stars – largely American or English – with "vehicles," or he could turn away from what he may have considered the commercial riff-raff, and attempt to write plays of literary merit. Many Canadian writers chose to follow this latter course, and they were probably influenced by the fact that a move-

[1]A reasonably complete, although not exhaustive list of published Canadian plays is to be found in Reginald Eyre Watters' *A Check List of Canadian Literature and Background Materials 1628–1950* (Toronto, 1959).

ment towards a literary and poetic theatre was relatively prominent in England. Before examining individual poetic dramatists, we should therefore take a glance at the source of their inspiration as it developed in the "old country."

This move to a poetic theatre, which took place in England at approximately the time experiments in realistic drama were being made, was a stalwart attempt to provide entertainment of a higher quality than the popular farce, pantomime, acrobatic display and extravaganza then rampant on the stage.[2] The experiment, however, was not an unqualified success. As William Archer noted when reviewing the poetic drama: "The indubitable fact remains, that while effort in the direction of poetical drama has been frequent and strenuous, success has been, to say the least of it, exceedingly rare."[3] Because it did not prosper, the movement received little critical attention.[4]

What was this literary and poetic theatre? It generally was known as "poetic drama," a term that became a familiar expression in the early part of the nineteenth century. However, its beginnings have not been studied to any extent and no full account of its development has yet been written. Originally it was generally a copy of Elizabethan drama, but in the latter part of the nineteenth century it underwent a change which altered its form. According to Priscilla Thouless, "The coming of naturalistic drama killed the old ideal of the poetic dramatists – romantic drama, written in a tradition alien to modern times," and forced some of the writers "to create new poetic forms of drama."[5] Ernest Reynolds also draws attention to the change in poetic drama when he notes that "it was not until Shaw's preaching of Ibsenism in the nineties had begun to take effect that there was any appreciable stirring of English poetic drama towards a new synthesis of social expression."[6] The new poetic drama was written by such diverse playwrights as William Butler Yeats, John Drinkwater, and George Bottomley. In examining the poetic drama of the Canadians we will find ourselves almost totally concerned with the pre-Ibsen or pseudo-Elizabethan variety. These were the plays of the old ideal, written by poets who, as Reynolds contends, "were plot-dramatists, dressing up their stories in Shakespearean peacock-feathers."[7]

There were attempts at the time to clarify the aim and purpose of these plays. The Earl of Lytton, for example, when looking back on the dramatic career of his father, Bulwer-Lytton, said: "To portray the great movements of the soul in such a manner as shall have the effect of elevating whole

[2]For a concise account of conditions see: Ernest Reynolds, *Modern English Drama: A Survey of the Theatre from 1900* (Norman, 1951), pp. 15–21.

[3]William Archer, "The Poetic Drama," *The Critic*, xxxvi, 24 (January, 1902).

[4]*The Modern Poetic Drama* by Priscilla Thouless is devoted to the subject. *Modern English Drama* by Ernest Reynolds, *The Victorian Theatre* by George Rowell, and *A History of Late 19th Century Drama* by Allardyce Nicoll deal with the subject accurately and at some length.

[5]Priscilla Thouless, *Modern Poetic Drama* (Oxford, 1934), p. 8.

[6]Ernest Reynolds, *Modern English Drama*, p. 73.

[7]*Ibid.*

masses of human beings into a perception of this 'ideal nature,' and a sympathetic contact with it, is the purpose of the poetic drama."[8] In the same vein, John Todhunter wrote that there were "some signs that what is wanted is something that will appeal to the imagination and stir the deeper springs of emotions; an art that will be sanely and vigorously romantic."[9]

A clear-cut definition of poetic drama is very difficult. However, it is possible to discern some of its general characteristics. It is often concerned with characters who move about in settings remote in time and place. As Richard Moody notes, "The clearest and most colorful traits of the romanticist are his loving and longing looks into the past and into the future, his delight in rosy recollections and fervid hopes, his easy and fanciful dreams of distant place and distant clime."[10] The action usually focusses upon a single historical occasion within which characters of recorded history and imagination play out their parts. The action also ranges outward to distant,

86

and often primitive or exotic lands in which reason is set aside and emotion is allowed to reign. Here the dramatist could follow his preference "to act on faith, to trust to the inner experiences of life, and to follow the sentimental longings of his heart." The ingredients usually found in such a play are violent action, escape and pursuit, intrigue, the supernatural, a liberal supply of sentimentalism, and a pervading idealism. The poetic drama as written and produced was essentially melodrama, with its appeal to those who merely wished to be entertained, but could be set apart from the melodramatic plays which were popular at the time chiefly because of the grandeur of its language.

Many of the English poets of the romantic movement turned their attention to the theatre at one time in their career, and although they were apparently interested in writing closet drama which would be read in the library, they were not entirely devoid of theatrical ambition. The failure of these poets to make any lasting contribution to the theatre, however, can be attributed to their refusal to come to terms with the demands of the stage. This lack of practical theatre knowledge is generally evident in poetic drama. Shelley's *The Cenci* stands out as probably the best of its kind, and exhibits at times a true dramatic force. But the total effect is untheatrical; the play is too lengthy and disjointed for the theatre. Byron turned his hand to the theatre and produced a number of plays which were eventually presented on the stage. They were performed in the following order: *Marino Faliero*, 1821; *Werner*, 1830; *Sardanapalus*, 1834; *Manfred*, 1834; *The Two Foscari*, 1837. Generally, however, when the work of the romantic poets took dramatic form it became closet drama, despite the encouragement they received from several theatre managers who hoped they would create a new and exciting drama for the stage.

William Charles Macready's attitude was significant. He was one manager of the time who genuinely preferred poetic drama and who made a real

---

[8]Earl of Lytton, "The Stage in Relation to Literature," *The Fortnightly Review*, xxxiv, New Series, 13 (July, 1883).

[9]John Todhunter, "Poetic Drama, and its Prospects on the Stage," *The Fortnightly Review*, lxxxi, New Series, 732 (January, 1902).

[10]Richard Moody, *America Takes the Stage*, Bloomington, 1955, p. 2.

effort to promote it. After first meeting Robert Browning he noted in his diary:

He said that I had *bit* him by my performance of Othello, and I told him I hoped I should make the blood come. It would indeed be some recompense for the miseries, the humiliations, the heart-sickening disgusts which I have endured in my profession, if, by its exercise, I had awakened a spirit of poetry whose influence would elevate, ennoble, and adorn our degraded drama.[11]

It was reasonable to expect that Browning could become a successful playwright. Many of his collections of poems, such as *Dramatic Lyrics, Dramatic Romances, Dramatic Idylls*, indicated by their titles that he had a natural inclination for dramatic form. However, his first play, *Strafford*, which he wrote in 1837, was a disappointment. His chief failing here was an inability to portray characters in action; and he was also bound by an obsession for historical accuracy. His detailed history of the outbreak of the American Civil War, for example, is almost unintelligible to the reader and would have been impossible for an audience to follow. Browning did, however, make one attempt to please an audience. His play *A Blot on the Scutcheon*, written in 1843, possibly at the prompting of Macready, was not hampered by detail; action predominated, but unfortunately the play failed to rise above a feeble melodrama.

With Bulwer-Lytton, Macready had more success. In 1838 he presented Lytton's *The Lady of Lyons, or Love and Pride*. The first performance proved popular and from that time until well into the nineteenth century it could be found in the repertoires of the leading English actors. Although not exceptional as dramatic literature, this play was respected by the romantic actor and was placed without question among the classics. It is interesting to observe that *The Lady of Lyons* played a special role in Canada: it was one of the plays of John Nickinson, one of the first professional actors to appear on the stage in Toronto. Lytton's play was part of a repertoire that included *Hamlet, Romeo and Juliet*, and *The School for Scandal*.

Lytton's other poetic drama was *Richelieu*, written in 1839, and also first performed by Macready. In his tour of America, Macready presented both of Lytton's poetic dramas as well as Byron's *Werner*. Jean Beraud, in his history *350 Ans de théâtre au Canada français*, recalls Macready's visit to Montreal and offers evidence of the early appearance of these poetic dramas in Canada:

On lui devait les tentatives scéniques de Robert Browning et d'Edward Bulwer-Lytton . . . dont Macready joua ici le *Richelieu*, ainsi que *Hamlet, Macbeth* et le *Werner ou l'Heritage*, de Byron, en juillet 1844.[12]

The attraction that followed Macready's performance at the Theatre Royal, Montreal, is worth noting as a comment on the theatre of the time. A Mr. Von Stavoren delighted the audience with a rendition of *The Hunters of the Pyrenees* or *The Chasm of Death*, and *Six Degrees of Crime*, or *Wine, Women, Gambling, Theft, Murder and the Scaffold*.

87

[11]William Charles Macready, *Macready's Reminiscences*, ed. Sir Frederick Pollock, II (London, 1875), p. 8 (from an entry in his diary February 16, 1836).
[12]Jean Beraud, *350 Ans de théâtre au Canada français* (Ottawa, 1958), p. 32.

Another important star performer to display a sympathy with the poetic drama was Henry Irving. Other than Lytton's works, however, he only produced one or two plays by Tennyson, of which *Becket* was the most significant.[13] Irving grew less and less inclined, as time passed, to attempt a new play of any description, and it was not until the advent of Herbert Tree and George Alexander as leading romantic actors in England, that the poetic drama received further encouragement. The poet and dramatist with whom these actors were associated was Stephen Phillips. Tree produced *Herod* in 1901 with moderate success, but it was Alexander's presentation of *Paolo and Francesca* in 1902 which made Phillips prominent as a poetic dramatist. The play was highly praised and considered by many critics of the time to be the first poetic drama to break from the crippling romantic tradition displayed in the dramatic works of the poets. Edmund Gosse noted:

Mr. Phillips succeeds in pleasing alike the seeker after delicate literary sensations, and the average sensual person in the stalls, he achieves a remarkable triumph of tact. That he does it without recourse to the Elizabethan Tradition is another proof of his adroitness.[14]

Allardyce Nicoll, on the other hand, feels that Phillips slavishly followed the Shakespearean model:

The Shakespearean plan Phillips has followed as a pattern, that is evident: Shakespeare's verse form becomes the model for his verse, and the characters are set forth in the manner of the great seventeenth-century tragedies.[15]

Contrary to the opinion of the contemporary critics, Stephen Phillips did not herald the approach of the new poetic drama. He stands, rather, as one of the last poetic dramatists of the "old ideal."

CHARLES HEAVYSEGE

The first poetic dramatist in Canada was Charles Heavysege. Very little is known of his early life except that he was born in England and followed the trade of cabinet maker until he came to Canada.[16] Before emigrating to Montreal in 1853, he had published a small volume of poems, *The Revolt of Tartarus*, but it was not until he had arrived in Canada and taken up his post as reporter for the *Montreal Daily Witness* that he seriously turned his attention to the business of writing. As Desmond Pacey has remarked in his *Creative Writing in Canada*, "something in the Canadian environment seems to have stimulated him to increased literary activity." Within a ten-year period he published two poetic dramas, *Saul* (1857) and *Count Filippo* (1860); three long narrative poems, *The Owl* (1864), *Jephthah's Daughter*

[13]The plays of Tennyson produced by Irving were: *Queen Mary* (1876); *The Cup* (1881); *Becket* (1893).

[14]Edmund Gosse, "The Revival of Poetic Drama," *Atlantic Monthly*, xc, 165 (August, 1902).

[15]Allardyce Nicoll, *A History of Late Nineteenth Century Drama* (Cambridge, 1946), I, p. 209.

[16]A few remarks about Heavysege's personal life are found in two sources: Bayard Taylor, "The Author of Saul," *Atlantic Monthly*, xcvi, p. 412–13 (October, 1865), and Lorne Pierce, *An Outline of Canadian Literature* (Toronto, 1927), p. 63.

(1865), and *Jezabel* (1867); and a novel, *The Advocate* (1865). Of all his publications, however, only one received acclaim: his first work written in Canada, the poetic drama *Saul*.

Saul, subtitled *A Drama, in Three Parts*, is a lengthy work. Briefly it is the story of Saul as given in the First Book of Samuel. The first part begins with the anointing of the Hebrew King by Samuel and ends with the expulsion of the evil spirit by David's witching music. The second part finds David hospitably received at Bibeah, then describes the overthrow of the Philistines at Elah, Saul's jealousies of David's growing popularity, and his marriage to Michal. The third part describes the incantations of the Witch of Endor, and then finally Saul's death.

The drama was not an immediate success. In Canada, where it was first published, it was totally ignored and would quite likely have remained a nonentity had it not been for the review that appeared in the *North British Review* in August of 1858. Here, the English critic Coventry Patmore hailed *Saul* as a masterpiece. Other literary reviewers soon became interested, and it was not long before it was receiving a great amount of praise – praise which has since been recognized as reaching far beyond the play's actual worth. At the time, however, it was generally agreed that *Saul* had scaled the literary heights. Patmore had set the pattern for the succeeding reviews in stressing the moral acceptability of the play and in pointing out that its greatness was derived in part from the fact that it had remained faithful to the Elizabethan tradition. He admired Heavysege's poetic ability and felt that the better passages were "scarcely short of Shakespearean." The play itself although "not a great work," was "indubitably one of the most remarkable English poems ever written out of Great Britain." It is disappointing to turn from this praise to the following typical excerpt. It is from the last act. Saul enters, mortally wounded:

> Now let me die, for indeed I was slain
> With my three sons. Where are ye sons?
> Oh let me find ye, that I may perish with you; dying,
> Cover you with my form, as doth the fowl
> Her chickens!

The quality varies, of course, but on the whole the play never becomes more than a poor copy of Elizabethan tragedy. Saul remains a pasteboard character and, to the modern reader at least, consistently fails to inspire a sympathetic response. Heavysege's attempt to reveal Saul suffering the torments of remorse falls short of expectations. It is the morning of the final battle with the Philistines. Saul is discovered at the Hebrew camp in the valley of Tezreel:

> O hell, upbraid me not,
> Nor, loathing, spit upon me thy fierce scorn,
> When like a triple-offspring murderer,
> I enter thee. O hell, I come, I come;
> I feel the dreadful drawing of my doom.
> O monstrous doom! O transformation dread!

How am I changed!—how am I turned, at last
Into a monster at itself aghast!
O wretched children! O more wretched sire!
Would that I might this moment here expire.

It becomes apparent that the critics' main interest in *Saul* was the moral lesson the author presented. A review of the play by Daniel Clark in *The Canadian Monthly* of August 1876 reflects this concern. In it he attempts to explain the greatness of *Saul* by examining the nature of poetic genius. His remarks are worth quoting in part:

Its gifts and graces may be prostituted for ignoble purposes, but that is an abnormal condition, and not natural to the possessor. True nobility of soul gives chasteness of expression, lofty sentiment and ardent aspirations after good. These are emblazoned as insignia on the escutcheon of poesy, for if it descends from this extreme level, the *afflatus* may be present, but not in its normal exercise.

90

Merely to say that there is moral earnestness here is to observe nothing more than what is to be expected, for moral earnestness was certainly a dominant characteristic of the age. But the density of the Canadian version will be particularly evident in the works of most of the Canadian dramatists examined.

It must have been gratifying for Heavysege to realize that his play *Saul* had received international critical acclaim and that as a result he had become a well-known figure in the literary world of his day. He was proud of this play. Not only did he arrange for two more editions (1859 and 1869), but in March of 1862 he gave it a public reading. He wrote in a letter that "I have no news worth communicating, except the circumstance of my having given a reading from *Saul* in Nordheimer's Hall, should be considered such. There was no reason to be dissatisfied with either the number or the behaviour of the audience."[17]

Presumably Heavysege paid for the use of the hall, for it was a commercial theatre used extensively by touring actors. Any loss incurred, however, was no doubt shared by the owner, a gentleman known for his generosity. This information about Mr. Nordheimer is offered by our old friend, Captain Horton Rhys who, as we have already noted, performed in Montreal in August of 1859 during his Canadian tour. His usually caustic remarks are softened when he recalls Nordheimer of Montreal:

Nordheimer is the name of the proprietor of the handsomest concert-hall in Canada. Remember it, my brethren, for good fellows are scarce, and he (Mr. Nordheimer), professionally or otherwise, is, in all senses of the term, one of the right sort. Liberal in his dealings, and assiduous in his attention, to which, through the good people of Montreal being awfully slow at "coming out," I attribute our not absolutely failing on our first appearance. I do not think there was the hire of the room *in*, on the first night; whereupon, the generous owner so materially reduced the said hire, that albeit disposed to "Up sticks and off!" after the first attempt, I was induced to try again, and we were rewarded by an eventual bumper.

[17]Lawrence J. Burpee, "Charles Heavysege," *Transactions of the Royal Society of Canada*, vii, 22 (Section ii, Series ii, 1901).

It would be idle to speculate whether or not Charles Heavysege was in Nordheimer's Hall when Rhys made his appearance. Chances are that he was, however, as he took an active interest in theatre. Although he wrote his play *Saul* originally for the reading public, he did not hesitate to rewrite it for the stage. According to Mr. William Boyd, a printer in Montreal who prepared the copy of *Saul*, Heavysege wrote a stage version at the request of a New York theatrical manager. It appears that Charlotte Cushman expressed the desire to play the part of Malzah, Saul's evil spirit. Unfortunately, Miss Cushman died and the venture was forgotten, but not before Heavysege had completed the script and received a payment.[18] The acting version of the play has unfortunately disappeared, and it is therefore impossible to determine how Heavysege revised it. The fact that Malzah was conceived as a male character should have caused Miss Cushman no trouble; in fact it may have had some influence on her choice as she was noted for her portrayal of such roles as Romeo and Hamlet. Indeed, one of her last performances was in the part of Cardinal Wolsey! She apparently considered the play to be stage-worthy and yet it is conceivable that even with her dominating personality the play could have failed. Here is Malzah's last speech before making his final exit from the stage:

> Alas, alas!
> If I were mortal I should now expire,
> From rumination and forced solitude;
> To be restricted to these palace walls,
> Is nearly as intolerably dull
> As to lie hutched i' the compass of Saul's skull.
> (As late I did), like chicks within their eggs:—
> 'T is more; for 'tween each moon's new birth and full,
> I could abandon it to stretch my legs.
>
> 'T was in an evil hour I came to tempt him;
> For this most vile transaction ends not here;
> But I shall ever self-upbraidings know
> Oft as I meet him in the realms below.

Literary conditions in Canada at the time of Heavysege could hardly be considered stimulating. John Richardson had written *Wacousta*, Canada's first novel of any significance, in 1832. In 1836 there appeared in Halifax the series, *The Clockmaker, or the Sayings and Doings of Samuel Slick of Slickville*. In 1838 the series was published in England and America as *The Clockmaker*, and Sam Slick, the smart Yankee who wins his way by "soft Sawder" and his knowledge of human nature, became a literary figure, and his creator, Thomas Chandler Haliburton, became famous. Except for these two works, the literary field remained barren. When Charles Heavysege published *Saul* in 1857 he became Canada's third writer to be known internationally. He also enjoyed the distinction of being recognized as Canada's first poetic dramatist.

Aware of his exalted position, Heavysege continued his literary work. In

[18]*Ibid.*, p. 27.

1860 he attempted to improve his distinguished position in the field of dramatic literature with the publication of *Count Filippo or The Unequal Marriage*. The play is founded upon the old problem of an unnatural and ill-omened union between youth and age. Count Filippo, an elderly nobleman and chief minister of state to the Duke of Pereza, marries a beautiful young girl named Volina. The Duke, Tremohla, who feels that he is near death, has, on the advice of Filippo, arranged a marriage between his son Hylas and the daughter of the Duke of Arno, much to Hylas' disgust. The young Prince bitterly resents what he takes to be Filippo's interference with his private affairs, and with the aid of Gallantio, a disreputable noble, the Prince determines to revenge himself upon Filippo by corrupting his young wife. Hylas arranges to meet Volina during Filippo's absence at Arno, and astonishes himself by falling in love with her. He modifies his original intention, but cannot avoid showing his love. Poor Volina withstands him for a time but she is inexperienced in love and the would-be-lover furnishes an all too attractive contrast to the ancient Filippo. She weakens and Hylas has his way. Volina then appeals to Hylas to stay with her but, beginning to show the other side of his nature, Hylas promptly makes a suitable excuse to leave her for a day or so. Volina is upset after his departure, and determines to seek forgiveness from Heaven. She goes to the cathedral where Filippo has also come in disguise. He sacrilegiously enters the confessional and hears his wife's tale of sin. Finally he reveals himself, and with threats tries to discover the lover's name, but Volina refuses to tell. Eventually the affair comes to the ears of the ancient Duke, and he calls them all before him. In this concluding scene, Volina is sentenced to do severe penance in a convent, and Filippo is dismissed from his position, and it is suggested that he become a cloistered monk. The aged Duke then very conveniently dies of shock and Hylas, rather than receiving a reprimand, succeeds to the dukedom.

In *Count Filippo* Heavysege obviously tampered with one of the basic rules of poetic drama. This is not a sentimental and idealistic conclusion; affairs are not ended in this fashion, at least not usually in poetic drama. The seeming unreality disturbed the critics. Bayard Taylor, who had followed general opinion and praised *Saul*, condemned *Count Filippo*:

The plot is not original, the action languid, and the very names of the *dramatic personae* convey an impression of unreality. . . . The characters are intellectual abstractions, rather than creatures of flesh and blood; and their love, sorrow, and remorse fail to stir our sympathies.[19]

It must be confessed that the plot has a familiar ring, but the suggestion that it fails to "stir our sympathies," because of an essential unreality of the characters is questionable. Heavysege attempted to replace declamation with normal expression, and the characters, rather than "intellectual abstractions," are allowed a degree of naturalness. The opening remarks in the scene in the confessional, for example, have a simple directness:

FILIPPO: Speak daughter: God is love; none need despair, –
     You keep the primal virtue, chastity?

[19]Bayard Taylor, "The Author of Saul," *Atlantic Monthly*, xcvi, 417 (October, 1865).

VOLINA: I ought; but, oh, who do that which they ought?
FILIPPO: Few; yet remember, if you have offended,
There was forgiveness even for Magdalen.
VOLINA: May Heaven forgive me, too, for I do need it:
More heinous sin than Magdalen's is mine;
Adultery, worse than a virgin's lapse, –
Adultery, for that I need forgiveness.[20]

The problem would seem to lie not in the unrealistic nature of the characters, but in the quality of the subject-matter and Heavysege's treatment of it. In the Introduction, Heavysege pointed out the purpose of the drama:

Next in enormity to a breach of the marriage relation, stands its mutual contraction by youth and years. To give a truthful, though fictitious, instance of the sad issue of such an ill-omened union as the latter is the aim of this drama.

This aim is accomplished. However, in the last scene Heavysege possibly went too far to be morally acceptable. By condemning the innocent and rewarding the guilty, he not only indicated "the sad issue of such an ill-omened union," but, in effect, condoned the breaching of a marriage relation. This unorthodox ending quite likely disturbed the critics, whether they were conscious of it or not, and partly led to the play's bad critical reception. Certainly *Count Filippo* did not receive the acclaim that was offered to *Saul*. It could not please the critic who believed that "True nobility of soul gives chasteness of expression, lofty sentiment and ardent aspirations after good." In fact it is possible that a critic like Daniel Clark believed the romantic world of the poetic drama to be sincere if it expressed emotional concepts and moral attitudes which he thought desirable. Any attempt to re-create natural human relations could have been considered undignified, disturbing and even insincere. *Count Filippo* would not have stirred his sympathies.

Heavysege continued to believe that *Saul* was his most impressive work. His daughter, Mrs. Middlemiss, recalled his making the rather pathetic prophecy that *Saul* would live long after he had died. It is true that as late as 1928 this play was still receiving favourable comment. J. D. Logan and Donald G. French in their review of Canadian Literature, referred to it as a singular achievement. "As a poetic drama there is no other poem which was written in Canada that is so much in the grand manner. Its theme is Biblical, and it is really treated with epic grandeur and romantic intensity."[21]

Although *Saul* is merely a literary curiosity today, there was a time when it was obviously read and appreciated by men of literary pretensions. The interesting and disappointing fact is that no would-be Canadian dramatist, on reading *Saul*, was provoked to criticize it or to seek out fresh approaches to the art of writing plays. There were no Ibsens in Canada. There were only followers of tradition and whether they were influenced by Heavysege or were merely attracted to the romantic conventions, they continued to write

93

[20]Charles Heavysege, *Count Filippo*, Act v, Scene ii.
[21]J. D. Logan and Donald G. French, *Highways of Canadian Literature* (Toronto, 2nd edition, 1928), p. 49.

the nineteenth-century style of poetic drama. Many of these Canadian poetic dramatists are examined for the first time in this book. We can see now that Heavysege was not a lone literary figure, but the first of a number of writers who followed the romantic tradition. Like Heavysege, their concern was with the universal passions of love, revenge, jealousy, and hatred as demonstrated in the lives of the heroes of faraway places and times.

The dramas can be roughly divided into two categories. One type, probably the most prevalent, presented a *dramatis personae* of quasi-historical characters against a romantic background of some distant locale. These plays were almost totally unrelated to the life of the time. The second type differed from the first in that it treated historical figures related to the Canadian scene. Only one play, *Santiago*, fails to fit into either category and will therefore be examined separately.

94 THE CONVENTIONAL POETIC DRAMA

One of the first plays of the conventional romantic type to follow *Saul* was *Sebastian or The Roman Martyr* which was written by Thomas D'Arcy McGee, M.P.P., in 1861. It is a rather extraordinary experience to read this play by a man recognized in his time as a literary connoisseur, poet, electrifying orator, and one of the founding "Fathers of Confederation." Here, surely, we could expect to find some reflection of the contemporary scene. But this is not the case. When McGee turned to drama, which he did on only one occasion, as far as I can ascertain, he selected a religious theme and set his scene in Rome at the time of the persecution of the Christians. His story of Sebastian was founded on Cardinal Wiseman's celebrated tale, *Fabiola*, and was written and published for schools and colleges – especially for a "Christian Brothers' School."[22] There is little of value in *Sebastian*. One suspects that any lay teacher with a burning desire to publish could have produced it. McGee's reasons for writing the play are stated in the Prologue:

> What is the purpose of the mimic scene,
> If not to show what may be and what has been?
> How glorious souls spurning the meanest state,
> May rise to God the source of all that's great.
> Such our bold task – presenting here to-night,
> Pancratius and Sebastian to your sight.
> The Christian's past, extending dim and far,
> Its chancel lighted yet by Bethlehem's star,
> Spreads its broad aisles and transepts to our gaze,
> Filled with the august forms of other days.

The past, with all its romantic and religious grandeur, was considered a suitable subject by this man, who, in his day-to-day affairs was struggling to create a nation. We should note also that it was published in New York and was presumably intended for schools in the United States.

[22]Thomas D'Arcy McGee, *Sebastian or The Roman Martyr* (New York, 1861), introduction.

Another play of the conventional school to follow *Saul* was *Ravlan*, written by Samuel James Watson and published in 1876.[23] Watson came to Canada from Britain in 1857 and "took up the work of reporting and writing for Montreal newspapers, and afterwards for the *Globe*, Toronto."[24] In 1871 he was appointed librarian of the Legislative Library of Ontario and it was while occupying this post that he wrote all his major works. As librarian he compiled a *Constitutional History of Canada* in 1874, and in 1880 produced *The Powers of Canadian Parliaments*. For his own pleasure he wrote a historical romance called *The Peace-Killer, or The Massacre of Lachine*, printed in the *Canadian Illustrated News* in 1870, and in 1876 had published *A Legend of Roses, a Poem; and Ravlan, a Drama*.

Ravlan and the poem were reviewed in *The Canadian Monthly* of January 1876. The critic was impressed by the work, but felt that the book, as a whole, was of such rare excellence that it might not be appreciated by the average Canadian reader. He said at the opening of his article: "The first thought that occurs to one in attempting a review of this book is naturally this – For what audience was it prepared, and where, in Canada are the sympathetic readers with taste for such compositions."

The reviewer admits that in Canada one could hardly say that conditions favoured literary aspiration, and he contends that for this reason alone it was important that "justice should be done it in the way of criticism." He states, moreover, that *Ravlan* deserves special attention because:

It should not be forgotten that it is in dramatic composition that Canada has won her greenest literary laurels abroad. Mr. Heavysege's drama of *Saul* and his later work "Jephthah's Daughter," both won the critical ear of England; and if our estimate of Mr. Watson's work is not astray, there is no reason why it should not meet with equal attention there.

Watson did not receive the international acclaim which his reviewer predicted. He does, however, deserve to be remembered as one who carried on the romantic tradition championed by Heavysege.

The story of *Ravlan*, faithful to the rules of poetic drama, looks back to the tenth century when the Saxon king, Athelstane, ruled over Britain. It consists of a series of intrigues by the chief Druidess, Britomart, to place her son on the throne, or at all events, to prevent the heir and hero of the story, Ravlan, from ascending to it. Her efforts cause general chaos, and the play ends tragically with the stage strewn with dead bodies.

The work has a certain competence of poetic style to its credit, but very little else. The ideas presented, when they are not commonplace, are obviously derivative; the movement of the blank verse is monotonous and shows little metrical invention; the characters involved are flat and rigid – their speech is declamatory. In short this play is obviously second-rate dramatic literature. And yet, according to the reviewer of the time, *Ravlan* displayed in many passages "great energy of expression, and a dramatic talent of no mean order."

[23]Samuel James Watson, *A Legend of Roses, a Poem; Ravlan, a Drama* (Toronto, 1876).
[24]Archibald MacMurchy, *Handbook of Canadian Literature* (Toronto, 1906), p. 103.

The critic made no attempt to select scenes to demonstrate Watson's dramatic talent. He chose, rather, a passage to reveal "the softer mould of the author's muse." The selection is from the scene in which Aidnai attempts to answer Ravlan's question about her love.

> I should have everything, because I feel
> That almost every creature seeks for love;
> And as we treat it, adds unto our pleasure.
> For our delight the brave and songful lark
> Mounts heavenward with his treasure-trove of mirth,
> To vaunt before the unseen choristers
> That waft the singing morning-breeze to earth,
> The gleeful glories of his meadow music.
> For this I love him, and along with him
> The faithful hound, whose big fond heart doth feed
> On a caress, and lives but for his master.

It is not likely that *Ravlan* would have had much success in the theatre, but it is also questionable whether Watson would have allowed it to be performed even if a theatre manager had shown an interest in the play; as we have seen, the theatre was considered by most "respectable" people to be a thing apart, and not a very desirable thing at that.

Occasionally, because of a special set of circumstances, a play by a Canadian poetic dramatist would be performed. Such was the case with Frederick A. Dixon's *Maiden Mona the Mermaid*, especially written for the children of the Earl and Countess of Dufferin. It was presented at Government House, Ottawa, on January 1, 1877. On another occasion he wrote *Canada's Welcome*, a masque which celebrated the arrival of His Excellency the Marquis of Lorne and Her Royal Highness the Princess Louise. The performance was held at the Opera House, Ottawa, on February 24, 1879.[25] Dixon does not stand out as a remarkable poetic dramatist. But his romantic leanings are obvious, particularly in his descriptions of the stage scene. Here is the setting for the first scene of *Maiden Mona the Mermaid*:

Cavern on the Sea Coast by Moonlight. — Opening in Rocks at Back, showing Sea. — The Waves are Rising and Running into Mouth of Cavern. — Introductory Music Descriptive of Storm; Thunder Heard Behind. — Music Gradually Changes to Soft Measured Air as Curtain Rises. —

Dixon of course was the exception; his plays were actually produced. Most Canadian poetic dramatists had to be content with having their plays published, as did John Hutchinson Garnier, whose play, *Prince Pedro*, was printed in 1877.

Garnier, a physician and a poet, came to Canada around 1850. He practised as a physician first at Hagersville, Ontario, and then at Lucknow, Ontario, where he died in 1898.[26] *Prince Pedro* is long and tedious but does manage to recapture something of the flavour of the Elizabethan drama. Basically the plot revolves around a forged will. The villain of the play,

---

[25]Dixon also wrote *Little Nobody*, which he described as a "Fairy Play of Fairy People," and *Pipandor*, a comic opera. They are of little importance.
[26]Charles Canniff James, *A Bibliography of Canadian Poetry* (Toronto, 1899), p. 23.

Ludro, Abbot of Centra, has been able by treacherous means to concoct a will which disinherits the rightful heir to the throne, Prince Pedro. Matteo de Castro, a royal sympathizer, makes a gallant effort to reverse the unfair order, but is unsuccessful and departs for the hills with his sister Inez and a few friends. There they meet Pedro, the banished Prince. An alliance is formed and from that time on they are bound together in common cause. The bonds are made even more secure by the marriage of Prince Pedro and Inez. It is on this happy event that Garnier concludes what could be considered to be the first half of the play. Actually it has taken him four acts to reach this point. But now the author has a great deal more plot in mind and very little time to develop it. Ignoring Artistotle's unities, he leaps ahead, and for his fifth act we find that Inez has not only borne the Prince two children, but that she and the children have all been murdered by the evil Ludro. Moreover, during the same interval, the Prince, with Matteo as his trusted aide and friend, has reclaimed his throne. The action now takes place in the various chambers of the royal court, and with the change of setting comes a change of mood. The pastoral scene and light-hearted tone reminiscent of *As You Like It* are abandoned in favour of a sombre Webster-like quality. Pedro is now obsessed with the desire for revenge. There are moments when he falls into a reflective mood, but only when he dreams of Inez:

> Aye, it is true, when one doth think thereon,
> That life is but a dream, a cloud, a mist,
> That passeth fleetly o'er the scythe of time!
> How oft in dreams, the shadow of the past,
> Tingeth our fancy as with rosy tints.
> Inez! and thou wert but a dream to me, —
> A happy dream, thou and our loving sons.
> Oh, thou didst promise with thy dying breath,
> To come once more, and be my comforter.
> How oft we sat together lovingly,
> With thy soft cheek laid gently on my breast,
> And thy fond arms encircling me in peace.

Gentle thoughts are quickly put aside, however, when the Prince finally captures the wicked Abbot Ludro. A simple execution is not sufficient; the villain must suffer, and so Pedro orders his guards to "stretch him upon the rack; Tear him from limb to limb, and sear his flesh." With classic restraint, Garnier has the torture take place offstage. While Ludro screams in agony offstage, Pedro dreams of Inez and prays that his actions will in some way help her rest in peace, believing perhaps that hate and lust for revenge characterize life beyond the grave. The play is essentially a romantic melodrama, and reflects the "big bow-wow style" of its time. In spite of the confusion inherent in the plot, it is, conceivably, stageworthy.

Most of Canada's poetic dramatists had very little contact with each other. Garnier, for example, seems to have been unaware of Hunter-Duvar, who was writing at the same time many miles away on the east coast of Canada. According to information contained in Archibald MacMurchy's *Handbook of Canadian Literature*, John Hunter-Duvar was born in Scotland on August 29, 1830. It is not known when he arrived in Canada, but we do know that he was appointed Dominion Inspector of Fisheries for Prince Edward Island in 1879 and held this position until 1889. His later years were spent in retirement at "Hernewood" in Prince Edward Island, where he died on January 25, 1899.

He wrote two plays: *The Enamorado* in 1879 and *De Roberval* in 1888. In the latter drama Hunter-Duvar made some attempt to reflect the Canadian scene, and therefore it will be considered later. *The Enamorado* was a straightforward romantic drama in the conventional pattern. The scene is set in the remote past, as the author notes in his Preface: "The main incidents dramatised in the text occurred in the reign of Henry III, of Castille, and during the incumbency of Henry de Villena as Grand Master of the Order of St. James, of Calatrava."

This description hardly supports the contention of the contemporary critic J. A. Payzant that Hunter-Duvar's works could only have been written by "a true Canadian, a man imbued with the true national instinct and aspirations of a Canadian."[27]

The play tells the romantic story of Mazias, a gentleman of Gallicia, who is enamoured of a girl named Clara. Clara de Lope is one of the ladies-in-waiting in the household of the Grand Master, Henry de Villena, and is officially betrothed to Tellez de Mendoza. She tries unsuccessfully to discourage Mazias. The Grand Master eventually steps in and sends Mazias off on a fictitious duty, planning while he is absent to have Tellez and Clara married. Mazias hears a rumour of the Grand Master's plans, however, and returns in time to disrupt them. The Grand Master then sends him to jail. By this time Tellez's jealousy has become uncontrollable, and he seeks out Mazias at the jail and kills him. And so ends the sad story of Mazias, the enamoured one.

It is not the type of story one would expect from a man "imbued with the true national instinct and aspirations of a Canadian." I think we can assume that in this play Hunter-Duvar was not attempting to reflect the Canadian scene or to capture the spirit of Canadianism. He was merely following the tradition of the poetic dramatist and the story of a Spanish love affair was suitable to his purpose. Upon this framework he was able to display his pseudo-Shakespearean poetry. Notice the familiar sound of the phrasing and imagery in Clara's description of the dawn:

> See the gates
> Are swinging on the hinges of the east,
> And out there wells the flush of morning-red
> That heralding the coming of the sun,
> Encarnadines our lovely ladies' cheeks
> Making them living roses.

The Fireworshippers, another conventional poetic drama, was written by C. F. Newcomb and J. M. Hanks and was published in 1882. Although the

[27]J. A. Payzant, "John Hunter-Duvar," *Dominion Illustrated*, v, No. 112, 127 (August 23, 1890).

collaboration failed to produce a worthwhile drama, there is some evidence that at least one of the authors had a sense of the theatre. The opening is unique. Three short scenes, rapidly presented to the reader (in much the same manner as black-outs are produced in a modern revue or variety show), depict the three main characters in general terms and foretell the dreadful events of the drama. The first character to appear is Zorotus, the High Priest. Although it appears that he is killed in the early scenes of the play, he actually survives and serves to close the play, as he opens it, with wise and holy utterances:

> Oh, thou invisible spirit of life! Doest thou
> dwell in the flame, or art thou in the winds
> that bear health and strength throughout the world.[28]

This is spoken while he is kneeling before a lamp in which burns the eternal light. Next the Prince speaks:

> Alas, what dire and fateful lot is mine.
> Doomed in youth's prime to be
> in all things, but the knowledge that I am not,
> an old and worn out priest. Alien to the priesthood,
> I am selected to fill the space of one who died
> and left no one of priestly blood to fill the place;
> and according to the thrice accursed law,
> I, being alien, must never enter that blessed and happy
> State of matrimony. Oh, the hopeless misery of my condition.

The evil-plotter follows directly, a Richard III in feeling, if not in expression:

> Blood, blood, always blood, everywhere.
> I see it when the lowering western sky
> doth hold the glowing sun, ere yet
> he hasteth to go down, and the river rushing
> to the sea with strong and majestic flow
> seemeth to boil and seethe with blood,
> and when the darkness is broken by the coming day,
> the eastern sky is crimson with the gory hue.
>
> Yea, and more blood! Though I slay the mother that bare me,
> though I kill my first-born, yet will I be King.
> Woe be to him that standeth in my way.

Following these opening speeches, the play begins and it is soon apparent that *The Fireworshippers* is merely a crude re-working of *Richard III*.

The conclusion, however, is worth noting for here again the work bears the marks of a stage play: Newcomb and Hanks adopted a particular type of stage business that was popular at the time – the *tableau*. This was the *pièce de résistance* of many melodramas and was used to great advantage in such plays as *Uncle Tom's Cabin*. The message was driven home by ending the scenes with significant poses. Good and evil could be pondered

---

[28]C. F. Newcomb and J. M. Hanks, *The Fireworshippers* (Toronto, 1882), Act I, Scene i.

by the audiences as they gazed at little Eva suspended between heaven and earth and with the organ gently playing off-stage. By the 1880s the *tableau* had become a part of the pageantry of the theatre.[29] Newcomb and Hanks were evidently aware of its effectiveness for they end the play in this fashion:

> KING KUROS [the Prince] stands before the throne of Gheba, the royal crown and the vestments of the Kings of Gheba upon him. By his side, clasping his hands, stands ALTHEA, clad in the royal robes also. In front, upon the sacred altar, burns the holy fire. ZORATUS, the chief priest, stands before it, facing the King and Queen with hands spread over them, apparently blessing them. Grouped around stand the nobles and great men of Gheba, in the robes of the nobility of Gheba. Slow music outside. Curtain slowly falls.

Another product of this indomitable pair is the play *Dermot McMurrough*, also published in 1882. Generally *Dermot McMurrough* adheres to the rules of poetic drama, but it certainly does not bring glory to the tradition. Indeed, unlike *The Fireworshippers*, it even lacks interesting theatrical features.

Briefly, the action takes place in Ireland in 800 A.D. and involves the trials and tribulations of Armagh, chief Man-at-Arms and trusted friend to Dermot McMurrough, King of Ireland. Apparently the King is going mad and many of the nobles, not wishing to turn against the throne and yet not wanting to serve the erring King, have gone into hiding. Armagh, as a friend to both parties, has the difficult and thankless task of mediating between the two. He does his job well, and at the end of the play when Dermot has been killed in battle, the nobles entreat him to succeed to the throne. Armagh piously rejects the honour saying,

> It must not be. Down false ambition,
> I will join the good old Priest, and
> spend the remainder of my life, leading
> my countrymen into the paths of peace and rectitude.

Unfortunately (or fortunately) there is no indication that this writing team prospered, and in fact all traces of Newcomb and Hanks have disappeared.

Two more poetic dramas which should be mentioned in passing are *Leo and Venetia* by William E. Anderson and *Jassoket and Anemon* by George Arthur Hammond. It seems unlikely that either play had a large reading public. A single copy of each is in the Theatre Collection of the Toronto Public Library. Apparently both authors were either printers or connected with the printing trade. Hammond was actually known as "the printer-poet of Kingsclear." There is no information about Anderson, but we do know that his play was printed not by a publishing house but by the *Pickering News* office.

Leo and Venetia, printed in 1895, is a conventional poetic drama. The scene is set in Benevento, Italy, at some vague time in the past. The characters and, to some extent, the situations seem to be borrowed from Shakespeare. The plot concerns Leo, a poor but noble youth, who through fortu-

---

[29]*Tableaux vivants* were presumably first introduced by Madame de Genlis but the story of their growth has not been recorded. According to Richard Moody (*America Takes the Stage*) the *tableaux vivants* were popular in American plays of the spectacular type in the 1840s.

100

nate circumstances manages to save the life of Venetia, the King's daughter. For his reward he naturally asks for her hand. Although the King agrees to the marriage, one of his ministers, the villain Ronolo, decides to intervene. The action is then concerned with Ronolo's attempts to murder Leo. In the end Ronolo is apprehended and the lovers live happily ever after.

Although in play form and composed of eighteen scenes, *Jassoket and Anemon* (1896) can scarcely be considered a dramatic work. As the author notes in the title, it is a "ramble"; Jassoket and Anemon, the two main characters, discuss and argue with a number of incidental characters the comforts of a religion and the pitfalls of scientific progress.

With the exception of Charles Heavysege, none of the writers so far considered became well-known literary figures. Many of them remained completely unknown. But in the 1880s and 1890s when some of these playwrights were writing, a group of Canadian poets did become prominent. They are sometimes referred to as the Confederation Poets and the four most important were probably Charles G. D. Roberts, Archibald Lampman, Bliss Carman and Duncan Campbell Scott. There were in addition several others of lesser importance: Frederick George Scott, George Frederick Cameron, Isabella Valency Crawford, William Wilfred Campbell and E. Pauline Johnson. Of this group, four attempted to write dramas: Bliss Carman, Duncan Campbell Scott, Frederick George Scott, and William Wilfred Campbell.

Bliss Carman's two plays *Daughters of the Dawn* and *Earth Deities* were educational masques. As he noted in the Preface to *Daughters of the Dawn*, they were originally planned by Mrs. Mary Perry King "to serve as a series of studies in her new educational movement." Carman wrote the dance librettos for the purpose of

disseminating Mrs. King's theory of the three rhythmical arts – poetry, music and dancing – and of training the youth of the country in them by impressing upon them the grave necessity of equi-development in morality, intelligence and physique in order that they might attain the highest degree of culture possible to man.[30]

The school that was founded to promote this movement was not a success, and Carman's association with it did little to enhance his reputation.

Something of the style and approach of these educational masques may be gained from a short excerpt from *Daughters of the Dawn*. The scene is described in the following words: "A wooded glade in Paradise. A running stream through a meadow. The sea line in the distance. Birds, butterflies, flowers, and creatures. Morning sunlight." Eve wanders into this scene and is supposed to accompany the following lines with "primitive expressive motion":

> Dear Life! Earth and sun and sea-line!
> Shadowy woods and shining river!
> Flowers and meadows fresh with morning,
> Calling birds that sway and flutter,
>   Soaring glad and free!

[30]Muriel Miller, *Bliss Carman, a Portrait* (Toronto, 1935), p. 102.

Carman's only other play, *Earth Deities*, was also written in collaboration with Mrs. King. Stress was again put on joining words and music.

The only play of Frederick George Scott which still exists is *The Key of Life*. It reminds us of the close relationship of religion and literature in Canadian culture. Scott was Canon of the Cathedral in Quebec from 1906 to 1925, and, in looking for suitable material which would lend itself to poetic treatment, it was natural that he should have turned to the Bible. In *The Key of Life* Scott tells the story of Joseph and Mary and the birth of Christ. His primary aim was to teach, and as his Prologue states, moral instruction was to take precedence over entertainment:

> We have no wit to bring you, nothing rare,
> In turn of speech or figure passing fair,
> But simply that great message from the past,
> That God's strong arms around the world are cast.

102

Bliss Carman, Frederick George Scott, and Duncan Campbell Scott[31] were primarily concerned with the land. An interest in nature, always evident in earlier poetry and novels in Canada, had become prominent in the work of Canadian artists and poets. The scenery of Canada, rather than the people, attracted and inspired the artists. As Roy Daniells has noted "The preoccupation with the land . . . has left its mark on the form of traditional Canadian writing."[32] Strangely enough, this reverence for the Canadian landscape is not noticeable in Canada's poetic drama. True to the conventions of the romantic drama, almost all of the Canadian dramatists, even those who were landscape poets, preferred remote and exotic settings.

William Wilfred Campbell's progress as a writer follows this pattern. In the beginning he was one of the nature poets and he wrote some of his best poetry under this influence. In later years he devoted most of his time to writing poetic dramas and thus turned his back on Canada and sought inspiration from Elizabethan drama.

As a poet, Campbell's fame is secure as long as anthologies of Canadian verse are published, and his memory will be cherished by all those who have been stirred by the beauty of his work.

> The lake comes throbbing in with voice of pain
>   Across these flats, athwart the sunset's glow;
> I see her face, I know her voice again,
>   Her lips, her breath, O God, as long ago.[33]

As a nature poet he drew great praise. Professor Horning, echoing the views

[31]Duncan Campbell Scott, although establishing himself as an important poet during this period, did not write a drama until late in his life, at a time when there was little interest in poetic drama. In the 1920s he became a founder and active member of the Ottawa Little Theatre. He wrote and delivered the Prologue at the opening of the theatre on January 18, 1923, and was the author of a one-act play, *Pierre*, performed that evening. (E. K. Brown, *Selected Poems of Duncan Campbell Scott* [Toronto, 1951], p. xiv.) Another play of his, *Joy, Joy, Joy*, was presented by Hart House Theatre in Toronto, May 12–14, 1927. Scott's plays, however, are not poetic dramas, nor do they fall into the period under consideration.

[32]Roy Daniells, "Poetry and the Novel," in *The Culture of Contemporary Canada*, ed. Julian Park (Toronto, 1957), p. 11.

[33]W. J. Sykes, *The Poetical Works of Wilfred Campbell* (Toronto, 1922), p. 4.

held by the critics of the time, pointed out that "He is to be placed in the very front of our Canadian singers."[34]

But Campbell was not content with this place; he desired a larger field for his talents. It was perhaps his admiration for Sir John A. Macdonald that finally turned his thoughts to Empire. ("A British subject I was born and a British subject I will die," said that notable Canadian statesman when union with the United States was mentioned in his presence.) Sir John was responsible for obtaining for Campbell, when he severed his connection with the church and was looking for a place in the government, a position which he hoped would enable the poet to support his family and have more time for his writing. Approximately a month after this appointment Macdonald died. The emotional Campbell was stirred to public utterance and for the funeral wrote a memorial poem entitled "The Dead Leader." Carl F. Klinck, Campbell's biographer, comments: "For the first time in his life he wrote a national, it might even be called imperial, poem."[35] Campbell wrote of:

> Him of the wider vision
> Who had one hope, elysian,
> To mould a mighty Empire toward the west. . . .

It was a poem suitable for the occasion, a tribute to a great man, but in no way remarkable except for the effect which it had on Campbell himself. It is probable that while writing this tribute Campbell was stirred by a sudden realization that he was part of a great Empire, one upon which the sun never set, which "under God, was the greatest instrument for good the world had ever known." He was moved by patriotic fervour and under its stimulus, like many another writer, he wrote his worst poetry:

> England, England, England,
> Girdled by ocean and skies,
> And the power of a world, and the heart of a race,
> And a hope that never dies.

> England, England, England,
> Wherever a true heart beats,
> Wherever the rivers of commerce flow,
> Wherever the bugles of conquest blow,
> Wherever the glories of liberty grow,
> 'Tis a name that the world repeats.[36]

Campbell did not live to see the decline of the British Empire as a world power. He lived during its greatest days; his sentiments were not unnatural at the time and perhaps should not be scrutinized too severely from the viewpoint of the second half of the twentieth century. Actually, later in life, when his preoccupation with glory waned, he paused to consider the excesses of patriotism and wrote a lyric called "Afterglow" which, according

---

[34]Professor Horning's comment is to be found, along with about a dozen others, appended to *Poetical Tragedies*, by Wilfred Campbell (Toronto, 1908), p. 317.
[35]Carl F. Klinck, *Wilfred Campbell* (Toronto, 1942), p. 76.
[36]Wilfred Campbell, *Sagas of Vaster Britain* (Toronto, 1914), p. 10.

to Klinck, could very well be called a Canadian "Recessional." But with all deference to his biographer, though the aim was high, Kiplingesque, the resulting poem was in my opinion closer in tone to Edgar Lee Guest.

> After the clangour of battle
> There comes a moment of rest,
> And the simple hopes and the simple joys
> And the simple thoughts are best.
>
> A simple love, and a simple trust,
> And a simple duty done,
> Are truer torches to light to death
> Than a whole world's victories won.[37]

As we have noted, early in his career Campbell was in love with the Canadian countryside, and did his best work while under its spell. But with success his ambition grew. It was at this point that his poems, such as "Afterglow," took on what Campbell would have called a "larger view" – he ventured on themes which he felt called for more vigour, a more urgent appeal. And, as with his patriotic poetry, so with his drama; in straining for greatness, he lost the simple beauty that had characterized his work.

Commenting on the source material for drama in the Preface to *Mordred* in his *Poetical Tragedies*, Campbell noted that the particular function of drama was to "lift the thought and imagination to a loftier plane." He went on to say that if a tragedy is to recapture the glory of the Greek and Elizabethan ages it must be: "concerned only with man's personality in his relationship to those more sublime and terrible laws of being which mysteriously link him to deity." Or we might say, briefly, that Campbell, like Eugene O'Neill, and many other playwrights throughout history, was concerned with the relationship of man to God, and like most of them, found himself out of his depth. O'Neill wanted to be a modern Aeschylus; Campbell turned to Shakespeare, and because men of genius are the worst possible models for men of talent, signs of strain appear in the work of each. But at this point, the comparison ends. O'Neill was an innovator of stage technique; Campbell's knowledge of the stage was limited.

In O'Neill's plays, for example, the characters taken from Greek originals are placed in a modern setting; Campbell went to the past for his heroes without forging any psychological links with his own time. Campbell could not conceive of a "man-to-God" relationship in the context of the contemporary world. He therefore chose to divorce himself from the present, and, at the same time, he discarded thoughts of Canadian nationalism.

Four plays of Campbell's were published. *Mordred* and *Hildebrand* first appeared in 1895 and then were reprinted with *Daulac* and *Morning* in his book *Poetical Tragedies* in 1908.[38] All of the plays are related to the past. *Mordred* is a tragedy based on the Arthurian legend; *Hildebrand* tells the story of Gregory VII; *Daulac* turns to the early history of the New World

---

[37] W. J. Sykes, *The Poetical Works of Wilfred Campbell* (Toronto, 1922), pp. 93–4.

[38] Three other unpublished plays, *The Brockenfiend, Sanio the Avenger*, and *The Admiral's Daughter* are stored at Queen's University, Kingston. They do not throw much further light on Campbell as a dramatist.

and dramatizes the personality and achievement of Daulac des Ormeaux;
Morning "is set in a remote period anterior to Christianity."[39] Campbell's
choice of subject-matter indicates his lack of dramatic interest in Canadian
history. In referring to *Mordred* he wrote of the attraction of the classical
themes: "There is something in the story akin to those themes of the great
Greek Tragedies, and of the greater Shakespearean dramas, which associates
it with what is subtly mysterious and ethically significant in the history and
destiny of mankind."[40] With this inspiration, Campbell set out to write a
great drama. But *Mordred* is essentially a melodrama, as are all his plays,
with the possible exception of *Morning*. They are composed of murder,
revenge, and horror, with very little of "what is subtly mysterious and
ethically significant." Apparently Campbell was unable to translate his ideas
into dramatic terms. Critically, he had formed some opinions about the new
drama and the old. He expressed some of his views in an article called
"Shakespeare and the Latter-Day Drama":

It is not that the old tragedy and comedy are not so interesting, but that the
play-going public have been gradually educated up to an almost hysterical appetite for the gruesome and the nasty; the suggestive, the unnatural and the
immoral, so that the quieter, more human and saner depiction of life fails any
more to satisfy.[41]

Campbell the critic was inclined to be at cross-purposes with Campbell
the dramatist. When he wrote a play he was not necessarily concerned with
the "saner depiction of life." He was, on the contrary, very much the show-
man and, aware of the public appetite, always favoured the melodramatic
scene. Furthermore, according to some, in his treatment of the Arthurian
legend in *Mordred*, he was guilty of the very qualities he confessed to des-
pise. For example, the *Toronto Globe* of July 6, 1895, had this to say of
Mordred:

The simple, heroic, illuminating figures of the period of Merlin, of the Holy Grail,
of chaste knights and modest maidens are metamorphosed into others, grotesque
and revolting, and for no purpose evidently but to disgust.

Campbell's first play immediately attracted much critical attention.[42] It
is certainly the most actable of his plays and it was unfortunate that when
it was submitted to Henry Irving on the suggestion of friends, Irving already
had in his hands a play on the same theme written by Comyns Carr, which
he eventually produced. *Mordred* was never produced on stage.

Little of the "illuminating" story of King Arthur and his Knights of the
Round Table appears in Campbell's play. In this dark and tragic story
Mordred is the son of King Arthur and his sister Gawaine, as he appears in

---

[39]Campbell, *Poetical Tragedies*, Preface to *Morning*, p. 203.
[40]*Ibid.*, p. 11.
[41]Wilfred Campbell, "Shakespeare and the Latter-Day Drama," *Canadian Magazine*,
xxx, 16 (November, 1907).
[42]Campbell, *Poetical Tragedies*, p. 319. A collection of favourable reviews are reprinted
by Campbell. The editor of *Walsh's Magazine* is quoted as saying: "Unless I am
greatly mistaken . . . *Mordred* . . . is the greatest work yet accomplished by any
Canadian poet. . . ."

Malory's *Morte d'Arthur*, instead of Arthur's nephew, as in other legends. Mordred, born twisted and ugly, instead of being a joy to his father, is treated with contempt and disgust. As the years pass his resentment turns to hate and desire for revenge. Queen Guinevere's love affair with Launcelot, Arthur's trusted friend, of which Arthur has been blissfully unaware, gives Mordred the opportunity, and he tells the King of it. Having set the former friends at each other's throats, Mordred seizes the throne. But his reign is short-lived, and in the battle following Arthur's reclamation of the throne, both Arthur and Mordred are killed.

From this legend Campbell presumably felt he had written a play to "lift the thought and imagination to a loftier plane"; in fact, he merely created a blood-and-thunder spectacle of the Marks Brothers type. This comparison is made with some reason, for it was in Ottawa, Campbell's home for many years, that the Marks Brothers played most frequently and where they seem to have been continually assured of large and appreciative audiences. We do not know if Campbell attended often, but we can see what could be a Marks Brothers' stamp on his plays. Consider the following scene between Launcelot and Guinevere in which, after falling in love at first sight, they discover their love is actually a crime:

GUIN: All life hath been but shaping up to this.

LAUN: Oh, could this sunset be but gold forever!

GUIN: My lord, Arthur!

LAUN: (*starts back*) Great God!

GUIN: Kiss me. Why Great God!
Thou art my God when thy lips are so sweet.

LAUN: Why calledst thou me Arthur?

GUIN: And art thee not?

LAUN: Oh, who art thou that callest Arthur lord?

GUIN: As thou art Arthur, I am Guinevere.
(*Launcelot starts back in horror.*)

LAUN: Guinevere! Make thick your murky curtains!
Day, wake no more! Stars, shrink your eye-hole lights,
And let this damned earth shrivel!

GUIN: (*clutching his arm*) And art thou not great Arthur?
Who art thou? O God! Who art thou?

LAUN: Not Arthur, no! but that foul Launcelot,
Who 'twixt his hell and Arthur's Heaven hath got.

GUIN: Then am I a doomed maid! (*swoons.*)

LAUN: Black, murky fiend of hell! come in thy form
Most monstrous, give me age on ages here,
And I will clang with thee and all thine imps,
Bind me in blackness under Hell's foul night,
And it were nothing, after dreams like this.

GUIN: (*rising up*) Oh, mercy! damned or not, I love thee still!

The melodramatic style is obvious in Campbell's other plays also. *Hildebrand*, for example, which was published at the same time as *Mordred*, examines Pope Hildebrand and his conflict between his desire:

> To separate humanity from the Church,
> And re-create a world within this world,
> A kingdom in these kingdoms, alienate
> From all the loves and ties that weaken men,
> By rendering all the priesthood celibate,
> Espousèd only unto Holy Church,

and his tender concern for his daughter, Margaret, who is married to a priest. Campbell aimed high, but the play again conforms to the melodramatic standard. Because of the Pope's decree, Margaret's husband must leave her and their infant. Despite her pleading, he leaves them, saying:

> I can hear the Holy Father's voice,
> Though he's in Rome, saying nay, nay, to thee.
> Farewell, Margaret, we will meet in heaven.

Margaret, now alone and destitute in her humble cottage, is approached by the villain, Ariald, a decretal preacher. He has always loved her and now sees his chance to take her for his own. But Margaret refuses his advances:

MAR.   Out! Out! blasphemer! If the Church be vile,
      If justice swept from earth and pity dead,
      Though devils walk this world, though God be gone,
      Know there be left one righteous woman's scorn
      For such as thee!
AR.   When thou dost see bleak desolation come,
      Gaunt, burning hunger fill thy baby's eyes,
      Thou'lt come to me.
MAR.   If thou be Satan, thou black Prince of Fiends,
      Thou wearest this man's form, thou firest his heart.
      (*To Ariald*) Go! Go! I forget my womanhood.
AR.   (*Going out*) Remember!
MAR.   If there be nothing in this world for me,
      I have a friend no priest nor Pope can take,
      Whose name is death.

The tragedy mounts as Margaret loses her child, her sanity and finally her life, culminating in Hildebrand's uneasy doubts of the wisdom of his strict principles as he dies:

HILDE.   This world-ambition hath eaten up my heart,
       And my life with it. Better to be there
       Where she doth lie than to be God's Vicar.

Mordred and *Hildebrand*, Campbell's early attempts in the dramatic form, were published in 1895. Eighteen years passed before he again presented the reading public with two new plays, *Daulac* and *Morning*. In *Daulac* we find that the intervening years had not changed Campbell's melodramatic style; the heroes and villains are even more clearly defined. By his choice of Daulac des Ormeaux as hero, however, Campbell was able to transfer a good deal of the action to Canada (the climax is a dramatization of the famous exploit of Daulac, that is, Adam Dollard, Sieur des

Ormeaux, who died defending a small village of settlers against an Indian attack) and thus he wrote one of the first Canadian plays about French Canada. According to Carl F. Klinck, *Daulac* was the "first noteworthy English play on the subject of French Canadian history." It is questionable, however, whether *Daulac* is a more noteworthy play than *De Roberval*, which was written twenty years earlier and also dramatizes an incident in early French-Canadian history.

Neither play, unfortunately, stressed its Canadian content. Campbell's main interest lay in the intricacies of a melodramatic plot, and in *Daulac* the Canadian incident is insignificant. The purpose of the play was:

> to depict the ultimate triumph of the fate of an unsuspecting innocence over the wiles and plots of a clever and scheming malice, and to show that the final heroic deed was but the natural outcome of an unusually noble nature in the personality of Daulac.

108

Desjardin pursues the hero with the illogical motivation of the conventional stage villain: there is no motivation. On one occasion he manages to contrive a situation in which the hero, Daulac, is helpless to defend himself. The scene is a room in an inn where Daulac is sitting with two friends, Piotr and Fillet. According to plan, Desjardin, cloaked and masked, and with two assassins, rushes in on the seemingly defenceless hero:

DES. Ha, ha, ha!
PIO. (*under the table*) Murder! murder!
FIL. (*at side, calling*) Murder! thieves! murder!
  They fight harder. Daulac kills one, then wounds the second, fighting his way out.
DES. Damn him! damn him! he still lives, still lives! But wait! the *lettre de cachet*! ha, ha, ha! I'll have him yet! I'll have him yet!

It is hard to accept such writing from a man who was apparently interested in creating literary dramas. The expression *lettre de cachet*, for example, was so familiar that actors were known to use it as an *ad lib* when they forgot lines. It is more understandable, however, if we keep in mind that this sort of thing was the theatrical fare of the time.

Both the Marks Brothers and the touring companies which came from the United States and England had as the largest percentage of their company's repertoire such plays as *The Black Flag, A Soldier's Sweetheart, The Duke's Daughter, Uncle Tom's Cabin, The Two Orphans, A Rash Marriage, Ten Nights in a Bar-Room* and *East Lynne*, and these were presented to the public with unrelieved regularity. The influence of these plays on Campbell merely strengthened his natural inclination. His early prose work is essentially melodramatic; the tendency is revealed quite clearly in his short stories.[43]

There is no indication that, as a playgoer, Campbell ever took a serious interest in the plays of the New Movement. He never referred to the performance of *A Doll's House* which took place in Ottawa on November 19,

[43]Wilfred Campbell, "Love's Tragedy at Scratch's Point," *Canadian Magazine*, III, 325–31 (August, 1894).

1895, the year in which he published his first two plays. He was aware of this revolution in the theatre, however. As a critic he formed his own conclusions, and some years later revealed them in his article "Shakespeare and the Latter-Day Drama."[44] It is in effect an answer to Tolstoy and Shaw, whose recent criticism of Shakespeare had caused Campbell much irritation. He forgave Tolstoy for, as he said, "who can speak without admiration for his earnestness?" but for Shaw he had nothing but criticism and scorn: "It might be as easy to compare the author of *Man and Superman*, criticizing Shakespeare to a fly buzzing at a mountain, or to a pigmy tilting with a titan, and so leave him to posterity." It is unlikely that Campbell saw the production of *Man and Superman* in Montreal on January 21, 1907. If he had, he would probably have agreed with the critic of the *Montreal Daily Star* who wrote in part:

It is this quality to shock which is at once one of the greatest gifts and the greatest defects of the genius of Shaw. It is a gift in that it is original – stirs the mind and jostles the people out of their mental stagnation. It is a defect, however, when Shaw approaches subjects sacred to every man in the same manner.

A melodrama could usually be counted on to approach "subjects sacred to every man" in a conventional manner and therefore would have been acceptable to such a man as Campbell. The new social dramas, on the other hand, were dangerous in his opinion. One of his main concerns, expressed in the Preface to *Morning*, was that they lacked "the larger belief, centering in the idea of God." Campbell wanted to correct this error by writing a play which would comment on modern times and yet not lose the idealism of the old poetic drama. The old romantic tradition had not been employed to handle modern social situations such as those found in the new or problem plays, but had considered the conventionally moral problems within the doubly removed safety of time and space. The question was, could the modern scene be dealt with in that old and noble style?

Morning, Campbell's last serious attempt to write a poetic drama, was his answer to this question. It is quite conceivable that he may have been offering this play as an object lesson to such writers as Shaw, for in *Morning* he wrote a poetic drama which was presumably his version of a problem play. He noted in the Preface that "its theme is plainly modern, and deals with the tremendous problems of modern society." It does not deal merely with man in society; this would be trivial in Campbell's eyes. "The central problem of the play," according to the author, is "the belief in God and larger hope, as vitally affecting man's whole life, actions and ideals."

C. F. Klinck considers *Morning* to be a rather exceptional type of play. "It is one of the most unusual products of a Canadian pen, a distinctively Canadian attempt to face a new world without a sacrifice of the best traditions of the old."[45] It is true that the language, though still pseudo-Shakespearean, is much nearer standard speech than in his other plays. The villain, Vulpinus, for example, manages to reveal his villainy without becoming

[44]Campbell, "Shakespeare and the Latter-Day Drama," *Canadian Magazine*, xxx, 14 (November, 1907).
[45]Klinck, *Wilfred Campbell*, pp. 146–47.

completely unnatural. We are introduced to him at the opening of the play. He enters alone:

> He must not prosper. Every honor he wears,
> But makes my toil the harder. Nature dread
> Did fashion deceit to make my soul its dwelling.
> I am a man! although I doubt all men.
>
> Wreck him? Yea, I will. I'll use this world
> To confuse its high imaginings. . . .

Vulpinus may not be as sensational a villain as Ariald or Desjardin, but there is no mistaking his melodramatic origins.

Morning is, in fact, the story of virtue harassed but triumphant, of villainy baffled but indefatigable. Leonatus, a noble-minded citizen and chief Senator of the city of Avos, is toppled from his high position by the clever scheming of Vulpinus. There is little attempt to give Vulpinus a motive for his actions; he is an evil force, and in this case stands for cynicism. He is opposed to Leonatus, who stands for faith. The problem which Campbell raises is "which ideal is to prevail in society, that of the cynic or that of faith and hope – Vulpinus or Leonatus?"

Campbell intended to write a problem play – but there is no problem! There is no great trial of Leonatus' faith, as in Job, with Job's tremendous affirmations of faith, and his ultimate vindication. Leonatus, though deprived of all his wordly goods through the machinations of Vulpinus, retains his faith. Shortly after his expulsion from the city, the citizens rally to Leonatus and seek him out in the forest, where he has sought a home. But too late; he is dying. In his last moments, the old man, re-established in his friends' regard, makes his peace with them and looks forward to a better world:

> Believe me, friends, we are all good citizens;
> Leonatus did ever love your city,
> And built its virtues. Sit you down, good friends,
> I am no lord, but just a poor old man
> Whom his loved city, in mistaken dream,
> Did banish for his misdeeds. Believe me, friends,
> They did not mean it; God for some good reason
> Did blind them to it. Look not so cold upon us,
> We will not stay; yea, we will go without,
> Where our poor woes and wants may not offend you.
> Come, my sweet daughter, take your father's hand!
> We are alone, the very inclement night
> Doth freeze us, the stars refuse us bread,
> The world is aged and ruined, dread and dark,
> My poor limbs fail me. All, yea, all but God!
>   (*He staggers; they hold him.*
> (*half rising up*) Nay, nay, you lie, you doubters; back of all
> This wintry age, this iron of dread and dark,
> I see a glimmer. I do feel a dawn
> Breaking! Breaking! (*Dies.*)

110

Campbell, the minister, has the last word; no problem is solved, but a sermon has been preached.

Poetic Drama

SANTIAGO

Strangely enough, there seems to be only one play that does not fit into the category of the conventional poetic drama, or the group yet to be considered, the poetic drama as related to the Canadian scene. *Santiago* gains its distinction by a slight, but interesting irregularity. Unlike the conventional poetic dramatists who looked to the remote past, the author of this play seems to have received his inspiration from a contemporary incident. It was not a Canadian incident, however, although it appeared prominently in most Canadian newspapers and magazines.

In 1863 the Campania Church in Santiago, Chile, burned to the ground. The doors, unfortunately, opened inward and the people gathered there were trapped. As a result, some two thousand worshippers perished. In 1866 Thomas Bush used this ghastly incident as the climax of his play, *Santiago*, published in Toronto. Actually it is more accurate to say that he used it as a final scene, for there is no single plot. The burning of the worshippers apparently struck Bush as good material for a scene and it obviously acted as a springboard for his imagination and suggested a locale as well. So, with little concern for the end of the play, which he presumably had tentatively worked out, Bush began.

The early scenes show that he intended to compose an allegorical and theological treatment of man in search of his destiny. This theme is quickly sacrificed in favour of his stronger desire to construct a melodramatic thriller. The play is a failure because it lacks a sustaining plot, has no focus, nor even a very intelligent theology. But it does remain one of the most interesting plays by a Canadian in the period under consideration.

In such a large undertaking as the one chosen by Bush, the plot necessarily becomes merely an expedient device with which to move the characters, who consequently appear only in profile and owe their existence to one or two dominating traits. Credulous, for example, the first character we meet, is essentially a good man with the one serious failing that his name implies. He has lost his way and finds himself on a path surrounded by dangerous pitfalls. There is little doubt that Bush is suggesting that Credulous has wandered off the straight and narrow to find himself beset with dangers. Will faith alone enable him to survive? Bush supplies the answer when eventually he has Credulous meet a stranger of whom he asks the way. The stranger's reply and ensuing action suggest that faith is not enough and that a man must be acquainted with evil:

> The road? I've travelled it in safety often.
> Come – time's pressing; let me plant your foot
> Safe on that jutting rock; *that* firmly gained,
> Most of the danger's passed; come nearer.
> *Timorously approaching, is pushed off; shrieking, descends.*[46]

[46]Thomas Bush, *Santiago* (Toronto, 1866), Act I, Scene ii.

111

The force of the object lesson is somewhat diminished when we find Credulous has later been rescued. His rescuer is called Vampries, and with the advent of this character we realize that the author has shifted his interest to the problem of good and evil. The setting, of course, does not change. The action still takes place in the mountains of Chile and the characters involved apparently continue their course in the direction of Santiago. But Vampries now becomes the main character through whom Bush seeks to throw light on the problem.

Vampries is an extraordinary mixture. He has the heart of a Robin Hood and the mind of a Machiavelli, and although he appears quite often as God's representative, he is at all times capable of the Devil's deeds. His evil nature is recognized in the latter part of the play. Vampries is talking with Gorman, a reporter who is in Santiago at the time, when Gorman's companion Diaz returns from the scene of the fire:

GORMAN: Speak Diaz, from the fire?
DIAZ: No, from a black tartarus full of stench
And images of terror, outraging Hell!
(*Exit Vampries*)
I've touched the talisman – did you observe it?
My citing hell has sent the devil packing![47]

Vampries, however, is not just the Devil in disguise, but rather an individual with two identities. When he does a good deed it is not for an evil purpose. When a man of virtue falls into danger, he aids him, as he did Credulous. It should also be noted that the punishment he hands out to evil-doers is in the name of God. But there is malice in his correction, as we can note by turning to the scene in which he is attacked by a thug known as Gripos, friend of Treacher, the murderer who attempted to take the life of Credulous. Vampries proves to be too strong for Gripos, disarms him and holds him at his mercy:

GRIPOS: My arm is broken – powerless – at your mercy.
VAMPRIES: Wretch! Know you that word? Thou, the unbranded Cain,
Crying to all thou meet'st for public vengeance.
Felon! know this arm doth ne'er relinquish
Nor this heart relent. Body and soul are mine.
Ha! start ye? Body and soul, I said!
GRIPOS: Lord – has it come to this. (*Trembling, sinks on his knees.*)
VAMPRIES: Mercy, is it villain? Yes, such as thou'st shown.
I'll treat thee to a sight which, doubtless, thou
Hast oft bestowed on others; come on, then.
(*Thrusting him to the precipice*)
Look there! – what, sick? I soon restore thee.
(*Holding him by the hair over gulf*)
Poor craven wretch – to shriek so dastardly!
I did but act the gibbet.
(*Laying him back on the rock. Walking to and fro.*)

[47]*Ibid.*, Act v, Scene v.

>Another sentence of this dismal story
>Comes to a rueful stop. Such paragraphs
>And periods illustrate the page
>Of this dull book of life. See: he revives;
>Just one more glance. (*Turns his face over the edge*)
>Look down – thou seest those pointed rocks?
>Right down among the shadows, and near by
>A skeleton? Pleasant remembrancer;
>Well, think now of thy journey through the air –
>Then what a smash these cracking bones and thews –
>This quivering flesh – will make on yon hard bed;
>All to wind up in Hell.

GRIPOS: My God! my God!! my God!!!

VAMPRIES: Ha, ha, ha! (*Swinging him to and fro over the abyss*)
>Thy prayers are profanation. Heaven is dumb.
>Go, taste of retribution.
>(*Casts him off amid shrieks of terror.*)

Unlike Credulous, Gripos does not reappear.

It seems at this stage that Bush is using Vampries as a kind of Christian superman or prophet. He arrogates to himself the attributes of God, judgment and the power of retribution. I do well to be angry, he seems to say, as he views his fellow man.

It is in the city of Santiago where, under Vampries' control, events reach their hideous climax. There is little forewarning of the tragedy. The actual fire in the church was an unfortunate accident; but in the play it is the result of an evil scheme. According to the plot, the elders of the church are divided on the question of materialism. The majority of the elders wish to do away with gaudy displays, but one elder, Urango, and a few supporters, argue in favour of such spectacles. Vampries then enters and joins the altercation; with subtle care he takes every opportunity to support Urango. On the occasion of a festival in the church, Vampries lays the ground-work for his master plan. He offers to prepare a fireworks display for the festival. Urango at first hesitates to go this far, but Vampries, likening fireworks to Pentecostal fires, persuades the simple priest:

>None doubts the fact – the essential spirit
>Of quick and active fire dwells in these fluids
>But then remember tongues of living flame
>Announced at Penticost the coming in
>Of this great dispensation! wherefore then
>This dubious dread of heaven's selected sign?

The priest gives his permission, and Vampries begins his preparations as the scene ends.

The church burns and thousands of worshippers perish. Now, one would have thought there would have been an opportunity for Vampries to declare himself, to point a moral or issue a warning, as prophets did on such occasions. But he does not. No attempt is made to justify the massacre.

Events, on the contrary, turn at this point to a small and rather pathetic incident that occurs during the fire. It has no relation to the Vampries story other than possibly echoing the theme of materialism.

It seems that at festival times many of the poor rent the special clothing required for participation in the services from a haberdasher called Sheeram the Jew. When Sheeram discovers that two ruffians who have rented his suits have no intention of returning them, he follows them, and thus they all eventually arrive at the church. Because of the crowd Sheeram is unable to get inside, but he does get as far as the doors, where he plants himself firmly. The fire breaks out, the people panic, there is a rush for the door, but Sheeram won't move. He cannot bring himself to run from the danger for fear of losing sight of his property. Eventually he is trampled to death. Some time later two men appear carrying a body:

114

1ST MAN: Some people appear to run into danger for no end in life but to make trouble. Here stood this poor creature stretching his neck into the mouth of the furnace – everybody else rushing away, down he went, everybody treading the life out of him.

2ND MAN: That's so. Is he dead? Turn his face –
Who of all else in creation?
Old Sheeram, the Jew.

Though Bush does not make it clear whether Vampries is God's agent or the Devil in disguise, there is no doubt about the feelings of the people. The play ends abruptly with a mob seeking the priest and his "familiar." They enter an inn and question the owner:

1ST MAN: Has old Nick been here?

MANY
VOICES: The priest's man who fired the church?

HOST: No such person visits my house, what think you friends, would it not be better to go home and pray for the souls of those poor creatures lying dead in the church?

1ST MAN: That's just what we're after, first settle the score with these devils about their murdered bodies, then pray for the souls, eh Mister? (*Cheers from the mob.*)

HOST: It seems very shocking – the city drowned in grief and you . . . (*Loud cries, there he goes, there he goes! Tullio boys. Exit mob.*)

The result of the chase and the fate of Vampries are not disclosed. When the noise and confusion die down, the host turns to Gorman, the reporter, the only other person who has remained, and suggests that he no longer stay at his inn as he has been seen too often in the company of Vampries. And so *Santiago* ends as it began, abruptly, inexplicably.

The play has many faults of construction and form which constantly expose the playwright's inexperience. But the work retains interest despite structural failings simply by presenting a sequence of highly imaginative scenes. It seems unlikely that an author who was capable of writing a play such as *Santiago* did not publish further. I have not, however, discovered any other publications nor found any information about the author, Thomas Bush.

Looking back over the work of the Canadian poetic dramatists we become aware of a remarkable lack of interest on the part of these writers in their own country. This seems to be a common attitude in writers in new or pioneer countries. The production of dramatic work often requires a certain atmosphere of emulation, both critical and encouraging, created by people with similar aims. In Canada, the poetic dramatists were apparently unaware that such conditions were developing and that there was a growing nationalistic outlook which would make writing on Canada welcome. They disregarded national affairs and turned their attention to what they obviously considered more important, the classic theme. A number of dramatists who did utilize the history of their own country will now be considered. The three major playwrights in this group are Charles Mair, Sarah Anne Curzon, and James Bovil Mackenzie. Two others who made a sincere attempt to write poetic plays with a distinct Canadian imprint were J. M. Harper and John Hunter-Duvar.

It might be helpful here to take a brief look at some of the actual conditions of the times. Between 1857, when Heavysege's *Saul* was published, and 1886, when Charles Mair wrote *Tecumseh*, one of the first important attempts to dramatize Canadian history, falls the achievement of Canadian Confederation. To most educated people it signalled material and cultural progress. Nationhood could mean more roads and railroads and a better climate for the growth of the arts. In fact, the promise of increased literary activity throughout the country presented itself to Canadian writers in the form of a threat. It was suggested that they publish or perish! The villain, of course, was the United States. Henry J. Morgan took occasion in 1867 to encourage Canadians in his *Bibliotheca Canadensis*:

We are just entering upon the commencement of a new, and it is sincerely to be hoped, – a bright and glorious epoch in our history – an epoch which now sees us firmly implanted on the American Continent as a vigorous and highly promising State, Federally constituted, full of brilliant hopes and fond yearnings for national greatness and renown – of important achievements to be performed – of high purposes and resolves to create for Canada an independent position, and a name which shall be symbolical of wisdom and enlightenment worthy of our British lineage and antecedents.

Now more than at any other time ought the literary life of the New Dominion develop itself unitedly. It becomes every patriotic subject who claims allegiance to this our new northern nation to extend a fostering care to the native plant, to guard it tenderly, to support and assist it by the warmest countenance and encouragement.[48]

Pleas such as this appeared in various magazines and eventually there was a return. The first notable answer in the field of drama was Charles Mair's poetic drama *Tecumseh*.

Tecumseh, a play in praise of Canadian attitudes and principles, looks back to the war of 1812. In that event the author finds ample room for the

---

[48]Henry James Morgan, *Bibliotheca Canadensis* (Ottawa, 1867), p. viii.

expression of the new spirit. When the Canadian soldiers are forming to fight the American foe, they burst into song:

> Our hearts they are one, and our hands they are free
> From clime unto clime, and from sea unto sea!
> And chaos will come to the States that annoy,
> But our Empire united what foe can destroy?
> Then away! to the front! march! comrades away!
> In the lists of each hour crowd the work of a day!
> We will follow our leader to fields far and nigh,
> And for Canada fight, and for Canada die.

The particular brand of nationalism that Mair exploits rests on two strongly felt sentiments: love for England and antipathy towards the United States. Although *Tecumseh* was the first play to express these sentiments, they were hardly a sudden revelation.[49] For some time the common prejudices for England and against the United States had generally been accepted.

The anti-American, pro-British sentiment, with its considerable influence on Canada's cultural growth, did not have an exact beginning, but once the general feeling was established contemporary magazines aided its growth. The *Anglo-American Magazine*, published in Toronto from 1852 to 1855, reflects a popular attitude. A statement in the prologue to "Sederunt 1" of "The Editor's Shanty" outlines the policy of the publication. Realizing that the educated Canadian was becoming interested in literary matters, the writer, hoping to attract readers to his magazine, turns a critical eye on the American publications. He reminds the reader that the American journals are "more abundant than profitable," and then goes on to explain his attitude in more detail:

It is with no desire to detract from their literary merits that we venture this bold assertion. The talent displayed in many of the original compositions which they contain, is unquestionable; the industry evinced in their compilation is most commendable; we have no doubt also, that much discrimination is employed in selecting such articles as are best suited to the tastes of the majority of the people among whom they circulate; but it is precisely in this particular that we deem them deficient and inapposite for the Canadian public.

It is with the hope and intention of remedying this defect that the *Anglo-American Magazine* has been commenced. By making our selections from sources seldom used by our contemporaries and by regulating the nature of the articles published in our pages, we shall endeavour to maintain in their integrity, what we believe to be, those characteristic elements of the genius of British Colonists – monarchical principles.

The editor of and the writers for the *Anglo-American* simply did not like Americans and they were mortally afraid of American politics and institutions. They were pro-British and proud of it.

The sentiments expressed in this magazine soon spread and entered deeply

[49]Pro-British spirit is found in F. A. Dixon's *Canada's Welcome*, 1879 (p. 8):
"From that great land which gave us rule and right,
Whose guiding hand we held through gloom to light,
Whose greatness, honour, friendships, fame we share,
From England, England's daughter claims our care."

into a wide portion of Canadian thought, and it is sometimes shocking to find that they still exist. Certainly no record of the thought and taste of the Canadian people would be complete if it did not take into account the extraordinary forces of attraction and repulsion at work with respect to Great Britain and the United States.

In Charles Mair's *Tecumseh* these forces are central to the action. Basically the play is concerned with the heroic attempts of the brave Tecumseh, leader of the Indian tribes, to check the advance of the evil Americans. He fights alone until in 1812 the Americans commit an act of aggression against Canada, and at this point the two forces of good come together in joint effort to crush the aggressor.

Much in the same manner as the writer in the *Anglo-American*, Mair exalted the Indian and Canadian by discrediting the American. Here is Tecumseh's appraisal of the average citizen of the United States:

> Who does not know your vaunting citizens!
> Well drilled in fraud and disciplined in crime;
> But in aught else – as honor, justice, truth –
> A rabble, and a base disordered herd.

Mair, not satisfied to refer merely to the American rabble through the eyes of Tecumseh, wrote three rude caricatures into the play. Here they discuss the value of an Indian:

TWANG.   What arthly use air they – plouterin' about their little bits o' fields wi' their little bits o' cabins, and livin' half the time on mush-rats? I say let them move out, end give reliable citizens a chance.

SLAUGH.   Wall, I reckon our Guvner's kind's about played out. They call themselves the old stock – the clean pea – the rale gentlemen o' the Revolooshun. But, gentlemen, ain't we the Revolooshun? Jest wait till the live citizens o' these United States end Territories gits a chance, end we'll show them gentry what a free people wi' our institooshuns *kin* do. There'll be no more talk o' skoolin fer Injuns, you bet! I'd give them Kernel Crunch's billet.

GERKIN.   What was thet, General?

SLAUGH.   Why, they say he killed a hull family o' red skins, and stuck 'em up as scar'-crows in his wheat field. Gentlemen, there's nothing like original idees!

TWANG.   Thet war an original idee! The Kernel orter hev tuk out a patent.

In this travesty, intended as comic relief, Mair betrayed his real feelings.

In the first three acts the action takes place in the United States. In Act IV, however, we are suddenly transported to Canada, the scene of the succeeding action. We are ushered into this land of freedom, by the way, with great dignity. It is as if Mair wished to inform us that he was now ready to deal with great and glorious matters. A chorus enters to set the scene:

> War is declared, unnatural and wild,
> By Revolution's calculating sons!
> So leave the home of mercenary minds,

And wing with me, in your uplifted thoughts,
Away to our unyielding Canada!
There to behold the Genius of our Land,
Beneath her singing pine and sugared tree
Companioned with the lion, Loyalty.

The martial air is struck, and with it the pro-British conviction. Here, for the first time, Mair discloses the secret of Canada's strength. It resides, not in any political idealism of the kind rampant in the United States, and not in mechanical know-how or industrial growth but in loyalty to England.

General Brock, who comes on the scene in the fourth act, and almost replaces Tecumseh as the hero, opens his mouth only to utter loyal sentiments. He is possibly at his best when giving a pre-battle oration.

Ye men of Canada!
Subjects with me of that Imperial Power
Whose liberties are marching round the earth:
I need not urge you now to follow me,
Though what befalls will try your stubborn faith
In the fierce fire and crucible of war.
I need not urge you, who have heard the voice
Of loyalty, and answered to its call.

Then forward for our cause and Canada!
Forward for Britain's Empire – peerless arch
Of Freedom's raising, whose majestic span
Is axis to the world! On, on, my friends!
The task our country sets must we perform –
Wring peace from war, or perish in its storm!

In a war of such magnitude there must be no half-hearted Canadians. Loyalty to Canada is demanded from all, including the newly arrived American settlers. On one occasion Brock finds it necessary to lecture a deputation of these Yankee settlers:

But think on this as well! that traitors, spies,
And aliens, who refuse to take up arms,
Forfeit their holdings, and must leave this land,
Or dangle nearer Heaven than they wish.
So to your homes, and ponder your condition.

We can note here that Mair was one of the "Canada First" group which cherished loyalty to the Federation as its aim. His chauvinistic attitude can be partially explained by the fact that he dedicated this drama to the survivors of the Canada First Association.

In this latter part of the play a little love affair is set in motion. A white man, Lefroy, a poet-artist, and now a soldier fighting with the British, has fallen in love with Iena, niece of Tecumseh. Separated earlier in the war, they both search for each other and eventually stumble into each other quite by chance. But their time together is to be short. Lefroy must follow with the troops as Tecumseh makes an advance. Iena, however, disguises herself as a brave and follows. In a furious battle she is able to save Lefroy's life by stepping in front of a bullet that was meant for him.

There is no evidence that Mair ever offered *Tecumseh* as a stage play. It is true, as Norman Shrive points out in his article "Poets and Patriotism" in *Canadian Literature* (spring, 1964), that as he wrote the play there was a "growing conviction that the work might be staged." His wife apparently had faith in him as a playwright, and Mair himself makes a number of references to such a possibility in his letters. But nothing came of it. His interest was probably very fleeting for in his "Memoirs and Reminiscences" he makes no mention of the theatre and in his list of favourite authors Shakespeare is the only dramatist.[50]

Mair had very little opportunity to familiarize himself with contemporary drama. He was born in the little village of Lanark, situated deep in the northern timberland of Ontario. At approximately the date of his birth, 1838, Thomas Marks settled with his wife at Christie Lake, about fifteen miles away. It was not until fifty years later, however, that Marks's sons, the Marks Brothers, became nationally known as a theatrical family. As Robert Marks (the eldest boy) can be considered, in some respects, a pioneer of Canadian touring theatricals when he ventured forth in the 1880s, it is understandable that Mair in his early days was a stranger to the stage. Moving westward in the early part of his life, he continued to live at a distance from the theatre. When Robert Marks was first performing in Winnipeg (a town considered at that time, 1879, to be on the periphery of the civilized world), Mair had left Manitoba to settle yet further west in Prince Albert, Saskatchewan.

Tecumseh is technically actable, in spite of the fact that it has twenty-eight scenes, is divided into five acts, and contains a cast of thirty-odd name-characters and as many more extras. It was probably not its size which condemned it to the library shelf. The passion for gigantic literary works was an obsession of the time; Mair was merely following precedent. The chief obstacle to its production lay in its subject-matter. It was only suitable for a Canadian theatrical company, and unfortunately no manager was interested in it. As a result, *Tecumseh* has no stage history. It does, however, stand as a vigorous attempt to re-mould the form and the content of the closet poetic drama.

The next poetic dramatist to look to Canada for inspiration was Sarah Anne Curzon who was a leading feminist of her day. She was active in a number of women's literary clubs and spent a good deal of time working with the Canadian Woman's Suffrage Association for the rights of women to admission to University College, Toronto. Her interest in Canada, therefore, was somewhat coloured by an intense concern with the rights of women. It was natural, therefore, that in her search through Canadian history, she found herself fascinated by the story of Laura Secord. In the Preface to *Laura Secord: The Heroine of 1812*, she recalls how the story of this unsung heroine came to her attention:

[50]*Toronto Star Weekly*, November 14, 1925.

It was with feelings of the deepest interest that she [*sic*] read such of the contributions to the newspaper press as came in her [*sic*] way during the debate with regard to the pensions asked of Government for the surviving veterans of 1812 in 1873–4. Among these was incidentally given the story of Mrs. Secord's heroic deed in warning Fitzgibbon. Yet it could not pass without observation that, while the heroism of the men of that date was dwelt upon with warm appreciation and much urgency as to their deserts, Mrs. Secord, as being a woman, shared in nothing more tangible than an approving record. The story, to a woman's mind, was full of pathos, and, though barren of great incidents, was not without a due richness of colouring if looked at by appreciative eyes.

Mrs. Curzon also noted that her drama was written (in 1887) to "rescue from oblivion the name of a brave woman, and set it in its proper place among the heroes of Canadian history."

Mrs. Curzon was determined to dramatize the true story of Laura Secord. At the opening of the play we discover that the Americans have successfully fought their way to Queenston, Ontario, and have billeted their men in various Canadian homes, including Laura Secord's. By chance Laura hears of the plans that have been made to ambush and destroy the small force commanded by Captain Fitzgibbon at Beaver Dam. She recognizes her duty immediately. Beaver Dam is within walking distance; she will make the trip alone, warn Fitzgibbon and thus save the day for Canada! The action of the play is then concerned with her trip and its successful conclusion.

This story offers ample opportunity to point up the anti-American and pro-British theme. When Laura arrives at St. David's Mill, a stop-off on her journey to Beaver Dam, she pauses to watch a sergeant put some new recruits through their paces. The following scene takes place:

> (*The band falls in, three little fellows have fifes, two elder ones flutes, one a flageolet; the owners of the cornet, bugle and bassoon take up their instruments, and a short, stout fellow has a trombone.*)
>
> SERGEANT GEORGE: (*to band*). Now show your loyalty, "The King! God bless him."
>
> (*They play, the squad saluting.*)
>
> SERGEANT GEORGE: (*to band.*) That's very well, but mind your time.
>
> (*To the squad.*) Now you shall march to music.
>
> (*To the band.*) Boys, play "The Duke of York's March."
>
> (*To the squad.*) Squad – attention. Quick march.
>
> (*They march.*) Squad – halt.
>
> (*At a signal, the band ceases playing.*)
>
> Yes, that's the way to meet your country's foes.
>
> If you were Yankee lads you'd have to march to this.
>
> (*he takes a flageolet*). Quick – march.
>
> (*Plays Yankee Doodle with equal cleverness and spite, travestying both phrase and expression in a most ludicrous manner until the boys find it impossible to march for laughter; the Sergeant is evidently delighted with the result.*)
>
> Ho! Ho! That's how you march to "Yankee Doodle."
>
> 'Tis a fine tune! A grand, inspiring tune,
>
> Like "Polly put the Kettle on," or
>
> "Dumble-dum-deary." Can soldiers march to that?

Can they have spirit, honour, or do great deeds
With such a tune as that to fill their ears?

In *Laura Secord*, and, for that matter, the other poetic dramas based on Canadian themes, something is curiously lacking. Although the dramatist usually chose an outstanding person in Canadian history, he managed without fail to reduce that person to a caricature. The little things that make a character human, the details, the idiosyncracies of the personality, never appear. This, of course, is a common characteristic of the conventional poetic drama; the plays are idealistic, not realistic. This trait in the regular romantic dramas seems to become all the more disturbing in plays which profess to reflect contemporary matters. In *Laura Secord*, for example, there are two characters, Pete and Flos, who as Negro slaves are rare specimens on the Canadian scene. (They are also rare in Canadian drama, this being the only play to present a Negro in the period under discussion.) Their inclusion, one might think, would have had some special significance. But such is not the case. In a scene in which the American soldiers have demanded dinner, Laura turns to Flos and Pete and asks if there is enough food. Their answer reveals the conventional "blackie."

121

> FLOS.   De mistis knows it aint much, pas' noo bread
> An' two – three pies. I've sot some bacon sisslin',
> An' put some taties on when Pete done tole me.
>
> PETE.   Give 'em de cider, mistis, an' some beer,
> And let 'em drink 'em drunk till mas'r come
> An' tell me kick 'em out.
>
> FLOS.   You! – jes' hol' yer sassy tongue.

Apart from establishing their loyalty to their mistress and their dialect, which presumably catches the flavour of the Deep South, Mrs. Curzon makes no further attempt to develop Pete and Flos. They are clearly fugitives from the minstrel show. The vogue which T. D. Rice had started in the 1840s was by this time a frequent and popular attraction at the Canadian opera houses and probably Mrs. Curzon had ample opportunity to study the type. She was evidently quite satisfied to take the black-face of the music hall and insert him in her poetic drama. And it may be argued that this was the sensible thing to do; she was merely following an accepted stage practice: these characters had very little to do in the play and thus making them stereotypes simplified their portrayal. But in doing so, she side-stepped an important issue. The fact that slavery did not exist in Canada during the time of the rebellion of 1814 is ignored. An act had been passed forbidding the introduction of slaves in Upper Canada after 1793. Those people who did have slaves at this time were allowed to keep them, but any children of these slaves were to be free on reaching maturity. We can assume, therefore, that Flos and Pete were representative of the last slaves in Canada, or were, indeed, Canadian citizens. Had Mrs. Curzon been a more subtle playwright, she might have found drama in the presence of Negroes in Canada, but this did not happen. She was not to be diverted from her main purpose: the telling of a plain tale of feminine heroism.

The heroine, Laura Secord, is also never developed as a character, she stands merely as a noble example to women in dangerous times. When she has delivered the message, Fitzgibbon finds time to gather his men around and speak on her behalf:

> Men, never forget this woman's noble deed.
> Armed, and in company, inspirited
> By crash of martial music, soldiers march
> To duty; but she, alone, defenceless,
> With no support but kind humanity
> And burning patriotism, ran all our risks
> Of hurt and bloody death, to serve us men,
> Strangers to her save by quick war-time ties,
> Therefore in grateful memory and kind return,
> Ever treat women well.

122   Laura Secord as an example to be followed becomes wearisome; her constant display of heroism palls. After she has eluded a sentry and is deep in the forest, she breaks into tears, a sign of weakness that soon passes. Quickly she dries her eyes and gazing in the direction of the Heights declaims:

> And Brock! McDonnell! Dennis!
> All ye hero band, who fell on yonder Heights!
> If I should fall, give me a place among ye,
> And a name will be my children's pride,
> For all, – my all – I risk, as ye, to save
> My country.

The intense and rhetorical quality of this eloquent expression of her patriotism hardly varies and inevitably becomes tedious, especially to those who know the legend.

W. S. Wallace has made the most accurate and complete examination of Laura Secord in his paper, *The Story of Laura Secord: A Study in Historical Evidence*. After a searching investigation, he came to the conclusion that the legend had little foundation in fact. Setting forth the true facts as he found them he states:

Truth compels one to say that the story she told from memory in later years (and no doubt sincerely believed) was seriously at variance with the facts, and that she played no part in determining the issue of the battle at Beaver Dam.[51]

But he rather weakens his own contention by prefacing to this paragraph the sentence, "Of her courage and patriotism there is no question." Perhaps Dr. Wallace found that in spite of his investigations, he regretted his destruction of a charming myth. In any event, the truth of the story has nothing to do with the play. Even if Mrs. Curzon was aware of the doubts cast on Laura Secord's story, she would have been justified, in her own mind, in ignoring such details for the purpose of exploiting the romantic idea. Laura was a perfect vehicle for Mrs. Curzon's message. The theme was loyalty, and Laura was the loyal heroine; there was no need to look beneath the surface.

Laura Secord was never produced. Like *Tecumseh* it had an anti-American

[51]W. Stewart Wallace, *The Story of Laura Secord* (Toronto, 1932), p. 26.

and pro-British bias. American companies would not have welcomed such a play, the British were uninterested, and there was not at this time a Canadian company capable of translating it into stage terms. The play nonetheless reveals many features which indicate that it may well have been written with the stage in mind. There are, for example, only eight scenes requiring a change of scenery. This is not typical of the closet drama. Indeed, it offers a production more manageable than many of the plays toured by the Marks Brothers. Apart from the number of scenes there is also much more description than was normally required in a closet drama. By comparison, the opening of *Thayendanegea*, a "historico-military" drama to be considered in this section, follows the typical form of description. There is no attempt made to cramp the broad picture to the dimensions of the stage. The reader is on one occasion told that the place is "Fort Niagara – Encampment of the British Army of Investment." In the circumstances this is all that is needed and the reader's imagination is left to do the rest. Mrs.

Curzon, however, was not content with such a general setting. She took the trouble to describe the scene for action, with a good feeling for detail. The opening scene in Act III is worth noting:

The parlour, with folding doors which now stand a little apart. A sentry is visible, on the other side of them. The parlour windows are barricaded within, but are set open, and a branch of a climbing rose with flowers upon it, swings in. The sun is setting and gilds the arms that are piled in one corner of the room. A sword in its scabbard lies across the table, near which, in an arm-chair, reclines Lieutenant Fitzgibbon, a tall man of fine presence; in his right hand, which rests negligently on the back of the chair, he holds a newspaper of four pages, "The Times," from which he has been reading. Several elderly weather-beaten non-commissioned officers and privates . . . together with a few militia-men and two cadets share the society of their superior officer, and all are very much at their ease both in appointments and manner, belts and stocks are unloosed, and some of the men are smoking.

The author has made a definite attempt to describe the scene for the coming action, to note the season and to point out the time of day. The description is stage-worthy.

There are times, however, when the descriptions are not consistent with stage production; there is one scene, for example, in which "bats are on the wing, the night-hawk careens above the trees, fire-flies flit about, and the death-bird calls." At another time, when the heroine makes her initial break through the enemy lines, she approaches a cow! Of course staging a scene with a cow was quite conceivable. Animals were frequently seen on stage, the most notable being the bloodhounds in *Uncle Tom's Cabin*. Such an effect was expected to add to the entertainment value of the show. Mrs. Curzon was likely more interested in telling the story as she knew it, however, than "out-Tomming the Toms" as, according to some reports, Laura Secord managed to trick the sentry by leading a cow through the enemy lines.

Mrs. Curzon wrote one other play, *The Sweet Girl Graduate*, concerning the attempts of a young feminist to obtain a higher education in an all-male college. It was never performed, but according to the author it "appeared in *Gripsack* for 1882 and was written at the request of the editor of *Grip*, who was . . . in full sympathy with all efforts to secure the rights of women."

The two so-called minor plays of this section, *De Roberval* and *Champlain* can be considered together; both deal with the early history of the French in Canada. The subject-matter is not common in the English-speaking drama. The only other poetic drama to deal with the French Canadian is Campbell's *Daulac*.

De Roberval, the play that has already been noted as preceding Campbell's *Daulac* chronologically, was written by John Hunter-Duvar in 1888. It tells the story of a young Frenchman who, at the request of the King of France, sails to the shores of the New World for the purpose of establishing a New France. De Roberval is supplied with some colonists of a rather dubious nature, whom he describes to a friend:

> Among my colonists are the choicest thieves,
> Cut-throats and galley-slaves, and monstrous drabs,
> Trulls of the camp, and all the market jades
> That could be found in all the prisons of France.

The journey across the ocean takes place between acts. On reaching Quebec, De Roberval immediately turns to his colonists and outlines their duties:

> Gentlemen Colonists! Our voyage o'er
> Your duty now is quickly to get housed;
> The ladies, who have honored us and shared
> Our tiresome passage o'er the stormy sea,
> Expect that much, and long to have a home
> Where each may busy her with women's cares,
> And rear up sons to people this fair land.
> For the land, fresh from Nature, is right fair,
> Though wild, indeed, compared with pleasant France,
> Yet, soon the patient hand of industry
> Will turn the mighty woods to fertile fields.
> Set them to work.

However, only one season passes before the King abruptly recalls them. France is at war and needs the help of every Frenchman.

The main body of the play is concerned with the period in Canada and describes the hardships and problems of the colonists. The story of Margaret (niece to De Roberval) and her lover is a strange and dramatic thread in the play. Margaret, who has apparently been indiscreet, now wishes to marry her lover to conceal the guilt. De Roberval, her guardian, refuses to give her his permission, but agrees to take them both to the New World where they can begin anew. He isn't true to his word, however, and before arriving he leaves the two young people and an old lady stranded on a small island off the coast of America. The man who was detailed to take them there tells De Roberval about it after they have settled in Canada:

> The wind had fallen, and our idle sails
> Lay pinned against the mast. Some twenty hours
> We lay in a dead calm, and from aloft
> Could see the fragile, gently-nurtured dame

Dragging huge stones and staggering under faggots,
Helping the man and witch to build a hut.
Then, as a breath came round by nor'-nor'-east,
We spread our wings and left them to their fate.

On this cruel note the author concludes Margaret's story. She apparently pays for her sin by remaining a prisoner on this rocky island for the rest of her life. The play ends with De Roberval and his colonists leaving Canada, and Hunter-Duvar takes this occasion to have his principals glance at the future of this new country expressed in terms of a prophetic vision from a dying holy man. England is eventually to rule, of course, and to rule wisely. The divided parts of Canada are to become one whole and this is to be achieved "under a statesman genial, strong and sage." There is no doubt to whom Hunter-Duvar refers. The play itself is dedicated to The Right-Honourable Sir John Alexander Macdonald, G.C.B., Prime Minister of Canada.

In *De Roberval* we also have a love affair between a white man and an Indian maid. As far as I can determine, there is only one other example of such a union in Canadian poetic drama. Charles Mair had already explored this romantic idea in *Tecumseh* by bringing together that strange character Lefroy and the Indian girl, Iena. It is rather difficult to imagine the reaction of the Canadian public if a mixing of the races in such a romantic fashion had been presented on stage. Actually, however, in both cases, the love affair was highly romanticized and, it should be noted, very similar. The heroine, in each case, suffered a tragic end.

In Hunter-Duvar's play, the hero, De Roberval, falls in love with a young Indian girl named Ohnáwa. At the last minute before embarkation, the French discover that one of their members has been captured by the Indians. Ohnáwa, risking death, prepares to guide De Roberval and a band of troops to the Indian settlement where the Frenchman is being held prisoner. They have almost arrived at their destination when Ohnáwa, who has been scouting in advance discovers an ambush. She reveals her hiding place by calling out to De Roberval:

OHNÁWA:　Back! Back! retreat, brave Chieftain if you love me!
　　　　　Our outlying scouts are crouching all around;
　　　　　Come but a few steps more I could not save thee,
　　　　　But must stand by and hear thy death-song sung.
　　　　　Even now our deadliest Knife is on thy track;
　　　　　I stand between thee and the arrow's point –
　　　　　Oh!
　　　　　(*an arrow whizzes from the covert; it strikes her; she falls;
　　　　　Roberval bends over her.*)
　　　　　My chief, my warrior, e'er my lips grow cold,
　　　　　Clasp me close – closer – kiss me – for I love thee. (*Dies*).

DE ROB:　(*Rising*) Dead. She is dead. The truest loving maid.
　　　　　Here thou, Jean Bourdon, and thou Jacques Richaud,
　　　　　Ye both have wives at home in Picardy:
　　　　　Take post behind this tree, guard her corse well,
　　　　　Treat her as reverent as ye would a queen.
　　　　　Forward the rest! no quarter for them now!

Unlike most of the Canadian poetic dramatists, Hunter-Duvar pointed out in his Preface that his drama was "not written for the stage." A reading of the play supports his intentions: *De Roberval* tends to be dramatic prose rather than a poetic drama.

The other play set in a French-Canadian milieu, *Champlain*, by John Murdoch Harper, was published in 1908. In his Argument to the play Harper outlined his ponderous object:

The various scenes portray the nobility of Champlain's perseverance in presence of the meanness of spirit inherent in the recurring trading companies and their representatives, who were for ever breaking faith with their obligations, to the detriment of the pioneers. The elaboration of the contrast between the constancy of the beneficence and the inconstancy of self-seeking is the main intention of the piece.

126

This theme dominates the work and tends to blur the story. Champlain is pitted against a number of villains, and his altercation with one of them leads eventually to a trial on board ship. The scene is "the vessel's deck arranged as a tribunal, with awning overhead and a dais erected on the quarterdeck." Here the traitor, Duval, who had previously sought Champlain's life, is put on trial. The scene is given a brief dramatic moment when Duval breaks from his guard and stabs an accomplice who confessed. Before leaping from the ship in a vain attempt to escape, Duval turns to Champlain and the judges:

> Ha, ha, Champlain, you trader's gilded tag,
> With prick of knife receive my benediction,
> Should aim direct aright my strength of cast.
> (*Throwing his blood-stained dirk at Champlain's head, Duval finally leaps from the bulwarks of the ship into the river.*)

It is hardly necessary to note that he misses, is eventually caught and put into jail, where he obviously belongs. Champlain continues on to the colony, where he is plagued by hardships and constant fighting and bickering. He comments to his wife:

> This colony is but a crisis-bag,
> Trade throating trade, and creed a-cursing creed,
> With sordid passions slinking everywhere.

Discouraged by the lack of support he receives from France, Champlain eventually decides to leave to look after his own interests.

Champlain is not an outstanding example of the poetic drama, in fact it does not compare well with most of the Canadian plays considered in this book. However, Dr. O'Hagan, a distinguished man of letters in Canada at that time stated that Harper was "one of the greatest dramatists in Canada since Heavysege."[52]

We can now turn to J. B. Mackenzie's *Thayendanegea*, our last play to be considered. Unlike *Tecumseh* and *Laura Secord*, it was obviously never intended for the stage. Indeed one is inclined to wonder if, even as a closet

[52]Comment by Dr. O'Hagan in *The Canadian Men and Women of the Time*, p. 502.

drama, it was intended for the average reader. The author's inscription at the front of the book stands as a warning:

To the Reverend William Clark, M.A., LL.D., *Professor Mental and Moral Philosophy, in the University of Trinity College, Toronto*: Whose friendly encouragement – Grace accorded only after his, an expert's scrutiny of a portion of the timber being used – extended to the author whilst it was as yet reposing on the stocks, emboldens him to test the sea-worthiness of the thin-ribbed craft, now launched on the choppy billows of latter-day criticism, the drama of *Thayendanegea* is inscribed.

Thus, with deadly seriousness did J. B. Mackenzie present, in 1898, his historico-military *opus* to the Canadian reader. He obviously wrote the play about Thayendanegea (Joseph Brant) from a sense of duty. He notes in his Preface:

I formed the opinion, first, that it was the bounden duty of *someone* to enter the breach, in order to rid the situation of the singular – not to say affronting – anomaly to be traced through the circumstance of the character and actions of Tecumseh having enlisted the machinery of the drama for their attractive exposition, whilst those of the earlier companion upholder of British supremacy on the continent – one endowed with a many-sided capacity, plainly denied to the other (barely his compeer even in the way of military distinction) one who acquired equal celebrity for his bearing in the martial camp, beside the Council-fire, and in the field of diplomacy, remain unchapleted by any memorial tribute tendered him of the kind.

Unfortunately Mackenzie's abilities do not match his aspirations and Thayendanegea's memory does not gain much eminence by this dedicated work. Mackenzie endeavoured to present every detail of this Indian's life, but lacked the skill to make a living portrait of the man.

The play covers a period from 1759, the year of the British victories in the war against France, through the War of Independence, to its conclusion in 1783. The heroic record ends at this point, and obviously the play should too, but Mackenzie adds a scene which tells of possibly the greatest tragedy of Thayendanegea's life. Although it has relatively little relation to events which precede it, the scene seems acceptable in dramatic terms despite Mackenzie's apology for it. No glorious death on the battlefield for Thayendanegea, nor sunset years laden with honours, but a fading out with bitter memories of a defeat in a matter nearest his heart; the making of a worthy man of his own son. Thayendanegea's son, crazed with liquor, attacks his father one night and in the encounter is killed. The play ends with Thayendanegea cursing the evils of drink.

It should be noted that in this historical drama, Mackenzie, like Mair and Curzon, speaks as a Canadian patriot and achieves this status by discrediting the American and waving the British flag. On one occasion he has Guy Johnson, a high-ranking British officer, reprimand a group of revolutionaries:

Reckless, purblind incendiaries, take thought!
Strife-fanners, – were a rupture justified –
What genuine assurance of success,

127

In guilty call to arms to realize
Your pestilent theories, poor fools; which this
Opening of the floodgates of your turbulence;
Hasty unbottling of an ogreish force?

Has our age-owned supremacy become
So slight a thing – so shaken, tottering –
That Albion's stewards overseas could not
Cohorts enough control to crush your mad
Revolt? Your beggarly militia – they
With Britain's seasoned veterans contend!

On this chauvinistic note the section concerning plays which utilized a Canadian historical background concludes. It is not a very impressive showing and could hardly be considered as a significant variant of the poetic drama of the English-speaking world. In the total number of Canadian poetic dramas, however, this group represents an important contribution.

This survey of the poetic dramas in English-speaking Canada is not exhaustive. Now that the Dominion Archives and many libraries throughout the country have become interested in Canada's theatrical past, it is to be hoped that more plays and more information about them and their authors will be gathered enabling further and more comprehensive studies to be made.

Certain similarities can be noted in the poetic dramas discovered so far. Many of the authors employed melodramatic violence apparently in the belief that it contained the essence of drama. They were no doubt influenced by the melodramas of the time. Subtlety, irony, and other more sophisticated components are almost completely lacking. This could be attributed to the circumstances of the authors' lives in this pioneering country where the atmosphere was unfavourable to formal culture. Moreover, we must remember that puritanism laid a heavy hand on the arts, especially on the stage. It may seem strange at first, then, that these writers should have attempted playwriting at all. A partial answer seems to lie in what appears as another common trait of all the Canadian poetic dramatists. Shakespeare was their guide and Shakespeare had always been regarded as "cultural" even by the sternest Puritan. Children at school were encouraged to memorize long passages and in many a lonely shack or cabin the extent of a man's library would be the Bible and Shakespeare. The poetic dramatist therefore followed the pattern dictated by the pioneering environment. There was, apparently, no genius who could transcend these limitations, as Judge Haliburton had done in prose when he produced one of Canada's only masterpieces up to this time, *Sam Slick, the Clockmaker*, by imaginatively and realistically interpreting the local scene.

Another similarity evident among the various authors is their lack of interest in the work of the contemporary dramatists of the New Movement. Deprived of this influence, Canada's poetic drama remained static. It did not, as Ernest Reynolds has suggested of the English poetic drama, take on "a new synthesis of social expression." Indeed, the New Movement appears to have had no effect at all on the Canadian poetic dramatists.

A common misfortune of the two dozen poetic dramas covered in this section is that to our knowledge not one was given a professional production. The authors were not encouraged by theatrical people to prepare plays well suited to the stage, and although a number of the writers would no doubt have enjoyed seeing their plays come to life, they were neither actively aided nor encouraged. Circumstance and bad luck also contributed to this unfortunate lack of production. For example, Heavysege's *Saul* lost its chance with the death of Miss Cushman, and Campbell's *Mordred*, although attractive to Irving, arrived after that actor had already accepted another play on the same subject. Mainly, however, the failure to bridge the gap between the closet and the stage was caused by the lack of an interchange of ideas and information between the theatrical world and the writers. The poetic drama in England suffered from the same problem and had the same meagre stage history. Indeed, if it had not been for the efforts of such stage managers as Macready and Irving it is possible that the English poetic dramas would have remained on the shelf as did the Canadian poetic dramas.

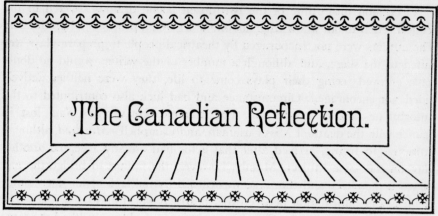

The Canadian Reflection.

130   The plays to be discussed in this chapter are only recently discovered and have been brought together here for the first time. It is hoped that more of them will eventually be found and thus enable future generations of scholars to extend these tentative beginnings and examine the individual plays from a broader perspective. At present it is necessary to consider them individually for there is no single aim which unites them. The few plays which have been discovered to date are obviously not from a group of playwrights with a common purpose, but from individuals with particular concerns. On the whole, however, we can discern a number of common characteristics. These playwrights were not concerned with the literary or poetic drama, nor is there any evidence to indicate that they were influenced by the realistic plays of the New Movement. Although the dramatists have chosen to locate the action in Canada they are, without exception, incapable of creating a distinctly Canadian impression. There is a lack of what is sometimes called "reportage," that quality in writing which induces character definition and attention to realistic detail in the matters of locale and atmosphere. Realism was not the primary aim of these dramatists. Regardless of their original intentions, their plays descend into melodrama, farce, or musical comedy. The *dramatis personae* are inevitably conventional types: villains and heroes substitute for authentic characters.

    The dramas related to specific localities have been grouped together under the title of Regional Plays. A few others, generally national in viewpoint and concerned with contemporary politics, have been placed under Political Reflections. W. A. Tremayne's work is treated separately.

REGIONAL PLAYS

The Female Consistory of Brockville by Caroli Candidus was printed in Brockville in 1856 and seems to be the first Canadian play dramatizing a local incident.[1] It appeared one year before Heavysege's *Saul*, usually singled out as the first play written in English in Canada.

[1]The fact that this play was printed in Brockville is interesting. Why the author should assume a pseudonym and then proceed to have his play printed at the local printing establishment is difficult to understand. A good deal of mystery surrounds this play.

The event was the ousting of the town's minister by pressure from a body of church women. In his Preface, significantly dedicated to the ladies of Brockville, he said, "None know better than you whether it be true in fact. None know better whether the portraits are drawn from life. None know better whether they are daubs or photographs." But the author did not proceed to give merely the alleged facts of the familiar scandal. Instead he deliberately presented the other side of the case to them and in play form showed the victimization of the innocent and undefended cleric by the machinations of some militant and presumptuous church women. The mocking title, which in affixing the adjective "female" to the name of the usually august advisory board of the church, reveals the author's bitter scorn.

The facts of the case are recorded in *The Acts and Proceedings of the Synod of the Presbyterian Church of Canada,* and at the time of this report the minister, Mr. Whyte, had already made a protest and an appeal against the accusations laid by the ladies of Brockville, which were as follows:

It was next moved by Dr. Mathieson [that] . . . inasmuch as there is sufficient evidence now before the Court, both in the general tenor of the Record, and in the manifest unsuitableness of the disposition and feelings both of Mr. Whyte and many of the members of the congregation of Brockville towards each other, and also proving the general charge of Ministerial misconduct on the part of Mr. Whyte, and a spirit and temper unbecoming the character of a Minister of the Gospel, which if unchecked would be subversive of religion, and injurious to the interests of this Church, the Synod, in full view of the evidence confirming the general charge in the libel, find Mr. Whyte guilty of frequently acting toward his wife in a way inconsistent with the duties and happiness of those united in the marriage bond . . . and the Synod find him to be liable to such punishment as the nature of the offence and the laws of the Church demand; and further, in accordance with this finding, the Synod, with a view to mark their abhorrence of the offence charged and of which Mr. Whyte has been found guilty, dissolve the pastoral connection subsisting between Mr. Whyte and the Congregation of Brockville and declare the Church vacant, and, further, suspend Mr. Whyte from his Ministerial functions, aye, and until he give satisfactory proof of genuine repentance."[2]

It would seem clear from this that Mr. Whyte had been guilty of a serious offence and had received a just sentence. Had the play not been written, the case would have been forgotten in time, with only the church record for history. But such was not the case. *The Female Consistory of Brockville* remains to refute the findings of the Synod and stand as a proud testimonial for the minister. How well the author achieved his purpose at the time we cannot say, but at least he managed to keep the scandal alive by trying to even accounts.

The play is not written in a realistic fashion. It is not a social drama, as we understand it, in which the serious purpose is achieved in a serious mood, and the story unfolded in an atmosphere of naturalness. The style here is

---

[2]*The Acts and Proceedings of the Synod of the Presbyterian Church of Canada in Connection with the Church of Scotland,* Session XXVII, Diet VI, Montreal, 1855, pp. 20–21.

more typical of an early nineteenth-century farce: the setting is insignificant, the language is stilted and the characters are stock types with fictitious names such as Mrs. Noheart and Miss Prim Proboscis.

The plot focusses on four characters: the elderly Mulish, his daughter, Lady Mulish, her friend Lady Dowager Mooress and the minister. The two ladies are the aggressors and lead a group of women who would like to prove their equality, if not superiority, to men. Old Mulish defends the male position as well as the minister, who, although under attack, never appears on stage to speak for himself.

As far as the ladies are concerned, the minister is an irritating man with an insufferable attitude toward women. They would like the power to decide for themselves who will run their church and, more particularly, in what manner. The unco-operative cleric must be removed, and the obvious and easy way to do this, considering the precarious nature of a churchman's position, is to start a slander campaign against him. Malicious gossip quickly produces the desired effect and he is ostracized by most of the good people of the town for being a cruel wife-beater and a very unchristian man. However, the proud minister refuses to leave town as expected. The ladies therefore take a more decisive step and prepare evidence against him so as to bring him to trial and have him ordered out of town. They are aware, as is the reader, that since the minister is innocent, their evidence will have to be gathered by dishonest means. Mrs. Mulish calls in her friend Miss Prim Proboscis, and together they decide on the most plausible scheme. Miss Proboscis must persuade any maids ever employed by the minister to give evidence that would prove their allegations. The plan is simple, but the corrupting of the maids proves difficult, as the following scene indicates:

PRIM PROB: You saw a very strange scene in the minister's house once, Marjory?

MARJORY: I did.

PRIM PROB: What was that, Marjory?

MARJORY: I saw the minister lying sick on the floor of a bedroom in great agony, with a pillow under his head, when in slipped Madame Noheart, [the minister's wife,] and kicked the pillow away.

PRIM PROB: Hush! Hush! Marjory! You must not speak of that. Have you seen nothing else?

MARJORY: . . . I have seen Madame Noheart bathe her face with opium liniment and wrap it up in a napkin and tell me to say it was caused by the minister striking her.

PRIM PROB: . . . Oh Marjory! Marjory! You must not speak of these things.

Eventually Miss Proboscis is able to extract a promise from the various maids that they will memorize certain statements and repeat them faithfully as witnesses. The necessary preparations completed, the ladies set a date for the trial. This unusual step, perhaps called for by the narrative to show the determination of the women, would surprise any lawyer.

The ladies' quarry never appears on the stage. Because his actions are only reported our picture of him is hazy. This method has a dual purpose for the author. He is able to concentrate our attention on the cruelty and maliciousness of the females, while the minister is raised above the sordid scene and presented as the innocent victim. The character Mulish speaks for the minister, and of course the author. After the trial, which thoroughly condemns the minister, Mulish speaks directly to the audience:

OLD MUL: Oh! What a trial! Trial did I say? It is a sham. The greatest sham that e'er was played before the face of man – a farce, a solemn farce, – a mockery of justice; a foul conspiracy to blast the name and reputation of an upright man; an envious machination of the Presters to pull him down and cast him to the dust, because he is a brighter and a better man than they. Oh! It is the story of Joseph and his brethren enacted once again.

Lady Mulish then enters and Mulish levels an accusation at her which is certainly intended by the author for all the ladies involved:

OLD MUL: I'm satisfied that you have done what never can be undone; – what may cost you many a sigh and many a pang. Ay, and alas! your children too! Yes them! For this goes deeper than you think. You've struck the sceptre – the parental sceptre – from your own frail grasp, and broke it in your rage, when you struck him who bore the moral rule. You've satisfied your rage – but at a cost for which you should not have bought the world, had it been offered you at such a price.

Lady Mulish is unimpressed with his lecture, and replies abruptly:

LADY M: Stop, father, stop – you over-rate the cost. One minister is sacrificed – that's all.

This unwarranted female attack on "him who bore the moral rule" is more than a cruel assault on human dignity and privacy, it is a threat to male authority. Mulish claims it was his daughter's insistence on foolishly believing that she was man's equal which originally prompted her attempt to destroy the position and dominance of the minister. However she defends herself by saying:

LADY M: The Rights of Women are now beginning to be better understood, and to bring to light her long-buried capabilities. It has lately been discovered that woman is the equal of man: equal in counsel – equal in debate – equal in judgment – equal in eloquence – equal in courage – equal in every quality, but that of brute force, – a poor superiority, enjoyed by them in common with the beasts of burden.

Considering that the year was 1856, this may be one of the earliest statements of the suffragette's point of view in Canada. It was not until 1880 that Canadian women became actively engaged in securing their rights as citizens and even then, when the excitement was presumably at its height, the force of the movement was slight. It failed to generate much interest, and the suffrage leaders believed this was caused not by a reaction from the men but by a lack of interest on the part of the women. Candidus ridiculed the views of feminine equality, but his concern indicates that the women of Brockville were anything but apathetic.

At the end of the play a unique *tableau* is presented. The female consistory is gathered at a meeting into which the corpse of the minister is carried. It lies there for a length of time and then suddenly starts to rise.

There is something farcical about the body coming back to life to terrify its former tormentors, but the end is not comic. As the confusion dies, the consistory shout, "At last he speaks!" But pathetically the corpse stands mute, unable to defend, accuse, or even explain. And finally we assume the curtain drops. Perhaps the play was intended as the defence of the corpse, or the destroyed minister. Or was this the case of a proud man being judged by those he considered inferior and not deigning to speak? Was there a biblical reference to "he opened not his mouth"? Were perhaps some of the accusations true but personal and undefendable? A number of possible meanings can be read into this little *tableau*.

The play, its *raison d'être*, its relation to the truth, and its effect on the ladies of Brockville to whom it was dedicated, all form a fascinating mystery. The quality of the writing, the phraseology, and the strong prejudice in favour of the minister, suggest that the anonymous author, "Caroli Candidus, Esq., A Citizen of Canada," might have been the angered minister himself. Some elementary detective work shows that the *nom de plume*, Caroli Candidus, which appears casually to be "frank singing" is on closer examination a cleverly constructed cryptonym. Candidus is the Latin word for "white" and also implies, in its archaic meaning, "clear and pure," a thoroughly satisfactory and appropriate pseudonym for Mr. Whyte. With regard to Caroli, we discover that Carolus in mediaeval latin was synonymous for Charles and that Carol II of Rumania was often referred to as Charles II. The reason for the form Caroli is still unsolved. It will be intriguing to try to decipher this whole riddle one day. At least Mr. Whyte has left us certain of one thing; he was no ordinary man.

Another play which reflects a rural area in Southern Ontario is *The Shrievalty of Lynden*, by J. W. Keating. It was printed on March 11, 1889, in St. Catharines, Ontario, in the County of Lincoln. To date it has been impossible to trace the local incident, if indeed there was one, that prompted this little one-act drama. The fact that it was dedicated to the Crown Attorney for the County of Lincoln, John McKeown, Esq., however, suggests that the play may have been concerned with the duties of the Sheriff of this county. This suspicion is strengthened when we note that the Crown Attorney in the play is called John McMahan. There are indications also that the character of Frederick Dickson, the newly appointed Sheriff of Lynden, was possibly drawn from the actual Sheriff of Lincoln County at that time, T. C. Dawson, and that T. B. Clench, his Deputy Sheriff, may have inspired the character of Walter G. Tench.

The play opens in the Sheriff's office in the town of Arcona where Tench and an associate, called Green, await the arrival of the new Sheriff, whom they expect to be a highly qualified person. When Dickson finally arrives, they are not disappointed. In appearance he leaves nothing to be desired, and when he turns his attention to some routine assignments, his skill is immediately evident. Green and Tench leave, assured that their association with the new Sheriff will be pleasant and secure. Left on his own, Dickson confesses to the audience that he really knows very little about his job, and that although he is sure he will soon learn to master his routine duties, he is

afraid he is too soft-hearted and overly sentimental. He would find it
extremely difficult to commit a man to prison, for as he says:

> Oh! The stern duties of a Sheriff thus to part,
> A man from wife and child, so near his heart.

Several weeks pass, and Dickson does nothing to jeopardize his position, in
fact he enhances his reputation by the particular care he spends on his dress.
The Crown Attorney remarks:

> Thou hast done nobly well my friend and much
> Capacity shewn, in thy acquirements of
> The laws and usage pertaining to thine office.
> Your princely bearing whilst in open court,
> Hath not been by me unnoticed, nor hath
> Thy courtly gear in vain sought admiration.
> Clad as thou wert, in regulation coat,
> And on thy head cocked hat with stately plume,
> And at thy side a courtly sword didst wear,
> Which made thee the observed of all observors.
> In appearance thou well hast made thy mark, . . .

Not only is a Gilbert and Sullivan flavour occasionally noticeable, but the
character of the Sheriff bears a resemblance to that of Koko in *The Mikado*.
Like him, the Sheriff finds the task of imposing prison sentences unpleasant
and the prospect of killing a man horrifying. Yet unlike Koko he never tries
to evade his duties as chief executioner, when this position becomes his after
the unexpected resignation of the hangman. Later, when a murderer by the
name of Frank Dardanus is brought before him, he does not question the
fact that the convicted man must die, although he does rebel against the
means of death. His protests are in vain, however, and Dardanus is taken
to the scaffold where the Sheriff prepares to carry out his disagreeable chore.
Fortunately at the last moment Dardanus, who is actually innocent, is par-
doned, and with this solution, the play ends.

The *Shrievalty of Lynden*, like *The Female Consistory*, presented a
serious question in a light, farcical fashion. The question of whether the play
was based on an actual incident is not important as it seems probable that
the author was trying to draw the Crown Attorney's attention to the fact
that hanging was a brutal act and should not be practised in a civilized
community. Keating was not questioning the death penalty, but he was
obviously suggesting that the people in authority should make some effort
to examine alternatives to hanging. His suggestion is made by the Sheriff:

> Oh! Why do they not invent some newer method
> To put to death, those malefactors, in manner
> Less repugnant to a tender hearted man?
> For instance, a battery charged with electricity
> Of such force and power, that when applied,
> Would instantaneously kill the victim.

This appeal in *The Shrievalty of Lynden* preceded by a year the first legal
execution of a criminal by electrocution. In 1890 at Auburn Prison, New

York, William Kemmler, a convicted murderer, became the first human being to be legally executed by electricity.

Keating, in common with the other prose dramatists to be considered in this chapter, was interested in a certain aspect of the society in which he lived, and his interest was deep enough to prompt him to write a play about it. Unfortunately, although he started with a serious issue, he soon reduced his potential drama to a shallow farce. This tendency to draw away from reality, common in nineteenth-century drama, was predominant in Canada. *The Female Consistory* and *The Shrievalty of Lynden*, for example, focus on actual situations and raise specific issues, but remain quite lifeless. The characters are apparently copies of real people who lived in a particular part of the country and were involved in certain events; but as the plays evolve, we find only cardboard characters and contrived plots bearing little resemblance to the Canadian pioneering atmosphere of the time. The dramas are generally well removed from the emotional climate in which they were written.

It is well to consider this when making conjectures about plays which have survived only as titles. *Louis Riel, or The Northwest Rebellion* is one example. It was presumably played at the Grand Opera House, London, Ontario, in 1886. No more information about the production has been discovered. How pleasant to think that this play, which lies waiting to be found, could reveal an exciting new insight into that period of Canadian history. That it may very well have dealt with highly controversial matters of the time, is evident when we consider that Riel was captured, tried for treason, and hanged in 1885, with repercussions verging on civil war. And yet, on the basis of similar plays that have come to our attention, we are led to suspect that the Riel affair, in its dramatized form, was no more than a farce or musical comedy. We can note, for example, that one play about the Riel rebellion which still exists is described as "A Musical and Dramatic Burlesque in Two Acts." This play, *The 90th on Active Service or Campaigning in the North West* was written by George Broughall and was performed at the Princess Opera House, Winnipeg, on July 19 and 30, 1885.

In the Preface the author explains that it was conceived, written and rehearsed at Fort Pitt, one of the longer stops on the way home from the successful campaign in Saskatchewan. It generally follows the pattern of a typical army show. Comical scenes of inspections and mess parades, etc. are tied together by songs in which all the cast joins in. The Gilbert and Sullivan ditties were given original words to suit the occasion. *The 90th on Active Service* is a light and frivolous romp and would deserve no further examination if it were not for the fact that in this burlesque we discover that many of the comic lines are spoken by or refer to characters who would have been well known in Winnipeg at the time. George Ham is singled out, for example, and a great deal of fun is poked at a war correspondent called J. Michael Caesar O'Flynn. He represented, as he says:

. . . the organ, happily called after that bright orb of day, which rolls like a fiery chariot, across the broad blue ethereal space above; and which also is thrown at the doors of thousands of eager subscribers, for five cents a copy, strictly in advance.

At another time he informs his audience that he must rush to the wire and, "make the columns of the great luminary in the East ring with news and sensation." There is little doubt that we are being offered a crude caricature of a correspondent from the *Globe*, of Toronto. The man's style of writing is also ridiculed. Description is apparently his *forte*:

To paint the beauties of nature, the babbling brooks, the rugged cliffs, and the stormy meteorological reports of the weather, in that soft mellifluous language which falls gently on the ear, leaving a tender touch of romance behind, and the charm of the bygone scenes, is a portion of the business of a perfect correspondent.

In listing the qualifications necessary for a war correspondent O'Flynn stresses the fact that the job ". . . requires a man of varied experience, a refined culture, a $14 a term education, and a poetical instinct."

J. Michael Caesar O'Flynn was, of course, an easterner, and on this count alone would have been subject for laughter. There may also have been a character of this description active at the time in Winnipeg. But it seems to me that many of the citizens who witnessed this play, could not have failed to see a resemblance between O'Flynn and Charles Mair. Mair's exciting experiences in and around Winnipeg during the Red River uprising of 1869–70 are well documented.[3] During this time he acted as a war correspondent for the *Globe*, and was at the centre of a good deal of controversy. His name in Winnipeg was not to be forgotten for many years. As his biographer, Norman Shrive, points out: "Mair's enemies made certain that their impressions of his early conduct at Red River would never be forgotten."[4] It should also be pointed out that in 1885 Mair was with a regiment at Humboldt which was posted there for the purpose of guarding the telegraph station. It was to this station that "the reports of action had to come . . . for transmission over the wires."[5]

One other play by Broughall, *The Tearful and Tragical Tale of the Tricky Troubadour; or the Truant Tricked*, was written in 1886. There is no sign of Mair among the characters.

For Canada and the Empire, by Hal Newton Carlyle, was produced at the Grand Opera House, London, in March 1900. Although referred to as a war drama and given publicity as a play concerned with the dramatic significance of the Boer War, the actual performance, according to the reviewer for the *Free Press*, was essentially a variety show:

Mr. J. McDonald sang "Soldiers of the Queen," as one of the "Christmas diversions," and was encored. Mrs. Jas. McCormich sang "What We Have We'll Hold," in a spirited manner, being the recipient of an elegant bunch of flowers handed over the footlights.

[3] Norman Shrive, *Charles Mair: Literary Nationalist* (Toronto, 1965). See chaps. four and five.
[4] *Ibid.*, p. 74.   [5] *Ibid.*, pp. 175–6.

From the advance publicity, *For Canada and the Empire* could have been imagined as an important drama examining this country's role in the Boer War. The discovery that it was no more than part of a social evening is most disappointing.

Two further frustrations may be the scripts, when found, of *The Big Boom* and *The Man from Ottawa*. *The Big Boom* was performed in Winnipeg on November 23, 1886. It was written by Charles Handscomb who was Winnipeg's chief drama critic and the self-appointed defender of public morals. The reviewer for the *Winnipeg Free Press* noted that *The Big Boom* generally resembled an "average melodrama" but suggested that Handscomb added a modern touch by placing some of the scenes in Winnipeg. The contemporary setting apparently delighted the audience and "gave the actors the opportunity of getting off local hits." A Gilbert and Sullivan influence is again noticeable. The favourite song of the evening was called "The Busted Boomer," and it was sung to a *Mikado* air. One of the verses survives:

> Oh I ne'er will forget the cry,
> Nor the deep succeeding gloom
> When A. W. Ross, the real estate boss,
> With Edmonton bust the boom.

The Man from Ottawa was written by George Summers, known on the road as "The Canadian Comedian," and was presented by him at his Mountain Theatre in Hamilton, May 24, 1911. The critic for the *Hamilton Spectator* said that the play was one that would "appeal to Canadians, owing to the fact the scenes are laid near home – the Rosedale section of Toronto being the spot in which all the mix-ups occur." It again was probably an unpretentious farce and there is not much likelihood that it contained many searching comments on that exclusive locale.

Probably one of the first English delineations of the French-Canadian character was attempted in the novel, *Border Canucks*, by George Cameron Rankin. Shortly after its publication in 1890, Rankin and his brother McKee Rankin adapted it for the stage. The play was known in Quebec as *L'Habitant* and in the English-speaking parts of Canada as *The Canuck*. The novel is still available but the script has disappeared. It is possible, however, to make a general comparison by referring to the reviews of the performances in 1897. This production was obviously not the *première*, since on April 13 a reviewer for the *Montreal Gazette* wrote: "McKee Rankin, in his palmy days made a great hit (being a Canadian himself) in the delineation of *L'Habitant*, and in the character of Jean Cadeaux scored an unqualified success." There is no record of any earlier performance, but as the novel was published in 1890, we can assume that it preceded the 1897 performance by a number of years. The reference to Rankin's palmy days would be merely an allusion to the fact that Rankin's career as an actor was passing through one of its recurring periods of depression. At this time he was playing the smaller towns in Ontario and was billed to play at Belleville on

April 22, 1897. One year before, however, he had produced his own play, *Judge Not*, in Philadelphia, with great success.

Border Canucks, the novel, is the story of an American family named the Rathbones; and it is the author's examination of this family and the part it played in society that comprises the main portion of the book. As a secondary theme Rankin introduced the French Canadian. This was done in a sub-plot in which the hero, Jack Rathbone, against his father's wishes, visits from time to time his French-Canadian friends in Quebec.

It was in his description of the French Canadian that Rankin struck out into new fields, for at that time this particular Canadian had not received very much attention in English literature. William Henry Drummond, the well-loved and in some respects the most original of all Canadian poets, did not publish *The Habitant* until 1897. Jock Laforge, the principal French Canadian in *Border Canucks*, was thus well launched before the famous Johnnie Courteau was born. Indeed, Jock Laforge was renamed Jean Baptiste Cadeaux and brought to life on the stage some years before the appearance of Drummond's famous French-Canadian character. It is quite possible that *L'Habitant*, which was so successfully produced in Montreal sometime in the early nineties and then again in 1897, may have had some influence on Drummond.

The fact that George's brother, McKee Rankin, was an actor no doubt prompted the author to make a stage version of his novel. It is also possible that McKee persuaded him to select the French Canadian as the main character. Jock had already been developed in the novel as a likeable Canuck with a peculiar dialect:

Bah gosh, de chiles comes so fass at de fust of eet, dat's fright me. Before the fuss wan wus got toots on hees head, ah! hoorah bye! annuddair was on de cradle.[6]

The problem was to revise the plot in order to make the French Canadian predominant. The novel is not melodramatic and the sub-plot involving the French Canadian is incidental. Here again, it is logical to suppose that McKee influenced his brother. Rankin, the actor-manager, would have wanted a play which could promise commercial success and lend itself to his particular skills. The play apparently answered these two requirements. That it achieved these ends by cleaving strictly to a melodramatic line is suggested by the critic for the *Montreal Gazette*:

Kearney . . . looked and played the part to perfection, and in the scene where his erring daughter returns to her home and begs for forgiveness, he was applauded to the echo. Mr. Kearney appears to have a proper conception of the part and at once sinks his personality into the delineation of the French habitant. Mr. Kearney was ably assisted by Miss Beryle Hope, who took the part of Archange, his daughter, most acceptably and won the deserved plaudits of the audience. Mr. Alexander Gaden was the villain of the piece, and in the

[6]George Cameron Rankin, *Border Canucks, Our Friendly Relations* (Detroit, 1890), p. 12.

scene where he attempted to burglarize the premises of Jean Baptiste, was very effective.

Though the Rankins, possibly for commercial reasons, chose to offer a strict melodrama, the portraits of the people were evidently quite accurate. As the reviewer in *La Minerve* for April 15 remarked: "L'Habitant est une peinture très réussie des mœurs villageoise."

Minnie Trail; or, the Woman of Wentworth, written by W. P. Wood of Ancaster and printed at the *Evening Times* office, Hamilton, Ontario, in 1871, is a play which has a local setting. But the melodramatic structure of the plot completely removes it from reality. If it did retell a story that might have been familiar to the residents of Ancaster, the details have now long since disappeared.

Part of the action takes place in the barroom of the Royal Hotel which could have been in Ancaster, where the author lived, or seven miles east in Hamilton where the book was published, or in the County of Wentworth (southern Ontario at the head of the Lake) where presumably the heroine lived. The author no doubt had a reason for choosing this specific locality for his play, but the reason for doing so is never revealed.

The story is not unique; it is broad enough to allow for a number of melodramatic scenes, but not concise enough for character development. However, the scenes are stage-worthy and I wouldn't be at all surprised to find, one day, evidence that it had been produced.[7] Four leading characters command the stage: Mungo Trail, Ned Grailing, Mugley, and Minnie Trail. When the curtain rises we are led to believe that Mungo, Minnie's husband, has offended Ned Grailing, an acquaintance, sometime in the past. The action is controlled, for the most part, by Grailing's scheme to get revenge. Briefly, the plot is as follows. By sending letters to Mungo which appear obviously to be from women, he has managed to convince Minnie that her husband is unfaithful. At the appropriate moment, he suggests to Minnie that she leave Mungo, and when she does, to take with her the chest of money which he has secretly hidden in the house. In true melodramatic fashion, Minnie agrees. As far as the reader can determine, Mrs. Trail absconds successfully with the money, but a young man, Brunow, who unwittingly helps her remove the money, is apprehended. This complication of the plot allows Wood to create a prison scene in which to prove that love can truly conquer all. It is quite amusing, and so I have taken the liberty of reproducing a large part of the scene. Brunow's lover, Jeanie, arrives playing a guitar:

JEANIE: This is the prison where they keep poor Brunow. Could I only see him once again, or cheer him in his lonely cell with one sweet song, once music to my ear – but now it pains my heart – yet if it could cheer his lonely hours, or tell him that his Jeanie is here, those fingers would flit over the chords like madness; my poor heart would leap for joy to-night.

(She plays "Wandering Willie" and sings. Brunow sees her from the win-

---

[7]The reader may recall the Thespian Society that was active in Ancaster when Sol Smith arrived in 1828–29. It is possible that a similar club may have existed to serve Mr. Wood.

dow, but she has not noticed him. She is close to the gate, drops the guitar in despair, lays her left hand on the door, her right on her brow. She stands in a pleading position. Brunow waves a white handkerchief, which attracts her attention; he drops it at her feet.)

JEANIE: Thank heaven! that is the one I gave him last in Wentworth. This was my pledge to Brunow. Now will he soon be free as I; no cage can keep thee longer from my heart. I will ask him when will be the best time to venture such a risk.

(She pulls out some paper – writes – ties it up, putting a pencil inside: attaches it to the end of a long rod, and hands it up to Brunow. Brunow writes and drops a letter at her feet.)

(JEANIE: *reads*) Dearest Jeanie, midnight is the hour when all are still. Let me have those files at ten, and God help us both, my own Jeanie.

(JEANIE, *aside*) Yes, God will help us when we help ourselves. The irons once filed from his wrists, his manly arm will soon displace those bars. I will then raise him the rope which will bring him to my heart once more, if free from guilt and shame.[8]

Brunow proves to be free from guilt, and this little sub-plot has a happy ending. The major plot is stark tragedy. Minnie, prompted by a guilty conscience, returns home. But her wilful deed has caused irreparable damage to her physical being. When we see her again she is described as "an old care-worn looking woman." Her worst fears have been realized: "Ah, cruel world, that parts me from my children! Yet I am not fit to be their mother now." Her self-pity grows and finally she stabs herself. But it is a theatrical "stab" which allows her time to die. Her dying, in fact, takes the entire length of the last scene during which Wood is frantically trying to resolve his play. We now find Grailing is the apprehended villain, and it appears that he has been living with Minnie. He has thoroughly disgraced Mungo as he had set out to do. Mungo, now a veritable Othello, turns on Grailing and stabs him. Minnie, who has raised herself during the struggle, mistakenly believes that it is Mungo who has been stabbed, and is therefore given the opportunity to cry out a line that has an echo in all the favourite melodramas of the time: "Ah! Grailing, you have killed my poor Mungo. He will never know that his poor Minnie loved him to the last." And at this point she dies. Mungo alone lives, but as he says: "Are not my children motherless? My home desolate? And I – Oh, God." Just what this last exhortation implies is left to the readers' imagination because on this line the curtain falls.

Some years later, in 1895, the Hamilton area served as the setting for another entertainment. This was a comic opera entitled *Ptarmigan* which was dedicated to the Canadian Club of Hamilton and was written by Jean Newton McIlwraith with music composed by John Edmund Paul Aldous, B.A. It deals with the problem of emigration and is probably the first original comic opera in this country to comment on the prevailing tendency among Canadians to abandon their own country in favour of the United States. The subject receives light treatment in true comic opera fashion, but the serious undertone is there.

[8]W. P. Wood, *Minnie Trail; or, The Woman of Wentworth* (Hamilton, 1871), Act II.

141

Ptarmigan, the leading character, is the culprit, but as it is pointed out in the descriptions in the cast list, he is an "Unconscious Villain." The reason why he is listed as a villain is not explained until the end of the first act. When the opera begins, it appears that Ptarmigan has just returned from a trip and has joyfully joined a group of typically wholesome and healthy Canadians at a winter carnival. It isn't long before he is identified by two French Canadians. They are described in the cast list as Al. Louette and Corbeau, "French Canadians in love with British Rule." We would assume today that this was a comic or satirical description, but there is nothing in the play to indicate this. Are the Frenchmen actually good Britishers? No comment on bi-culturalism or bi-lingualism clouds the issue. All in the play are good Canadians and are greatly concerned when the two French Canadians expose Ptarmigan. The other men soon realize that Ptarmigan is a villain, and for the girls who still don't understand, Robin, a muscular musician starts to explain:

> *Solo* – ROBIN
> You ask me what he's done? I'll tell his story,
>   Although the tale corrupts my wholesome tongue.
> We all knew him of old, but never more he
>   Shall be our guest, nor join our friends among.
>
> He left his father's house for sake of money –
>   Alas! His crime will turn you into Fates –
> Lower he sank, until, the trait'rous one, he
>   Signed papers to be fused into the States.[9]

At this point he breaks down and cannot go on. Dick Cissel, "Sergeant of Volunteers," continues, with appropriate choral comment from the group as they gradually become aware of the full meaning of the crime:

DICK CISSEL. Be it known that on the 29th day of February 1893, P. TARMIGAN [*sic*], a native of Ottawa, Canada, reported himself for naturalization, and declared his intentions preparatory to being admitted a Citizen of the United States.

PART CHORUS. Oh, horror without name!
    Unutterable shame!
    Our highly prized! He's naturalized
    And now must bear the blame.

DICK CISSEL. He proves, by the examination of two competent witnesses, his residence in the United States more than five years, his attachment to the principles of the Constitution of the United States, and favourable disposition to the good order and happiness of the same.

PART CHORUS. Oh hateful, perjured hand!
    With us you cannot stand.
    We'll let you know before you go
    You've got a native land.

DICK CISSEL. Thereupon, said PTARMIGAN is duly sworn in open Court, and makes oath that he will support the Constitution of the United States, and

---

[9] J. N. McIlwraith and J. E. P. Aldous, *Ptarmigan; or, A Canadian Carnival* (Hamilton, 1895), Act I.

that he does absolutely and entirely renounce and abjure all allegiance and fidelity to every foreign Prince, Potentate, State or Sovereignty whatever, and particularly to the Queen of Great Britain and Empress of India.

PART CHORUS. You've ta'en a sacred oath
    That you will not be loath
    To fight our Queen! Oh dastard! Mean!
    You're knave and coward both.

But Ptarmigan is not content to remain silent. He had reason for his move, as he says:

PTARMIGAN. See here! That's coming it rather strong. I aint no knave nor coward. How was I to know what sort of boom you were getting on over here? Before I went away these (*indicating* AL. LOUETTE and CORBEAU) were the only Canadians, now you're all "in it."

This interesting observation receives no answer. The young Canadians will not be placated, but out of deference to the ladies, they decide not to hang him. At the suggestion of one of the characters, Bob O'Link, they choose rather to confine him in the ice palace where they expect he will freeze to death and in that condition serve as "a monumental warning to youthful Canadians so long as the ice palace itself shall endure." The first act ends in a tableau: "Ptarmigan, tied to a toboggan, and the centre of fixed bayonets."

In the second act we find Ptarmigan free but disguised as a painter. The escape has been engineered by a newspaper lady called Hepatica, who is described as a "New Woman." An Indian friend of hers has kindly consented to take Ptarmigan's position in the ice palace. In the role of artist, Ptarmigan has cause to speak generally about Canadian culture. At the opening of Act II we find him in discussion with Blue Belle, "A Wealthy Widow of literary tastes, in love with Browning." They are looking at some paintings:

PTARMIGAN. . . . Are these all Canadian artists?
BLUE BELLE. Every one! We wouldn't give space on our walls to any man who was not a Canadian.
PTARMIGAN. Wonderful! Wonderful! And are you so far advanced in the other arts? Excuse my ignorance. I've been abroad, you know, and find things greatly changed on my return.
BLUE BELLE. No doubt. Canada is now synonymous with culture. BEETHOVEN will soon be studied in all our kindergartens and BROWNING used as a first reader. . . .

She then sings for him, in the way of demonstrating the singular development of Canadian musicology.

The opera, of course, must have a happy ending. Ptarmigan is recognized and captured again, but Hepatica steps forward and offers the solution:

HEPATICA. Is it possible to conceive of any one, man or woman, in full possession of his or her senses, deliberately renouncing his or her British birthright and electing to become amalgamated with the mobocracy upon our southern boundary?

143

ALL. You're right! It is not possible! He must have been crazy!

HEPATICA. Since I have demonstrated that Ptarmigan signed those fatal papers during a fit of temporary insanity, will you be satisfied if he here and now destroys them?

ALL. Why, certainly!

HEPATICA. Ptarmigan, to escape the fury of these inquisitors which your own criminal folly, in a moment of mental aberration, has drawn upon you, will you, in the presence of these witnesses, tear up your naturalization papers?

Ptarmigan happily agrees to do so, and the opera ends with the full chorus singing in praise of Victoria's reign.

We note at this point that an examination of Canadian characters yields little reward. Unlike the Americans, for example, Canadians failed to exploit their ethnic groups. Because the number of Negroes in Canada was relatively insignificant, it is possibly not fair to expect to find a Canadian minstrelsy, but it is within our rights to question why no play, even briefly, remarked on the common attitude to the Negro, when we recall that Canada was the destination of the "underground railway," and that it was in Canada that the actual Uncle Tom eventually made his home. The Métis were a particularly colourful and purely Canadian group of French-Canadian and Indian mixture, which, led by Louis Riel, made a significant mark on Canadian history. Until recently, however, they were ignored as dramatic material. The many varieties of English-speaking Canadians were never given individual attention. There were any number of Canadian types which could have been developed, but only one was significantly presented, and that was the Canuck. Here indeed was a character who could have become as familiar as the American Yankee. But the incentive was lacking. The Canadian dramatist moulded his characters to comply with the accepted conventions. The "Canadians" in Brockville, St. Catharines, Ancaster, Hamilton and Quebec became indistinguishable from the common stage characters in all the melodramas and farces of the time.

POLITICAL REFLECTIONS

It is probably safe to state that the Canadian Confederation was influenced by two broad factors: a strongly felt need for British North American unity – in effect a desire to remain loyal to England – and a basic dislike and fear of the United States of America. These two important factors received the greatest amount of comment in the journals of the day, and, it might be added, are still noticed frequently in the present social and political commentary. In the plays which reflect the political scene in the period preceding and following Confederation, we find a concern with these two themes. Loyalty to England and distrust of the United States are the guiding forces, but it will be noticed that we discover here for the first time a satirical point of view which was not reserved entirely for the Americans, as it was in the poetic drama, but directed often against individual Canadian politicians and sometimes at the government. But no licensing act loomed. The writers generally followed the style of Gilbert and Sullivan and commented on contemporary politics in a burlesque fashion. Their primary aim was to please, and although their criticism was at times severe, the plays were obviously not expected to cause any serious reaction.

The only Canadian play dealing directly with Confederation is *Dolorsolatio*. It was performed at the Theatre Royal, Montreal, on Monday, January 9, 1865. The author remains unknown, having preferred to write under the pseudonym of Sam Scribble. The play hardly warrants this precaution, which leads us to conjecture that the author was either a prominent citizen or possibly a civil servant.

The action takes place in Grandpapa Canada's house. During the course of the burlesque, his sons and daughters and a number of guests arrive. Among them are Master East, his elder son, a gentleman of French education; Master West, his younger son, an overgrown boy; Montreal, a fashionable young lady; Toronto, a young lady with a very good opinion of herself; and Ottawa, another young lady just at the point of entering into society. We soon discover that the members of this family are at odds with each other, the two most obstreperous being Master East and Master West. It seems that these two cannot discuss or argue without eventually fighting, but as they match each other in clumsiness, there is never any harm done. On the occasion of the gathering of the clan an innocent remark leads to the usual brawl and Master East receives some rather hard knocks before Canada finally intervenes. Grandpapa Canada first quite obviously consoles East, before reprimanding them both.

> My darlings, let's agree, for so we ought
> *Fighting* at any rate is not our *forte*!
> You silly boys let each concede a point: –
> [To East] What matter if your nose is out of joint.[10]

Toward the close of Scene ii, while the members of Canada's family are still bickering, a noise is heard from behind the house. Everyone knows it is the familiar sound of the warring neighbours, Mr. Abe North and Mr. Jefferson. The family are all eager to see the fight, except Canada, who has misgivings. His hesitation reflects generally the Canadian attitude.

> . . . I fear that this admission
> May pr'aps be construed into *Recognition!* –
> I'm strictly neutral! and my feelings smother!
> I hate one side! and can't a-bear the other! . . .

He is finally persuaded to go, however, and in Scene iii Canada and his family gather in the back yard to watch the fight. The scene was no doubt presented as a lesson for the Canadian audience.

> (*Great noise of fighting outside – Enter* c., *knocking down paling.* Mr. A.
> North, *and* Mr. J. South, *fighting down to front – Tableau.*)
> LONDON. Bully for you!
> QUEBEC. By Jingo! ain't this prime?

---

[10]Sam Scribble, *Dolorsolatio* (Montreal, 1865), Scene ii.

TORONTO. I'll back the old 'un –

MONTREAL. I the young 'un –

CANADA. Time!

> (*Combatants glare at each other fiercely*, R.C., *and* L.C. *– characters forming ring*, Canada C.)

CANADA. Not in my house! I won't have such marauders
Spoiling my garden, trampling on my borders!

> (*Combatants glare at each other – they appear as if to fight, but don't.*)

MR. SOUTH. I'll gouge him that's a fact!

MR. NORTH. Snakes! there's a figure!

MR. SOUTH. You tarnal Yank!

MR. NORTH. You everlasting Nigger!

> (*Same business, after which Mr. North and South skedaddle in opposite directions.*)

146

Having witnessed such a disgraceful exhibition, the children are encouraged to forget their small grievances and, as Grandpapa suggests, "stick together." But they are unable to find a way. At last an old man enters bearing some miraculous medicines. He presents them with a demijohn labelled, "Dolorsolatio," of which the sole ingredient is "Federation." Sample drinks are taken by all and the miracle happens. The children forget their differences and fondly join hands. Canada then steps down stage and addresses his audience:

> You've seen how I've been cured, – to make me stand
> Firm in my new resolve, give me *your hand*!
> I see you will – then you approve – that's certain –
> Thank you! now then, blue fire! and down the curtain![11]

It is conceivable that *Dolorsolatio* was written and presented as a piece of propaganda. The eventual discovery of the identity of Sam Scribble may throw more light on this possibility. At the present we only know that Scribble presented "Federation" as the medicine which would give Canada an immunity against the various diseases of its neighbour, the United States of America. In the same year, Scribble also wrote *Not Dead Yet; or, The Skating Carnival*, a one-act farce which did little to enhance his reputation as a dramatist.

One of the first plays to comment satirically on the Canadian political scene was *The Fair Grit, or The Advantages of Coalition*. It was written by Nicholas Flood Davin in 1876. A few details about Davin's life are known to us. He was a lawyer, journalist, and politician before coming to Canada from Ireland in 1872. After a brief period as a reporter for the *Toronto Globe*, he resigned and spent a year touring the Dominion giving lectures. Although there is no record of the route he took, we do know that he spoke at Shaftsbury Hall, Toronto, in April 1873.[12] In the early eighties, after a

---

[11]Michael Booth, in his *Hiss the Villain* (London, 1964), p. 21, points out that, "New inventions in stage fire . . . made . . . the spectres of melodrama possible, for this was an age that first saw in the theatre blue and red fire. . . ." These flashes of colour were produced by burning various chemicals: the red represented evil, the blue good. See also Bernard Shaw, *Man and Superman*, Act III, the Devil's descent into hell.

[12]This lecture was published in the same year. Nicholas Flood Davin, *British Versus American Civilization* (Toronto, 1873).

stay of some years in Toronto, he went to Regina where he established the *Leader*, which flourishes yet as the main newspaper in the capital of Saskatchewan. In 1887 he was elected Conservative member for West Assiniboia, Saskatchewan, and from that date until 1900 he sat as a Conservative in the Canadian House of Commons. He blossomed briefly as a poet in 1889 when he published *Eos, an Epic of the Dawn*, a slim volume containing a selection of his verse. It was highly praised at the time even though it is little more than a curiosity now. Although at one time Davin had every expectation of achieving greatness, by 1901 his political influence had diminished as his personal problems increased, and at 58 he committed suicide. The only reason for his action is contained in a poem written shortly before he died:

> As for me, I'm time-weary,
> I await my release.
> Give to others the struggle,
> Grant me but the peace;
> And what peace like the peace
> Which Death offers the brave?
> What rest like the rest
> Which we find in the grave?[13]

Davin nurtured a dislike of American ways most of his life, but it seems his loyalty for England came unexpectedly. As he pointed out in his work *British versus American Civilization*:

When I was in London I often criticised the Queen and our Monarchy adversely. But since I touched these shores I find a loyalty I had never suspected one of the deepest passions of my heart.

These sentiments can be found in most of his work, but are not stressed in his only known play, *The Fair Grit*. Here Davin devoted himself to an examination of Canada's two parties, the Tory, or Conservative Party, and the Grit, or Liberal Party.

The Fair Grit is a simple farce presenting the trials and tribulations of young love. The young man, George St. Clair, comes from a Tory family, while Angelina, his beloved, is the daughter of the Grit Senator, Alexander McPeterson. The course of their true love, of course, cannot run smoothly until some political adjustment is made between the two families. This occurs at the last moment when the elder St. Clair suddenly changes parties. In keeping with the farcical style, the shift in his political beliefs is not only done abruptly but with great ease. As St. Clair says, "I was born and bred a Tory, but I was really *au fond* a Grit." To which McPeterson replies, "Yes, you were always a fond Grit." Apart from the implication that there is very little to choose between the two parties, in this play on words Davin also reveals the country-yokel qualities of the Grit leader, then the Prime Minister, Alexander Mackenzie.

The Fair Grit was written during the time when Mackenzie had taken

[13]Roy St. George Stubbs, *Lawyers and Laymen of Western Canada* (Toronto, 1960), p. 21.

over the government from John A. Macdonald. The change had occurred in 1874 and for two years the Mackenzie government had been beset with unending problems. It is only natural that Davin, in the role of political satirist, and as an active Conservative, would ridicule Mackenzie (McPeterson). The satiric thrusts against the Prime Minister, however, are mainly personal. On one occasion McPeterson is giving an informal speech. Rude interruptions bring this rejoinder:

My friends, I don't think it shows much good manners on your part to call a man of my dignity "Sandie." I am a Dominion Senator, and even when I say my prayers I always ask the Lord to bless not "Sandie" but the Honourable Alexander McPeterson, Senator of the Dominion of Canada, and the Lord feels honoured by being addressed by a person of my dignity.

In this little scene Davin has caught something of the character of Mackenzie. The Grit leader held himself with great dignity but although his outward appearance was commanding, he was essentially a timid man: an intellectual without vision. His actions, possibly as a shield for his inadequacies, sometimes tended toward exaggeration, and his honest self-respect in his early struggles as a poor labourer later turned to arrogant boasting, thus providing easily caricatured qualities for the satirist. Goldwin Smith once observed – and Frank Underhill draws our attention to it in his *In Search of Canadian Liberalism*: "If his strong point as prime minister consisted in his having been a stone-mason, his weak point consisted in his being one still."[14]

Davin was irritated by Mackenzie's mannerisms, as were many people, but he was seriously disturbed by the low quality of Canadian politicians as a whole. He made no effort to hide his disgust of the government, as further examination will show. In the opening scene, George St. Clair is at a loss to understand why he should have difficulties in his love affair with Angelina. Since George has been abroad some years, a cynical friend, Ronald, attempts to advise him on recent developments and in doing so hints that all is not well in Canadian politics. Encouraged by George's questions, Ronald interprets the political scene in more detail. The basic problem for most politicians is apparently to determine the degree of honesty required by various situations. But Ronald also has specific complaints:

We have ministers talking like children about political economy – a science they never studied, and if they had, they couldn't have mastered it. We have persons who don't know the rudiments thoroughly, dogmatizing about free trade, as if any man of mark ever held that free trade was applicable to the conditions of every country. We talk about constitutionalism. But we are at present ruled by a personage responsible to no one. If taxation without representation is tyranny, still more is power without responsibility.

This criticism is blunt, but justified at least in part. The Mackenzie government, following English liberalism, stood for free trade; it was part of the platform on which they were elected. Unfortunately the time was not right for such a policy. Ironically, upon their election the country fell into a

[14]Frank H. Underhill, *In Search of Canadian Liberalism* (Toronto, 1960), p. 39.

deep depression, and this free trade Liberal government was forced to increase tariffs in order to get revenue.

Davin could find no excuse for such conduct. Mackenzie may have been
honest, but his government was proving inept, and the country was consequently suffering. In Davin's opinion, the only solution was a return to a
strong leader. It is possible to see a Conservative's description of the head
of his party, John A. Macdonald, at that time the Leader of the Opposition,
in the following oration:

George, let us here in Canada make no mistake; to have a real society, that
shall have good form, you must have a real head of society, and that head
should find his or her inspiration not in the brackish waters and moral poverty
of imitation, but at the springs and fountains of principle and nature, and in
no elevating companionship with the ideal heights of human character, round
which blow for ever more the breezes which keep the heart fresh, and the
bloom on the cheek of the soul.

149

Davin was an idealist, and as a journalist he was possibly able to maintain
his faith by using his newspaper column, as it were, as protection against
the sordid business of politics. When he became an active politician, he no
doubt found it expedient to close his eyes occasionally. But he was under no
delusion when writing *The Fair Grit*. When George, for example, exclaims
that surely Canadian party politics could not have fallen so low, he has
Ronald reply:

Yes, but we have. It is a rivalry in indecent hypocrisy in which practice and
profession are more than usually apart. They out-vie each other first in pro-
fessions of purity, and then out-do each other, as far as it is possible, in acts of
corruption. It is a buncombe struggle – a battle of quacks. Each has his sham
nostrum, his delusive specific, and the poor country is the patient whom the
betraying drug of the blatant and brawling Pharmacopola [sic] leaves worse
than he was.

This harsh criticism voiced the opinion of an intellectual minority. A similar
jaundiced view of the political affairs of the country can be found in two
discriminating journals of the time, *The Canadian Monthly* and *The Nation*.
Frank Underhill has defined the essence of their editorials:

Both these journals of the intellectuals pointed out, with a constant succession
of fresh examples from the news of the day to illustrate their point, that Canadian governments kept their followers together and themselves in office by a
continuous system of bribes to sectional, class, racial, and religious interests,
and that this was all that party policy ever meant in practice.[15]

The Fair Grit describes one aspect of the political scene of the early
seventies with boldness. Unfortunately the play, for all its political astute-
ness, fails to be theatrically effective. There is no record of a performance
and the play was apparently overlooked in the literary periodicals.

In 1874 there appeared in the *Canadian Illustrated News* a parody by
William Henry Fuller entitled "The Unspecific Scandal." It was a satire

[15]*Ibid.*, p. 68.

written at the expense of the Conservative party which, as led by John A. Macdonald, had fallen in ignominious defeat as a result of the part it had played in the Pacific Railway Scandal. The author suggested in his Preface that the affair was: "An Original, Poetical, Grittical, and likely to be Historical Extravaganza performed by Her Majesty's Servants at the Great Dominion Theatre, Ottawa."[16] Fuller was able to see the humorous side, but on the whole the scandal was considered a grave incident; the country was shocked by the disclosure of such political corruption. William Buckingham's remarks reflected the general attitude:

It was long suspected that Sir John Macdonald, either by himself or by his authorized agents, had frequently drawn upon Government contractors for election purposes. Never before, however, had it been known the extent to which such drafts were made, and never before was it thought that ministers would become so emboldened in corruption as to ask over their own signatures for such large amounts of money . . . . the almost universal feeling was that the honour of Canada was irreparably compromised.[17]

Four years later the scandal was apparently waived by the majority of Canadians, and John A. Macdonald and his Conservatives swept back into power. The incident, of course, was not forgotten. One anonymous satirist celebrated the occasion by writing the following:

> From slough of scandals as Pacific deep,
> Where he had sunk, all hoped for aye to sleep,
> See John A. rise, all oozing o'er with slime,
> Wriggle his frame and rear his head sublime.
> Reposed in filth, a season dark he lay,
> Absorbing vigour from congenial clay,
> He wakens now, his form appears once more,
> He spurns the envious mire and mounts the shore.
> From his foul frame the dripping ordures run,
> Form into pools and quicken in the sun.
> New forms arise, the creatures of his power,
> Share with their chief, the fortune of the hour.
> By dubious ways they wander, till elate,
> Like maggots swarm the carcass of the state,
> With ill got gains reward precarious toil,
> Feed while they may, and fatten on the spoil.[18]

The Macdonald party remained fair game for political satirists for many years. Only one play, however, was written and performed at their expense. Fuller apparently took his parody "The Unspecific Scandal," which was

[16]William Henry Fuller, "The Unspecific Scandal," *Canadian Illustrated News*, IX, 8 (January 3, 1874). It is noted among the dramas in Reginald Eyre Watters' *A Check List of Canadian Literature and Background Materials 1628–1950* (Toronto, 1959), as "An Original, Political, Critical and Gritical Extravaganza, performed at the great Dominion Theatre, Ottawa, in the year of grace 1873. [Anon] Ottawa, Woodburn, 1874." One may get the impression that this Extravaganza was an actual performance. But this is not so. Fuller merely means that the show he was observing and ridiculing in his verse was taking place in the Dominion's capital, Ottawa.
[17]William Buckingham, *The Honourable Alexander Mackenzie* (Toronto, 1892), p. 351.
[18]Anonymous, *Canada, a Satire*, Theatre Collection, Toronto Public Library, p. 13.

essentially a rewording of *H.M.S. Pinafore*, revised and expanded it, incorporating Sullivan's famous music, and had it produced as *H.M.S. Parliament, or The Lady Who Loved a Government Clerk.*[19]

Despite its ancestry, the play retained an originality of its own, according to a reviewer who watched the opening at the Academy of Music, Montreal, on February 16, 1880:

It has been erroneously supposed by many that the burlesque is only a plagiarism on *H.M.S. Pinafore*. It is nothing of the sort; true much of the charming music of that opera is introduced and the construction of the play is similar, but, outside of this and the fact that it and its prototype are satires on political questions of the day, there is nought in common.

Today it is almost impossible to read the play without Gilbert's lines and Sullivan's music instantly coming to mind. But in 1880 it is doubtful if many in the audience had had the opportunity of seeing *H.M.S. Pinafore*, since it was first presented in England only two years previously. The fact that *H.M.S. Parliament* attacked the chief men in the government with gay abandon obviously did much to draw attention away from comparisons with the original too. The Montreal critic felt it was a particularly Canadian triumph:

Last night's performance . . . may not ineptly be considered as marking a new departure in the theatrical world so far as Canada is concerned. Certainly the production of a play purely Canadian in its bearing, with a plot, the notion of which is supplied only from home sources, with its scenes located in this "Canada of ours," its *dramatis personae* culled from the foremost men of our country today, and portrayed in a vivid and realistic manner . . . is a novelty in Montreal.

It should be noted that *H.M.S. Parliament* followed *Dolorsolatio* and that it is the latter play which should rightfully be considered as having marked a "new departure." Fuller's musical comedy was larger and more professionally produced, but it was not the first of its kind. The two plays do, however, share the honour of having been the first political satires written, directed, and performed by Canadians. *Dolorsolatio* was produced by a local stock company and *H.M.S. Parliament* was presented by E. A. McDowell, who, as we have noted, was well known throughout Canada as a theatre manager.

The chief politicians involved in *H.M.S. Parliament* were the Prime Minister, John A. Macdonald; the Opposition Leader, Alexander Mackenzie; and Sir Samuel Tilley, the Minister of Finance. They were represented on stage by Captain Mac. A., Alexander MacDeadeye, and Sir Samuel Sillery, K.M.G. The plot concerns the love affair between Angelina, the Captain's daughter, and Sam Snifter, a government clerk. For political reasons, Captain Mac. A. has arranged a match between his daughter and Sir Sillery, but when he insists too strongly, the young couple decide to elope. They are apprehended, and it is at this point that the secret is

---

[19]As we have seen, it was given a "try-out" performance in Emerson by E. A. McDowell in 1877–78.

discovered: the young clerk is actually Sir Sillery's nephew. Proof follows in the best *Cox and Box* tradition, and so the play ends happily. The plot is incidental to Fuller's purpose: his main interest is in the individual characters and the sallies he can make at their expense.

There is no indication that Macdonald saw the production, but if he had, one wonders whether he would have enjoyed hearing his double, Captain Mac. A. sing, "Corruption is a thing I detest like anything – and it never will be charged to me." And on being questioned, "WHAT! NEVER?", reply, "Well, *very seldom*." The part played by Macdonald in the "Pacific Scandal," to which this comment obviously refers, is concealed in the vagueness of political motives. The fact remains that as leader of his party he accepted large sums of money for which he was expected to give political preference. As a result of the exposure, Macdonald not only received bitter personal criticism but was forced to retire in humiliation. Despite this some of the sting of the satire may have been removed since he was already back in power as Prime Minister.

It should be noted here that Fuller had singled out John A. Macdonald as an object for satire in 1873, two years before the scandal. Although there is no bitterness in this early piece, an attitude of amiable disrespect is clearly evident. Fuller called the poem, "Ye Ballad of Lyttel John A."

> Oh merrye it is in the free foreste
> Amonge the levés greene,
> To hunt the deer bothe easte and weste
> Wyth bowes and arrowes keene.
>
> But weary it is in the Commons house
> Where men talke loud and longe,
> And Grits abuse ye Mynisteres
> With wordés hot and stronge.
>
> Sir John he satte in ye Commons house
> All wearye and ye rout,
> And he almost wished ye Grits were in
> And ye Mynisteres were out.
>
> And he syghed and sayd, Oh, woe is me
> That ever they brought me here,
> I had rather keepe a beere saloone
> Than be a Premieere.[20]

Sir John was not the only one to be satirized in *H.M.S. Parliament*. Sir Samuel Tilley is the target when Sillery recalls his past and suggests the reason for his rise in politics. His explanation owes a great deal to Sir Joseph's Song in *Pinafore*, but it is neatly revised to fit Tilley's background. He rose from humble beginnings:

> As dispensing clerk I made such a name
> That a partner in the firm I soon became;

[20]W. H. Fuller, "Ye Ballad of Lyttel John A.," *Canadian Illustrated News*, VIII, No. 9, 135 (August, 1873).

I prescribed for my customers' little ills,
And totted up the totals of their yearly bills.
I totted up the totals in a way so free,
That now I am a minister and K.M.G.

Fuller did not dwell on Tilley's past. He was mainly interested in satirizing him as the instigator of a government project known as the National Policy, or more familiarly, as the N.P. It was on the lips of everyone, as the chorus says:

Wherever he may show,
Up, up, the prices of all things go.
Shout! for the great N.P.,
And Sir Samuel Sillery, K.M.G.

According to Donald Creighton "The National Policy was borne away towards success on the swift wheels of an accelerating prosperity."[21] By 1880, however, some observers, including Fuller, were beginning to question its advantages:

Oh, we ne'er shall have real prosperitee
Till we knock on the head the horrid N.P.,
This horrible sham, the N.P.

Fuller was obviously annoyed by the N.P. and was so hard on it and Tilley that it was noted in "Music and the Drama" in *Rose-Belford's Canadian Monthly and National Review* in April 1880 that "Sir Samuel Tilley and the N.P. are so mercilessly satirized that, notwithstanding the disclaimer of the author . . . it is hard to acquit him of the charge of partisan bias." Fuller regarded it as a creation of vested interest in no way beneficial to the average Canadian. He even felt the policy could be considered a disloyal act, for although the N.P. was passed ostensibly to better the conditions of the Canadian manufacturer and to erect an effective barrier against the economic giant to the south, it also acted as a direct rebuff to England's policy of Free Trade. To a "loyal" Canadian, any action that was not true to England was disgraceful. The terms loyal and disloyal were frequently used at this time to signify not the relationship of a Canadian to Canada but the attitude of the Canadian with respect to the Mother Country. Fuller was well aware of this important bias.

In the last scene, essentially a tableau, Fuller emphasizes the duty of the Canadian government toward England. Two ladies are brought on stage, suitably draped to represent Canada and Britannia. After some inconsequential chat they come to the point. Britannia is worried about her daughter's spending habits. She reproaches Canada for "building all those long railways" reminding her that the English coffers have a bottom. Canada's reply is that she can borrow from Cousin Jonathan. And this, of course, is the crucial point. Where do Canada's sympathies lie? Britannia raises the question:

BRIT: . . . I don't want to meddle with your domestic affairs, and, although I

21Donald Creighton, *John A. Macdonald* (Toronto, 1955), p. 275.

153

can't say I approve of your going back on your *mother's free trade* principles in the way you have done, still I don't feel called upon to interfere, but I am told you are carrying on a flirtation with your "Cousin Jonathan," and some people are even talking about an alliance between you. (Reproachfully.) Oh! Canada, *I would never have believed it of a well-conducted girl like you!*

Canada proves to be loyal and gives a straightforward answer:

CANADA: (Indignantly.) *It's a horrid story mamma*, I like "Jonathan" very much as a near neighbor and a cousin, but I should never dream of a closer connection, and I don't believe he desires it either.

The cast then joins Canada and Britannia for the conclusion.

CANADA: ... I may flirt a bit, of *course*,
    but for better or for *worse*
    I will never be untrue to *thee*.
    (Addressing "Britannia.")
ALL: No; never!
BRIT: What, never?
ALL: No; NEVER!!
    We will never be untrue to thee.
GRAND CHORUS – *Air, "Rule Britannia"*
Hail Britannia! the ruler of the sea,
Canada to Britain ever true will be.

While considering the ways in which the English stage in the seventies and eighties regained respectability, George Rowell points out in his *The Victorian Theatre* that W. S. Gilbert played a notable part by "recalling political satire to the English stage after more than a century of exile at the sentence of Robert Walpole's Licensing Act."[22] It might be added that Gilbert and his partner Sullivan played a minor but similar role in Canada. The gentle satire on English politics was ideally suited to the taste of the conservative Canadian public. It gave them the opportunity to laugh at political situations much like their own, while maintaining a comfortable detachment. The social awareness implicit in the musicals also interested a discriminating audience, while the wholesome appeal attracted theatre-goers of a wide but respectable variety. The Gilbert and Sullivan operettas, in fact, did much toward creating an audience that was ready and willing to accept the theatre as a part of their culture.

Fuller took advantage of the fact that the English satires were popular and highly respected when he chose to base his play on *H.M.S. Pinafore*. But even with this precaution, he was far from certain about the Canadian response to a satire which, although clothed in the Gilbert and Sullivan tradition, was aimed at Canadian statesmen. In the Preface to the printed version he remarked: "If any expression or allusion in this extravaganza should give reasonable cause of offence to any person, he will be sincerely sorry, and hereby apologizes for it in advance. . . ." As it happened, there was no need for him to apologize. Canadians were apparently quite happy

[22]George Rowell, *The Victorian Theatre* (London, 1956), p. 93.

to accept this light form of satire and, we might add, have continued to
appreciate the genre; the popularity of *Spring Thaw* is current evidence.
H.M.S. Parliament received only the highest praise. It is rather disappointing, in fact, to find that not one of the men concerned felt compelled to
comment. They all maintained a discreet silence, the politically correct thing
to do. There were, no doubt, some offended persons, but they either hid
their embarrassment by joining in the laughter or remained silent. One
senator, particularly, could have felt quite free to defend himself, strictly on
personal grounds. His name in the play is Ben Burr, but unfortunately his
true identity remains a mystery. Mrs. Butterbun, the purveyor of refresh-
ments for the Members of Parliament, serves to draw him out:

BURR: What about apples, today,
        Mrs. Butterbun?
        An apple sweet,
        I think 'tis meet
        That I should eat.
        That's poetry, Mrs. B. You ought to give me one for nothing for such
        an exquisite stanza.
BUTT: Certainly, Mr. Burr; here is one.
BURR: But this is rotten, Mrs. Butterbun.
BUTT: So is your poetry, Mr. Burr, so that's all right.
BURR: Are you aware, profane woman, that I am the Poet of Canada? that
        the roar of the mighty cataract, beside which I have been nurtured, finds
        an echo in my verses? Do you not know that I am to be appointed the
        Poet Laureate of the Dominion?

The victim of this caricature was wise; his silence preserved his anonymity.

Further political satires would probably have been welcomed in the
Canadian theatre, but no one accepted the challenge. Fuller himself continued to write musical comedies, but he never returned to the political field.
His next musical, *Off to Egypt or An Arab Abduction*, had no social or
political significance despite its title. News events at this time were concerned
with the fierce fighting in Egypt caused by Great Britain's attempts to
establish a protectorate over that country. Presented by Augustus Pitou, who
had been manager of the Grand Opera House a few years earlier and was
at this time an independent producer in the United States, it apparently
opened somewhere in the United States and then was taken on tour, eventually arriving in Toronto on December 22, 1884. The comedy involved a
simple musical description of a group of tourists *en route* to Egypt, using for
material the situations in which characters such as Major Babadil Binks of
the Bombay Bombadiers and Miss Zenobia Gushington found themselves.
No script exists. The story line appeared in a Toronto newspaper, the *Globe*,
on December 20, 1884.

Some of the production details are worth noting. It was mentioned in one
of the reviews, for example, that the play was mounted in a most elaborate
fashion with new scenery which was "carried in the company's own car."
As the custom of transporting a show complete with cast, costumes, and
scenery became an accepted practice only in later years, the *Off to Egypt*

production could be considered one of the first of its kind in Canada.[23] It is also interesting to note in passing that Pitou went to such lengths as to include a group of Arabs "specially imported into the play" for the purpose of abducting the tourists during an exciting climax.

Off to Egypt was a great success in Toronto. One reviewer was impressed by the fact that "the applause and encores and recalls were almost continuous." There is no further information about the play in Canada or the United States, however, and we are led to suspect that the initial enthusiasm was short-lived.

Fuller's next dramatic work appears to have been *A Barber's Scrape*. Our knowledge of this work is limited. There is only a brief statement by Henry James Morgan in his review of the arts in 1886: " 'A Barber's Scrape' is the title of a musical burlesque, from the pen of Mr. W. H. Fuller, still better known as the author of 'H.M.S. Parliament.' "[24] In *Histrionic Montreal*, Graham notes that it was presented at The Lyceum Theatre in February, 1896, under the production of Richard Goldon.

We know of only one other dramatic work by Fuller, and that was a trifling farce called *A Fair Smuggler*.[25] There is no record of a performance, but it is presumed that one could have taken place for on the front page of a surviving script is stamped "Property of N. Y. Smyth, Belasco Theatre, New York." With W. H. Fuller's signature on the last page is a statement to the effect that the play was written by him and that his address at the time was 210 West 25th St., New York. This last play, *A Fair Smuggler*, if indeed it was the last play, stands as a pathetic finale to Fuller's career as a dramatic author. It is a simple curtain-raiser, and historically has little value. In relation to the times, however, we must remember that these one-act nonentities were an important item for the theatre managers. Few evenings at the theatre were without the curtain-raiser or the comic after-piece, and the short innocuous farce which could be dashed off in a short time was in constant demand. Still, it is disappointing to think that Fuller may have ended his days as an unknown hack writer.

A glance back through this chapter reminds us once again of the gap that has existed in this country between the play and the performance. Of the various farces, melodramas, and musical comedies just considered, only a few found a place on the stage. W. H. Fuller was obviously the most successful. But his career as a playwright hardly ranks high. He may become more important, historically, as details about his life become available. As his association with E. A. McDowell implies, he did take an active interest in the theatre. But, as a rule, we are left with the isolated incident; an odd performance and the odd play appearing in different parts of the country at different times, with few if any links between them. The would-be playwrights had little knowledge of the theatre world, and the actors and managers in the professional theatre obviously had little interest in them.

---

[23]Dion Boucicault was in Toronto at approximately the same time travelling in his own "combination car." See Appendix C.

[24]Henry James Morgan, *The Dominion Annual Register and Review* (Montreal, 1886), p. 226.

[25]One script survives in the Theatre Collection, New York Public Library.

There was one playwright who might well have been considered by the Canadian touring companies. William A. Tremayne was neither interested in recapturing the glory of the Elizabethan age nor was he tempted to examine the social or political aspects of life in Canada like an Ibsen or Shaw. Tremayne wrote conventional farces and melodramas and usually had a good stock of them for sale. None of the Canadian touring companies were known to present one, and this is strange, for of all the playwrights Canada produced, Tremayne was the most popular and the most commercial.

Born in Portland, Maine, Tremayne spent most of his life in Montreal, Quebec, and it was there that he died on December 2, 1939. Although he was well known in that city during his lifetime, little information about him is available today. In 1912 he was honoured by being included in James Morgan's *The Canadian Men and Women of the Time*, where he was noted as being

The most voluminous dramatic author Canada has so far produced; is a young man of merit, with some wonderful conceptions, and is deserving of encouragement.

But in W. Stewart Wallace's latest *Dictionary of Canadian Biography*, William A. Tremayne is not mentioned – a mere fifty years later!

It is not known exactly when Tremayne turned to playwriting. We do know that as a youth he spent some time as an actor, and in that capacity reached a degree of prominence as a member of James O'Neill's touring company. No record of his experiences with this company remains, but we can assume that they made some impression on the budding young writer. James O'Neill (father of the playwright Eugene O'Neill) had a seemingly potent "fatal look" which may have had some interesting effect on the youth. Reference to O'Neill's devastating effect upon his actors is noted in a poster printed in Halifax, Nova Scotia. The theatrical publicity maintained that in the power of his gaze lay the secret of his success as an actor, and that the gaze was often fatal to the career of the recipient:

The most impressive scene in *Virginius* is in the fourth act, where Virginius claims the possession of his daughter from Appius Claudius, the tyrant. Caius Claudius, his hireling, has just made his plea for the maiden when Virginius turns toward him saying: "Look at me and I will give her to you." Caius Claudius replies, "Do I not look?" "Yes," Virginius answers, "Your eye does, but your soul does not." Saying so, O'Neill steps forward looking Caius Claudius in the eye with a look so intense, so sweeping, so penetrating, so all-absorbing, that Caius involuntarily shuts his eyes, turning away from Virginius. This is not only according to the text, but it is due to something else. It is because it is a physical impossibility for any man to face that look and not try to avert it.

Two actors last year gave up, unable to meet Mr. O'Neill's gaze every night. They said it burned into them like fire.[26]

[26]A copy of the poster is in my collection.

Perhaps Tremayne's aspirations as an actor were cut short by this fatal look. Whatever the case, he eventually left acting to write. According to Basil Donn, a close friend and associate, Tremayne began early to supplement his income as an actor by supplying the old Vitagraph Motion Picture Company with a weekly comedy script.

His first play, *Lost 24 Hours*, written in collaboration with Mr. Logan Fuller,[27] was either commissioned or selected by Robert Hilliard. It was not a brilliant piece of work, at least in the opinion of the reviewer for the *New York Dramatic Mirror*, who saw the opening night at Hoyt's Theatre on September 6, 1895:

> As an entertainment of a not very exalted order, the piece selected by Robert Hilliard for his starring tour may be pronounced a success. It is farce, pure and simple, and resembles both in plot and treatment, a dozen of farces – mostly of French origin – which have been based upon the infidelities of the husband during the absence of his wife.

The reviewer's suggestion that the play was not entirely original might very well have been right. Borrowing from the French was quite a familiar practice, and as Tremayne was bilingual he had ample opportunity to study the French farce. The critic noted also that though it was a "brightly written piece" and was found quite amusing by the audience, it made a number of suggestions which bordered on the "indecent." This may have accounted for the fact that it was never performed in Canada.

Whether the play was an artistic success or not, Tremayne had made rather an impressive beginning. *Lost 24 Hours* was probably the first play by a Canadian to be produced in New York. Furthermore, the fact that his play had been toured throughout the country by a star of some rank placed him immediately in a class by himself. No other Canadian could claim this distinction. He understood one of the basic rules in the commercial theatre: if a play was to be produced on stage it had almost invariably to be written for a star. Tremayne, either by good judgment or good fortune, managed to secure the services of stars whose abilities did not exceed the quality of his plays. His first play was presumably suited to the talent of Robert Hilliard; his second was tailored to fit Robert Mantell.

Robert Bruce Mantell was essentially a romantic actor. He may not have had O'Neill's fatal look but he was handsome and passionate, adroit with a sword, and endowed with a commanding yet mellifluous voice. He was seen at his best in such plays as *Monbars*, *The Corsican Brothers*, *The Marble Heart* and *The Lady of Lyons*,[28] and as the swashbuckling hero he no doubt often had occasion to perform in Montreal. There are no records of his early performances in this city, but on October 28, 1889, the newspapers note his production of *Monbars* at the Grand Opera House, Toronto. It was his first appearance there and he was an immense success. According to the critic of the *Empire*, "Mr. Mantell was called before the curtain upon every possible occasion, and fully deserved the honours heaped upon

[27]No relation to W. H. Fuller as far as I can ascertain.
[28]For a list of the plays with which he toured Canada, see Appendix C.

him." It seems that his interpretation of the role was "at once vigorous and powerful, as well as tender and emotional." The critic then proceeded to point out the particular scenes in which Mr. Mantell excelled: "The great scene where he cauterizes the wound inflicted by the mad dog was thrilling, but not more so than the duel in the last scene."

It is no exaggeration to say that Mantell took Canada by storm. He became the favourite in Opera Houses throughout the country, and, it should be noted, unlike the top performers of the United States and England, he played in the towns as well as the cities. As a result his name became as familiar to the average citizens as did that of the Marks Brothers. Walter McRaye recalled Mantell's days of glory with obvious nostalgia:

Only to people of that generation will he be remembered as perhaps one of the handsomest of romantic actors. Like James O'Neill he was born in Ireland, and had all the romance and fire that birth in the emerald isle gives to her sons.[29]

Tremayne surely recognized the similarity between this matinee idol and James O'Neill, with whose acting style he was very familiar.

Tremayne wrote several plays expressly for Mantell. The first was called *The Secret Warrant* and was performed at the Academy of Music, Montreal, on January 24, 1898. The play no longer exists, but a summary of the plot does. Granting that an outline rarely gives a favourable impression, it still must be admitted that it appears to have been one of the most extraordinary conglomerations of romantic nonsense ever to have graced the stage. The reviewer for the *Gazette*, on January 25, made a gallant attempt to reveal the bare outline of the plot:

The scene of the play is laid in Paris in 1720 during the licentious days of the Regency of Phillipe Duc d'Orleans. The plot turns upon the issue of a *lettre de cachet* or blank warrant, for the confinement in the Bastille of Louis de Beaumont, a captain in the King's Guard. De Beaumont has spurned the love of a gay vindictive court favourite, Gabrielle de St. Victor, a friend of the Regent. There is, of course, another motive. It seems that her brother, a profligate, Heneri de St. Victor, has challenged Louis to a duel for having defended his (the former's) promised bride from the maudlin insults of her dissipated and indifferent suitor. Henry is supposed to marry a wealthy heiress and so it is in the interest of Gabrielle and her father to protect him from possible death.

The critic at last concluded with, "Louis manages his release through influence and it ends on a note of all's well." It should be noted that he considered the play "a well rounded, consistent and logical piece of dramatic writing." The audience was evidently also very impressed. At the end of the third act their applause and calls for the author were so prolonged that "Mr. Tremayne appeared before the curtain and in a brief and courteous speech thanked his towns people for their appreciation."[30]

[29]Walter McRaye, *Town Hall Tonight!* p. 10.
[30]The play was also a great success in Winnipeg according to the critic of the *Free Press*, June 25, 1898: "This is a beautiful play full of intense human interest, permeated with striking dramatic and picturesque situations and elegant dialogue."

Within the week another play of Tremayne's was produced in Canada. It was called *The Rogue's Daughter* and was performed by a stock company in Montreal on January 31, 1898. Again, with the aid of the *Gazette* review, we notice Tremayne's reliance on the most familiar type of plot:

The Rogue's Daughter is the story of an unscrupulous father who uses the beauty and wit of his daughter to entice men into his fraudulent schemes. The daughter has been brought up to this sort of thing and uses her accomplishments well in her father's interest. It is only when she finds herself in love with one of the intended victims that she throws off her mask and refuses to do her father's bidding. It concludes in the accustomed way, and there are the usual little side issues the way of silly young lovers to make up a little comedy of fun.

These comments indicate the play was following the popular trend; it was wholesome and lighthearted.

160   *The Rogue's Daughter*, incidentally, did not make up the complete evening's entertainment, but was followed by a variety show. The vaudeville acts treated the audience to "Juno Salmo," a gentleman who could "twist himself into any odd shape," and was "entertaining, but just a trifle gruesome." There was also a soft-shoe dancer. The main performer, however, seems to have been a man by the name of Mr. C. Gaven Gilmaine, who did character impersonations of great actors. It was rather disturbing for the critic, who was unable to decide from "just what point of view to regard Mr. Gilmaine, the sublime or the ridiculous."

The habit of combining vaudeville with so-called legitimate drama was an established practice. Many theatres were finding it increasingly difficult to attract customers without the added variety show, and if the manager was unable to locate live performers, he would turn to the newer and more sensational "moving picture" machines which were known by a variety of different names: the Vitascope, Cinématographe, Kinetograph, Bioscope, and Ametomagnoscope. Toronto in 1897 already had a theatre, owned by Mr. H. H. Lamkin, which presented a double bill of vaudeville and cinematograph. And in London, Ontario, one of the theatres had introduced the vitascope as a between-the-acts attraction. It was not, therefore, a unique situation to have a variety show presented at the conclusion of *The Rogue's Daughter*; it was all a part of the evening's entertainment.

On March 5, 1900, Robert Mantell performed on the stage of the Royal Opera House, Toronto, in a new play by Tremayne called *The Dagger and the Cross*. On the same night, at the Grand Opera House, Henry Irving was starred in *Robespierre*. It was the occasion of Irving's fourth tour of the United States and Canada and, as advertised, it was supposed to be his last visit.[31] As a result these performances were considered even more of an event than was normally the case. The fact, therefore, that the Royal Opera House was "taxed to its utmost to accommodate the audience" is rather remarkable, and attests to Mantell's great popularity in this country. As the reviewer for the *Evening News* mentioned on this occasion, "Mr. Mantell

---

[31]He made one more trip in 1904. Between 1884 and 1904 he visited North America five times.

scarcely needs an introduction to Toronto playgoers; he is well and most favourably known as one of the first in the ranks of tragic artists."

That the manager anticipated losing some of Mantell's admirers to his competitor, however, is indicated in the advance publicity where it was stated that his performance would be seen at popular prices. The advertisement in the *Evening News* on March 3, 1900, went to some lengths to explain this innovation.

Mr. Mantell has been a star ever since he left Miss Fanny Davenport's company in which he was leading man. When he became a star it was not long before he was at the head of romantic actors in this country, and he has always been what is known as a "high priced" star. Mr. Small's feat in securing him as an attraction with the stipulation that the regular prices of the house shall not be increased during the engagement, is certainly very creditable to him.

Actually the retention of the regular prices probably had something to do with the fact that the house was full, indicating the shrewd management of Ambrose Small.

But *The Dagger and the Cross* also contributed to the success of this occasion. Tremayne had managed to fashion a play that was, according to the critic of the *Evening News*, "admirably adapted to Mr. Mantell's strength in dramatic scenes." As usual, the author had contrived a perfect setting for the romantic star, but beyond this there seems to have been little merit in the play.

Roubillac, a Venetian painter, grows jealous of his wife and is given some grounds for it by her confession that she is under the spell of her husband's friend, Villetto. They go to England to escape the false friend and he follows them, forcing Roubillac to play the priest and marry him to a Miss Talbot. Finally, in a quarrel with a man called Reuben Clegg, who really loves Miss Talbot, Villetto is stabbed and Clegg is condemned to death. On her dying bed, Francesca, who has guessed the secret that Roubillac stabbed Villetto, extracts a promise from him that he will confess the deed. He carries out his promise. Reuben is cleared, and Roubillac pays with his life.

Here we have a plot which probably had little but its mechanics to recommend it; a series of scenes set up to display the athletic skill and the variety of emotions of the romantic actor. And yet with this vehicle, Mantell was able to compete with the greatest actor of the time.

There is a lapse of six years before we encounter another play by Tremayne. In this case we find that he was again acting as a collaborator, but as with *Lost 24 Hours*, his name is the prominent one. In this third play, *The Triumph of Betty*, his co-writer, Irving L. Hall was unknown and has remained so.

There is no indication that it received any more than its run of performances at the Russell Theatre in Ottawa from May 2 to May 5, 1906. It was produced by Miss Adelaide Thurston, and received the attention of only one of the critics in this city. The favourable review of the *Ottawa Free Press* included some remarks on the plot which are of interest to us:

The authors have endeavoured to represent the American girl as she really is, and have brought humourous contrasts of manner simply by placing her in the midst of a rather narrow-minded circle of friends and acquaintances in a foreign country – where words and actions that are perfectly legitimate and right, are looked upon with censor [*sic*] and suspicion. How she, by sheer force of wholesome personality and downright honesty of purpose, triumphs over her enemies and brings happiness to all those who have loved and trusted her, is told in an exceedingly interesting and at the same time, humourous manner.

In this play Tremayne took his first step in the direction of the contemporary scene. There is, however, no indication here that Betty was another Daisy Miller; it is more likely that the play was a typical melodramatic comedy.

In all of Tremayne's plays to this point there are no topical references or attitudes which would single them out as the products of a Canadian pen. That he makes a rather pathetic gesture in this direction in his next play only serves to stress the difficulty he found in the task. It was as if Tremayne felt that Canadian subject-matter lacked interest and was unsuitable for a commercial play, and yet he still desired to touch on the Canadian scene. In the end he compromised. He wrote a British melodrama and allowed himself to make the odd comment on Canada. The resulting play was neither one thing nor the other: the simple inclusion of some typically Canadian names cannot make a play typically Canadian.

This of course, seems to be one of the enduring difficulties for Canadian dramatists: to write about things that are Canadian. It has been, and still is, the constant theme of critics of Canadian culture. John Coulter, for example, could very well have been commenting on Tremayne's dilemma when he wrote in the preface to his *Deirdre*:

The art of a Canadian remains with but little differentiation the art of the country of his forebears and the old world heritage of myth and legend remain his heritage to be used for suitable ends though the desk on which he writes be a Canadian desk in a Canadian house, and though his work be designated Canadian.

The Black Feather, which was produced at the Grand Opera House, Toronto, September 8, 1916, is an example of what John Coulter had in mind. In it Tremayne has actually mentioned Canada, and indeed his heroine has now become a Canadian girl, but the play as a whole retains the old-world heritage. It is essentially an English melodrama couched in farce. The critics of the time were impressed nonetheless. It was hailed as a sensational success; a play "made in Canada." Tremayne also must have felt that it was one of his better works, for in 1918 he had it published under the new title of *The Man Who Went*.

The leading role, played by a now unknown actor named Albert Brown, is a character called Dick Kent, son of a British diplomat. Throughout the play he puts on the appearance of a mere idler, but as we discover in the last act the pose is cultivated for professional reasons. Dick Kent is in love with a Canadian girl who has been brought up by her uncle, a well-meaning but not very bright official of the Foreign Office. The girl's brother, weak like his father, works in the same office. The period of action is July, 1914.

The plot becomes obvious. We are soon introduced to a German and an Austrian who are quite naturally intent on seeking valuable secrets from the Foreign Office. They almost succeed, but at the last minute, Dick, in not quite as flamboyant a fashion as Hawkshaw, reveals his true identity as a member of British Intelligence. The villains are apprehended, the family name is upheld, and the hero gets his girl.

A slight Canadian flavour is added to this conventional plot by references to various Canadian localities, Winnipeg and Edmonton, for example. On one occasion, just after the first tentative love scene between Dick and his Canadian girl, Eve, she leaves, pressing a flower into his hands. He stands looking after her in admiration, and then, lifting the flower to his lips says, "Made in Canada." This, of course, would have impressed the Canadian audience for it was a direct reference to a government-sponsored drive to make the citizens conscious of their duty to buy Canadian goods. However, these references hardly made a Canadian play. As the critic for the *Evening Telegram* put it when considering *The Black Feather* as a Canadian product, "it is like certain of our manufactures, we import the parts and merely put them together in Canada."

Throughout his life Tremayne was constantly turning out plays. *A Free Lance*, written for Mantell, had a performance in Montreal sometime in 1902, but the full record is lost. *The Light of Other Days* is noted as being one of his plays and is listed along with some others in his obituary. Henry James Morgan cites nine more plays which may have been produced, but have since vanished without a trace. They are: *A King of Tramps*, *J. Brown, M.D.*, *Les Aveugles*, *The King's Rival*, *Blind Love*, *A Happy Pair*, *The Cavaliers* (an opera), and *A Romantic in Bohemia*.[32] A number of other scripts now in my possession include: *Changing Times*, *A Cowboy's Conversion*, *Set a Thief to Catch a Thief*, *Nance*, *A Made Marriage*, *The Wife of a Diplomat*, *A Night at the Chateau*, *Her Last Chance*, *In the Days of Mazarin*, *The Ruling Passion*, and *Phra the Phoenician*.

Tremayne was one of the few practising playwrights in Canada and, as far as we can tell, one of the most successful. He perhaps owed part of his initial success to the fact that many of his earlier plays were designed for such popular actors of the times as Robert Hilliard, Robert Mantell, Miss Adelaide Thurston, and Albert Brown. By writing for a specific actor he was pursuing the tradition of the theatrical journeymen of nineteenth-century England in which writers, following the set patterns of melodrama and farce, were able to dash off pieces designed to enhance a particular actor's talent. A certain amount of prestige was gained by this association with a star and there was a fair assurance of financial reward. But as the years passed and the new forms of drama developed, Tremayne obviously found fewer actors for whom he could write. He was popular in his day, but with hindsight we can see now that even when most successful, he was lagging behind the times, as were the majority of Canadians who applauded his plays.

[32]The last play was called *A Romance in Bohemia* according to Basil Donn who retains a criticism of the play by B. K. Sandwell printed in a paper called the *Weekly Tattler*.

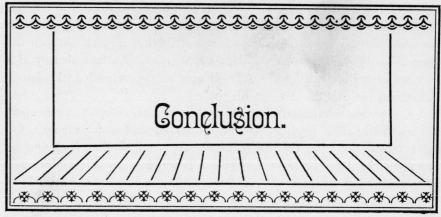

Conclusion.

164   Although a number of scholars and reviewers have searched back into Canada's theatrical past, few have been able to discover a coherent pattern on which to base their critical judgments.[1] One obvious reason for this is that there have been relatively few researchers in the field to build a background of fact.[2] There has also been the disturbing suspicion that early Canadian drama is of such low quality that it doesn't deserve serious criticism. The facts revealed in this book may indeed stand as proof to some readers that the native drama is surely barren ground and had best be forgotten. But this would be the case only for those who persist in thinking that the dramatic literature of Canada must be placed in a world perspective. The dearth of critical works, in fact, would indicate that this evaluative view has been dominant. Perhaps it is time for Canadians to admit that although criticism of early Canadian drama has value in that it can determine Canada's position in world drama, this need not be the only end. There can be little doubt that as Canadian dramatists develop and look forward to world recognition, they must compete at that artistic level. But, looking back, we may receive more value from our study by recognizing the fact that early Canadian drama is important primarily because it is a mirror of Canadian life, just as Elizabethan drama can be regarded as a mirror of that period. This has been my aim. I have sought out Canadian playwrights, critics, and actors not for the purpose of placing them at their various levels on the ladder of success, but hopefully to allow them to speak, to tell us something about themselves and their work in this early period of our country's growth.

I realize, of course, that the Canadian drama of future years may very well reflect a unique mosaic sustaining no one ethnic point of view. In such a broad context it may be impossible to single out characteristics that could be termed "Canadian" and all of our fussing about it will just be noted as a peculiar syndrome of the time. But this has so far not been the case. The

---

[1]Among those who have formulated specific points of view that place some of the details of the past in a particular perspective are Herbert Whittaker, Nathan Cohen, Michael Tait, and Mavor Moore. Some other writers are noted in the text. (See Bibliography under the section on Canadian Stage.)

[2]This situation is improving. Theses on Canadian theatre are now being encouraged in a number of Canadian universities.

35 / The remarkable Marks Brothers, with headquarters at
Christie Lake, Ontario, sent tours through Canada and the
United States in the latter part of the 19th and well into the
20th century. (See Chapter Two.)

36, 37, 38, 39 / The Marks troupe on the road (*upper left*). The
seven brothers (*lower left*). Red Cedar Villa, where the family
gathered (*upper right*). A scene from a Marks' production,
Under Two Flags (*lower right*).

40, 41, 42, 43 / Souvenirs of the Marks
Brothers: Tom Marks, two of his company
and his dog, Buster; Kitty Marks, wife of
Ernie Marks and his leading lady. A show is
coming to town! — a familiar sign on the
theatrical train. (*right*) The leading lady,
par excellence: May A. Bell, as she sometimes appeared in the opera houses across
Canada.

CANADIAN
Illustrated News

VOL. XXI.—No. 9.   MONTREAL, SATURDAY, FEBRUARY 28, 1880.   { SINGLE COPIES, TEN CENTS. } { $4 PER YEAR IN ADVANCE }

SCENES IN THE NEW POLITICAL BURLESQUE ENTITLED "H. M. S. PARLIAMENT."

44 / Scenes from *H.M.S. Parliament* by W. H. Fuller. (See pp. 151–155.) Adapted from Gilbert and Sullivan's operetta, it was first presented on the road by E. H. McDowell's company. The burlesque, which ridiculed contemporary Canadian political figures, was produced in Montreal in 1880. (*Canadian Illustrated News*)

45 / Miss Ida Van Cortland, who got her start with Mrs. Morrison at the Grand Opera House, Toronto, became a popular theatrical figure in eastern Canada. Here seen with some of her company, which was managed by her husband Albert Tavernier.

 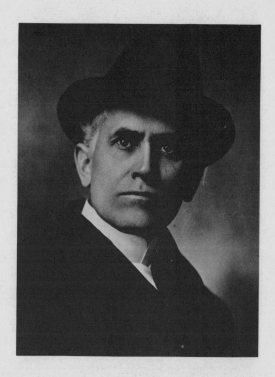

46 & 47 / Albert Tavernier in and out of
character. He attempted to improve the
artistic quality of the fare offered by many of
the touring companies.

48 / (*right*) Ida Van Cortland playing a
romantic scene with an unknown actor.

49 & 50 / Ida Van Cortland's last engagement was possibly with Stuart Robson in *The Meddler*. She is shown above seated at left with the company. (*right*) A publicity picture taken in 1899.

51 / Charles Mair (*top left*) might have written for the Marks Brothers or the Tavernier Company. Instead he wrote poetic dramas that remained on the shelf.

52 / D'Arcy McGee, our martyred politician (*top right*), was also a playwright. (See page 94.)

53 / A scene from *At the Point of the Sword*, a swashbuckling Marks Brothers production.

54 / Sarah Anne Curzon, poetic dramatist, best remembered for her patriotic play *Laura Secord: The Heroine of 1812.*

55 / Charlotte Cushman, the famous American actress who allegedly expressed a desire to play a part in *Saul*, the poetic drama by Charles Heavysege that gave him international acclaim.

56 / The Canadian poet Bliss Carman was also the author of several masques.

57 / William Wilfred Campbell, another Canadian poet who contributed to the poetic drama.

current emphasis is, in fact, on nationalism. Canadians are very busy trying to find their identity and to do this they sometimes look hopefully into the past for significant cultural phenomena. Ideally, Canadian drama should offer some rewards for this research, and I must confess that I had hoped to find some hint of the beginnings of our present drama when I began my research. But comparisons of this kind have for the most part proved useless.

The development of Canadian theatre in the period under consideration was in many respects an isolated phenomenon. This may strike the reader as strange in a country with so little past. But Canada's history is not only short, it is also disjointed. The country has passed through various phases of growth with amazing rapidity, too fast indeed to establish much in the way of traditions. The period that terminates rather neatly in 1914 witnessed a certain development in the theatre, but unfortunately it was of a type that precluded any chance of creating a particular cultural attitude, and it is chiefly for this reason that the present state of theatre in Canada has little to do with past developments. Recognizing this fact may be valuable for historians in Canadian theatre. The tendency is to be "present-minded," to look for and to designate as important those aspects of the past which seem to lead directly to some present condition. This approach is not altogether reliable. The old theatres, diligently copied from English models, have disappeared; only a few rebuilt examples linger on. The Stratford Festival Theatre and the O'Keefe Centre belong to a world that has forgotten the opera house. Our early actors, none of whom attained distinction, did not devise a style that was noticeably Canadian, certainly nothing that would compare with the Stratford Shakespearean actors who are finding their own way somewhere between the English and American acting styles. No playwright produced anything of enduring significance and most of the plays reflect a cultural climate that has ceased to exist. No national type emerged, such as the Yankee character still noticed in contemporary American plays by the earnest student. As the total picture takes shape, we become aware that the character of activities of the years 1790 to 1914 was informal, not rooted in deep cultural habits and desires, but tossed together from the ideas and physical assets of other countries. It is therefore not surprising to find practical Canadian touring groups copying the American commercial successes, and a few lonely intellectuals trying to emulate their British peers by producing poetic dramas.

The imitative characteristics predominant in this early period are now being replaced by an inner conviction that the Canadian way of life is capable of generating a viable culture of its own. In various ways we are now taking tentative steps toward self-determination. We speak on our own behalf in the political arena, we hopefully determine the means of our defence and in the cultural world we occasionally offer theatre productions that are not just typically English or American. These moves toward some sort of independence are no doubt signs of our growing maturity.

The early period of our growth in the theatre reflects our ties with England, and the proximity of the United States precluded the desire (if indeed there was any) for independence. Or perhaps independence was denied us from the beginning. Whatever the case, the conditions were not of the best for the creative writer. We find almost constantly that Canadian dramatists were incapable of attaining originality of expression or form. Too often the dramatists reached out for models from other countries without attempting to inject new life into the old forms. The poetic dramatist chose to follow the literary trend of Romantic melodrama. Some writers preferred to take Gilbert and Sullivan as their model and a number found American melodrama a useful example to follow. The Canadian playwright was truly "other directed." He sought his examples outside his own country in everything he attempted, whether it was farce, musical comedy, or poetic drama, and unfortunately he usually chose the wrong models for emulation. The actors, as well as the playwrights, were satisfied to be imitators. The English and Americans supplied the models: the Canadians accepted them. This state of affairs I believe to be one of the main factors that makes early Canadian theatre a separate entity. It precludes in fact any continuum; the early stage is a separate block and cannot be the base of the pyramid growth. The base, I hopefully submit, is being formed now.

166

In early Canadian theatre we can find little evidence of a positive approach, and there was little in the way of government aid to foster such an approach. Canadians thus capitulated to the foreign commercial interests such as touring companies. These groups were interested in financial profit and, as melodrama appealed to most theatre patrons, it became the staple commodity. Canadians became the receivers of some of the best and most of the worst American and English commercial successes. The Golden Age of theatre in Canada, often referred to by reviewers, was therefore an artificial one: fool's gold, with little value. There was no substantial base. When the movies began to replace stage performance, the effect on the theatre in Canada was severe, but the replacement didn't represent a deterioration in the dramatic form, it was a change of media merely. The early movies were essentially an extension of stage melodrama, and the advantages of this were obvious. The film could travel in a can at a fraction of the cost of a touring company, and the product was superior. Canadians willingly gave up one form of dependency and immediately accepted another. When I noted in the preface that the theatre age was coming to an end around 1912 because stage performance was beginning to be replaced by the movies, I was, in effect, saying that one phase of our dependence was ending. Similarly, when I stated that the First World War ended a phase in our professional theatre, I was alluding to the fact that most of the theatre in Canada was provided by English and American touring companies that remained in their own country or were disbanded during the war. (Although they returned in the 20s in reduced numbers the effect was different and deserves to be considered separately.) The early theatre in Canada owed its existence to outside forces. When the theatrical imports were curtailed, Canada's so-called professional theatre was seriously affected. This fact is often overlooked. The 1951 edition of *The Oxford Companion to the Theatre*, for example, furnished us with this:

Forced by the conditions of their life to depend very much upon themselves for amusement, Canadians in town and country have been enthusiastic advocates of the Little, Amateur, or Community Theatre movement. The infrequent visits of English and American touring companies have been welcomed in the larger towns . . . and have no doubt done much to encourage the local amateur groups.

It might appear that conditions were such that Canadians were "forced to depend very much upon themselves," but the opposite is the case. It seems clear to me that Canadians depended too much on the United States and England, and it was the onslaught of the touring companies, not the infrequency of their visits, that made it so difficult for the local amateur groups to survive. It is true, however, that following the First World War, the stage was partly kept alive by amateur groups. This stage of our history, leading to the Dominion Drama Festival, the vital Hart House performances, and other interesting developments, has yet to be written.

If on the national scene we find that Canadians as a whole were unable to detach themselves from the sentimental ties with England and defend themselves from the physical encroachments of the United States, inside Canada we find a strange proliferation of isolationism – the individual parts of society were determined to exist within their own confines. As the lack of independence from the world scene had a tendency to perpetuate our childhood, so the lack of cohesion within the country weakened our resistance to the outside pressures.

In the theatre world itself we are immediately aware of isolated developments. The playwright, more often than not, was divorced from the theatre, as a number of critics have pointed out.[3] This separation is most noticeable in the work of poetic dramatists. Here evidence seems to suggest that many of the playwrights were eager for productions of their plays but were rejected by the professionals. However, we must note that with few exceptions there was no effort made by the playwrights to become members of theatrical groups. Also, prose playwrights appear to have been unaware of the movement toward social realism in the theatre and were generally unwilling to examine their own society in depth. There was, moreover, very little contact between the acting groups. It is doubtful, for example, whether Albert Tavernier and the Marks Brothers ever met. Censorship was superimposed on the theatre by do-gooders, who chose to be watchdogs rather than active participants. Everywhere we find isolated little groups working within their own narrow confines.

Many sensible excuses for this condition can be offered: the country was very young and the population was small in a large tract of land. But there must be more pervasive reasons, perhaps having to do with the Canadian psyche and the desire for independent expression within our mosaic culture.

A compelling approach to this aspect of our society is offered by Northrop Frye in his examination of the growth of our early communities. He notes that these early communities were essentially isolated pockets surrounded by

167

---

[3]This fact is drawn to our attention in two excellent pieces by Michael Tait: "Drama and the Theatre," *Literary History of Canada*, and "Playwrights in a Vacuum," *Canadian Literature*, No. 16, 5–18 (Spring, 1963).

a "huge, unthinking, menacing, and formidable physical setting" – and he suggests that "such communities are bound to develop what we may provisionally call a garrison mentality." In the garrison, "a closely knit and beleaguered society," the individual feels secure and has little desire to step outside into the unknown. The easier solution, as Frye says, is to "multiply garrison, and when that happens, something anti-cultural comes into Canadian life, a dominating herd-mind in which nothing original can grow."[4]

The fact that the Canadian dramatist did not attempt to imitate the plays that emerged from the New Movement bears witness to a tendency among Canadians to which Michael Tait refers when suggesting causes for the lack of artistic achievement among early Canadian dramatists. The playwright "capitulated to certain social pressures which were inimical to the free exercise of what rudimentary dramatic talents he possessed."[5] This is quite true; a writer inevitably reflects his social context to some extent. We

have sufficient evidence to prove that the theatre was not generally accepted and the poetic dramatists, recognizing this, made a rather futile effort to produce respectable drama. By doing this they divorced themselves from the ("vulgar") stage. Social pressures forced them in the wrong direction and presumably the antipathy shown by the public towards the new ideas of Ibsen and Shaw also affected their attitude.

We might expect the odd individual to resist this kind of pressure, but strangely enough there is no record of such independence in this early period. This is all the more puzzling when one remembers that Canadian dramatists were perfectly free, after all, to write for the American or English stage where there was more freedom of expression. But apart from Tremayne, who produced stock melodramas in any case, the Canadian dramatist on the whole failed to explore this possibility.

Although it might be true that the history of this country is not studded with many dramatic moments, there are sufficient areas that stand out as material for the dramatic artists and are, even more importantly, indigenous to this country. The early relations with the Métis, for example, and the juxtaposition of the French and English are fraught with the sort of conflicts that are the life blood of the theatre.[6] But until recently such moments in Canadian history have been ignored by Canadian playwrights. Instead we find that any subject that was volatile or had in it the stuff of drama was inevitably skirted as "controversial." A "Canadian" play was one in which you would find Indians acting essentially Shakespearian roles, or Gilbert and Sullivan on Parliament Hill. The characters were not real and it was presumably because their "realness" was assiduously avoided by the Canadian dramatist.

The treatment of the Métis, French-English cross-cultural problems, and slavery all received the same decorous treatment. It would seem, in fact, that decorum (or as I have mentioned a number of times throughout this book,

[4]Northrop Frye, *Literary History of Canada* (1965), pp. 830–31.
[5]Michael Tait, "Playwrights in a Vacuum," p. 16.
[6]See Chapter Four.

a wholesome and proper attitude) was both the natural and necessary posture of Canadians during this period. Was it the limitations of the sensibilities or a preferred stance that made it virtually impossible for a Canadian dramatist to write about intimate human relations in a mature fashion? Ibsen was certainly examining the sensitive area of human relations and in England and the United States the reaction was sudden and violent. But in Canada the reaction was a combination of apathy and bewilderment; there was just no room for such ideas. As C. W. Handscomb put it when reviewing Ibsen's *Ghosts*: "The Ibsen cult may be all right but in this morally healthy western community we want none of his gruesome dissections." This attitude was not just western or Canadian, it was typically Victorian. But in Canada it was of a particular density because of unshakable faith in moral values. Writers, critics, and the public took a moral point of view that constantly served as a substitute for exploration and understanding. Here indeed is the garrison mentality.

The outstanding characteristic of our early dramatic and literary history may have been this passion for wholesomeness, and this quality may be the one thread that ties some of our present attitudes to the past. At the present time we are described as industrious, penny-pinching, and conservative in dress and social habits; we talk a great deal, according to reports from the Bell Telephone Company; we usually benefit from comparisons with the "ugly" American, but we are not usually singled out as being "wholesome." But possibly this is our most dominant trait. Variety columnists today have quite correctly noted that Wayne and Shuster, our stars in the television comedy field, are wholesome and quite at odds with the general trend in England and the United States where "sick" comedy is currently the vogue. In the drama we generally find Canadians to be rather shy about the *avant-garde*. Canadians have been reluctant to accept new ideas. Moreover, Canadians have constantly avoided the head-on conflict; the baptism of fire does not excite their imaginations. Historians are quick to notice, for example, that Canadians have been "deprived" of a bloody revolution, and consequently prefer to stand at a respectable and wholesome distance from reality, to observe rather than to participate.

Obviously there was in Canada a built-in predisposition to accept melodrama. As we have discovered, it became the basic ingredient of the musicals, farces, poetical dramas, and so-called social plays. Canadians in this respect were like Americans of whom George Jean Nathan observed, "[They] . . . love, honor and obey melodrama above every other form of dramatic art."[7] But in the United States there were attempts by individuals and select groups to nourish other forms of the theatre. Experiments in the new realistic style were the concern of many leading literary figures of the time. We know that in the 1890s a group of men actually met with the purpose "to consider plans for the establishment of a distinctively American theatre."[8] And in

[7]George Jean Nathan, *Another Book on the Theatre* (1916), p. 307.
[8]Arthur Hobson Quinn, *A History of the American Drama from the Civil War to the Present Day*, Vol. I (New York, 1927), p. 141.

the universities there was also a growing interest in the theatre. George Pierce Baker's course in playwriting at Harvard began in 1905. The foundation of the Society of Dramatic Authors in 1906 was also significant. But in Canada there was no experimentation, nor was there any consistent attempt to give direction to the theatre. The forces against the theatre were many and vocally effective. Unfortunately there were not a sufficient number of sophisticated and well-educated theatre supporters to create a demand for what the bourgeois considered questionable. There were too few people willing to accept the theatre as an art. To most Canadians it was just a pastime; to some an unnecessary evil. In a larger sense, the latter reaction represented a well-intentioned attempt to conserve the wholesome Canadian society against what were regarded as the forces of evil.

At the beginning of this book a comment was taken from *A Statistical Account of Upper Canada* by Robert Gourlay to show the slowness with which the theatre arts gained a hold in Canada. Gourlay pointed out that in the 1820s Canada was ". . . too young for regular theatric entertainments and those delicacies and refinements of luxury which are the usual attendants of wealth." Almost a hundred years later Canada was still "too young" to create a theatre of its own.

Appendices.

A

COPY OF C. P. WALKER'S NOTEBOOK

Manager of the Winnipeg Opera House and the Walker Theatre, 1897–1911

The notebook was sent to me by Walker's daughter, Mrs. Ruth Harvey. As she suggested in an accompanying letter, it was probably done in slack time by one of his office staff. It is not an accurate account; dates are sometimes confused and productions are occasionally listed twice by mistake. Many items, therefore, have had to be checked against the theatre columns of the *Winnipeg Free Press*. Major errors have been corrected, the chronology revised, gaps filled, and footnotes to each season's record have been added where it seemed appropriate or necessary. The figures listed in a column on the right for the first six seasons pose something of a mystery. They could be the actor's "take" or Walker's profit; it is unlikely that they represent the box-office returns for the performance. These entries are, however, related to the productions and do in a sense act as a ruler with which we can judge the commercial success or failure of the various touring companies.

I have made no attempt to give a complete record of the plays in Winnipeg during these years. Plays which were presented in Walker's theatre and not mentioned by him, and the productions at other theatres in Winnipeg, are faithfully recorded in the *Winnipeg Free Press* and await the ardent scholar.

The year in which the notebook was begun coincides with the opening of the new theatre, which was actually the rebuilt Bijou. The *Manitoba Morning Free Press*, May 8, 1897, notes: "Mr. C. P. Walker, the manager and lessee of the Fargo Theatre, will also under lease manage the Winnipeg Opera House."

SEASON 1897–1898

Julius Caesar (*Wed.*)	James, Louis[1]	Sept. 8	$436.50
Romeo and Juliet (*Thur. mat.*)	James, Louis	Sept. 9	177.00
Othello (*Thur.*)	James, Louis	Sept. 9	305.50
Old Curiosity Shop	Kate Putnam[2]	Nov. 11–12	
Pulse of New York	[Mayhew & Lang]	Nov. 19–20	172.00
Othello	Sanford Dodge[3]	[Nov. 25]	133.50
Merchant of Venice (*Sat. mat.*)	Thomas Keene[4]	Apr. 30	
Richard III (*Sat.*)	Thomas Keene	Apr. 30	
The Face in the Moonlight	Robert B. Mantell[5]	June 25	
Sweet Lavender	Neill Stock Co.	July 18–19	178.75
Jim the Penman	Neill Stock Co.	July 20–21	223.50

[1]Louis James opened the new Winnipeg Opera House with a production of *Spartacus, the Gladiator,* on Monday evening, September 6, 1897. On Tuesday, he presented *A Cavalier of France,* advertised as "the first time on any stage." He closed his four-day engagement with *Othello.*

[2]Kate Putnam was either getting tired or old. She attempted a new play, *Tom Tinker's Kid,* on the afternoon of November 13 with little success. At the conclusion of her performance in *Old Curiosity Shop* that evening, she announced her retirement.

[3]Sanford Dodge presented *Damon & Pythias* in the afternoon of November 25, 1897. In the evening he performed in *Othello.* In spite of the advertising that preceded his arrival, the reviewer for the *Free Press* was not impressed: "The interpretation given the piece was certainly a disappointment although Mr. Dodge warmed to his work in the second act."

[4]Thomas W. Keene opened on April 28, 1898, with *Richelieu.* On April 29 he presented *Louis XI.* His last performance in Winnipeg was *Richard III.* He died June 1, 1898.

[5]Robert B. Mantell returned to Winnipeg in this year for a three-day engagement: *Monbars,* Thursday, June 23, 1898; *A Secret Warrant,* June 24; *A Face in the Moonlight,* June 25. Albert Tavernier is discovered here playing Doctor Daniel in *Monbars.* (See Chapter Two.)

SEASON 1898–1899

The Span of Life	[Valentine Stock Co.]	Oct. 3–4	$210.00
The New Dominion	Clement Clay	Oct. 31–Nov. 1	458.75
Recital	E. Pauline Johnson	Feb. 3	139.25
The New Dominion[1]			
[Return engagement]	Clay Clement	[Apr. 29]	230.25
Uncle Tom's Cabin	Young Brothers	May 19–20	300.00
Banker's Daughter	Neill Stock Co.[2]	[May 28]	
London Assurance	Neill Stock Co.	June 2–3	320.00
Alone in New York	Frank E. Long	June 26–July 1	12.50
Heart of Chicago	Lincoln J. Carter	Aug. 26–27	312.25

[1]*The New Dominion* was written by Clay Clement who also played the lead. On April 28 he presented his new play *A Southern Gentleman.*

[2]The Neill Company was highly respected in Winnipeg. They rarely came to this city for less than a week. In this season they presented *The Dancing Girl* on May 29 and 30; *A Parisian Romance* on May 31 and June 1; and *London Assurance* on June 2 and 3.

SEASON 1899–1900

Macbeth	Modjeska	Nov. 1	$1119.25
Much Ado About Nothing (mat)	Modjeska	Nov. 1	301.00
London Life	[Lawrence Griffith Co.]	Jan. 1–2	
A Lady of Quality	Eugenie Blair	Jan. 9–10	639.25
The Little Minister	[Miss G. Heyer Co.]	Jan. 19–20	523.75
Shenandoah	[Jacob Litt's Co.]	Jan. 22–23	309.50
Hamlet	Walker Whiteside[1]	Feb. 15	276.50
Hamlet	Walker Whiteside	Feb. 17	314.00
Merchant of Venice	Fred. Warde[2]	Apr. 3	301.00
Crust of Society	Valentine Stock Co.	July 9–10	125.00
Human Hearts	[Frederick Fairbanks Co.]	Oct. 26	314.75
Uncle Tom's Cabin	[No trace]	Oct. 27–28	
Hamlet	Walker Whiteside	Nov. 1, 2, 3	362.00

[1]Walker Whiteside was well known in Winnipeg. He had apparently performed Hamlet there in 1886, and at that time was advertised as "The Boy Tragedian" [*Free Press*, March 3, 1899]. It is strange that C. P. Walker recorded Whiteside's appearance and then did not mention Otis Skinner who opened at the Winnipeg Theatre on February 19 and played until February 21 with *The Liars*.

[2]Frederick Warde opened with *The Lion's Mouth* on April 2, 1900.

173

SEASON 1900–1901

The Little Minister	[Chas. Frohman's Co.]	Oct. 12	$352.25
Human Hearts	[Frederic Fairbanks and Co.]	Oct. 26–27	
Hamlet	Walker Whiteside	Nov. 1	
The Marble Heart	W. Owen	Dec. 6	179.50
Othello	Wm. Owen	Dec. 7	210.75
The New Magdalen	Wm. Owen	Dec. 8	183.75
The American Citizen	Neill Stock Co.	Dec. 10	332.75
A Lady of Quality	Eugenie Blair	Feb. 4	196.50
The Christian	[Lionel Adams, Julia Stuart & Co.]	Feb. 26–27	
Tess of the D'Urbervilles	Mrs. Fiske[1]	Mar. 13	769.00
A Midsummer Night's Dream	James and Kidder[2]	Apr. 2	495.25
A Midsummer Night's Dream	James and Kidder	Apr. 3	429.50
King John	Modjeska[3]	Apr. 23	584.50
Macbeth	Modjeska	Apr. 24	439.25

[1]Mrs. Fiske first presented *Becky Sharpe* on March 12.

[2]Louis James and Kathryn Kidder travelled with a large company. The reviewer for the *Free Press*, April 2, 1901, mentions that the company numbered forty-one players including "a ballet and chorus." He notes also that the production had "music, dancing and revels, all of the songs and dances of the Shakespearean text, as well as the Mendelssohn music written upon this story, having been restored for this revival."

[3]Modjeska also performed in *Mary Stuart* at a matinee on April 24. Again we find the company to be a large one. "The play calls for massive, almost archaic settings." Modjeska played the part of Constance in *King John*.

SEASON 1901–1902

A Little Outcast[1]	[Lincoln J. Carter]	[Sept. 17–18]	$576.00
Romeo and Juliet	Harold Nelson[2]	[Sept. 6]	
Rip Van Winkle	Thomas Jefferson	Oct. 25–26	407.75
Human Hearts	[Frederic Fairbanks Co.]	Dec. 31, Jan. 1	313.00
The Taming of the Shrew	Chas. B. Hanford	Feb. 26–27	
Henry VIII	Modjeska and James	Mar. 1	
Uncle Tom's Cabin	[Stetson's Co.]	May 2–3	
Shadows of a Great City	Ellis-Lennon	May 15	
East Lynne	[No trace]	Aug. 2	

[1]The opening production of this season, *A Little Outcast*, was financially successful, but it didn't meet the approval of the drama critic C. W. Handscomb. (This appears to be the first review to which he signed his name.) Having poked fun at the many ludicrous situations in the play, he ends by saying, "If we can't relish melodrama, we don't have to patronize it, other people can, and they call for it. That is why the Carpenters and the Lincoln Carters produce it, and the theatre managers book it." (And that is probably why he wrote *The Big Boom* some years later!)

[2]Harold Nelson presented *Hamlet* on September 5 and *Richelieu* on the evening of September 6. Handscomb was very impressed by this young man. Writing about the audience's response to Nelson's Hamlet, he felt obliged to say, "It was a gathering calculated to inspire the young Canadian actor . . . and surely his flattering reception by so large an audience must have seemed some reward for years of toil, of struggle and of sacrifice."

SEASON 1902–1903

A Celebrated Case	Harold Nelson[1]	Sept. 4	$ 50.45
Hamlet	Harold Nelson	Sept. 5	
The Tempest	James and Warde	Sept. 11–12	
The Merchant of Venice	Harold Walker	Sept. 15	407.25
A Poor Relation	Horace Lewis	Oct. 15–16	
Shore Acres	[Miss Melville & Co.]	Oct. 24–25	471.75
Rip Van Winkle	Thomas Jefferson	Nov. 3–4	
Richard III	Walker Whiteside	Jan. 12	
Hamlet	Walker Whiteside	Jan. 13	
The Only Way	[Frawley Co.][2]	Jan. 18	418.00
Othello	Harold Nelson	Jan. 23	
Romeo and Juliet	Harold Nelson	Jan. 25	
Much Ado About Nothing	C. B. Hanford[3]	Feb. 2	
The Taming of the Shrew	C. B. Hanford	Feb. 3	
Two Orphans	Kate Claxton	Feb. 12–14	
Macbeth	John Griffith	Feb. 23–24	

[1]Harold Nelson came under Walker's management in this year. He was being billed as "The Eminent Canadian Actor." On October 10, 1903, he and his company put on "an Elaborate Scenic Production of the Great Religious and Historical Play, *Quo Vadis*."

[2]Frawley's production of *The Only Way* was probably a pirated version of Sir John Martin-Harvey's play. It may have come as a surprise to Martin-Harvey to realize that his famous role, Sydney Carton, was not unknown to many of his audiences when he toured Canada in 1914. The people of Winnipeg, at least, would have remembered the striking last scene which impressed the reviewer of the *Free Press*: "Carton outlined against a morning sky, standing on the platform of the guillotine" (*Free Press*, January 19, 1902).

[3]It's amusing to note the reviewer's remarks about Hanford's presentation of *Much Ado about Nothing*: "Mr. Charles B. Hanford's performance at the Winnipeg theatre last night was given under circumstances somewhat disconcerting to the players for interest was distracted and illusions destroyed by announcements at intervals of the progress of the hockey game in Montreal."

174

SEASON 1903–1904

Sherlock Holmes	Kelcy and Shannon[1]	Sept. 28–29
The New Dominion	Clay Clement	Oct. 14–15
Human Hearts[2]	[Tom Logan & Co.]	Dec. 30–31
Katherine and Petruchio	Harold Nelson	Feb. 16
Twelfth Night	Marie Wainwright	Feb. 17–18
Ghosts	Alberta Gallatin	Mar. 9–10
Hamlet	Harold Nelson	Mar. 21
The Merchant of Venice	Harold Nelson	Mar. 23
Living Canada	Pictures	May 6–7
East Lynne	Inez Forman	Aug. 26–27

[1]Herbert Kelcy and Effie Shannon acted together for years. Their production of William Gillette's adaptation of *Sherlock Holmes* was a sensation in Winnipeg. Handscomb is quite gay in his review: "We're a bit out of the way geographically, according to the map, but while organizations of this calibre journey to us we are quite in it, theatrically, don't you think? Well rather!"

[2]*Human Hearts* was obviously a favourite in Winnipeg. It had, apparently, all the ingredients necessary for the average playgoer. As Handscomb says: "*Human Hearts* gives a pure, wholesome lesson that touches the heart strings in the pathetic scenes and excites the risibilities in the humorous ones. The pathos and comedy are so well blended that the audience is in tears one moment and convulsed with laughter the next."

175

SEASON 1904–1905

Pretty Peggy[1]	Jane Corcoran	Jan. 9–11
Octoroon	Courtney Co.	May 26–27
Twelfth Night	[Ben Greet & Co.][2]	July [3]
Much Ado About Nothing	[Ben Greet & Co.]	July 4
A Midsummer Night's Dream	[Ben Greet & Co.]	July 5
Rip Van Winkle	Thomas Jefferson	Oct. 24–25
Candida	Lester Lonergrin [*sic*]	Dec. 22–24

[1]*Pretty Peggy* was a critical success. This was the type of play for Jane Corcoran, according to Handscomb: "not that Ibsen rubbish." He was obviously charmed: "There is certainly a new star in the theatrical firmament, and she sparkled with more than ordinary brilliancy at the Winnipeg theatre last night."

[2]Ben Greet's Shakespearean Co. opened at the Winnipeg Theatre on July 3, 1905 with *Twelfth Night*. The other plays put on during the week were: *A Midsummer Night's Dream, Comedy of Errors, The Merchant of Venice,* and *As You Like It.* Handscomb reminds his audience that "the majority of the plays will be given in the quaint Elizabethan manner. . . ." *A Midsummer Night's Dream* was given an open-air performance on "the pretty lawn of M. J. R. Waghorn, at Armstrong's Point."

SEASON 1905–1906

Human Hearts[1]	[Tom Logan & Co.]	May 1
Yankee Doodle Girls[2]	[Yankee Doodle Combination]	Jan. 25–27
The Merchant of Venice	Louis James	Feb. 17
Macbeth	Nance O'Neil	Mar. 13
Uncle Tom's Cabin	[Washburns Co.][3]	Apr. 13–14
Bernhardt, Mme. Sarah	At Auditorium	May 1

[1]Although the lead actor and some of the minor roles were changed occasionally, the Human Hearts company remained essentially the same. According to Handscomb this was their tenth year of appearances in Winnipeg. He staunchly supports the old vehicle: "Good plays like good wine, improve with age" (*Free Press*, Jan. 19, 1906).

[2]*Yankee Doodle Girls* was one of the first big vaudeville shows to arrive in Winnipeg. A large and appreciative audience turned out. "Of course," said Handscomb, "there is a pretty free display of limb and lingerie as is customary in this character of frivolous entertainment, but there is nothing actually offensive. Indeed, for a burlesque show, it is remarkably clean."

[3]In Washburn's *Uncle Tom's Cabin* production, it is advertised that "real bloodhounds were to be used for the famous scene where Eliza escapes on the ice."

SEASON 1906–1907

The Yankee Consul	Harry Short	Jan. 14–19
Uncle Tom's Cabin	Stetson's	Apr. 5–6
Mrs. Warren's Profession	Rose Coghlan[1]	Apr. 30, May 1
A Yankee Tourist	Raymond Hitchcock	May 22–25
The Duel	Otis Skinner	June 27–29
As You Like It	Scenes – Viola Allen	July 4–6
The Merchant of Venice	Scenes – Viola Allen	July 4–6
Romeo and Juliet	Scenes – Viola Allen	July 4–6
The School for Scandal	Scenes – Viola Allen	July 4–6
Twelfth Night	Scenes – Viola Allen	July 4–6

[1]For further information about Rose Coghlan see Chapter Two.

SEASON 1907–1908

Alice in Wonderland[1]	[Local production]	Oct. 25–26
The Awakening	Olga Nethersole	Nov. 23
Uncle Tom's Cabin	Stetson's	Apr. 10–11
The New Dominion	Clay Clement	Apr. 13
The Bells	Clay Clement	Apr. 14
The Second Mrs. Tanqueray	Mrs. Patrick Campbell	Apr. 29
The Notorious Mrs. Ebbsmith	Mrs. Patrick Campbell	Apr. 30
Hedda Gabler	Mrs. Patrick Campbell	May 2

[1]*Alice in Wonderland* was produced by a group of amateurs, and involved over two hundred children and grown-ups.

In this season the Walker Theatre opened its doors to the public. Winnipeg was now starting to look like a theatre town. Handscomb's column which was starting to flow over more than one page, at least on the Saturday editions, can list five houses of entertainment: The Walker Theatre, The Winnipeg Theatre, The Dominion Theatre, The Bijou Theatre, and the Y.M.C.A. Auditorium.

SEASON 1908–1909

King Lear	Robt. B. Mantell	Aug. 3
The Merchant of Venice	Robt. B. Mantell	Aug. 4
Hamlet	Robt. B. Mantell	Aug. 5
Othello	Robt. B. Mantell	Aug. 6
King Richard III	Robt. B. Mantell	Aug. 8
Macbeth	Robt. B. Mantell	Aug. 8
The Rivals	Thos. & W. W. Jefferson[1]	Sept. 7–9
The Clansmen	A New York Co.	Sept. 10–12
Uncle Tom's Cabin	Downie's Co.	Sept. 25–26
The Great Divide	The Ben Greet Players	Nov. 12–14
Rip Van Winkle	Thomas Jefferson	Dec. 14–16
A Doll's House	Nazimova	June 9–10
Hedda Gabler	Nazimova	June 11

[1]Thomas and William Jefferson were the sons of Joseph Jefferson. They performed together in *The Rivals* and Thomas starred alone in *Rip Van Winkle*. His performance was patterned after his father's. In fact, it was said that he wore his father's clothes and shoes for the role.

177

SEASON 1909–1910

The Second Mrs. Tanqueray	Olga Nethersole[1]	Mar. 4
Camille	Olga Nethersole	Mar. 5
The Great Divide[2]	Henry Mordant & Co.	Mar. 14–16

[1]Olga Nethersole performed in *The Writing on the Wall* on March 3 and ended her engagement on March 4 with *Sapho*.

[2]*The Great Divide* was presented at the Winnipeg Theatre. Walker had recently bought this theatre and planned to use it to house the attractions sent out by The Klaw and Erlanger Syndicate. It is noted in the *Free Press*, March 5, 1910, that the Walker Theatre would be dedicated to "the highest class of vaudeville," and that this policy was to "continue from week to week until further notice."

SEASON 1910–1911

Becky Sharpe	Mrs. Fiske	Aug 15–16
Pillars of Society	Mrs. Fiske	Aug. 17
The Nigger[1]	Guy Bates Post	Nov. 14–16
Billy	Sidney Drew	Nov. 24–26
Sweet Lavender	Edward Terry	Feb. 13–18
The Chimney Corner }	Earl Grey Dramatic	{ Apr. 24–29
David Garrick }	Trophy Competition	{ Apr. 24–29

[1]*The Nigger* was one of the first race problem plays to reach Winnipeg. It caused little reaction. One can tell from the review that the critic (initials, E. B.) considered the problem of the negro to be extremely remote. However, he felt that the possibilities of the theme may have frightened the audience as it did him. The play could conceivably have been brutal and embarrassing. But, as he points out, "when the curtain went up, [the audience was] relieved to find that it was an intensely strong and powerful play written to entertain."

B

178   THEATRES IN EASTERN CANADA, C. 1900

I found it virtually impossible to describe all the theatres, with their dates, for Eastern Canada. More research at the local level will have to be done before a complete record can be attempted. However, by extending and editing Julius Cahn's *Official Theatrical Guide* for the years 1896–97 and 1900–1, it has been possible to recreate a partial picture of theatre in Canada for the year 1900. Cahn's *Guide* itself is not complete; if theatre managers did not bother to fill out the questionnaire he sent, their theatres were omitted from the book, as were many of Montreal's and Toronto's theatres.

As it is unlikely that any scholar will wish to pursue this task farther, I have included a good deal of detail; some of the information, in fact, may appear to be trivia to the average reader. Prices of seats, seating capacities, stage dimensions, peculiarities of theatres, and the newspapers and hotels in the particular towns are noted whenever possible.

A manager of a theatre company, whether he was Canadian, English or American, was wise to consult Cahn's *Theatrical Guide* when he contemplated a tour of Eastern Canada. Copies of this book no doubt travelled far and wide, tucked between the railroad schedule and the list of "opening dates." Very few of them survived this treatment; one copy is in my collection and another is resting in the Library of Congress. The large centres, of course, were Montreal and Toronto and so they will be examined first. As Ontario was the most popular area for the travelling company, I have selected the information which deals with the theatres in the towns and cities of this province.

MONTREAL
[Population approximately 350,000]

Academy of Music

MANAGER	J. B. Sparrow
PRICES	25 cents and $1.50
SEATING CAPACITY	Orchestra, 500
	Balcony, 400
	Gallery, 900
LIGHTING	gas and electricity
STAGE DIMENSIONS	Width prosc. opening, 36 ft.
	Height prosc. opening, 36 ft.
	Footlights to back wall, 40 ft.
	Stage to rigging loft, 64 ft.
	Grooves can be taken up flush with fly gallery
SCENIC ARTIST	R. J. Garand
ORCHESTRA	Full
	L. Gruenwald, leader

[This theatre was built in 1875, and opened with a production of *Rosedale* by E. A. McDowell and Co.

It was rebuilt in 1896 and was under the management of Jacobs and Sparrow for a number of years.

In 1900 the companies arriving in Montreal would have had the following selection of "dailies" in which to advertise: *Star, Gazette, Herald, La Presse, La Patrie* and *Le Journal*.]

Her Majesty's Theatre

MANAGER	John A. Gease
PRICES	25 cents to $1.50
SEATING CAPACITY	Orchestra, 550
	Dress circle, 450
	Gallery, 600
	Family circle, 250
	20 Boxes
LIGHTING	gas and electricity
STAGE DIMENSIONS	Width prosc. opening, 34 ft.
	Height prosc. opening, 32 ft.
	Footlights to back wall, 45 ft.
	Stage to rigging loft, 67 ft.
	Grooves standard height
ORCHESTRA	10
	Otto Zimmermann, leader

[Built in 1898 and destroyed in 1963. Further particulars are found in Chapter One along with comments on other theatres in Montreal.]

Theatre Royal

MANAGER	J. B. Sparrow
PRICES	10¢, 20¢, 30¢, 50¢, and 75¢
SEATING CAPACITY	2,005
LIGHTING	gas and electricity
STAGE DIMENSIONS	Width prosc. opening, 33⅓ ft.
	Height prosc. opening, 32 ft.
	Footlights to back wall, 45 ft.
	Height to rigging loft, 38 ft.
	Eight grooves

[This is the second Theatre Royal which was built in 1852 and was still operating as a theatre in the early 1900s. We can see from the prices, however, that it has lost some of its prestige by 1900. The "ten, twenty, thirty" expression usually referred to the fare of melodrama. For the companies that were doing well there was the Windsor Hotel with rooms at $3.50 and up. For the less fortunate there were the hotels, Richelieu and Victoria, with rooms from $1.00 and up.]

179

TORONTO
[Population approximately 260,000]

Grand Opera House

MANAGER	O. B. Sheppard
PRICES	Orchestra, $1.00
	Balcony, 75¢
	Gallery, 25¢
SEATING CAPACITY	Orchestra, 592
	Balcony, 359
	Gallery, 800
LIGHTING	gas and electricity
STAGE DIMENSIONS	Width prosc. opening, 34 ft.
	Height prosc. opening, 55 ft.
	Footlights to back wall, 50 ft.
	Height of grooves from stage, 22 ft.
SCENIC ARTIST	George Drake
ORCHESTRA	9
	Frank Jennings, leader

[O. B. Sheppard had a long career in Toronto. He was manager of the first Grand Opera House in 1878. In the early 90s he was working for the Whitney chain, which included the Grand, The Academy of Music, and in 1896, The Princess. He was an Alderman in Toronto (ward 3), in 1896 and in this year became General Inspector of Fisheries for Ontario. He takes a look back on his career in an article by T. H. Scott, "Gas Lights and Radiant Stars in the old Grand Opera House," *Evening Telegram*, October 23, 1924.

The first G.O.H. was built in 1872 for Mrs. Morrison. The second G.O.H. referred to here in Cahn's Guide was opened in 1880.]

Princess Theatre

MANAGER	O. B. Sheppard
PRICES	Orchestra, $1.00
	Balcony, 75¢
	Gallery, 25¢
SEATING CAPACITY	Orchestra, 650
	Balcony, 365
	Gallery, 800
LIGHTING	gas and electricity
STAGE DIMENSIONS	Width prosc. opening, 35 ft.
	Height prosc. opening, 50 ft.
	Footlights to back wall, 45 ft.
	Grooves can be taken up flush with fly gallery
	Number of grooves, 5
	Stage to rigging loft, 65 ft.
SCENIC ARTIST	George Drake
ORCHESTRA	9
	W. Culligan, leader

[C. J. Whitney secured the lease of this theatre in 1896 for a yearly rental of $4,000. It housed many of the more ambitious productions in Toronto during the period being discussed, one of the last dates I have noted being a production of *Lady Windermere's Fan*, starring Margaret Anglin, on November 16, 1914. A number of hotels are listed: Queen's, $2.50 and up. Rossin, $2.00 and up. The cheapest hotel was the Albion, $1.00 and up.

The newspapers: *Mail, Globe, World, News, Star, Telegram,* and *Sunday World.*]

180

Toronto Opera House

MANAGER	Ambrose J. Small
PRICES	Orchestra, 50¢ and 75¢
	Balcony, 25¢, 35¢ and 50¢
	Gallery, 15¢
SEATING CAPACITY	Orchestra, 700
	Balcony, 500
	Gallery, 700
LIGHTING	gas and electricity (110 volt., Edison)
STAGE DIMENSIONS	Width prosc. opening, 31 ft.
	Height prosc. opening, 25 ft.
	Footlights to back wall, 45 ft.
SCENIC ARTIST	William Drake
ORCHESTRA	10
	Will J. Obernier, leader

[A. J. Small disappeared without a trace on December 2, 1919. He started work in the theatre as an assistant to O. B. Sheppard. In a business-like manner he quickly took control of a number of theatres in Eastern Canada. He purchased the Grand from the Manning estate in 1906. In 1910 he extended his circuit to the Maritime Provinces assuming control of the Academy of Music in Halifax. By this time, all his theatres were part of the Klaw Erlanger Syndicate.

The Opera House was built in the 1880s. In 1896 it was controlled and sometimes called Jacob and Sparrow's Theatre. Destroyed by fire in 1903 while still under the management of A. J. Small.]

Grand Opera House

MANAGER	Joseph Frank
SEATING CAPACITY	1,400
LIGHTING	gas and electricity
STAGE DIMENSIONS	Width prosc. opening, 30 ft.
	Height, 30 ft.
	Depth footlights to back wall, 28 ft.
	Height of grooves from stage, 18 ft.
	Four grooves
ORCHESTRA	7

[The Grand was built in 1874 on Albert St. near Metcalfe St. and for many years was the cultural centre of Ottawa. In 1897, the new Russell Theatre dimmed its glory, and by 1900 it was booking the second-rate shows. According to an article in *Ottawa Journal*, Feb. 18, 1946, it, "went up in smoke" on the night of July 5, 1913.

Hotels available at this time were: The Russell, with rooms at $2.00 and up. The Windsor and Grand Union at $1.50 and $1.25. And the Brunswick at $1.00.

The newspapers were: *Citizen, Journal, Free Press* and *Le Temps*.]

181

The Russell

MANAGER	W. A. Drowne
SEATING CAPACITY	Orchestra, 700
	Balcony, 400
	Gallery, 700
STAGE DIMENSIONS	Width of prosc. opening, 33 ft.
	Height of prosc. opening, 32 ft.
	Depth footlights to back wall, 40 ft.
	Stage floor to rigging loft, 64 ft.
	Grooves can be taken up flush with fly gallery
SCENIC ARTIST	J. Quinn
ORCHESTRA	12
	James McGillicuddy, leader

[An article in the *Globe*, April 9, 1901, notes: "The loss of the Russell Theatre . . . cost $90,000. The building . . . recently was leased to Ambrose J. Small, the Toronto theatrical man, who intended to assume control early next season. Until a meeting of the directors it will not be known whether the theatre will be rebuilt." Then on April 15: "Ottawa will have a new theatre. Mr. A. J. Small, the new lessee, was notified tonight."

It was demolished in the 1930s to make room for Confederation Square.]

ARNPRIOR
[Population approximately 4,000]

Town Hall

MANAGER	John Tierney
SEATING CAPACITY	650
LIGHTING	electricity

[This would be a stop for the smaller touring companies; a "one-night-stand."]

BARRIE
[Population approximately 7,500]

Grand Opera House

MANAGERS	Powell & Kennedy
SEATING CAPACITY	1,000
LIGHTING	electricity
STAGE DIMENSIONS	Width prosc. opening, 33 ft. Height prosc. opening, 27 ft. Footlights to back wall, 32 ft. No grooves; all scenery braced
SCENIC ARTIST	Mr. Davis

[There is evidence of the Grand in operation in 1897. Pauline Johnson and Owen Smilie appeared here on June 22. It was also a frequent stop for the Marks Brothers; here Edith Ellis Baker played in 1903. See Chapter Two.]

BERLIN
[Population approximately 12,000]

Berlin Opera House

MANAGER	Geo. O. Philip
SEATING CAPACITY	825
PRICES	"vary"
LIGHTING	gas and electricity
STAGE DIMENSIONS	Width prosc. opening, 26 ft. Footlights to back wall, 27 ft. Three sets of grooves Stage to rigging loft, 43 ft.

[This town, of course, changed its name to Kitchener. There were two dailies here in 1900: the *Berlin Record* and the *News*. These two apparently amalgamated; a reviewer from the *Berlin News Record* reviewed *Ghosts* in 1903. See Chapter Two.]

BOWMANVILLE
[Population approximately 3,000]

Town Hall

MANAGER	John Lyle
SEATING CAPACITY	400
LIGHTING	electricity
STAGE DIMENSIONS	Width prosc. opening, 19 ft. Height, 13 ft. Footlights to back wall, 18 ft.
ORCHESTRA	8 or 10 David Morrison, leader

Theatre on second floor

[This town would probably be considered a "one-night-stand." There were, however, three hotels to choose from if one was stranded: Balmoral, Bennett House, Station Hotel. No room prices are mentioned.]

BRANTFORD
[Population approximately 16,000]

Stratford's Opera House

MANAGERS	Tuttle and Fyle
SEATING CAPACITY	1,000
PRICES	25¢ to 75¢
LIGHTING	gas
STAGE DIMENSIONS	Width of prosc. opening, 24 ft. Height of prosc. opening, 23 ft. Footlights to back wall, 28 ft. Four grooves

Theatre on second floor

[This Opera House was playing host to the travelling stars in the 1890s. Robert Mantell was a frequent visitor, and Julia Stuart performed *A Doll's House* here in 1898. See Chapter Two.
The Marks Brothers returned yearly; their last performance at Brantford recorded on Feb. 30, 1911.]

182

BROCKVILLE
[Population approximately 10,000]

Grand Opera House

MANAGER	John L. Upham
SEATING CAPACITY	950
PRICES	25¢ to $1.00
LIGHTING	gas
STAGE DIMENSIONS	Footlights to back stage, 20 ft. Stage to rigging loft, 15 ft. Three grooves
ORCHESTRA	10 F. H. Fulford, leader

Theatre on second floor

[There is no evidence of early theatre in Brockville where Reverend Whyte wrote his *Female Consistory of Brockville*. See Chapter Four. Ada Gray presented *East Lynne* here in Sept. 1881. It was another regular stop for the Marks Brothers. They "packed" the houses, Nov. 28–30, 1898.]

COBOURG
[Population approximately 5,500]

Victoria Opera House

MANAGER	Charles H. Simmons
SEATING CAPACITY	900
PRICES	25¢ to 50¢
LIGHTING	gas and electricity
STAGE DIMENSIONS	Width of prosc. opening, 35 ft. Height of prosc. opening, 22 ft. Footlights to back wall, 30 ft. Height of rigging to loft, 36 ft.

Theatre on second floor

[There is not much information about the theatre in Cobourg. The first theatre was apparently a renovated distillery. At the turn of the century the Victoria Opera House had competition from a place of entertainment called the Bijou Dream Theatre.
Cahn's *Guide* does not list a theatre for Cobourg for the years 1896–97.]

183

CHATHAM
[Population approximately 12,000]

Grand Opera House

MANAGER	R. A. McVean
SEATING CAPACITY	1,336
LIGHTING	gas and electricity
STAGE DIMENSIONS	Width prosc. opening, 37 ft. Height prosc. opening, 30 ft. Footlights to back wall, 38 ft. Five sets of grooves
ORCHESTRA	9

Theatre on second floor

[In April 1885 the famous Daniel Bandmann played the Grand. It was reported in the New York *Dramatic Mirror* that "when he was supposed to be performing in *Richard III*, he lounged around the Hall and gave as his excuse that a Chatham audience could not appreciate good acting! His insufferable manners will not be tolerated by Canadian audiences."]

GALT

Scott's Opera House

MANAGER	R. McMillan
SEATING CAPACITY	1,000
PRICES	according to attraction
LIGHTING	electricity
STAGE DIMENSIONS	Width of prosc. opening, 25½ ft. Height of prosc. opening, 15½ ft. Footlights to back wall, 27 ft. Height to rigging loft, 32 ft.
ORCHESTRA	10 George Baker, leader

Theatre on second floor

[Some early events in Galt's theatre are described in Chapter One.]

GANANOQUE
[Population approximately 5,000]

Turner's Opera House

MANAGER J. B. Turner
SEATING CAPACITY 1,000
LIGHTING electricity
STAGE DIMENSIONS Width of prosc. opening, 24 ft.
Height of prosc. opening, 22 ft.
Footlights to back wall, 30 ft.
Six grooves
Grooves can be taken up flush with fly gallery
ORCHESTRA 6
Theatre on second floor

184

The Opera House

MANAGER S. A. McKenzie
SEATING CAPACITY 1,000
PRICES 25¢ to 50¢
LIGHTING electricity
STAGE DIMENSIONS Width of prosc. opening, 22 ft.
Height of prosc. opening, 15 ft.
Footlights to back wall, 28 ft.
Four grooves
Height of grooves from stage, 13 ft.
SCENIC ARTIST W. F. Grant
ORCHESTRA William Reese, leader
Theatre on first floor

[Gananoque was a small town. The fact that it had two good-sized opera houses is rather remarkable and prompted me to make a note of them here.]

GUELPH
[Population approximately 15,000]

Royal Opera House

MANAGER AND
LESSEE A. J. Small
SEATING CAPACITY 1,400
LIGHTING electricity
STAGE DIMENSIONS Width of prosc. opening, 30 ft.
Height of prosc. opening, 32 ft.
Footlights to back stage, 35 ft.
Stage to rigging loft, 60 ft.
ORCHESTRA James Johnson, leader

[The Royal opened on November 5, 1894, and was first leased by Albert Tavernier. W. A. Mahoney was manager in 1897, and A. J. Small appeared in 1899. The daily newspapers of the time were the *Herald, Mercury,* and *Advocate.*]

HAMILTON
[Population approximately 55,000]

Grand Opera House

LESSEE C. J. Whitney
MANAGER A. R. Loudon
LIGHTING electricity
SEATING CAPACITY 1,120
STAGE DIMENSIONS Width of prosc. opening 30 ft.
Height of prosc. opening, 25 ft.
Five grooves each side
Stage to rigging loft, 60 ft.
ORCHESTRA 7
A. Lomas, leader

[There is every indication that Hamilton will prove rich ground for the theatre historian. It was linked to Toronto in the early days (see Chapter One). Amateur productions of a sustained nature reach back into the 1880s, the Garrick Club being noteworthy. It was also on the main route of all the professional touring companies.]

LONDON
[Population approximately 40,000]

Grand Opera House

Destroyed by fire

[The Grand was built in 1880. It occupied the third and fourth floors of the Masonic Temple built at the corner of King and Richmond Streets. It was destroyed by fire in 1900. The new Grand Opera House was opened in 1901 and is now the home of the London Little Theatre. The theatre history in London, Ontario, is quite impressive. See article by F. Beatrice Taylor, *London Free Press*, June 15, 1955. Orlo Miller is something of an authority on the theatre in London and Western Ontario. See his article, "Old Opera Houses of Western Ontario," *Opera Canada*, V, 7–8 (May, 1964).]

PETERBOROUGH
[Population approximately 13,000]

Bradburn's Opera House

MANAGER	W. H. Bradburn
SEATING CAPACITY	1,000
LIGHTING	gas and electricity
STAGE DIMENSIONS	Width prosc. opening, 22 ft. Height prosc. opening, 17 ft. Footlights to back wall, 38 ft. Stage to rigging loft, 23 ft. Four grooves

Theatre on second floor

[Little information about the theatre in Peterborough is recorded. However, an obvious opportunity awaits the researcher. Cahn notes that there were three drama critics in this town in 1900; F. D. McKay of the *Evening Review*; F. R. Yokome of the *Examiner*; and W. H. Robertson of the *Morning Times*.]

STRATFORD
[Population approximately 14,000]

Opera House

MANAGER	Albert Brandenberger
SEATING CAPACITY	Orchestra, 375 Balcony, 350 Gallery, 400
PRICES	25¢ to $1.00
LIGHTING	gas and electricity (Joe Bart)
STAGE DIMENSIONS	Width of prosc. opening, 25 ft. Height of prosc. opening, 28 ft. Footlights to back wall, 38 ft. Height to rigging loft, 48 ft. Three traps Grooves can be taken up flush with fly gallery
ORCHESTRA	7 Madam Haush, leader

Theatre on main floor

[The Opera House was also known as the Brandenberger Theatre and The Theatre Albert. It has been rebuilt and is now part of the Stratford Shakespeare Festival complex.
Stratford's drama critic was R. R. Lang of the *Beacon*.
There was also a "Typewriter – Miss Russell" available.
The theatre was opened on January 4, 1901.]

ST. THOMAS
[Population approximately 15,000]

Duncombe's New Opera House

MANAGER	T. H. Duncombe
SEATING CAPACITY	1,027
PRICES	25¢ to $1.00
LIGHTING	gas and electricity
STAGE DIMENSIONS	Width of prosc. opening, 30 ft. Height of prosc. opening, 30 ft. Footlights to back wall, 35 ft. Stage to rigging loft, 48 ft. Five grooves; can be taken up flush with fly gallery
ORCHESTRA	11 Fred Dunn, leader

Theatre on main floor

[There were two dailies in St. Thomas at the turn of the century, the *Journal* and the *Times*.
All the hotels were reasonable: One dollar was the price at the Columbia, Wilcox and Dake House.
Little information was known about theatre in St. Thomas at the time of writing.]

New Grand Opera House

MANAGER	R. A. McVean
SEATING CAPACITY	1,200
LIGHTING	gas and electricity
STAGE DIMENSIONS	Width prosc. opening, 30 ft. Height prosc. opening, 35 ft. Footlights to back wall, 38 ft.
ORCHESTRA	9

Theatre on ground floor

[Preparations for building the New Grand were going on in May 1894. It was to be part of Whitney circuit.]

WOODSTOCK
[Population approximately 10,500]

Grand Opera House

MANAGER	W. D. Emerson
SEATING CAPACITY	1,200
PRICES	25¢, 35¢ and 50¢
STAGE DIMENSIONS	Width of prosc. opening, 28 ft. Footlights to back wall, 24 ft. Height of grooves from stage, 18 ft. Stage to rigging loft, 48 ft.
ORCHESTRA	7 Frank Windsor, leader

[The newspapers were the *Sentinel-Review* and the *Times*.]

186

G

The companies vary in their importance, but in an effort to be reasonably complete, I made a selective list. For clarity, I have placed them in three categories: THE TOURING STARS, SOME LESSER-KNOWN COMPANIES, AND THE RANK AND FILE OF THE ROAD.

*SOURCES OF INFORMATION:

New York Dramatic Mirror, New York, 1880–1914; *The New York Clipper*, New York, 1881–1914; T. Allston Brown, *History of the American Stage* (New York, Dick and Fitzgerald Publishers, 1870); W. Browne and E. De Roy Koch, *Who's Who on the Stage, 1908* (New York, B. W. Dodge and Co., 1908); W. Davenport Adams, *A Dictionary of the Drama* (London, Chatto & Windus, 1904); Ruth Harvey, *Curtain Time* (Boston, Houghton Mifflin Co., 1949); Marie Dressler, *My Own Story* (Boston, Little Brown and Co., 1934); *The Oxford Companion to the Theatre*, edited by Phillis Hartnell (London, Oxford University Press, 1951).

ADAMS, MAUDE, & CO.

Her first starring role was Lady Babbie in J. M. Barrie's *The Little Minister* in 1898. As a leading lady, she performed in the following plays: *Romeo and Juliet* (1900), *L'Aiglon* (1901), *Quality Street* (1903), *The Little Minister* (revival, 1905), *Peter Pan* (1905), *The Jesters* (1908). She toured eastern Canada in 1910 with Barrie's *What Every Woman Knows*.

ANGLIN, MARGARET, & CO.

She was an internationally famous actress who was born in Ottawa, April 3, 1876. Her father was Speaker of the House at the time, and her birth, according to the legend, took place in the Speaker's Chamber. Her first professional appearance was at the Academy of Music, New York, in 1894. In 1897–98 she organized with E. H. Sothern, "a company for a tour of Lower Canada, playing Rosalind in *As You Like It*." (*Who's Who on the Stage, 1908*). Further tours in Canada: 1903, *Cynthia* (with Henry Miller); 1914, *As You Like It, Taming of the Shrew, Twelfth Night, Antony and Cleopatra, Lady Windermere's Fan*. For an interesting and amusing glance at Anglin see *Curtain Time*, p. 165.

ARLISS, GEORGE, & CO.

Remembered chiefly for his film work, this actor had a long career on the stage. He first attracted attention when playing Cayley Drummey in Mrs. Patrick Campbell's production of *The Second Mrs. Tanqueray* which she took on tour in 1901–3. He was probably with the company when it played at the Princess Theatre, Toronto, in February 1903. He toured Canada again in 1909 with Molnar's *The Devil*.

BARRETT, LAWRENCE, & CO.

This well-known American actor died in 1891. During the 70s and 80s he was in the leading ranks of Shakespearean actors. His tour of Canada took place in 1880. In November of this year at the Grand Opera House in Ottawa, he presented *Hamlet* and *Julius Caesar*.

BARRETT, WILSON, & CO.

This rather extraordinary jack-of-all-theatrical-trades was known as an actor, playwright, and theatrical manager. It is noted in *A Dictionary of the Drama* that he "made his debut as an actor at Halifax, in 1864." Among the long list of plays he claimed to have written are: *Pharaoh* (1892), *The Manxman* (1894) and *The Sign of the Cross* (1895). He died in 1904. He toured the cities and towns in eastern Canada in the following years: 1892, *Ben-My-Chree, Pharaoh, Hamlet*; 1894, *Virginius, The Stranger, Hamlet, Othello, The Silver King, Ben-My-Chree*; 1895, *Othello, Hamlet, Ben-My-Chree, The Silver King, The Manxman*.

BERNHARDT, SARAH, & CO.

Bernhardt was born in Paris in 1844 and in 1880 she made her first appearance in the United States and Montreal. While in Montreal she presented, *Adrienne Lecouvreur, Froufrou, La Dame aux Camélias*, and *Hernani*. She was threatened with excommunication by the Bishop of Montreal. Later appearances in Canada were: 1896, *Izeyl, Gismonda*; 1910, *L'Aiglon, Camille, Jeanne d'Arc*.

CAMPBELL, MRS. PATRICK, & CO.

An amusing picture of Mrs. Campbell is given by Ruth Harvey in her *Curtain Time*. She remembers Mrs. Campbell's visit to Winnipeg: "Papa often regretted that before Mrs. Patrick Campbell started her tour . . . he had not equipped the theatre with a seismograph." She recalls the commotion of Mrs. Campbell's visit, pp. 212–16. This tour was probably in 1903, and her repertoire included *The Second Mrs. Tanqueray, The Joy of Living*, and *Magda*. In 1907 she returned with *The Notorious Mrs. Ebbsmith*.

CARTER, MRS. LESLIE, & CO.

Sometimes hailed as the American Bernhardt, Mrs. Carter's career started in 1890. In 1911 she presented *Two Women* on a tour through eastern Canada. While in Montreal, it was reported that a "Mr. Germain Beaulieu, advocate of this city, has had a notarial protest against the production of the play in Canada served on Mrs. Carter. Mr. Beaulieu claims that the play is an infringment of copyright of a drama which he wrote" (*New York Dramatic Mirror*, March 29, 1911). No further information about this altercation has been found.

188

DRESSLER, MARIE, & CO.

Although she became a famous comedienne in the United States, Canadians claim her for their own as she was born in Cobourg, Ontario. She toured Canada with a production of *Tillie's Nightmare* in 1912. She refers to the role in her book, *My Own Story*: "It was shortly after my distressing experience in bankruptcy that I was offered the role which proved my nearest approach to immortality. This was the part of the boarding-house drudge in *Tillie's Nightmare*. For five years I was Tillie. And for many years after, the public remembered me not as Marie Dressler but as Tillie" (p. 146).

FISKE, MINNIE MADDERN, & CO.

Born in New Orleans, December 19, 1865, she was an accepted star by the time she was sixteen. Her schooling was a problem, in that she was forced to spend brief periods of time in "French or convent schools in the cities of New Orleans, St. Louis, Montreal, and Cincinnati" (*Who's Who*). Her tours in Canada were made in the following years: 1896, *The Queen of Liars, A Doll's House*; 1899, *Tess of the D'Urbervilles*; 1909, *Salvation Nell, Rosmersholm*; 1910, *Becky Sharp, The Pillars of Society*.

FORBES-ROBERTSON, GERTRUDE ELLIOT, & CO.

Toured in eastern Canada in the following years: 1904, *The Light That Failed*; 1907, *Caesar and Cleopatra, Hamlet, Mice and Men*; 1910, *The Passing of the Third Floor Back*.

GREET'S SHAKESPEAREAN CO., BEN

Ben Greet was one of the first managers in the nineteenth century to consider presenting Shakespeare's plays in the open air. Most of the productions took place on the grounds of universities. In Toronto, during convocation week in 1904, for example, his "Shakespearean Pastorals" were presented in the Dean's Garden, University of Toronto. In June of that year, his company performed *As You Like It* and *A Midsummer Night's Dream* on the grounds of Western University. He returned to Canada with the same theatrical fare for the next two years: 1905, *Two Gentlemen of Verona, As You Like It, A Midsummer Night's Dream, The Tempest*; 1906, *Merchant of Venice, Macbeth*.

IRVING, HENRY, & CO.

Toured eastern Canada in the following years: 1884, *The Bells, Charles I, Louis XI, Much Ado about Nothing, Hamlet, The Merchant of Venice*; 1894, *Becket, The Bells*; 1895, *Faust, Merchant of Venice, King Arthur, A Story of Waterloo, The Bells*; 1900, *Robespierre, Merchant of Venice*; 1904, *Merchant of Venice, Waterloo, The Bells*.

IRVING, LAURENCE, & CO.

1914, *Crime and Punishment*.

KEENE, THOMAS W., & CO.

Keene was born in New York on October 26, 1840. He spent most of his active life on the "road," and it is worth noting that he seemed to prefer the Canadian circuits. William Seymore in his article, "Some Richards I Have Seen," *Theatre Magazine*, XXXI, 502 (June, 1920), makes a few remarks about Keene: "In 1888 I was associated with Thomas W. Keene, the most spectacular Richard of them all, yet withal a brilliant performance. Keene gave tremendous emphasis to the more violent passages, and evinced a sardonic humor, not unlike John Wilkes Booth. If Thomas Keene had taken himself more seriously, he would have ranked among our foremost tragedians. But 'Tom' would have his fun on the side." His tours in Canada were made in the following years: 1883, *Richelieu, Richard III, Hamlet*; 1884, *Richard III, Richelieu, Hamlet, Julius Caesar, Macbeth*; 1887, *Hamlet*; 1888, *A Rag Baby, Held by the Enemy*; 1889, *Hamlet, Julius Caesar*; 1893, *Hamlet, Richard III*; 1894, *Merchant of Venice*; 1895, *Hamlet, Merchant of Venice, Richard III*; 1897, *Richelieu, Ingomar, Othello, Richard III*; 1898, *Richelieu, Richard III*. According to Graham in *Histrionic Montreal*, his last appearance was in Hamilton, Ontario, on May 23, 1898. He was playing *Richelieu* when he was stricken. "Then fell a rugged oak, over whose prostrate trunk the sunshine was gleaming broadly through the vistas of a beautiful life" (p. 261).

LANGTRY, MRS., & CO.

Toured Canada in the following years: 1883, *As You Like It*; 1886 (with Maurice Barrymore), *A Wife's Peril, The Lady of Lyons*; 1887, *A Wife's Peril*.

LORRAINE, ROBERT, & CO.

In September 1905, Lorraine appeared at the Hudson Theatre, New York, in *Man and Superman*, playing the role of John Tanner. This production was taken on tour. It played in Toronto in November, 1906.

MANSFIELD, RICHARD, & CO.

Toured in Canada in the following years: 1883, *Parisian Romance*; 1901, *Henry V*; 1902, *Beaucaire, Beau Brummell*; 1906, *Merchant of Venice, Richard III*.

MARLOWE, JULIA, & CO. (see also SOTHERN)

Marlowe was born in England in 1865. She attained her greatest success in the following roles: Parthenia in *Ingomar*, Rosalind in *As You Like It*. Juliet, and Viola in *Twelfth Night*. Her tours in Canada were in the following years: 1889, *Sweet Lavender*; 1893, *Twelfth Night, Romeo and Juliet, Much Ado about Nothing, As You Like It*; 1908, *As You Like It*.

MARTIN-HARVEY, JOHN, & CO.

Martin-Harvey came to Canada in 1914 under the auspices of the British and Canadian Theatre Organization Society (see Chapter Two). His repertoire was: *The Bread of the Treshams, The Only Way* and *The Cigarette Maker's Daughter*. His life and acting career (especially in Canada) are examined in a radio programme called The Grand Tour which was produced by the author and is now in the archives of the Canadian Broadcasting Corporation.

MILLER, HENRY, & CO.

This actor-manager who became famous in the United States was born in London, England, in 1854, and was educated in Toronto. "He made his first stage appearance just before he was nineteen in a stock company performance of *Macbeth* at a Toronto theatre" (*Who's Who on the Stage*). He toured Canada in later years: 1886, *The Three Students*; 1902, *D'Arcy of the Guards*; 1909, *The Great Divide*.

MODJESKA, HELENA, & CO.

She toured Canada in the following years: 1883, *As You Like It*; 1899, *Mary Stuart, Antony and Cleopatra, Macbeth, Much Ado about Nothing*; 1900, *King John, Macbeth*; 1901, *Henry VIII, Macbeth*.

NAZIMOVA, MADAME ALLA, & CO.

She was recognized as a leading actress and was most frequently associated with Ibsen's plays. Her tours of Canada were in the following years: 1908 and 1909, *A Doll's House*.

O'NEILL, JAMES, & CO.

This well-known romantic actor was born in 1847 and died in 1920. In 1883 he toured Canada in a play called *An American King*.

SOTHERN & JULIA MARLOWE

Toured Canada in 1910 with *Romeo and Juliet, Merchant of Venice, As You Like It, The Taming of the Shrew, Hamlet, Twelfth Night*.

TERRY, ELLEN, & CO.

This actress was born in England in 1848. Her first appearance was with Henry Irving's Company at the Lyceum, London, in 1878. She remained with him as his leading lady until 1902. Terry toured eastern Canada with her own company in 1907 playing Lady Cecily Waynflete in *Captain Brassbound's Conversion*.

SOME LESSER-KNOWN COMPANIES

ARTHUR, JULIA, & CO.

This actress was born in Hamilton, Ontario on May 3, 1869. At the age of eleven she "played Zamora in *The Honeymoon* in private theatricals in her father's home" (*Who's Who on the Stage*). Her first professional appearance was in 1881 with Daniel Bandmann's Company. In 1898 she was touring Canada in her production of *A Lady of Quality*.

BANDMANN, DANIEL, & CO.

Bandmann was born in Germany. His first acting in English took place in 1863 in New York. In the 1880s he was touring in the United States and Canada. His repertoire included *The Merchant of Venice, Richard III*, and *Narcisse*. While playing at the Grand Opera House in Toronto in December 1884, he presented *Called Back*. One critic was not pleased: "So little did any of the company know the play that neither the hero or heroine could find the doors through which to make their exits from the stage" (the *Globe*, December 13, 1884).

BOUCICAULT, DION, & CO.

This actor, writer, manager, was born in 1820. He set out for the United States in 1853 and from that year on performed many of his own plays alternately in the United States and in England. He made one tour into Canada in 1884 playing *The Shaugraun* and *Colleen Bawn*. When he played at the Grand Opera House in Toronto, December 1884, a reviewer for the *Globe*, December 1, pointed out to his readers that "he travels in his own combination cars, built specially for his use. 'The Shaughraun,' as the dwelling car is called, is a model of comfort, elegance, and utility."

CLAXTON, KATE, & CO.

Kate Claxton was the original Louise in *The Two Orphans* which opened in New York in 1875 under Mr. Palmer's management. After it closed, "Kate Claxton made an arrangement with Mr. Palmer whereby she became its exclusive possessor, and played in it almost continuously for twenty years." (*The Theatre*, III, 63 (March 1903)). She toured Canada in the following years: 1880, *The Two Orphans*; 1884, *Sea of Ice*, *The Two Orphans*; 1885, *Sea of Ice*, *The Two Orphans*; 1903, *The Two Orphans*.

COGHLAN, ROSE, & CO.

This English actress was born in 1851 and died in 1932. She toured Canada in the following years: 1885, *Idol of the Hour*; 1894, *A Woman of No Importance*, *Diplomacy*; 1906, *Mrs. Warren's Profession*.

CORCORAN, JANE, & CO.

Toured Canada in 1908 with *A Doll's House*, *East Lynne*, *Hedda Gabler*. For more information about this actress, see Chapter Two.

EYTINGE, ROSE, & CO.

This American actress was born in 1835. She toured Canada in the following years: 1881, *Miss Moulton* (see Annie Russell); 1885, *Niagara*; 1907, *Cymbeline*. (On this tour she was associated with a Mr. Sam Reed. She retired shortly after this date.)

FAVERSHAM, WILLIAM, & CO.

Apart from noting his eminence in the theatre world, it is reported in *Who's Who* that he was "one of the biggest breeders of bull terriers in America." He toured in Canada in 1914 with *Othello*, *Julius Caesar*, and *Romeo and Juliet*.

GALLATIN, ALBERTA, & CO.

Her tour of Canada in 1903 with *Ghosts* is considered in Chapter Two.

GILLETTE, W. H., & CO.

1882, *The Professor*; 1885, *The Private Secretary*, *The Rajah*.

GLASSFORD, KATE, & CO.

1881, *East Lynne*, *Camille*, *Led Astray*.

GRAY, ADA, & CO.

1881, *East Lynne*; after a week in Toronto at the Royal Opera House (August) they played Peterborough, Cobourg, Belleville, Kingston, Brockville and Montreal; 1884, 1886, 1887, 1895, *East Lynne*.

GRIFFITH, JOHN, & CO.

1898, *Richard III*; 1902, *Macbeth*, *Searchlight of a Great City*, *Caste*; 1906, *Richard III*; 1908, *Othello*. (He was at the Russell Theatre, Ottawa on October 17. According to a release in the *Dramatic Mirror*, his route was then Brantford, Woodstock, St. Thomas, Stratford, and London.)

HACKETT, JAMES K., & CO.

This actor-manager was born on Wolfe Island, Ontario, on September 6, 1869. He went to the United States as a child and grew up there, eventually taking up a career in the theatre. He toured *Othello* in eastern Canada in 1914.

HARE, JOHN, & CO.

1896, *A Pair of Spectacles*, *Caste*, *The Hobby Horse* (see Chapter Two).

HARKINS' CO., THE W. S.

1890, *Shadow of a Great City*, *The Black Flag*, *Woman against Woman*; 1893, *Master and Man*.

HORNIMAN PLAYERS

1912, *The Silver Box*, *Reaping the Worldwind*, *She Stoops to Conquer*, *Nan*, *Candida*.

JAMES, LOUIS, & CO.

After approximately five years, during which he was leading man to Lawrence Barrett, James started his own touring company. His repertoire was almost exclusively Shakespearean. 1897, *Romeo and Juliet*, *Julius Caesar*; 1901, *A Midsummer Night's Dream* (with Kathryn Kidder); 1902, *The Tempest* (with Frederick Warde); 1905, *The Merchant of Venice*; 1908, *Merry Wives of Windsor*, *Comedy of Errors*. He died in 1910 while on tour in the United States.

KENDAL, MR. & MRS., & CO.

1894, *The Second Mrs. Tanqueray*.

191

MANTELL, ROBERT B., & CO.

Mantell was born in Scotland in 1854. By 1878 he was performing in the United States. He was constantly on the "road," and spent many of his last active years in Canada. 1887, *Monbars*; 1888, *Monbars, Marble Heart*; 1889, *Othello, Monbars*; 1894, *Othello, Hamlet*; 1896, *Hamlet, Othello, Romeo and Juliet, Monbars*; 1897, *The Face in the Moonlight*; 1898, *The Secret Warrant*; 1900, *The Dagger and the Cross*; 1901, *Romeo and Juliet, Hamlet, Othello*; 1906, *Richard III, Lear, Othello*; 1908, *Hamlet, King Lear*; 1910, *Merchant of Venice*; 1911, *Julius Caesar, King Lear*; 1913, *Merchant of Venice, King Lear*. Mantell wrote his "Personal Reminiscences," in *The Theatre*, XXIV, 194–196 (October 1916). He avoids any comment on Canada. For his connection with W. A. Tremayne, see Chapter Four.

MARKHAM, PAULINE, & CO.

Although famous in her day as a vaudeville artist, she essayed dramatic roles when she toured Canada. 1885, *The Two Orphans, East Lynne, Led Astray*; 1886, *The New Magdalen, Camille, The Ticket-of-Leave Man, East Lynne, Lady of Lyons*.

MATHER, MARGARET, & CO.

1884, *Romeo and Juliet*; 1897, *Cymbeline, Romeo and Juliet*.

NEILSON, ADELAIDE, & CO.

Miss Neilson made her *début* in 1865 in England. She opened the rebuilt Grand Opera House, Toronto, in 1880 playing in *As You Like It, Romeo and Juliet*, and *Twelfth Night*. This was probably on the occasion of her second visit to the United States. She died in this year after returning to Europe.

RANKIN, MCKEE, & CO.

Rankin should be remembered as one of the first Canadian actors to attempt to portray a French-Canadian character (see Chapter Four). He was constantly touring in Canada: 1885, *Notice to Quit*; 1897, *True to Life* (with Nance O'Neil); 1905, *Macbeth* (with Nance O'Neil); 1906, *The Sorceress* (with Nance O'Neil and Lester Lonergan). He died in April, 1914. At the funeral were Margaret Drew (daughter of John Drew), Mrs. Harry Davenport (daughter), Mrs. Lionel Barrymore, Arthur Barrymore, and Sidney Drew.

RUSSELL, ANNIE, & CO.

This actress was born in England in 1864, but spent her childhood in Canada. "She made her first public appearance at the age of seventeen, as Jeanne in *Miss Moulton* with Rose Eytinge at the Academy of Music, Montreal." (*Who's Who on the Stage*.) In 1907 she was touring Canada with Catharine Proctor in *A Midsummer Night's Dream*.

WHITESIDE, WALKER, & CO.

Whiteside ended his career playing character parts in New York. When on the "road" in Canada, however, he played mainly in Shakespeare. 1895, *Merchant of Venice, Hamlet, Richelieu, Othello*; 1896, *Hamlet, Merchant of Venice*; 1897, *Hamlet, Merchant of Venice*; 1900, *Hamlet*; 1902, *Heart and Sword, Merchant of Venice, Hamlet*; 1903, *Richard III, Hamlet, Merchant of Venice*.

THE RANK AND FILE OF THE ROAD

ALDRICH & PARSLOE CO.

1883, *My Partner*.

ARNOLD & FARLEMAN CO.

1883, *East Lynne*.

BAKER, EDITH ELLIS, & CO.

1903, *Ghosts* (see Chapter Two).

BAKER AND FARRON CO.

1882, *Max Muller*; 1883, *Government House* (presented for the first time at the Grand Opera House, Toronto, May 22); 1885, *A Soap Bubble*.

BARRY & FAY CO.

1881, *Muldoon's Picnic*; 1884, *Irish Aristocracy*.

BAUM'S DRAMATIC CO.

1883, *Maide of Arran*.

BEER'S COMBINATION, NEWTON

1886, *Lost in London*.

BELLOW & CO.

(See Mrs. Potter.)

BEN HUR CO., THE

1896, *Ben-Hur*

BINDLEY, FLORENCE T., & CO.

1887, *A Heroine in Rags*.

BLAIR, EUGENIE, & CO.

1898, *Camille, East Lynne, The New Magdalen, Jane Eyre*; 1900, *A Woman of Quality*; 1906, *The Woman in the Case.* Miss Blair was still performing in 1922. In this year she was playing the part of Marthy Owen, in Eugene O'Neill's *Anna Christie* in New York.

BOGEL, CLAUS, & CO.

1905, *Ghosts* (see Chapter Two).

BOKEL, WILLIAM, & CO.

1884, *Othello, Merchant of Venice, Richelieu.*

BONIFACE, GEORGE C., & CO.

1885, *The Streets of New York.*

BOUCICAULT, AUBREY, & CO.

1903, *Captain Charlie.*

BROOKS AND DICKSON CO.

1883, *The Romany Rye.*

CARNER, J. W., & CO.

1881, *Rip Van Winkle.* Joseph Jefferson, who was closely identified with the character of Rip Van Winkle for most of his long career, turned to the role of Bob Acres in *The Rivals* at about this time. Lesser talents were bound to use this vehicle. Carner was one. See also, THOMAS JEFFERSON and GEORGE H. SUMMERS.

CAUFFMAN, ALEX, & CO.

1881, *Lazare, A Life's Mistake.*

CHANFRAU, F. S., & CO.

1882, *Sam.*

CHASE, HETTIE BERNARD, & CO.

1891, *Alaska.*

CLARKE'S DRAMATIC CO., MARLANDE

1886, *Streets of New York.*

CLEMENT, CLAY, & CO.

1898, *The New Dominion*; 1903, *The New Dominion*; 1907, *The New Dominion.* (See Appendix A.)

COLEMAN, HELEN, & CO.

1882, *Widow Bedott.*

COLLIER, J. W., & CO.

1882, *The Banker's Daughter, Lights O'London*; 1885, *Lights O'London.*

CONLAN, WARREN, & CO.

1897, *Othello, Fool's Revenge, Damon and Pythias.* This company played Kingston in October and then were scheduled to move on to London. Like so many of these little groups, they just fade away.

COURTNEY, EDA, (?) & CO.

1885, *Her Last Hope*; 1904, *Pretty Peggy.*

CROSS ROADS CO., THE

1894, *The Cross Roads.* This type of company would be formed for the season, perform for a set number of engagements and then disband.

CUMMINGS, ROBERT, & CO.

1898, *The Wages of Sin*; 1899, *Lights O'London*; 1900, *The Power of the Cross.* The "home" for this company was the Princess Theatre, Toronto.

DAILY'S COMBINATION

1881, *Needles and Pins.*

DAVIES, R., COMBINATION

1892, *The Fast Mail.*

DAVIS, CHARLES L., & CO.

1887, *Alvin Joslin.*

DAY'S INTERNATIONAL THEATRE CO.

1886, *Queen's Evidence.*

DELMORE, RALPH, & CO.

1887, *A Ring of Iron.*

DE WOLFE, ELSIE, & CO.

1902, *The Way of the World.*

DODGE, SANFORD, & CO.

1897, *Othello.*

DOWLING, JOSEPH J., CO.

1882, *Nobody's Claim.*

DRAPER'S COMBINATION

1885, *Uncle Tom's Cabin.* This was a standard production. But as the years went by, more liberties were taken with this play. (See IDEAL UNCLE TOM'S CABIN CO.)

EGBERT DRAMATIC CO.

1886, *Engaged, Our Boys, Euchred, Monte Cristo.*

EMMETT, KATIE, & CO.

1895, *The Waifs of New York.*

EVANS, LIZZIE, & CO.

1886, *Foggs Ferry.*

FAY, ANNA EVA, & CO.
1896, *Mystifying Powers.*

FIFTH AVENUE CO., THE
1881, *Hazel Kirke, The Gov'nor, The Galley Slave, Fairfax, The Banker's Daughter, False Friend.*

FISH & HASSAN'S CO.
1887, *A Gold Day.*

FOSTELLE, CHARLES, & CO.
1881, *Mrs. Partington.*

GOODRICH, E. T., & CO.
1881, *Grizzly Adams.*

GRISMER-DAVIES CO.
1886, *Wages of Sin.*

GUY FAMILY COMBINATION
1885, *Uncle Tom's Cabin.* The play was noted as being "cleverly burlesqued" when it played in the Lyceum Dime Museum, Halifax, October 19. This is an exception; *Uncle Tom's Cabin* was usually given seriously in this early period.

HAMPTON, MARY, & CO.
1888, *Gwynne's Oath, Little Em'ly.*

HANFORD, CHARLES, & CO.
1893, *Julius Caesar*; 1903, *Much Ado about Nothing, Taming of the Shrew.*

HARRISON, MAUD, & CO.
1892, *American Girl.*

HARRISON-GOURLAY CO.
1883, *Skipped By the Light of the Moon.*

HAVERLY'S COMIC OPERA CO., J. H.
1882, *Patience, The Pirates of Penzance*; 1885, *Strategists.*

HEDLEY, KING, & CO.
1885, *After Dark.*

HERN, J., COMPANY
1882, *Hearts of Oak.*

HINDS, J. T., & CO.
1880, *Shaugraun, Colleen Bawn.*

HOLLAND, JOSEPH, & CO.
1896, *A Social Highwayman.*

HOUGHTON, EDWARD, COMBINATION
1895, *In Darkest Brazil.*

HOYT & COMPANY
1885, *A Bunch of Keys.*

HUNT, JULIA A., COMBINATION
1882, *Florinel.*

HUNTINGTON, AGNES, & CO.
1890, *Captain Therese.*

HYDE & BEHMAN CO.
1882, *Evangeline.*

HYER SISTERS, THE
1880, *Uncle Tom's Cabin.*

IDEAL UNCLE TOM'S CABIN CO.
1883, *Uncle Tom's Cabin.* This elaborate production was noted by a reviewer when it played at the Royal Opera House, Toronto, on January 8, 1883. He draws our attention to the fact that it had "two Topsys and two lawyer Marks." He continues, "The first Topsy that appears is a little girl realizing in a great measure the idea of the weird creature who 'growed' that is formed in reading Mrs. Stowe's celebrated works, and the second edition of Topsy appears to be the same plant a little more mature. The two Marks appear on stage at the same time." Mr. James T. Fanning was "the best Uncle Tom that has been seen in Toronto."

IRWIN, THOMAS, & CO.
1903, *Her Marriage Vow.*

ISHAM, JOHN W., AND W. H. LYTELL'S AMUSEMENT SYNDICATE
1897, *My Friend from India.*

JACKSON, PETER, & CO.
1894, *Uncle Tom's Cabin.*

JANAUSCHEK & CO., MADAME
1893, *Macbeth* (supported by Edmond Collier).

JEFFERSON, THOMAS, & CO.
1901, 1902, 1903, *Rip Van Winkle.* Thomas was the son of the famous Joseph Jefferson.

KEANE, J. H., & CO.
1881, *Hazel Kirke.*

KELCY, HERBERT, EFFIE SHANNON & CO.
1907, *Widowers' Houses.* This play was first presented by Miss Horniman in Manchester, October 7, 1907 (see Chapter Two).

KYLE, HOWARD, & CO.

1903, *Nathan Hale*. This play was anti-British. A report reached *The New York Clipper* when it was being presented at London, Ontario, in January. "After the London performance of *Nathan Hale*, Manager Sackett cancelled the balance of his Canadian tour — realizing how unsuitable it was."

LACY, HARRY, & CO.

1884, *Planter's Wife*.

LINDLEY, HARRY, & CO.

1885, *Young and Old America*. This fascinating character toured Canada for years. According to Walter McRaye in his *Town Hall Tonight!* (p. 26), "he toured the smaller towns playing a lot of pirated plays he had stolen from New York."

LONERGAN, LESTER

1904, *Candida* (see Chapter Two).

LONG, FRANK E., & CO.

1898, *Alone in New York*.

LONGEE, KITTIE, CO.

1880, *Uncle Tom's Cabin*.

LUDLOW, HENRY, & CO.

1907, *Merchant of Venice*.

LYCEUM DRAMATIC CO., THE

1886, *Nobody's Child*.

LYTELL, MAYER, & SNYDER DRAMATIC CO., THE

1881, *The World*.

LYTELL, W. H., & CO. (SEE ALSO ISHAM)

1883, *The White Slave, Galley Slave, Youth*; 1884, *The Silver King, Uncle Tom's Cabin*; 1885, *Romany Rye, Silver King, Separation*; 1886, *Romany Rye*; 1902, *A Milk White Flag*.

LYTELL AND NATHAN CO.

1882, *Michael Strogoff*; 1883, *Youth*.

MARKS BROTHERS, THE

See Chapter Two.

MATHEWS AND BULGER CO.

1898, *By the Sad Sea Waves*.

MAUBURY & OVERTON CO.

1885, *The Wages of Sin*.

MCDOWELL, E. A., & CO.

See Chapter Two.

MCWADE, ROBERT, & CO.

1882, *Rip Van Winkle*.

MILLS, JOSIE, CO.

1893, *The Black Flag*.

MINER, HARRY, & CO.

1885, *The Silver King*.

MITCHELL, MASON

1889, *The Fugitive*.

MOORE, ADELAIDE, & CO.

1886, *Excerpts from Shakespeare*.

MORRISON'S CO., LEWIS

1886, *May Blossom*.

MURPHY, JOSEPH S., & CO.

1885, *Kerry Gow*; 1891, *Bouchal Bawm*; 1896, *Shaun Rhue*.

NEILL STOCK CO.

1897, *Jim the Penman*; 1898, *Banker's Daughter, London Assurance, The Span of Life*; 1900, *The American Citizen*.

NELSON, HAROLD, & CO.

1902, *Hamlet, Richelieu, A Celebrated Case, Romeo and Juliet, Ingomar, The Merchant of Venice, Othello*; 1903, *Quo Vadis*. This actor was in association with Walker in Winnipeg.

NETHERSOLE, OLGA, & CO.

1899, *The Profligate, The Second Mrs. Tanqueray*; 1907, *The Awakening*; 1909, *Camille, The Second Mrs. Tanqueray*.

OWEN SHAKESPEAREAN CO., WILLIAM

1896, *Hamlet, Romeo and Juliet, Much Ado about Nothing, The Lady of Lyons*; 1900, *The Marble Heart, Othello*; 1903, *The School for Scandal, Othello, Romeo and Juliet*.

PECK AND FURSHMAN'S CO.

1888, *Uncle Tom's Cabin*.

POMEROY, LOUISE, & CO.

1885, *As You Like It, Romeo and Juliet, Twelfth Night*.

POST, GUY, BATES & CO.

1910, *The Nigger*.

POTTER, MRS., MR. BELLOW, & CO.

1896, *Charlotte Corday, Camille, She Stoops to Conquer*.

POWERS, W. H., PARAGON CO.

1881, *Galley Slave, My Geraldine, Matrimony*.

195

PUTNAM, KATE, & CO.
1897, *Old Curiosity Shop.*

REDMAN-BARRY CO.
1885, *Rank and Fame.*

REEVES, FANNY, & CO.
1889, *The School for Scandal, Led Astray.*
She was the wife of E. A. McDowell.

REHAN, ADA, & CO.
1895, *Twelfth Night, Railroad of Love,
Midsummer Night's Dream, The Taming
of the Shrew, The School for Scandal.*

REHAN'S CO., ARTHUR
1893, *A Modern St. Anthony, Satanella.*

REID'S COMPANY, W. L.
1899, *Ten Nights in a Bar-Room.*

RHEA, MLLE., & CO.
1886, *A Dangerous Game, Frou Frou,
Pygmalion and Galatea, The Country Girl,
Camille, Fairy Fingers*; 1894, *The New
Magdalen.*

ROBERTS, SIR RANDAL, & CO.
1881, *A Celebrated Case.*

ROBSON, MAY, & CO.
1914, *Martha-by-the-Day.*

ROBSON AND CRANE
1887, *Musicals and Shakespeare!* This
interesting combination was at the Royal
Opera House, Toronto, in May of this year.

RUSSELL, SOL SMITH, & CO.
1888, *A Poor Relation*; 1893, *A Poor
Relation*; 1894, *Peaceful Valley, The Heir-
at-Law*; 1895, *An Everyday Man.*

SANFORD'S DRAMATIC CO.
1889, *Under the Lash.*

SELMAN, PAIGE AND FOLEY'S CO.
1904, *Othello, Merchant of Venice,
Richard III.*

SHEPPARD'S COMBINATION
1887, *Night Off.*

SHOOK AND COLLIER CO.
1885, *A Prisoner for Life.*

SMITH, C. H., & CO.
1881, *Uncle Tom's Cabin.*

STAFFORD, WILLIAM, & EVELYN FOSTER CO.
1884, *Hamlet, Romeo and Juliet, Othello,
Ingomar.*

STELLA COMBINATION
1880, *Octoroon.*

STOVER'S COMBINATION
1890, *Uncle Tom's Cabin.*

STUART, JULIA, & CO.
1895, *A Doll's House.* See Chapter Two.

SUMMERS, GEORGE H., STOCK CO.
1903, *The Prodigal Son, Pawn Ticket
210, Resurrection, Rip Van Winkle, A
Wife's Honor, La Belle Marie, True Irish
Hearts* (see also Chapter Two).

TAYLEURE, B. L., DRAMATIC CO.
1885, *Octoroon.*

TERRY, EDWARD, & CO.
1911, *Sweet Lavender.*

ULMER, LIZZIE MAY, & CO.
1882, *The Danites.*

VALENTINE COMBINATION, THE
1899, *Romeo and Juliet, Crust of Society*;
1900, *The Private Secretary*; 1901, *Jim
the Penman, The Black Flag, Uncle Tom's
Cabin, Merchant of Venice, East Lynne.*

VAN CORTLAND, IDA, & CO.
See Chapter Two.

WAINWRIGHT, MARIE, & CO.
1893, *The School for Scandal, As You Like
It, The Social Swim*; 1903, *Twelfth Night.*

WALLACK, THE J. H., CO.
1885, *Victor Durand*; 1887, *Bandit King,
The Cattle King.*

WARD, GENEVIEVE, & CO.
1881, 1882, *Forget-Me-Not.*

WATERMAN, G., & CO.
1882, 1883, *Uncle Tom's Cabin.*

WEBBER, HARRY, & CO.
1882, *Nip and Tuck*; 1889, *Uncle Tom's
Cabin.*

WEED'S COMBINATION
1884, *Power of Money.*

WELLESLEY-STERLING CO.
1885, *Danites.*

WREN, FRED, & CO.
1881, *Uncle Tom's Cabin.*

Bibliography.

GENERAL WORKS

BROOKS, VAN WYCK. *The Confident Years*
New York: E. P. Dutton & Company, 1952.

CAHN, JULIUS. *Official Theatrical Guide*
New York: Publication Office, Empire Theatre Building, 1900.

DUNLAP, WILLIAM. *History of the American Theatre*
New York, 1832.

EATON, WALTER PRICHARD. *American Stage of Today*
New York: Small Maynard and Co., 1908.

HORNBLOW, ARTHUR.
A History of the Theatre in America from its Beginning to the Present Time
2 vols. New York: Lippincott, 1919.

LOGAN, J. D., and FRENCH, DONALD G.
Highways of Canadian Literature 2nd edition
Toronto: McClelland and Stewart, 1928.

LOWER, ARTHUR R. M. *Canadians in the Making: A Special History of Canada*
Toronto: Longmans, Green & Co., 1958.

MACMURCHY, ARCHIBALD. *Handbook of Canadian Literature*
Toronto: William Briggs Company, 1906.

MOODY, RICHARD. *America Takes the Stage*
Bloomington: Indiana University Press, 1955.

NICOLL, ALLARDYCE. *A History of Late Nineteenth Century Drama* Vol. 1
Cambridge University Press, 1946.

ODELL, GEORGE CLINTON DENSMORE. *Annals of the New York Stage*
London: George Redway, Covent Garden, 1888.

PIERCE, LORNE. *An Outline of Canadian Literature*
Toronto: The Ryerson Press, 1927.

QUINN, ARTHUR HOBSON.
A History of the American Drama from the Civil War to the Present Day
New York: Harper & Brothers, 1927.

REYNOLDS, ERNEST. *Early Victorian Drama*
London: Heffer and Sons Ltd., 1936.

————. *Modern English Drama*
Norman: University of Oklahoma Press, 1951.

ROWELL, GEORGE. *The Victorian Theatre*
London: Oxford University Press, 1956.

SACHS, EDWIN O. *Modern Opera Houses and Theatres*
London: B. T. Batsford, 1896.

WALLACE, WILLIAM STEWART, ed.
The Dictionary of Canadian Biography 2nd edition
Toronto: The Macmillan Company of Canada Limited, 1945.

WATSON, ERNEST BRADLEE.
Sheridan to Robertson: A Study of the 19th Century Stage
Cambridge: Harvard University Press, 1926.

WATTERS, REGINALD EYRE, ed. *A Check List of Canadian Literature and
Background Materials 1628–1950*
Toronto: University of Toronto Press, 1959.

198

THE CANADIAN STAGE

ANON. "Early Play Houses of Winnipeg" pamphlet for the formal opening of the
Walker Theatre, Winnipeg, Manitoba, February 18–19, 1907.

BERAUD, JEAN. *350 Ans de théâtre au Canada français*
Ottawa: Le Cercle du Livre de France, 1958.

BOOTH, MICHAEL. "Pioneer Entertainment: Theatrical Taste in the Early
Canadian West," *Canadian Literature*, 4, 52–8 (Spring, 1960).

BOSSIN, HYE. *Stars of David*
Toronto: The Jewish Standard, 1956.

BRAULT, LUCIEN. *Ottawa Old and New*
Ottawa: Ottawa Historical Information Institute, 1946.

CAMPBELL, MRS. WILLIAM. "Toronto Theatres in the Old Days,"
York Pioneer and Historical Society, Annual Report, 13–15 (1930).

CHARLESWORTH, HECTOR. *Candid Chronicles*
Toronto: Macmillan, 1925.

————. "Horse and Buggy Theatre,"
The Civic Theatre Magazine, 1, 12–14 (October 1945).

COHEN, NATHAN. "Theatre To-day: English Canada,"
Tamarack Review, XIII, 24–37 (Autumn 1959).

COLGATE, WILLIAM G. "Toronto Theatres in the Eighties,"
The Canadian Magazine, LVII, 279–82 (May–October, 1921).

CRAIG, IRENE. "Grease Paint on the Prairies,"
Historical and Scientific Society of Manitoba, III, 38–53 (1947).

DENISON, MERRIL. *The Barley and the Stream.*
Toronto: McClelland and Stewart Ltd., 1955.

DISHER, MAURICE WILLSON. *The Cowells in America*
London: Oxford University Press, 1934.

DURANG, JOHN. *Memoir of His Life and Travels*
Original manuscript property of the Historical Society of York County, Pennsylvania. Published as *The Memoir of John Durang, American Actor, 1785–1816.*
Pittsburgh: University of Pittsburgh Press, 1967.

GAISFORD, JOHN. *Theatrical Thoughts*
Montreal: Lovell and Gibson, 1884.

GRAHAM, FRANKLIN. *Histrionic Montreal*
Montreal: John Lovel & Son Publishers, 1902.

GUILLET, EDWIN CLARENCE. *Early Life in Upper Canada*
Toronto: Ontario Publishing Company, 1933; Toronto: University of Toronto Press, 1963.

————. *Toronto from Trading Post to Great City*
Toronto: Ontario Publishing Company, 1934.

HAM, GEORGE H. *Reminiscences of a Raconteur*
Toronto: The Musson Book Co., 1921.

HARDY, ALISON TAYLOR. "The Ottawa Little Theatre – Past and Present,"
Curtain Call, XII, 3–4 (January 1941).

HARRINGTON, GEORGE M. "Toronto and Its Early Theatrical Entertainments,"
Rose-Belford's Canadian Monthly and National Review, G. Mercer Adam, ed.,
VIII, 600–13 (January 1882).

HARVEY, RUTH. *Curtain Time*
Boston: Houghton Mifflin Co., 1949.

IRVING, LAURENCE. *Henry Irving, The Actor and His World*
London: Faber and Faber, 1951.

JEWITT, A. R. "Early Halifax Theatres,"
Dalhousie Review, V, 444–59 (January 1926).

MASSICOTTE, E. Z. "Les théâtres et les lieux d'amusements à Montréal," in
L'Annuaire théâtral, George H. Robert, ed.
Montreal: n.p., 1908–9.

MASTERS, D. C. *The Rise of Toronto*
Toronto: University of Toronto Press, 1947.

MCRAYE, WALTER. *Town Hall Tonight!*
Toronto: Ryerson Press, 1929.

MIDDLETON, JESSE EDGAR. "Music and the Theatre in Canada,"
in *Canada and Its Provinces*, Adam Shortt and Arthur G. Doughty, eds.
Toronto, Glasgow: Brook & Company, 1914.

———— *The Municipality of Toronto*
Toronto: Dominion Publishing Company, 1923.

MOORE, JAMES MAVOR. "The Theatre in English-speaking Canada,"
The Arts in Canada: A Stock Taking at Mid-Century, Malcolm Ross, ed., 77–82,
Toronto: Macmillan, 1958.

MURDOCH, BEAMISH. *A History of Nova Scotia or Acadie*
Halifax: James Barnes, Printer and Publisher, 1867.

PEMBERTON, EDGAR T. *Charles Dickens and the Stage*
London: George Redway, 1888.

PORTER, DANIEL R. "The Circus First Comes to Albany, 1798,"
New York History, XLIV, 1, 50 (January 1963).

Bibliography

RHYS, HORTON. *A Theatrical Trip for a Wager*
London: Charles Dudley, 1861; Vancouver: Alcuin Society, 1966.

SMITH, SOLOMON FRANKLIN. *Theatrical Management*
New York: Harper and Brothers, 1868.

TAYLOR, BEATRICE F. "British Garrison Officers Staged Hamlet in a Barn,"
London Free Press (June 15, 1955).

VAN CORTLAND, IDA. "Address to the University Women's Club of Ottawa,"
unpublished manuscript in the possession of Mrs. Ida C. McLeish, Ottawa.

WALKER, FRANK NORMAN. *Four Whistles to Wood-Up*
Toronto: Upper Canada Railway Society, 1953.

————. *Sketches of Old Toronto*
Toronto: Longmans Canada Ltd., 1965.

WALLACE, W. STEWART. "The Small Mystery,"
Maclean's Magazine, XLIV, 6 (July 1931).

WHITTAKER, HERBERT. "The Theatre," *The Culture of Contemporary Canada*,
Julian Park, ed., 163–180. Toronto: The Ryerson Press, 1957.

YOUNG, JAMES. *Reminiscences of the Early History of Galt and the Settlement of Dumeries in the Province of Ontario*
Toronto: Hunter, Rose and Company, 1880.

THE NEW MOVEMENT

CHENEY, SHELDON. *The New Movement in the Theatre*
New York: Mitchell Kennerley Company, 1914.

COBURN, JOHN. *I Kept My Powder Dry*
Toronto: The Ryerson Press, 1950.

ERVINE, ST. JOHN. *Bernard Shaw, His Life, Work and Friends*
New York: William Morrow & Co., 1956.

JACOB, FRED. *Peevee*
Toronto: The Macmillan Company of Canada Limited, 1928.

JONES, HENRY ARTHUR. *The Renascence of the English Drama*
London: Macmillan & Company, 1894.

MANDER, RAYMOND, and MITCHENSON, JOSEPH. *Theatrical Companion to Shaw*
London: Rockcliff Publishing Company, 1954.

PATCHETT, E. W. "Ibsen," *Queen's Quarterly*, XIV, 264–75 (April 1907).

WILLIAMS, RAYMOND. *Drama from Ibsen to Eliot*
London: Chatto & Windus, 1952.

THE POETIC DRAMATISTS

ANDERSON, WILLIAM E. *Leo and Venetia*
Pickering: *Pickering News* Office.

ARCHER, WILLIAM: "The Poetic Drama,"
The Critic, XXXVI, 23–7 (January 1900).

BURPEE, WILLIAM J. "Charles Heavysege," *Transactions of the Royal Society of Canada*, VII, 22–52 (Section ii, Series ii, 1901).

BUSH, THOMAS. *Santiago*. Toronto, n.p., 1866.

BYRON, GEORGE GORDON NOEL. *Byron: A Self Portrait*. Peter Quennell, ed. London: John Murray and Co., 1950.

CAMPBELL, WILFRED. "Shakespeare and The Latter-Day Drama," *Canadian Magazine*, XXX, 14 (November 1907).

—— *Poetical Tragedies*
Toronto: William Briggs, 1908.

CARMAN, BLISS, and KING, MARY PERRY. *Daughters of the Dawn*
New York: Mitchell Kennerley, 1913.

——. *Earth Deities*
New York: Mitchell Kennerley, 1914.

CLARK, DANIEL. "The Poetry of Charles Heavysege," *Canadian Monthly*, X, 127–8 (August 1876).

COTTON, W. L. "De Roberval,"
The Prince Edward Island Magazine, I, 1, 59–66 (March 1899).

CURZON, SARAH ANNE. *Laura Secord, the Heroine of 1812*
Toronto: C. Blackett Robinson, 1887.

——. *The Sweet Girl Graduate*
Toronto: C. Blackett Robinson, 1887.

DANIELLS, ROY. "Poetry and the Novel," in
The Culture of Contemporary Canada, Julian Park, ed.
Toronto: The Ryerson Press, 1957.

DIXON, FREDERICK A. *Canada's Welcome*
Ottawa: Maclean Roger & Company, 1879.

——. *Maiden Mona the Mermaid*
Toronto: Belford Brothers, 1877.

GARNIER, JOHN HUTCHINSON. *Prince Pedro*
Toronto: Belford Brothers, 1877.

GOSSE, EDMUND. "The Revival of Poetic Drama,"
The Atlantic Monthly, XC, 156–66 (December 1902).

HAMMOND, GEORGE ARTHUR. *Jassoket and Anemon*
Kingsclear, N.B.: Lashtok Publishing House, 1896.

HARPER, JOHN MURDOCH. *Champlain*
Toronto: Trade Publishing Co., 1908.

HEAVYSEGE, CHARLES. *Count Filippo; or, The Unequal Marriage*
Montreal, n.p., 1860.

——. *Saul*
Montreal: Henry Rose & Co., 1857.

HUNTER-DUVAR, JOHN. *The Enamorado*
Summerside: Graves & Co., Publishers, 1879.

——. *De Roberval*
Saint John, N.B.: J. & S. McMillan, 1888.

——. "A Legend of Roses and Ravlan,"
Canadian Monthly, IX, 72–82 (January 1876).

LYTTON, EARL OF. "The Stage in Relation to Literature,"
Fortnightly Review, XXXIV, 12–26 (December 1883).

MACKENZIE, J. B. *Thayendanegea: An Historico-Military Drama*
Toronto: William Briggs Company, 1906.

MACREADY, WILLIAM CHARLES. *Macready's Reminiscences*
Sir Frederick Pollack, ed. Vol. XI.
London: Macmillan and Company, 1906.

MAIR, CHARLES. *Tecumseh*
Toronto: Hunter, Rose & Co., 1886.

MCGEE, THOMAS D'ARCY. *Sebastian or The Roman Martyr*
New York: D. & J. Sadlier & Co., 1861.

NEWCOMB, C. F., and HANKS, J. M. *Dermot McMurrough*
Toronto: Hunter, Rose & Co., 1882.

————. *The Fireworshippers*
Toronto: Hunter, Rose & Co., 1882.

NORWOOD, ROBERT. *The Witch of Endor*
Toronto: McClelland, Goodchild and Stewart, 1916.

PAYZANT, J. A. "John Hunter-Duvar,"
The Dominion Illustrated, V, 127 (August 1890).

SCOTT, FREDERICK GEORGE. *The Key of Life*
Quebec: n.p., 1907.

SHRIVE, NORMAN. *Charles Mair*
Toronto: University of Toronto Press, 1965.

SYKES, W. J. *The Poetical Works of Wilfred Campbell*
Toronto: Hodder and Stoughton, 1922.

TAYLOR, BAYARD. "The Author of Saul,"
Atlantic Monthly, XCVI, 411–14 (October 1865).

THOULESS, PRISCILLA. *Modern Poetic Drama*
Oxford: Basil Blackwell, 1934.

TODHUNTER, JOHN. "Poetic Drama and Its Prospects on the Stage,"
The Fortnightly Review, LXXXI (New series), 713–25 (January–June 1902).

WATSON, SAMUEL JAMES. *A Legend of Roses, a Poem; and Ravlan, A Drama*
Toronto: Hunter, Rose & Co., 1876.

PLAYS RELATED TO THE CANADIAN SCENE

BROUGHALL, GEORGE.
The 90th on Active Service; or, Campaigning in the North West
Winnipeg: George Bishop, 1885.

————. *The Tearful and Tragical Tale of the Tricky Troubadour; or,
The Truant Tricked*
Winnipeg: *Manitoba Free Press*, 1886.

CANDIDUS, CAROLI. *The Female Consistory of Brockville*
Brockville, 1856.

DAVIN, NICHOLAS FLOOD. *The Fair Grit; or, The Advantages of Coalition*
Toronto: Belford Brothers Publishers, 1876.

FULLER, WILLIAM HENRY. "A Fair Smuggler."
Acting script held in the Theatre Collection, New York Public Library.

FULLER, WILLIAM HENRY.
H.M.S. Parliament; or, The Lady Who Loved a Government Clerk
Ottawa: *Citizen* Printing and Publishing Co., 1880.

KEATING, J. W. *The Shrievalty of Lynden*
St. Catharines, n.p., 1889.

MC ILWRAITH, JEAN NEWTON, and ALDOUS, JOHN EDMUND PAUL.
Ptarmigan; or, A Canadian Carnival
Hamilton: *Spectator* Printing Co., 1895.

SCRIBBLE, SAM. *Dolorsolatio*
Montreal: John Lovell Printer, 1865.

———. *Not Dead Yet; or, The Skating Carnival*
Montreal: John Lovell Printer, 1865.

WOOD, W. P. *Minnie Trail; or, The Woman of Wentworth*
Hamilton: *Evening Times* Office, 1871.

203

Index.

207

211

This book
was designed by
LESLIE SMART FTDC
with assistance from
LAURIE LEWIS.
The decorative linecuts
used throughout the book
come from the Printers'
Ornament collection
of Massey College.